WAR CAR

KINGDOM OF ENGINES

NATHAN VAN COOPS

Skylighter
Press

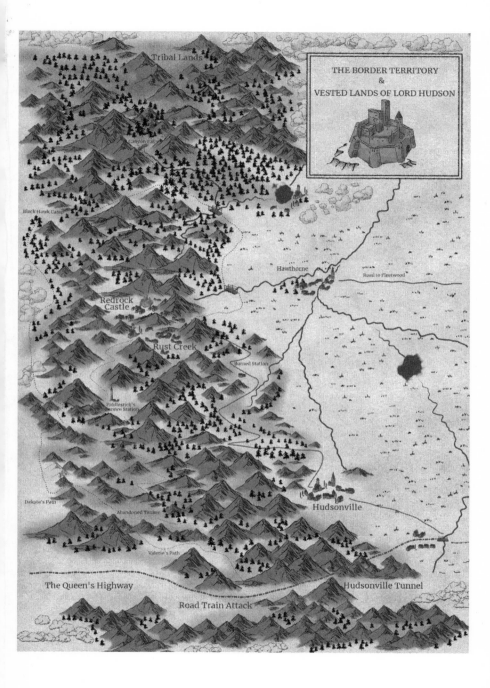

PROLOGUE

D akota Wren's inner thighs quivered, vibrating with every pulse of the engine between her legs. As the high-plains wind whistled through the darkened canyon and toyed with the loose strands of her jet-black hair, she clenched and unclenched her throttle hand, the soft leather of her fingerless glove flexing across her knuckles.

She took a moment to caress the motorcycle's fuel tank with her fingertips one last time. Every inch of this machine's steel body and gasoline-filled veins had come at a cost. Her own sweat and blood had given it life. But tonight it would be sacrificed for a higher purpose.

Her left hand adjusted the tension of the satchel slung across her back, and the weight of the portable welding tanks shifted against her spine. The discomfort was another sacrifice. It kept her alert, as did the crisp night air that bit at her cheeks through the open face of her helmet.

The low purr of the idling motorcycle was a whisper lost amid the wind-whipped crevices of the canyon. The machines of her companions were likewise inaudible, though she knew where each of her fellow riders were hidden.

She had clipped the wires to her headlight for tonight's excursion. The bulb sat dark in its socket, a blinded cyclops guided only by her touch. Darkness would be her ally and her weapon.

When pinpricks of light appeared on the horizon, Dakota's breath caught.

The wait was over.

She closed the visor to her helmet and pressed the toe of her boot downward to shift into gear.

Quietly she counted the racks of headlights coming into view. Seven enormous vehicles lumbered along the lonely highway.

Each giant road tractor would be pulling at least six trailer cars rigged in pairs side-by-side to take up two lanes of the road.

A seven-vehicle caravan would also be armed.

That was okay.

All part of the plan.

Her team remained in concealment a quarter mile from the road as the tractors rumbled past. When the last unit of the road train was parallel to her position, Dakota made her move.

Her fingers released the clutch and the motorcycle leapt into motion, scattering sand and gravel in a rooster tail behind her. Dakota plunged down the canyon path and into the open, shifting gears and accelerating toward the tail of the road train. Three other bikes erupted from hiding, the darkened figures streaking through the scrub brush with eyes fixed on their quarry.

The overcast sky lent cover to their pursuit.

Two of the bikes formed up to either side of Dakota but wouldn't overtake her.

This was her hunt.

Bold predictions and gallant oaths were easily made while sitting fireside under a smiling moon, but deeds weren't conjured by speech. These moments were born of silent courage and the audacity to act. This was the moment for Dakota to prove she was made of more than words.

Her heartbeat pulsed against the chinstrap at her throat as she closed on the last trailer of the road train. Steadying the bike beside the truck, she rose and planted one foot on the seat.

So far, no alarm had sounded from the road train's watch post. If there was a rear guard on the trailer, he was asleep or away from his post. The opening was all Dakota needed.

Wind blasted around the trailers and buffeted her as she edged closer, but she held tightly to the handlebars, rolling on the throttle.

She closed the gap.

A narrow, rusted ledge at the rear of the fuel tanker would be enough for a foothold if she could land it. She would have only one chance.

She caught a glimpse of the other riders at the edge of her vision. Lanja sat tandem on the back of Sprocket's bike, an arrow nocked and her bow at the ready. They were watching—waiting for their cue. If Dakota hit the asphalt and ended up as just one more bit of roadkill along the highway, there would be no need for them to proceed. It all hung on her.

Dakota gave the motorcycle a final burst of speed. Her bike didn't hold back. She wouldn't either. She raced within inches of the trailer, planted her second foot on the seat beneath her, then leapt.

Her hands came off the handlebars and stretched forward as she soared through the air. It was a matter of inches, but in the fraction of a second she was airborne, her heart seemed to stop. The sliver of a moment expanded, her mind taking in every millimeter of progress. The truck hurtling through space, the wind pressing hard against her chest—all of it resisted her.

But then her fingers gripped steel, and time resumed its flow in a rush of sound and wind. Blood pounded in her ears and threatened to drown even the rattling din of the trailer's lock chains. She exhaled.

Dakota glanced back in time to see her bike go off the road. It had stayed upright briefly, almost as though it had wanted to see her safely aboard the road train before losing its trajectory and careening into the ditch at the side of the road. The front wheel struck an embankment, and the rear wheel came up, flipping end over end before vanishing into the darkness.

The noise of the crash faded quickly as they sped away, but someone might have heard. Dakota scanned the trailer ahead, alert for any sign of trouble. But as she crept toward the front of the tanker, she encountered no resistance. She smiled to herself. This was going better than expected.

She crept around the tanker, pulling the pins connecting the trailer to its mate in the other lane and releasing the lock chains. Then she crept forward again to inspect the main coupler. The other pins had been easy enough to dislodge, but the tension on this shackle would be too much to disconnect while moving. She slung her satchel around to her front and extracted the blowtorch. She eyed the trailer ahead. It was a car carrier loaded with the dark shapes of vehicles.

"Hey! What do you think you're doing?" the shout came from her left and she turned to find a security guard gawking at her from the bed of the neighboring trailer. He reached for his belt. Instead of drawing a weapon, he chose a hand-held radio. But before he could key the mic, an arrowhead erupted through his forearm.

The man gawked at the tip of the arrow, the radio fell from his fingers, and then he lost his balance and toppled forward, vanishing into the darkness between the rigs.

And just like that he was gone.

Dakota stared at the space where he'd vanished, wondering if he'd missed the wheels. She was still frozen when the shout reached her ears. In the space beyond where the man had been standing, Lanja was fitting another arrow to her bow. Still aback Sprocket's motorcycle, she shouted something again and this time pointed. Dakota turned to find another rider had pulled up to her side of the rig. He tossed a second satchel to her, and she caught it. Inside, she recognized the hydraulic pressure accumulator that would allow them to apply the brakes to the trailer once she cut it loose.

Right. She had a job to do.

She pulled the wrenches from her bag and set to work installing the accumulator. In a matter of minutes, the brake system was ready, and she pocketed the remote. It was time to cut the trailer free.

As she eyed the coupler for the rig, she realized she had a problem. The tanker side of the joint was thick, hardened steel. The only place thin enough to cut through was close to the towing trailer, meaning she would have to cut from that side. If she timed it wrong, she could end up stuck aboard the road train as it sped away and would have no way to avoid capture.

She puzzled through the problem as fast as she could, finally arriving at the best possible solution. She would have to cut till there was just a thread of steel binding the joint together, jump back across, then apply the brakes to the trailer, letting it shear the rest of the way loose. It was dangerous, but every part of this plan was dangerous. There was no turning back now.

Dakota leapt from the fuel tanker to the car hauler and took position near the coupling. She sparked the torch to life and a blue-orange flame illuminated the night. Adjusting the gas valves until the center of the flame burned white hot, she flipped the secondary welding visor on her helmet and set to work.

As she carved through the hardened steel of the coupling, a crackle of static came over her helmet speaker. Someone had keyed a mic. Dakota flipped her visor up and looked around.

She and her team had vowed to keep radio silence unless it

was an absolute emergency to avoid anyone catching their chatter and tipping off the caravan's security.

This diversion from the plan wasn't as severe as someone speaking on the channel, but she knew something was up. Dakota glanced to either side and saw none of her companions, but when she rose and peeked into the slipstream of air coming around the trailer, she saw the problem. The dark shapes of the mountains were in view and that meant they were nearing the entrance to the Hudsonville Tunnel. If the road train reached the tunnel, their plan of escape would be worthless.

Dakota keyed her own mic once to acknowledge the signal.

The clock was ticking.

She moved back to her place at the rear of the car hauler and was about to flip her welding visor back down when a glimmer of light caught her eye. She turned to find the glow of her torch reflecting back at her from a chrome emblem on the car nearest her. She froze. Her eyes roamed over the sleek hood and the yawning intake scoop. The car's paint was murder black, taunting the night with its own deeper darkness, but the bear claw emblem on the grill was unmistakable.

Her gut clenched.

It shouldn't be possible.

Of the thousands of cars in New Avalon, what were the odds that this one would show up now, on this night, on this train?

A chill ran down her spine.

A sign? An omen? What did it mean?

The torch sputtered in a gust of wind, the flame bending and smoking, and for the first time tonight, her resolve wavered. If this car was a sign, it heralded something unexpected, a change in plans.

She mouthed a quick prayer to the spirits, seeking answers.

The microphone crackled twice. Two clicks. Time was running out.

Dakota took one more look at the car, then flipped her visor down and set to work cutting away the tangs holding the coupler together. Only a few more centimeters of steel held the tanker to the train. The metal groaned from the strain. Any instant it could give way. She fingered the remote in her pocket. She needed to jump across now. She should cut loose—go while she was still in the clear. Her plan was working, and all she needed to do was follow it through to the end.

But that car.

It pulled at the corners of her mind with the gravity of a dying star.

It meant something. She needed to know what.

She squatted low and aimed the torch at the last remaining width of steel binding the coupler. The metal glowed red hot and began to separate. She snuffed the torch and fetched the remote for the accumulator from her pocket. She took a firm grip on the frame of the car hauler and held on. Then she pushed the button.

A resounding crack split the air as the tanker trailer sheared away. The trailer she was aboard rocked and swayed. She kept steady pressure on the remote for the tanker's brakes, only letting up when one of the tires started to smoke. The tanker stayed true to course, decelerating rapidly as the rest of the road train sped away.

The headlights of her team's replacement tractor flicked on in the distance and flooded the road behind her with light. She glimpsed the shadows of the riders already encircling the tanker. Her crew knew what to do. They would have the stolen trailer hooked up and moving again in a matter of seconds. There was no element of surprise now and no use feigning secrecy.

The crew of the road train would know what happened too.

She had to move fast.

Dakota moved side-to-side on the back of the car hauler, pulling the pins for the boarding ramps. One after another the metal ramps fell, the ends striking the highway and sparking against the asphalt.

This was crazy, but she had left herself only one way out.

"What the hell, Dee?"

It was Sprocket's voice in her ear. It was clear he knew she wasn't aboard the tanker. She knew he'd be the one to call her out, too. There was no time for an explanation, and he wouldn't understand it anyway.

She tore the helmet from her head and hurled it aside, then opened the door to the war car. She tossed her welding gear into the passenger side, then slid into the driver's seat.

The smell of leather and gasoline. The polished dash. It took all of her willpower to not stop and simply admire this vehicle. It was everything she had imagined. She rummaged in her satchel and found a screwdriver, prying the access panel loose from the control column, then locating the ignition wiring.

An alarm was sounding somewhere, and the remaining rear trailer was weaving dangerously without its mate to keep it steady. The road train hadn't slowed. The driver was no doubt hoping to make the more defensible position of the Hudsonville Tunnel before stopping. It was going to be close.

Ignition wires sparked between her fingers. The starter jolted and kicked. She pumped the gas pedal and tried again.

This time the engine roared to life.

"Yesss!"

Dakota secured the ignition wiring and slammed the door.

A shadow passed over the windshield—movement in the row of vehicles stacked overhead.

Someone was coming.

Dakota eyed the narrow space ahead of the car. It was going to be a tight squeeze getting out from under the rack of cars above her and then onto the metal ramps trailing onto the highway. She shifted into gear and eased the car forward, gunning it over the hump meant to keep the car from rolling off the trailer. The car teetered on the brink.

She took a deep breath and prepared to take the plunge.

At that moment, a figure dropped from the racks above and landed directly on the hood of the car. Dakota found herself staring up into the face of a ferocious girl with violent eyes and a sword clenched in one hand. Light danced from the blade and glinted from a badge pinned to her jacket. The sword and crown of Avalon.

"Get out of my car!" the girl shouted.

There was something terrifying in the command. As Dakota took in the form of this girl with the flashing sword, her eyes ablaze with righteous justice, there was a part of her that wanted to listen, to shut off the car and surrender. Had it been another heist, on another night, she might have done just that. But tonight she had found herself sitting behind the wheel of the greatest war car in the history of cars.

And war cars never surrender.

Dakota gave the girl on the hood a smile, pulled her foot off the clutch, and stomped on the gas.

1

HIJACKED

V alerie Terravecchia kept her eyes on the knife in her attacker's hand. The masked man slashed at the air, forcing her to back away.

First rule of a knife fight?

Run.

The windowless walls to all sides eliminated that option.

Rule two? Get your hands on a weapon.

Valerie's sword was out of reach on the ground behind her attacker. The only way to it was past his dancing blade.

If that's the way he wanted it, who was she to disappoint?

She kept her hands up. When the next thrust came, she moved fast, seizing the man's arm. Her fingers slid down his forearm to his wrist and twisted, forcing the knife tip away. She trapped the man's knife hand against her hip, then struck at the flat of the blade with her forearm. The knife tumbled to the floor.

Despite this victory, the fight was far from over. The man snatched at her hair with his free hand, then went for a choke hold. Valerie pivoted, never letting go of his wrist, then lashed out with a kick to his knee that knocked the man's leg out from under him. He crashed to the floor.

This was her chance. If she was going to run, she ought to go now—at least snatch up her sword and turn on him.

She hesitated too long. The man swept her leg from under her, and she crashed to the floor beside him. He rolled, using the advantage of his muscled frame to try to pin her. She didn't wait for that to happen, instead whipping her body around and scissoring his neck and one shoulder between her legs. They rolled together as he struggled, but this time she ended up on top, the man's torso pinned beneath her.

He grunted, trying to get his head out of the scissor lock.

Valerie was panting. If she was smart, she would disengage and grab her sword while she had the advantage.

Instead, she released her grip on the man's neck, pivoted atop him mounting his abdomen, then leaned over and planted a kiss directly on his mouth. The masked man's eyes widened.

Valerie grinned and sat back.

The masked man slowly rose to his elbows. "Why do I get the feeling you aren't taking this seriously?" He reached up and pulled the ski mask from his head, revealing a rugged, stubbled jaw and a handsome face topped with a mop of unruly brown hair. The face of Damon Roark.

"I pinned you, didn't I?" Valerie replied. She ran her fingers over his chest and up his neck to his hair. "Besides, I thought it was time for a break."

"I've never had this trouble training the other knights in the king's employ," Damon said.

"I certainly hope not," Valerie replied. She leaned over and pressed her lips to his again. He kissed her back eagerly and rolled over, pinning her to the floor with his hips. Valerie felt herself melt as his mouth found its way to her neck.

A door hinge creaked and both Valerie and Damon looked up. Valerie's view was now upside down.

"Oh sorry, didn't know if you two were still awake." Rico Cabrera was standing in the doorway at the end of the trailer, his arms cradling a jacket. He placed a hand on the door jamb to steady himself as the trailer rocked. The highway noise was much louder with the door open, a rumbling of wheels and the clink-clink-clink of the connecting chains to the next car.

"It's fine. We were just getting in a little late-night sparring practice," Damon said. He climbed off of Valerie and stood, extending a hand to her.

"Is that what the kids are calling it these days?" Rico raised an eyebrow.

Valerie accepted Damon's hand and rose to her feet. She brushed some of the hay dust from her pants and pulled a few pieces of straw from her hair, then walked to one side of the trailer-turned-gym. She flipped a latch on the wall, then slid open a metal panel, revealing a thick glass window and a view of the darkened prairie beyond. She flipped another, smaller latch, then parted the panes, allowing the night air to whip through the window and fill the otherwise musty-smelling trailer. Wind picked up bits of straw from the windowsill and scattered them. Valerie suspected that the trailer must have been used for animal cargo on previous trips, or at least she hoped that was where the smell was coming from.

She stuck her head out the window, letting the night air whip though her hair and cool the beads of sweat that had formed on her neck. She was forced to squint in the blast of wind. Two cars ahead, she could make out the glow from the tractor driver's cab. There wasn't much to see out on the prairie. The low overcast hid the stars and whatever distant mountain features they might be passing were shrouded by the darkness.

When she pulled her head back inside, Damon had put away his knife and Rico was unfolding the canvas jacket. She recognized it as the one she had picked up prior to the trip, only now there was a newly stitched emblem on the back. The crest of the House of Terravecchia.

"You like it?" Rico was practically beaming as he held it up.

"Now you can have your house crest on the back and you can put your crown badge on the front. If you like it, I plan to make matching ones for Damon and me. Team Valerie!"

Damon brushed some dirt from his rolled-up shirtsleeves. "You do recall that I'm a *covert* agent, right?"

"Oh come on," Rico replied. "You don't want to rock one of these? The Terravecchia colors would look so good on you." He winked.

Damon shook his head, but the corner of his mouth quirked up with the hint of a smile.

Rico moved to Valerie and held out the jacket. "Fine. *You* tell me what you think."

Valerie slipped her arms into the jacket, trying out the fit.

"Now give me your badge."

Valerie fished the silver emblem bearing the crown and cross of New Avalon from her pocket. Her mechanic took it from her and fastened it to the jacket. "See? Perfection."

"It's a nice thought," Valerie said. "But don't you think it will look flashy, showing up in house branded gear? I don't want the other knights to think I'm putting on airs."

"Honey, you are the talk of the kingdom right now!" Rico objected. "Of course you should be flashy. At least I know I would be if I was in your shoes. Youngest knight to be invited to join the Round Table in a century. King's Tournament winner. Not to mention that you're from one of the most respected houses in the land. Of course you should look good. You're going to turn that palace on its head with jealousy. And why not? You earned it, girl."

Valerie let herself smile. "I'm glad you think so. I just wish I had your confidence. Youngest knight in a century means I also have the most to learn. They probably think I'm some upstart punk who got lucky. I know I would."

"You weren't lucky," Damon interjected. "You trained hard and fought harder. Rico's right. You earned this spot."

"If anyone doubts you, just run them over with the Guardian," Rico added. "No one will second-guess that."

Valerie laughed.

She couldn't argue there. Her father's war car, a Guardian 770, had been the most legendary car of its time.

It was hers now. Not only was it powerful and deadly, the paint work they had done on it prior to heading east ensured that it would exceed the standards of any knight at the Round Table. When she rolled up in that car, people would be foolish to doubt her. The thought calmed her nerves.

It had been over a month since she battled her way through the King's Tournament in Port Hyacinth, toppling the favored champions of the city and putting herself in front of the king. Her reward was an invitation.

She brushed her fingers over the badge on her chest. Knight Warden of the West.

It wasn't official yet. Not until she reached the king's court and formally accepted the invitation to join the Knights of the Round Table, but they would be there soon. The road train would get them across the frontier. Once they reached the border of the eastern territories, they could drive the rest of the way to Glastonbury Castle.

Valerie let herself imagine what it would feel like to enter the Courtyard of Kings and park her Guardian among that hallowed circle of warrior cars. The garages at Glastonbury Castle were rumored to be filled with the finest war cars ever made, deadly machines made of raw horsepower and cold steel. To see her family crest in that company would be an honor many drivers would kill for. Just the thought of all those cars made Valerie weak.

She could almost hear their engines in the distance, calling her.

Damon had his head cocked to one side, listening. It was as if her dreams were audible to him too.

But then she realized it was because there really were engines in the distance. Over the sound of the road train, there was a higher pitched popping coming from the prairie. Not a road tractor engine. Not a car. Valerie and Damon moved to the open window simultaneously, intent on the sound.

"Hey, what's going—" Rico began to speak.

"Shhh," Valerie said. Damon likewise held up a finger to silence him.

"It sounds like . . . trail bikes," Valerie said. "More than two."

"Raiders," Damon replied. He moved to the wall and snatched up his sword and scabbard. "Stay here. I need to warn the driver." He dashed to the door, disappearing the way Rico had come, toward the sleeper cars where they had been staying.

"Road raiders?" Rico's eyes were wide. "What are they after? We're just a private charter. If they want gold or trading merchandise, all we have is—"

"Cars," Valerie finished the thought. "They could be after the cars." She spun on her heel and snatched *Firebird* from the floor. The feel of the sword in her hand sharpened her senses. "Stay here!"

Rico flung his arms up. "What am I supposed to—"

But Valerie didn't wait for the rest. She snatched her scabbard from the wall hook, then slid the aft door of the train car open to reveal the wind-blown trailers behind them. She quickly counted the vehicles in sight. Damon's Easton Blackbird 900 sat at the front of the top rack, his primer-gray Vulcan was beneath it. There were two other project cars Rico had brought along for parts and salvage. The Guardian was somewhere beyond them, out of sight at the far end of the trailer.

A blue flash reflected off glass. It flickered white, then a brilliant blue again.

Torchlight.

Thieves.

How did they expect to get the cars free?

The car hauler trailer wasn't designed for pedestrians to navigate. Multiple vehicles divided her from whomever was on the far side. She would have to go over. She cinched her sword belt to her waist, then slid *Firebird* into its scabbard. Eyeing the structure of the upper car rack, she leapt, catching hold and swinging up to get a foothold.

The trailers rattled and moaned as the road train barreled down the highway. The wind buffeted Valerie and set her hair whipping about her face. She gained the top rack of the car hauler and climbed the hood of Damon's war car.

Up, then over.

From her perch on the car's roof, she had a view of the entire road train. If Damon had reached the driver's cab, there seemed to be no change. If anything, the tractor was accelerating. After a moment, Valerie spotted why. They were approaching a mountain ridge and the distant lights of a tunnel blinked at her across the prairie. The lead tractor of the caravan was nearly at the gates of the tunnel which yawned wide to swallow it up. The tunnel would offer protection, a defensible position to ward off the raiders.

Their driver planned to run, not fight.

A resounding crack drew Valerie's attention to the rear of the train in time to see the tanker trailer break free. She dropped to her knees and held on to the top of Damon's war car, expecting the fuel tanker to careen out of control. She waited for the catastrophic crash, but it didn't come. The tanker decelerated smoothly, braking and holding its course along the road before dropping away into the night behind them. That's when she saw the other tractor.

Riders in black moved like shadows along the road, forming up to guard the separated tanker. Then the spare tractor moved into position to hook up to the separated tanker.

Fuel.

They had only been after the fuel.

Valerie breathed a sigh of relief.

They had what they wanted. It was a loss for the caravan, but their road tractor could share fuel from the other trains in the group and pick up a spare fuel tanker at the next depot. It was a loss they could manage.

But then the ramps at the end of the car hauler fell, crashing to the concrete and scraping the pavement.

One of the thieves was still aboard.

Valerie squinted and peered down through the latticed structure of the car hauler. She caught a glimpse of movement as someone slipped around the Guardian and climbed inside.

Oh, hell no. Valerie leapt onto the junker ahead of her, scrambled over the roof to the hood, then leapt again, landing atop the car directly above the Guardian.

The Guardian's engine roared to life. Whoever this thief was, they knew what they were doing. She didn't have time to waste. Valerie slid down the windshield of the project car, positioning herself on the front bumper. There was a narrow gap between the ramps of the upper tier that allowed her a clear view of the Guardian's hood below her. She drew her sword, stepped off the bumper and dropped through the gap, landing astride the Guardian's hood scoop.

With one hand gripping the intake for the supercharger, Valerie glowered through the windshield at the thief behind the wheel. She was surprised to find it was a woman. A girl, really. Certainly not any older than she was. The girl's raven hair hung jagged and loose around her face, but her eyes were what held Valerie's attention. Rimmed in black and piercing in their intensity, this face was that of a wild creature, cheekbones that could cut you and a mouth made for devouring the weak.

"Get out of my car!" Valerie shouted.

The girl seemed frozen for a long second, as if sizing Valerie up, but then her fingers tightened on the steering wheel and her lips spread into a smile. The Guardian snarled and bucked beneath Valerie's feet. She fell forward as the hood sped out from under her. Her hip struck the windshield and she rolled onto the roof. She would have kept rolling had it not been for the sudden drop as the Guardian plunged down the ramps and the bumper ram sparked against the asphalt.

Valerie had only an instant to act, and she used it to lift her sword, her eyes focused on the subtle lines of rivets just visible beneath the Guardian's paint. Had it been any other car, she would have been guessing where the armored plates began. But this was her car, and she knew every inch of it. She knew that the roof armor had one weak point where the driver and passenger side roof plates joined. It was a gap of only a fraction of an inch but it was the exact place she drove the point of her sword, just as the thief inside the car stomped on the accelerator.

Firebird sank to its hilt in the top of the car and Valerie held on with both hands as the Guardian sailed into the black. Wind pulled at her hair and the jacket flapped and snapped around her.

The thief had yet to find the headlights or was deliberately ignoring them. Valerie clung to the hilt of her sword as the Guardian sped up, launching into the darkness. Valerie twisted to get one last look at the road train barreling away toward the mountains. The train was consumed by the night, even its sound swallowed up and lost amid the roar of the beast beneath her.

Whatever happened next, she was on her own.

2

SPLIT

When the sword blade came through the roof, Dakota Wren swore all the worst words she knew.

Who was this girl?

Only an insane person would hang on to the top of a speeding car. And she was still up there.

Dakota's heart hammered in her chest. The adrenaline from the heist was still running through her, and it was now tinged with fear. The fact that she had gone rogue and altered the plan was bad enough. She certainly couldn't show up to the rendezvous point with some mentally deranged swordswoman stabbing at her the whole way.

There was going to be enough trouble.

She had to end this.

She flipped on the headlights.

The highway ahead was smooth and straight for mile after endless mile. Not at all what she needed. She eyed the shoulder, then, spotting what she wanted, swerved hard and shot onto a bumpy cart track. A clatter and thump from the roof let her know that her freeloader was still hanging on.

Not for long. Dakota swerved and shot into the grass,

bumping over gopher holes and startling rabbits. The turbulent ride failed to unseat her guest, but she had plenty more tricks to try. She cranked the wheel hard, first right, then left, then stomped on the brake. A pair of legs appeared, boots flailing at the hood and knees scraping the windshield, but her passenger was still hanging on.

"Damn it," Dakota muttered. She floored the accelerator and shifted aggressively as she took a few more turns. She finally took the car into a 360-degree turn. The rear wheels churned up dust and debris that rained back onto the hood as she completed circuit after circuit. The girl on the roof cursed and shouted. Dakota swore back.

"Get off my car!" she screamed.

"This is my car!" came the reply.

"Not anymore," Dakota muttered. She accelerated again, shifting to second, then third. Finally she wrenched on the wheel while hauling up on the parking brake, torquing the car around 180 degrees. There was a shriek from the roof, the sound of metal on metal as the sword came free of the roof armor, then a thud as the girl hit the back of the car and vanished into the cloud of dust.

Dakota stepped on the gas and shot away a hundred feet before spinning the car around again, her headlights sweeping over the scrub brush and prairie grass. She scanned the dust cloud for signs of movement but saw none.

She considered barreling through the cloud and attempting to flatten her attacker with the ram at the front of the car, but something held her back. The cloud of dust moved and swirled in the light as though the spirits themselves were angered tonight. There was something about this girl that she wanted no part of. She was chaos, change. Dakota felt it in her bones.

She turned the wheel hard and raced away, her eyes flicking to the rear-view mirror. Whoever she was, she could eat dust tonight. This war car was hers.

Dakota's fingers settled into their places on the steering wheel.

He would be so proud . . .

Dakota let herself smile.

After tonight, everything would be different.

Damon Roark hung by one hand from the boarding door of the road tractor as the train pulled through the gates of the Hudsonville Tunnel. He didn't wait for the vehicles to come to a stop before vaulting onto the road. Rico's face appeared in the window of the passenger car as it squealed past him and then reappeared again at the rear door. He slid it open and leapt out to join him.

"What did they say? What are we doing? Did you see her? She jumped right onto the car. Do you know where she is?"

Damon did know, but the words wouldn't form in his mouth. He'd had a clear view from the tractor cab when he'd warned the driver of the attack. The glimpse of the Guardian vanishing down the ramps at the rear of the train had been just a flash in the mirrors, but he had seen it, and he'd recognized the girl clinging wildly to the top of the car.

The shouting match with the tractor drivers had accomplished nothing. They wouldn't stop. Not for curses, not for threats, not even for Damon's drawn sword. Not until they were through these gates.

They were through now, but now might already be too late.

Damon stormed past the last of the passenger cars. The car hauler trailer was still there, but the ramps were down, the Guardian missing.

"Oh my God. She could be dead," Rico stammered. "What do

we do?" The young man was shaking, his hands flitting from his face to his scalp.

"We stop talking and start getting these down," Damon said, his eyes roaming over the frame of the car hauler. He climbed onto the trailer. The Blackbird was blocked by two vehicles and too high up. His Rockwell Vulcan would have to do. Damon opened the door of the junker blocking his car in, released the parking brake, and moved around the back to push. "Get our gear. Hurry."

Rico nodded fervently and vanished back toward the passenger cars.

Damon's muscles strained as he shoved on the trunk of the junker. With the vehicle's engine in pieces, it had taken a winch and three men to get the vehicle up the ramps. It should have been as many men pushing it again, but Damon didn't have time to wait. He rocked the car once, twice, and then a third time before putting all of his strength into shoving it up and over the retaining hump. The rear wheels cleared the obstacle and Damon kept up the momentum, not relenting until the car hit the ramps and rolled off the trailer, coasting to a stop a dozen yards away.

Damon flexed his broad shoulders and turned back to the Vulcan. Primer gray and devoid of any insignia, the car lacked any specific details that would draw the eye, but the breadth of the hood betrayed the beast of an engine slumbering beneath. Damon's Easton Blackbird intimidated from the first glance. It bullied the eye, challenging anything and everything to fight. The Vulcan was a different sort of predator, anonymous and unassuming on the surface, concealing its sheathed claws and deadly fangs as it lay in wait.

He fished the keys from his pocket and slid into the driver's seat. The cylinders fired at the first hint of a spark, and the engine settled into its signature understated purr. Easing the car down the ramp, he was tempted to keep going, rocket down the road and into the night.

His fingers twitched as he put the car back in neutral. She was out there, alone and in trouble, but he had to wait. It twisted his guts to think about another moment wasted, but there was no part of his business that involved rushing into action without a plan.

He climbed out of the car and opened the trunk. As he did so, a resounding boom echoed through the tunnel. Rico reappeared with an armload of supplies and towing one of their weapons trunks on a tool cart.

"They closed the gate," Rico said, panting and out of breath.

Damon loaded the gear into the trunk and slammed it closed. "Stay with the train. I'll radio when I've found her."

"Hell no!" Rico replied. "I'm going with you."

"The frontier is no place for amateurs," Damon argued. "You'll be safer here and—"

"Nope!" Rico rushed around to the passenger door of the Vulcan and slid inside. The door slammed shut behind him.

Damon walked around the driver's side and leaned low to look across the interior. "You know I can pry you out of there if I need to."

"If you think you're the only one who cares about her, you're loco," Rico said. "And I'm going no matter what you say."

Damon sighed and climbed in.

When they pulled up to the tunnel gate, a trio of guards barred their way.

"This gate's closed until further notice. No one in or out," the nearest guard said. He had a lip filled with tobacco and dribbled a bit of juice down his chin when he spoke.

Damon leaned an arm out the window and stared the man down. "Our friend's out there. She went missing during the attack. We need to go after her."

"Our orders are clear." The man hiked up his pants. "Gates

stay closed until we're sure the attack is over. Nobody is getting out unless I say so."

"You must have some kind of sally port we can get a car through. We don't need you to open the main gates."

"We ain't opening nothing. Maybe you need your ears checked," the guard replied. "Not till we know these raiders have made themselves scarce. They likely feigned the attack just to draw us out and set a bigger party on us when we respond. But not tonight they won't. We won't budge till daylight."

"That's too long for us to wait," Damon argued. "Our friend needs help now. She's en route to become the newest knight of the Round Table. This is high priority."

"She could be the Queen of Sheba for all I care. If I don't have orders that say otherwise, that gate's staying closed."

One of the other younger guards wandered over. "If you want a sally port, there's one at Barrow Tower, ten miles north along the Back Ridge Highway. It's the long way around, but it's a double gate and they'll let you through at all hours for a toll."

"By the time we detour that far she could be dead," Damon growled.

"She's probably dead now." The first guard sucked at his tobacco and spit on the ground. "We won't be losing our jobs over your friend's poor choices. We have our orders."

Damon glowered at the man, but he knew this sort. Reason and logic would be lost against his blind adherence to structure and command. Short of running all three of the men over with the Vulcan, they had no choice. He backed the car around and shifted angrily into first gear, his rear tires biting asphalt with a squeal as he pulled away.

"I've got some maps in there," he said, gesturing to the glove box. "See if I have whatever backwater we're in and figure out how long it will take us to get around."

Rico rifled through the maps in the glove box, arranging them on his lap and trying to make out the names in the dim light. By the time they were past the rest of the caravan and out of the tunnel, he had found the one they needed. He spread the map open and located the Hudsonville Tunnel and Back Ridge Highway.

They were on the wrong side of a mountain, but at least they were moving.

Damon blasted along the twisting, inclined road and tightened his grip on the steering wheel.

"Hang on, Alley Cat," he muttered. "We're coming."

He could only hope they wouldn't be too late.

3

ABANDONED

V alerie Terravecchia lifted her head from the tall grass in time to see the taillights of the Guardian disappear over a ridge. She coughed, attempting to clear the dust from her lungs, and struggled to her feet. She swayed, still dizzy from the spin she'd taken atop the car and bruised from the subsequent tumble across the prairie.

Her fingers probed the sore points of her body, and she flexed her limbs. Miraculously, nothing appeared to be broken, though her wrist was tender, the knee of her trousers was torn, and her forearms were littered with scratches.

Her sword was missing. She parted the grass in her immediate area, squinting in the darkness and attempting to make out the weapon's shape. The path she had taken in her roll from the car was evidenced by broken stems and clumps of dirt that lay strewn about. A few divots along the path matched the stains on her elbows.

She looked southeast to the path of the distant highway. She'd come a lot farther than she'd expected in her journey atop the Guardian. The highway was invisible in the darkness, and the shape of the mountains was blurry. A few pinpricks of light dotted the lower end of the range. Somewhere along that route was the rest of the caravan. Damon, Rico. She had no way of knowing if they succeeded in warning the driver of the attack. Either way, the road train hadn't stopped.

As Valerie scanned the ground for her sword, a sound reached her ears and caused her to look up.

A motor.

Somewhere in the darkness between her location and the highway, the distinct pop-pop of an engine revealed the presence of another motorcycle.

A scout? A rear guard?

Valerie strode forward, trying to make out the shape of the bike. Her foot struck something solid and she looked down to find the cross-guard of her sword wedged beneath her boot. She sank to a knee to retrieve it, just in time, because the motorbike she had heard crested a rise in the terrain just south of her. The rider's headlight was out, and they seemed to be making their way cautiously along a deer trail or some other indiscernible path through the brush.

Valerie couldn't be sure, but it looked like the rider's route would take them not far from where she was hiding. The subtle hills and a scattering of rocks gave her a general idea of the likeliest of paths, and it looked like the bike would cut through a field of boulders to her left.

The feel of *Firebird* clenched in her fist gave Valerie a second jolt of adrenaline.

This wasn't over.

She stayed low and bolted through the grass, angling downhill and out of sight of the rider, but predicting where they would emerge. An overgrown pile of rock made for handy cover as she positioned herself. She would only get one chance.

Her breath came fast as she took a two-handed grip on her sword and tried to come up with the best method for an attack. Too aggressive and she might damage the bike, ruining her opportunity. Not aggressive enough and her quarry would escape.

The pop-pop grew steadily louder, and she coiled herself to spring. The rider was small, a good sign. The bike was close.

Twenty yards.

Ten.

Five.

Valerie sprang from her hiding place and sprinted for the front of the bike. She raised her sword and roared as she ran. The rider jolted in surprise and wrenched the handlebars, attempting to steer clear. Valerie swung with the flat of her blade, catching the rider in the face mask. She couldn't say if it was the force of the blow or the sheer shock of her appearance, but he lost control, laying the bike down in a low-side slide with a shriek of fear.

The bike skidded a dozen feet before hitting a boulder. The rider slid six.

Valerie raced after the rider, who struggled to rise, then, spotting her coming, fell over backward. The helmeted figure scrambled away, a mass of elbows and knees.

The rider looked top-heavy up close, his skinny frame seeming even more frail with the helmet on. He shrieked again inside the helmet, then pushed the helmet off and held up his hands. "'I'm sorry, I'm sorry. It wasn't my idea!"

Valerie froze. He was a teenager. Fourteen at most, and underfed if she had to guess.

"Who are you? And where's my car?" She brandished her sword at him.

The boy pointed past her. "He's got it!" Valerie turned to look, then swore as the boy used the opportunity to scramble to his feet and sprint away, his arms flailing as he high-stepped through the grass.

"Seriously?" Valerie muttered, angry at herself for falling for such a simple trick.

The kid may not be original in his tactics, but he was fast. His lanky frame made short work of getting away, stumbling once or twice in his frantic flight but keeping a fast enough pace to ensure Valerie wouldn't catch him.

Not on foot anyway.

She turned her attention to the motorcycle. The bike wasn't big . . . a single-cylinder Wellington Troublemaker that had seen its share of modifications. She sheathed her sword and picked the bike up, propping it on its kickstand for a quick inspection. The fuel tank was dented and scratched, but the frame looked straight, and nothing major had been knocked loose. It was impossible to be sure in the dim light, but it looked like it would run. Only one way to find out.

Valerie checked the ignition switch position, then threw a leg over, shifting to neutral and getting both hands on the handlebars. The starter button failed to do anything. She pressed it two more times to be sure, but the switch was useless. Fortunately, the bike had a kick start too, and when she gave it a try, the bike gurgled and popped.

It took three more firm kicks, then the bike came to life. She adjusted the engine speed by feel. She couldn't read the gauges without any instrument lights, but it wouldn't matter. She had a ride.

Valerie secured the scabbard of her sword beneath her on the seat, sitting on it. It was uncomfortable but infinitely preferable to having it wind up in the spokes of the rear wheel while riding.

She had a decision to make.

The scrawny kid likely hadn't made it far. She might be able to hunt him down, but getting him to talk would be another matter. Whatever role he had played in the tanker heist, she had no way of knowing if it would be useful.

She glanced southeast toward the mountain tunnel where the road train had disappeared. Damon and Rico would no doubt come for her. They could be on their way already. She could head that direction, rendezvous with them and continue the search.

But every second that passed, her car was getting farther away.

She was confident that Damon would be on her trail soon. He would have help and he could catch up.

Valerie recalled the brazen smile of the girl from the driver's seat of the Guardian.

If she thought this was over, she had another thing coming.

Valerie shifted into gear and rolled on the throttle.

She rode a few yards and scooped up the boy's fallen helmet, fitting it to her head.

The raiders were expecting one more rider, but she would give them a surprise.

Turning the bike around, she shot through the grass toward the hill where she'd last seen the Guardian. The trail wasn't hard to follow. The clouds overhead were breaking up, and moonlight spilled through the gaps, dappling the prairie with splashes of silver.

She followed the bent grass and tire marks northward. She was tempted to stop and figure out the headlight issue to make her job easier, but she couldn't afford the time.

The trail cut across the prairie, but then joined a dirt track that wound its way up into the foothills of the mountains.

The route grew rockier and the tire tracks more faint. She was forced to stop on several occasions to search for the telltale signs of the Guardian's oversized rear tires.

After what she guessed was more than five miles, the dirt track hit a junction and joined a broader road that snaked along a river. The Guardian's tracks were now interspersed among others, a number of motorcycle tire marks and one big vehicle. A few low points in the road had accumulated water, and the mud puddles showed signs of heavy dual tire marks.

The tanker trailer.

She was on the right path.

The trail wound along the river to a stone bridge that looked as though it had stood for a hundred years. The algae-covered rocks near the waterline gave evidence of a river that might overflow its banks in the peak of melting season. Now the water level was in decline, but the river still frothed and foamed as it rushed over its rocky bed.

The terror of the ride atop the Guardian, combined with the thrill of commandeering the bike, had left her clammy with sweat. Now the cool night air beside the pulsing river left her skin chilled. She let the bike idle while she stopped to take a drink from the river, then fastened her jacket tightly across her chest before continuing on.

As Valerie crossed the bridge, she scanned the tree line ahead. The shift from prairie to mountain foothills had been dramatic. A steady rise from the grassy plains ultimately stretched on to snow-capped peaks. In the darkness, the mountains were just a memory, but these trees were present and real. As the dirt road plunged onward into the trees, Valerie kept a wary eye out for trouble. The road twisted and turned, leaving her blind to what was coming. Her visibility was reduced to the few yards ahead of her, and she slowed the bike to second gear. Her eyes strained to catch any details along the route.

It was for this reason that when she rounded a curve and caught sight of the tanker trailer, it took her by surprise.

Valerie planted a foot and studied the road ahead. The fuel tanker wasn't moving. Its taillights were dark, and not so much as a bat moved in the vicinity. The trailer had been left in the middle of the road. There was no sign of the tow tractor or the motorcyclists who had absconded with it.

She stayed still, mistrustful of the scene, but when five minutes had gone by and there was no sign of movement, Valerie killed the engine, climbed off her bike, and walked cautiously forward.

The tanker had been emptied. Still-dripping fuel caps hung loose on their chains, dangling from the transfer lines. New tracks crisscrossed the road from smaller vehicles and possibly a trailer, no doubt loaded with portable tanks that would be easier to haul.

Hollowed out and motionless, the empty tanker resembled a carcass picked clean and left for the vultures.

It had been hastily devoured, then abandoned; an empty shell of its former usefulness.

But something wasn't right.

As Valerie neared the front of the tanker, her skin prickled. She froze in place, listening as best she could in the confines of the helmet. She'd made a mistake. It was too quiet, and the stillness was a lie.

The whiz of the arrow came so close that had Valerie been an inch to one side, it would have struck her. She spun on her heel and dove beneath the tanker, scrambling underneath and rolling to the far side. A second arrow embedded itself in the dirt in the same space her leg had occupied a fraction of a second earlier. The feathered flights quivered from the strike.

Valerie drew her sword, but it was of little consolation. She could see nothing. If there was more than one bowman, she was in trouble. Even if it was a single archer, she could easily be flanked.

Her breath came fast inside the helmet and fogged up the visor. She tore the helmet from her head and tried to calm her nerves. Whatever protection the helmet might have provided her was a sacrifice she had to make. She needed her ears.

A twig broke somewhere in the trees.

Her attacker was moving.

Valerie shifted to the rear of the tanker trailer, eyeing the distance to the bike.

"You follow us any farther, and I swear I won't miss the next shot!"

The voice was that of a woman. She sounded young.

Valerie peeked around the trailer, then ducked back immediately. She could see no one. She took a tighter grip on the handle of her sword, then shouted to the woods. "Give back the car you stole, and I'll leave you alone. I don't care about the fuel, but that car is personal. I mean to have it back."

"You're in no position to make demands." A pebble skittered across stone as the speaker moved.

Valerie retreated to the rear corner of the trailer, trying to watch two directions at once. "If you harm me, you're harming a Knight of the Round Table," Valerie shouted. "The king will have you strung up as traitors."

Her statement gave her attacker pause.

"I think you're full of it! You're probably just some squire with a fancy ride." The voice echoed off the rocks, making it hard to locate its source.

"I'm Valerie of the House of Terravecchia," she shouted back. "When I get to Glastonbury Castle, I'll be the new Knight Warden of the West. If you give me back my car, I'll tell the king to go easy on you. You may even get a pardon. Just give me the car."

"If I wanted a tall tale, I would have robbed a bard. You're never getting this car back, rich girl. Get lost."

As if to punctuate the statement, an arrow ricocheted off the tanker.

Valerie ducked back the other way, judging the distance to the trees on that side. But as she crept that direction, the voice was suddenly near.

"Hey there."

Valerie turned to find the girl from the car standing just forward of the tanker, an arrow nocked and the bowstring taut.

With war paint staining her cheeks and her eyes rimmed with black, the girl looked inhuman, a wraith born of moonlight and shadow.

Valerie's position was hopeless. There was no chance of reaching the girl before she released the arrow.

She held up a hand, then slowly, gently, she sheathed her sword.

"Throw your sword belt on the ground," the girl with the bow said. As she spoke, she relaxed the tension on the bowstring, and the arrow dipped toward the ground.

It was the only opening Valerie could hope for.

She turned on her heel and sprinted for the bike. Each step she ran, she expected an arrow in the back. When she heard the twang of the bowstring, she ducked and swerved. The arrow flew past, whizzing through the air and striking the bike ahead of her.

Valerie leapt onto the seat and knocked the motorcycle off its kickstand in one motion. Her heel flew back and kicked the starter into action, and she was applying throttle the moment the cylinder fired. The engine whined as she launched forward, shifting and swerving off road as she went, putting as many obstacles as she could between herself and the archer.

If more arrows followed her, she couldn't see them. She ripped through the woods, dodging rocks and trees. Branches lashed her, and she was forced to alter course repeatedly, but she managed to cover what she guessed was over a mile before stopping to get her bearings.

Her heart was pounding and she was out of breath, but at least she was out of danger for the moment.

Looking back the way she had come, she listened for sounds of pursuit. If anyone was coming, they were doing it quietly.

She put the bike in neutral, finally letting her death grip on the handlebars relax.

Then she felt the tingling against the skin of her leg.

She reached down to her right calf and felt the wet patch spreading across her pants leg. She sniffed at her fingers to be sure, but the smell was clear.

Fuel.

Climbing off the bike, she took a look at the damage.

The arrow hadn't missed her.

It had struck its target perfectly.

Fuel flowed freely down the arrow shaft, saturating the feathered flights before dripping into the dirt. The fuel tank was punctured an inch above the outlet port.

"Damn it," Valerie muttered.

She turned and looked back the way she had come.

She hadn't escaped after all. She had been allowed to leave. Whoever this thief was could have killed her with the shot far easier than taking out the bike. But whatever the reason for the archer's mercy, it didn't make the loss any easier to take.

Her war car was gone.

Valerie had lost.

The wooded hillside around her suddenly seemed a desolate place.

She opened the fuel cap and stuck her fingers inside the tank. Her middle finger just brushed the surface of the fuel. Hardly any tank remained below the arrow shaft. Not enough fuel to get her back as far as she had come. Assuming she could even find her way back.

She studied the dark woods to every side. It would be slow going until she found a road, then impossible going once she ran out of fuel.

This night was getting worse at every turn. Climbing back aboard the bike, she shifted into gear, squinted to make out a path, then rode onward into the darkness.

Dakota Wren climbed back up the hill and handed the

unstrung bow back to Lanja, who was leaning against a tree, waiting.

"I always knew you were a lousy shot under pressure," Lanja said. "I would've dropped her."

Dakota let the insult slide. She walked on without comment, unable to concentrate on anything Lanja had to say. Her mind lingered instead on the name the crazy girl had given.

Of course, anyone could have made up a name. But that name?

The wind in the trees whispered and moaned. The old spirits were awake, watching her.

One thing she knew for sure. A storm was coming.

At least now that storm had a name. Valerie Terravecchia.

4

FIDDLESTICK

T he fuel tank ran dry an hour before dawn.

Valerie had nursed the bike along a deer trail for as long as she could, coasting whenever possible and babying the throttle. Among the trees, it was nearly impossible to get an accurate sense of direction. When she emerged from the forest, she wasn't surprised to find that she was nowhere near where she had entered.

The overcast had dissipated, and the sky full of stars set the darkness of the prairie into sharp relief.

All except for one spot.

In the distance, a pinpoint of light glowed like a beacon amid the undulating prairie. It wasn't steady. It came and went, changing colors but always in the same sequence: white, blue, green.

There was a dirt track that ran from the woods north of her. It came close to her hilltop, then continued on toward the light. It was a sign of civilization at least.

Valerie stared at the light for several minutes before making up her mind.

She had no idea if the beacon belonged to friends or foes, but lingering in the dark was doing her no favors. It might be a trap, but she needed fuel, or help, or at least directions.

She set off to find it, pushing the little motorcycle as she went.

By the time she was within a half mile of the beacon, the sun was coming up. She had draped her jacket across the handlebars of the bike and was damp with sweat again despite the chill. The exertion of her night and the effort of pushing the bike had been more than enough to make her exhausted and sore. She hoped that whatever this outpost was, it would at least have water.

She was within view of the structure now. It was an odd shape, a miniature walled fortress, only in place of stone walls were mountains of used tires. They had been stacked and tied with barbed wire, then anchored to one another to create a barrier to vehicles or perhaps attackers. The beacon tower with the flashing light was not merely a beacon but was in fact a windmill. The blades were made of mismatched tin, two blades painted, the others flecked with rust, and its creaking was audible even from a distance. A number of cables and wires ran up and down the structure, and from the top, a series of rods stretched skyward. It looked like a combination of lightning rods and a homemade radio antenna.

There was a gate of sorts—an amalgamation of car parts, mostly bumpers, that created a strangely artistic entrance. There was no moat or drawbridge, but the area around the walls and the path to the gate was studded with concrete posts to prevent a car ramming its way through.

Valerie propped the crippled motorcycle on its kickstand and scooped up her jacket, then walked the remainder of the distance to the gate. The walls of the compound were a dozen feet high but there was no sign of guards or a watchman. She scanned the crow's nest of the windmill antenna tower, but that too was vacant.

Through the gaps in the gate, Valerie couldn't make out much of the interior of the compound, but she spotted a sun-faded gas pump, and the sight filled her with hope.

A chain, that she suspected might be for announcing visitors, dangled from one side of the gate.

She pulled it.

Instead of a bell, the chain triggered what sounded like a hundred tin cans falling from a height.

The crash of the cans was immediately followed by a cacophony of sound as at least ten different dogs rushed the gate and assaulted her ears with barking of every pitch and tone.

Valerie backed away from the snarling muzzles and bared teeth that snapped at her through chinks in the gate.

A moment later, a high whistle pierced the air. It trilled three times and the dogs went silent, all except for one tiny, wire-haired runt of terrier that continued to yip and snap as if it was the only defense the compound needed.

"Peaches! Shut your yap, you brainless fleabag."

The voice was that of a white-haired old man who wandered into view wearing a tattered bathrobe and unlaced boots. He carried a loaded crossbow.

The man disappeared from view as he walked to one side of the gate.

"Who are you and what do you want?"

Valerie turned toward the voice and spotted the old man's wizened face staring at her from a reflection in a side-view mirror. He had rigged a number of car door pieces at an angle, forming a sort of periscope that enabled him to view her from behind the safety of the wall.

"I saw you have a gas pump," Valerie said. "Also, my bike is damaged and needs repairs. And I could use some help finding my way back to the Queen's Highway."

"That's a lot of needin' from someone who ain't got a name," the voice replied.

"I'm Valerie Terravecchia of the House of Terravecchia. I'm a traveler on my way to join the Knights of the Round Table."

"Then I suppose I'm due to be elected Pope."

Valerie sighed. "I'm not making it up." She unclipped the silver badge from the front of her jacket and held it in the air.

"Come closer," the voice said. "Can't see nothin' that far away."

Valerie took a few steps forward, holding the badge up to the reflection in the mirror.

The eyes in the mirror squinted. "Ain't never seen one up close anyhow. You have any other proof?"

"If you have a telephone, I can make a call and prove it to you."

"No phone line out here."

"What about a radio?" Valerie offered. "I saw your antenna."

The man seemed to consider this. "What kind of motorcycle is it?"

"It's a Troublemaker 100. Has a hole in the fuel tank I need to fix."

"Terravecchia. Where have I heard that name before?"

"My family owns a vineyard in Briar Valley, near the west coast. Maybe you've had our wine?"

"How'd you come all the way from Briar Valley on a Troublemaker 100?"

"It's a long story to tell to a wall," Valerie said. "And it would be a lot easier to tell with some water. Will you please let me in? I can pay you for your services."

The man grunted, and then the reflection in the mirror disappeared. A chain rattled, and something behind the gate shifted. The gate swung open a few feet on creaky hinges.

"Leave the sword outside."

Valerie unbuckled her sword belt and held *Firebird* by its scabbard. "I ran into a gang of thieves in the woods. I'd prefer to keep it close if you don't mind."

"Set it inside the gate then. No further." The old man lifted his crossbow and made sure Valerie saw it.

The pack of dogs immediately set to sniffing Valerie the moment she stepped inside. Her hands received a few quick licks from the more affectionate ones. The tiny wire-haired dog that seemed the most ferocious at the outset was now pawing at her leg, vying for her attention.

"Down, Peaches!" the old man shouted. "You mangy wad of carpet."

Valerie rested her sword against the wall near the gate and moved inside.

The old man secured the gate latches, then gestured toward the central building of the compound. Valerie saw now that it was a service station. The fuel pumps were covered by an overhang, and beyond them, a pair of garage doors yawned open, revealing a partially disassembled car on a lift, several motorbikes, and a pile of unrecognizable parts.

"I appreciate the hospitality," Valerie said. "I won't bother you long. I just need to repair the bike and purchase some fuel. Then I'll be on my way."

"You won't be leaving here anytime soon then," the old man said. "Not on a road bike, repaired or not."

Valerie was taken aback. "What do you mean? Why not?"

"Can't sell you fuel I ain't got. Pumps ran dry two weeks ago. Delivery got held up from what they say. Robbers. Bandits. Purloinin' outlaws. They hit last month's delivery too. Due for another delivery in a day or two, but I ain't holding my breath."

"You don't have anything here that runs?" Valerie asked, scanning the lot.

"Well, I didn't say that," the old man replied. "But you asked for gas. And I ain't got none to sell." He turned his back on her and shuffled toward the service station office, the pack of dogs on his heels.

Valerie swore under her breath and followed.

The office was a dingy place. The windows below a certain level were layered in a hazy smear made by curious wet dog noses. The glass farther up wasn't much cleaner. Road dust clung to everything, and nearly every surface was speckled with smudges from greasy fingers.

The old man shuffled around the counter, latching a half-gate behind himself. The counter held a cash register, a coffee cup half-full of pens, and a nameplate that read J. Jeremiah Fiddlestick. Beside it, a few sun-faded flyers were strewn about advertising Fiddlestick's Garage and Road House.

When she looked up again, J. Jeremiah Fiddlestick was pointing the crossbow at her chest. Valerie put her hands up. "I thought you said you'd help."

"Out of the way," the old man said.

Valerie stepped aside and he fired. The bolt whizzed across the office lobby and struck a thatched target mounted to the wall. The arrow sank straight into the bullseye.

"Can't have too many of these things loaded and lying about. Right, then. You said you wanted to use the radio." Fiddlestick tossed the crossbow to the counter with a thud. "Who exactly are you trying to call?"

Valerie lowered her hands and took a breath. "I have friends who will be looking for me. With any luck, they'll be on the Citizens Band.

"Meet me around back," the old man said. "I'll power on the kit."

He scooped up Peaches, then vanished through a curtained doorway behind the counter.

Valerie wandered back out the front door, a half dozen of the other dogs trotting happily in her wake. As she made her way around back, she passed several wrecks of cars that had been stripped for parts, then noticed a second building that looked like it might once have been a diner. The sign over the door read "Rosie's." Whoever Rosie was, she wasn't in view, and while the door to the diner was open, there appeared to be no activity inside.

"We used to be a whistle-stop for the road trains in the old days."

Fiddlestick's sudden reappearance made Valerie jump. It was as though he had simply materialized out of the junk surrounding her. He set Peaches on the ground, then went on talking.

"Of course, that was before the Queen's Highway came through. Nowadays, ain't many have cause to come up this way. Hooligans mostly. Outlaws and brigands. Not many decent folk make the trek. Too far out of the way. I keep telling the regiment. We need more law and order out here before they can expect any more settlers to make it."

"Why do you stay?" Valerie asked. "Can't you move closer to the highway?"

"This is where the family is," Fiddlestick replied. He gestured toward an unruly flower bed dotted with tiny, stone grave markers. Valerie could make out only a few of the names. Tinkles. Chewy. Mister Buster. But there was another, larger grave marker that stood apart, closer to the wall. This one had a set of dates carefully carved into it, and the name read, "Tommy."

Valerie turned to study her host, but he was already shuffling away.

The windmill antenna array loomed even larger up close. Valerie was forced to crane her neck to make out the top of it. The mechanisms were noisy as well, squeaking and creaking as they turned a variety of devices at ground level. She was thrilled to see one such apparatus was a water pump. A steady trickle of water was coursing out of a pipe and collecting in various dog bowls on the ground, one of which was overflowing.

"Is that well water safe for drinking?" she asked.

"Help yourself," Fiddlestick replied. "There's a ladle by the spigot.

Valerie located the metal ladle and cleaned it with her shirt, then scooped several mouthfuls of water from the stream trickling from the pipe. She wiped her mouth as she filled the ladle again. "How far are we from the Queen's Highway?"

"As the crow flies, it ain't so far. But it's on the far side of Buffalo River. River's likely swollen this time of year, and it's a long way around by car." Fiddlestick opened a control panel on the side of the windmill structure, hung a pair of battered earphones around his neck, then started flipping switches. "Fastest way to connect is northeast. You can take Old Forge Road to Rust Creek. The village there has lodging, food—it's Lord Hudson's land. Redrock Castle is there. Lord Hudson himself could help you if you are who you say you are. The forge road runs south from there, meets up with the Queen's Highway near Hudsonville." He held one earphone to his ear and twisted a dial.

"Except I've got no way to get to Redrock Castle," Valerie said. "You're out of gas. We're stuck here."

"I've never been stuck in my life," Fiddlestick replied. He hung the earphones back on their hook. "Gas ain't the only ticket." He moved around the side of the windmill and pulled a tarp from atop a parts pile, revealing an odd contraption that Valerie vaguely recognized as a motorbike.

It was even smaller than the Troublemaker she rode in on.

Instead of an engine, it had a battery and electric motor.

"This here is Sparky," Fiddlestick said. "It's not the fastest ride in town, but it will make Rust Creek and back on a full charge. Comes in handy during the fuel draughts."

An electric bike.

"Are you willing to part with it?" Valerie asked.

"Nope."

Damn.

"What about a loan? You can have the Troublemaker."

Fiddlestick put a hand to his hip as he considered her. "I actually might be willing to do a loan, but only if you agree to a delivery while you're there. Been needing to make a trip, but it's hard to leave this crew long enough to do it." He gestured to the pack of dogs gathered around. "If you did the ride up for me today, I could take my time, hitch along with the farmers headed to town this weekend for market and bring Sparky back then. Is that agreeable to you?"

"That would be a godsend."

"Fine. I'll go get your cargo then. You see if you can make that radio work for you."

The old man waddled off, and Valerie made her way to the radio. The writing on the knobs was faded, and it was hard to make out which channel was which, but she selected what she hoped was channel twenty-eight and keyed the mic.

"Danger Dog, this is Alley Cat. You out there?"

She paused for twenty seconds, then repeated the call. Valerie twisted the knob to the channel to either side, trying calls there, then flipped back to what she thought was twenty-eight. "Danger Dog, this is Alley Cat. If you read me, I'm okay. Headed to a town called Rust Creek. If anyone else out there hears this and can relay a message, this is Alley Cat for Danger Dog. Meet me in Rust Creek."

J. Jeremiah Fiddlestick returned with a small basket covered with a blanket.

"I haven't heard a reply from anyone yet."

"I can keep the message going out while you're gone," he replied.

As Fiddlestick approached, Valerie noted that the blanket was moving. He pressed the entire basket into her arms.

"There you go then."

Valerie looked down just in time to have a reddish gold muzzle come out of the folds of the blanket and a tiny tongue licked her chin. The blanket fell away to reveal the oversized paws and eager eyes of a mixed breed puppy. It squirmed in the basket and licked at her again.

"He's the pick of the litter," Fiddlestick said. "See that he gets to a Miss Clara Foster up at the mercantile. Then we'll call it square." He grinned at her. "I'll go start the bike."

5

DELIVERY

Damon twisted the key in the ignition. The engine turned over, coughed a few times, then went silent.

"Still nothing," he shouted out the open driver's door.

A muttering of curses came from the front of the car where Rico was tinkering under the hood.

They had made decent time up the twisting mountain road, until the remnants of a rockslide cut off their planned route, forcing them to backtrack and detour on a route that had taken them far higher up the mountain than anticipated. The Vulcan wasn't having it.

"I think the wastegate on the turbocharger is part of the problem," Rico said. "It's stuck. When was the last time you lubricated this thing?"

The Vulcan's engine had lost power dramatically during the uphill climb, virtually gasping in the thinner air.

Damon clenched the steering wheel. "I've had a lot going on." An excuse and an admission. Vehicle maintenance had indeed taken a back seat in the last few weeks. His attention had been on Valerie Terravecchia, his protégé, his student, his obsession. The truth was he'd been soaking up their time together before heading east. Back at court, his time would belong to someone else again. His queen. But for the first time he could remember, his devotion to Queen Kimiko had serious competition.

It was a devotion that now left him fidgeting and agitated on the side of the road. "I'm turning the accessories back on. Trying the radio again."

They had tried hailing the Guardian all night, but so far, their designated channel only rendered static, an unanswered plea for news. Anything to keep his worst fears at bay.

He wasn't used to this. His professional life was complicated enough. He had always kept his personal life simple as a result. The job of a queen's agent required detachment, secrecy, and a willingness to sacrifice everything for the crown. It was a life he had relished until now—the danger, the adrenaline, but also the importance of doing work that mattered. There were lives being lived right now because he had saved them. And some that were ended because of him too.

Now here he was on a wild detour, chasing the girl who was systematically dismantling all of his defenses. His life was now anything but simple.

He squeezed the mic. "Alley Cat, this is Danger Dog. You out there?" He waited a few moments and repeated the call twice more, each time with fading optimism. He finally hung up the mic and laid his head back against the headrest. He was about to turn off the radio when a man's voice came over the speaker.

"I hear you, Danger Dog. This is J.J. Fiddlestick. Your Alley Cat is on the move. Lit out of Windtower Station about an hour ago."

Damon snatched up the mic. "Say again, J.J.?"

"I said your Alley Cat left Windtower Station an hour ago. She's headed for Rust Creek."

Damon snatched at the maps on the passenger seat and frantically searched for the town name. "Roger, J.J. You talked to her? She's okay?"

Rico appeared at the passenger side and leaned on the windowsill to listen.

"As well as can be. Came in on a shot-up 100cc Troublemaker. Judging by the arrow I found lodged in the fuel tank, I'm guessing some of the natives tried to use her for a pin cushion."

Damon and Rico's eyes met as they listened.

"She's headed up to Redrock Castle now. Suspect you'll find her with Lord Hudson before long."

"You're a saint, J.J.," Damon said. "I can't thank you enough. If you have any more contact from her, tell her we'll meet her there."

"Will do, Danger Dog. Over and out."

"Well, that's the best news we could've asked for," Rico said.

"Thank God," Damon muttered. He felt as though a cement mixer had been parked on his chest but now was gone. He hadn't realized how much he had been holding back from acknowledging the danger.

"At this rate, I'll have gray hair by the time we make the east coast."

"Speak for yourself," Rico said. "Drama keeps me young."

Damon studied the map again. "Rust Creek. We can be there in a few hours once we get running." He climbed out of the car and met Rico around front of the engine compartment. "So now all we have to do is figure out how."

Rico pulled a hammer from the tool kit. "Unjam that wastegate actuator spring for me. I'll go after the fuel mixture adjustment. Don't worry. We'll have this thing back on the road in no time."

Valerie reached over the handlebars for the third time in the last sixty seconds, doing her best to keep her canine cargo from leaping out of its basket. The puppy was cute, but an easy passenger it was not.

She had covered over fifteen miles, heading north-northeast on the dirt road that ran from Fiddlestick's service station. She was exhausted and covered in dust. On the positive side, the electric motorbike was easy to manage one-handed, even if it meant that free hand was constantly retrieving an excitable ball of fur with a death wish.

By the time she reached the road sign pointing the way to Rust Creek, she had almost given up hope of making it. "Sparky" was living up to its name. The battery compartment was hot and smelled strongly of evaporating chemicals, and she kept hearing disturbing crackling noises along the bike's frame. When she reached the outskirts of town, she turned down a main road and received a multitude of stares from villagers who seemed to have no problem stopping everything they were doing to watch her cruise by.

The town's outer wall was made of wood—thick, weathered tree trunks propped vertically and sharpened at the tops to discourage climbers. This perimeter barricade was guarded at a vehicle gate by a handful of men in mismatched armor. They eyed the sword slung across Valerie's back as she pulled up.

"All weapons must be surrendered while inside the wall," one of the guards said by way of greeting.

"You're wearing a sword," Valerie noted.

"We're City Watch," the man explained, tugging at the front of his uniform to display the crest of House Hudson.

"I've got one of those too," Valerie said, unclipping the badge from her belt and holding it aloft. "I'm Lady Valerie Terravecchia. King Logan has invited me to take the position of Knight Warden of the West, and I'll be keeping my sword."

The guard's eyes roamed over the cross and crown on the badge. He exchanged a glance with one of his companions, then he backed away with a grudging bow. "Your ladyship is welcome. If you follow the main road, it will take you to the gate of Redrock Castle. I'll announce your arrival to his lordship."

Valerie nodded, stuffed the badge into her pocket, then rolled on, noting the murmurs among the guards as she went.

Rust Creek was a town that could use a rinse if ever she saw one. The dust she had collected on her ride had nothing on the layers of dirt the few vehicles she spotted were sporting. It was as though each truck or tractor was in a competition to see which could go unwashed the longest. More than a few of the citizens seemed to be participating as well. After hours on the frontier, the scent of wood stoves, sweaty bodies, and questionable plumbing was an affront to the senses. Valerie kept her course down the main road and watched for any sign of the mercantile. She was eager to offload her tiny companion, whose excited yips were attracting more attention than she wanted.

The dog ceased being her primary concern when the motorbike suddenly sent an electric shock from the mirror support to one of her fingers.

She cursed in alarm, shaking her finger, then eyed the bike warily while trying to focus again. She came upon a town square or plaza, the busiest feature of which was a saloon surrounded by an array of motorcycles. Huge men in metal-studded leather eyed her as she attempted to steer the now faintly smoking motorbike across the square. Despite the law against weapons, she noted the majority of the men were armed in some fashion. Long knives and cudgels hung from belts, and one man had an axe slung across his back.

Another electric shock to her knee set Valerie cursing again. This time she leapt off the bike, snatching the puppy from the basket and letting the motorcycle go. It wobbled toward the side of the plaza, just missing someone's road bike, then teetered and fell. A loud pop was accompanied by a flash of light, then hissing and smoking followed. Valerie backed away as the compartment under the seat burst into flames.

Townsfolk were making an appearance on every nearby front porch and stoop. The saloon doors opened, and soon Valerie was surrounded by curious onlookers. One brave soul pushed through with a fire extinguisher and doused the smoking bike with extinguishing agent.

When the fire was out, Valerie was left standing in the middle of a circle of unmoving faces. Even the puppy had gone still, watching for what would happen next.

"That's what comes of riding sissy bikes," one onlooker said, drawing laughter from his companions on the porch.

"You need us to call your mommy, kid?" another asked. "Maybe she'll buy you another toy."

Valerie's face flushed. She tried to keep her anger in check, though it still crept into her voice. "I'm looking for the mercantile. Will someone point me that way please?"

A few glances turned up the street, and one man pointed a gnarled finger. Valerie followed the gesture to the building he indicated, then turned on her heel and headed that direction, doing her best to ignore the sniggers and laughter in her wake.

A bell dinged as she pushed through the door of the shop. The store was the cleanest space she'd encountered so far, recently swept and lined with neatly ordered shelves. Bread flour, sacks of nuts, dried fruit, and pickled preserves were popular. Odds and ends lined the walls, everything from braided rope to lamp oil. She found the proprietor at a cash register near a bay window.

The woman looked up, and a smile immediately spread across her face. She walked toward a door that led to some stairs and shouted up them. "Clara! Come down. You've got a surprise!"

A rustling overhead was followed by the clomping of small feet as a girl of perhaps six came thundering down the stairs. "Is it him? Is it him?" The girl spotted Valerie and immediately rushed over, then stopped short as she peered up at her. "Is that . . . is that for me?"

Valerie lowered the now squirming puppy to the little girl's hands. "I hope you two will be very happy together."

The little girl squealed, then rushed back to her mother. "Can I take him upstairs?"

"Why don't you find a crate out back first, and then go get him some water. Looks like these two have had a dusty drive. Didn't hear you thank our new friend."

"Thank you, ma'am," the little girl said, then rushed past her mother to the back.

The proprietor looked up to Valerie. "I take it J.J. couldn't make it to town?"

"He said he'd be up this weekend for the market. Sent me in his place."

"We're much obliged," the woman said. "Can I get you anything? A drink perhaps?"

"Wouldn't say no to some water. Is there anyone in this village that does vehicle repair? The bike Mr. Fiddlestick lent me is going to need work."

The proprietor filled a cup from a ceramic jug behind the counter. "The local mechanic is around the corner. He's out on a call right now, but I can have him find you when he gets back. Your bike rideable or is it going to need a pickup?" She slid the cup to Valerie.

"Definitely a pickup. It's in front of a saloon down the street."

"Make and model?" The woman snatched up a pen and pad of paper.

"Won't be hard to find," Valerie said. "The one that was recently on fire. Just tell him to store it for now. I'll figure out what to do about it later." Valerie took a sip from the cup of water, then looked out the window. "Who's the law in this town? Is there a constable or local peace warden? I need to report a theft."

"Sheriff Trammel is the one to talk to. You can find her in the tavern most likely. She takes appointments in there instead of the jailhouse."

"Which tavern?"

"We only have the one. Same one where you parked your bike."

Valerie muttered under her breath, then set the cup down. She unslung the scabbard from her back and affixed it at her hip instead.

"They don't allow swords inside the walls," the proprietor said. "Unless you're part of the sheriff's crew."

"I won't be staying long," Valerie said. "Thank you for your help and the drink. I didn't get your name."

"Leslie," the woman replied.

Valerie extended a hand and Leslie shook it. On her way out the door, the proprietor called out to her. "The town isn't as sleepy as it seems. Best watch yourself."

Valerie paused and studied the woman. It didn't seem as though any more information was forthcoming. "Like I said. I won't be staying long."

Leslie nodded. "Probably best."

6

BOUNTY

Valerie stepped out of the mercantile and took in the dingy buildings and dilapidated roofs of the town. The road, what she could see of it, couldn't have ever been straight. She supposed there might be some defensive advantage to having a maze of twisting avenues obscuring the path to the castle, but she thought it more plausible that the city engineer had simply been drunk and staggered around the village marking plots for buildings at random.

Valerie walked with growing dread back the way she had come, brushing the layer of dust from her jacket and doing her best to regain the dignity of her position. Mercifully, the wreck of Sparky seemed to have lost its appeal, and townsfolk were no longer gawking at it. She did her best to ignore the ignominious scene of her initial arrival and pushed her way through the doors of the local tavern.

The interior of the tavern still retained sconces for gas lamps on the roof supports, as though the addition of electric lighting might be a fad to be thought better of later. The long bar ran laterally across the back wall and bent in an L shape to cover three-quarters of the lefthand wall as well. A few multipaned windows meant customers seated at these stools were treated to a shortsighted view of the clapboard building next door.

Roughly a dozen customers were seated around tables, a scattering of loners with drinks in their hands and a small gathering of dice players having a raucous game of Shut-the-Box. More than a few pairs of eyes trailed her movements as she made her way to the bar, though no one accosted her. The barman met her with a polite smile. "What can I get for you, miss?"

"I was told I could find the sheriff here," Valerie replied.

"You were told right," the barman said. He gestured toward the corner of the tavern opposite the bar where a ponderous woman was seated at a booth littered with potato chip crumbs and loose paperwork.

Valerie nodded to the barman and walked over to the booth, sizing up the woman as she went. Sheriff Trammel did not look up as Valerie approached, instead keeping her eyes fixed on a fistful of receipts she was busy counting out and marking.

"Told you I don't want to be disturbed while I'm working," the woman said.

"I'm not staff," Valerie said. "Excuse my intrusion."

The sheriff did look up at this, but her mud-colored eyes roamed over Valerie without haste or any spark of interest. "You must be the stranger everyone was talking about. The one who left that flaming piece of—" Her voice cut off as her gaze landed on the hilt of Valerie's sword.

"There are no swords allowed—"

"Within the walls. Yes," Valerie finished for her. "But I won't be staying long. My vehicle has been stolen, and I require assistance getting it back."

Trammel's eyelids drooped and her upper lip receded as she spoke. "Becoming a victim of a crime does not authorize you to disregard local ordinance. Your sword should have been surrendered at the gate unless you have prior authorization from me. I'm the authority on weapons in this town, and I haven't authorized you."

"I had a prior authorization," Valerie said, pulling her badge from her pocket and cocking it toward the sheriff. "I'm en route to Glastonbury Castle, but the road train I was on was attacked. My war car was stolen. If you are the authority in this district, then I'd like to request your assistance in retrieving it."

Sheriff Trammel's gaze was still fixed to the warden badge as though disbelieving its existence and hoping to dispel the apparition through a sheer act of will. Finally, she grunted and rested an elbow on the table, waving her pen lazily with her fingertips. "Pursuit of car thieves is a job for a raised posse. Organization of such a group will require an authorization from me." Her jaw settled deeper into her face as she finished, vanishing somewhere amid the folds of her neck.

"That's why I'm here," Valerie said. "I'd like you to authorize such a group and help me pursue the thieves and bring them to justice. I've seen the culprits who did it and can identify one of them. I can take you to the last place I saw them. They also absconded with a fuel tanker from the train. Since the caravan was carrying noble passengers, that makes this a crime against His Majesty. I believe that requires additional urgency."

Sheriff Trammel swallowed, as if this new information had exceeded her capacity for consumption in one hearing. She took a deep breath, exhaling audibly through her nostrils, then set her papers aside. The booth creaked as she slid out, and the table groaned under the pressure of her hand as she used it to rise. Valerie noted that she wore the colors of House Hudson, though her tunic had faded to a murky impression of its original hue. A dagger hung at the woman's belt along with a silver badge, the lone item that appeared to have been recently cleaned.

Trammel turned and shouted to the barman. "Don't delay my lunch, Wyatt. I plan to be back for it."

The barman nodded and continued wiping out glasses.

Trammel stood at least an inch taller than Valerie and was easily twice her width. Valerie took a step back to allow the woman room to pass. The sheriff lumbered toward the door at a pace that befitted a glacier. Around the time she reached it, the street outside filled with noise. Valerie recognized the sound of at least a half dozen motorcycle engines along with a sound she couldn't place—a high-pitched, abrasive noise, like the steady scratching of spark plug threads against a wire wheel.

They stepped out into the daylight as the vehicles came into view. There were six motorcycles of various makes and sizes. Two were ridden by men that resembled those she had seen outside the tavern earlier. It was impossible to say if they were in fact the same men, as their bushy beards and dust covered leather jackets all projected the same "Don't mess with me" vibe. Two men had bandanas covering their faces, and all wore dark shades that obscured their eyes.

Two women were distinguishable among the group, one because she was flaunting a voluptuous chest via a red leather corset. Her bare shoulders were bronzed by the sun. The other woman was covered up entirely, but there could be no doubt about her sex. There was something in the way she sat astride the motorcycle that suggested she wasn't riding it so much as bending it to her will. She was dressed in form-fitting black pants and a jacket so tight that it left not a single surface for the wind to play with. Like the majority of the other riders, she wasn't wearing a helmet, but her hair was tucked up inside a hat with a stubby brim that jutted just above the rim of her shades. There was something sharp about the woman's figure, hard angles and a razor thin line of a mouth that suggested just looking at her could hurt you.

Valerie was fascinated by the woman, but her attention was diverted by the strange contraption bumping and scraping along the road behind her. It was a cylindrical cage made of twisted steel bars welded together at odd angles. It resembled a puzzle more than a cage—an artistic recreation of a mathematical impossibility. The motorcycle was towing the cage by means of a long pole and a central bearing that allowed the cylinder to roll.

The cage was occupied, and its occupant was screaming.

The prisoner appeared to be a man, bloodied and torn. There was little protection offered by the cage, other than the central bearing which acted as a sort of belt for the prisoner, pinning him in place at the center of the cylinder. Valerie tried to imagine how many stones had been kicked up by the bikes and how many more the cage might have collided with in its travels. Besides becoming sickeningly dizzy, there would also be the matter of the extreme heat that must have been generated by the friction of the cage against the road. A ride inside could only have been a surreal and merciless form of torture.

Valerie turned to observe the sheriff's reaction and was surprised to find a different version of the woman beside her. This Sheriff Trammel's eyes were bright and wide open, her chin was elevated and she took in the group with a look of what? Pride? Admiration?

It was clear the visitors were welcome in any case.

The six riders pulled up to the tavern. Engines cut off, boots crunched on gritty cobblestones, and the group dismounted. The cylindrical cage rolled to a stop, evoking new groans from the man inside.

A crowd of interested townspeople quickly gathered around the cage, gawking at the man inside, some with expressions of horror, others smiling and even laughing about the man's fate.

Valerie's stomach turned.

The woman towing the cage climbed off her bike and unfastened her gloves, tugging at each finger in succession, unhurried and unconcerned about the crowd. When she did look up, her gaze flicked to Trammel, then settled on Valerie and her sword. It was difficult to accurately read her expression behind her dark sunglasses, but Valerie thought she caught a flash of wariness—an involuntary tensing of her posture that lasted only an instant. Then she was striding forward, the soles of her knee-high boots tapping rhythmically up each step until she joined them on the porch. The woman's left hand rested on the hilt of a sword with a pommel in the shape of a viper's head.

"Nice of you to come out and meet us, Cissy. I'm touched." The woman was tall, close to 5'10" if Valerie had to guess, tall enough that she looked down on the sheriff.

Of all the monikers Valerie could have imagined calling the sheriff, "Cissy" would not have been one of them.

Sheriff Trammel hiked up her belt and didn't seem to mind the nickname. If anything, it made her look more relaxed. "Found Quintero quicker than I expected. I'd bet the ink on the wanted posters is still wet. Afraid I don't have your bounty payment written out just yet."

The bounty hunter patted Trammel on the shoulder. "I know you're good for it." She turned to the rest of the bikers and cocked a thumb toward the bar. "Drinks are on me tonight, you filthy heathens. It's time to get sloppy." Her fellow bikers trooped by, insulting one another and laughing as they went. More than a few eyes lingered on Valerie.

"Who's your new friend, Cissy baby?" the bounty hunter asked. She pulled her sunglasses from her face, revealing a pair of venom-green irises. She sized Valerie up before locking gazes with her.

"New arrival in town. She's crown law," Trammel explained. "A road train was attacked last night. Perhaps you saw something in your travels." The sheriff seemed to be fishing for something in particular, but Valerie couldn't discern what.

"Last night, you say? Can't say that I did. That must have been most frightening for you, though, miss..."

"Lady Valerie Terravecchia," Valerie said. Her fingers tapped against her sword hilt. "And it was only a temporary setback. I mean to bring the ones responsible to justice."

The woman's eyes flicked to Valerie's sword. "Crown law. Interesting. I'm Kai Nez. You've seen most of my crew pass by. Cissy here keeps us around to do her dirty work for her. Lord Hudson hates to see his town overrun by this sort of borderland filth." She gestured to the man in the cage who was now largely obscured by leering townsfolk. "He pays well for us to take out the trash." Her eyes came back to the sword at Valerie's hip. "What are you carrying there? Mind if I have a look?"

Sheriff Trammel turned and fixed her stare on Valerie as well, and Valerie felt suddenly as though she was being tested. She drew her sword from its scabbard, resting the blade carefully across the back of her opposite wrist.

"Impressive workmanship," Kai Nez said. "May I?" She held out a hand.

Something twisted inside Valerie. Her chest tightened as she had a sudden flashback to her brother Henry standing unarmed in a plaza in Port Hyacinth, her liege lord's son admiring Henry's sword, then plunging it through her brother's chest.

Kai Nez's eyes narrowed as she studied Valerie. It was as if she was peering into Valerie's past as well.

"Perhaps a momentary trade," Kai Nez said. She drew her own sword. The blade bore numerous scars, and there were notches deliberately cut into the cross guard. She tossed the sword in the air with a flourish, catching it again by the forte. She offered Valerie the viper-head pommel. "Careful. It bites." She feigned a strike with the pommel, causing Valerie to take a step back. Kai Nez laughed. She offered the sword to Valerie again, this time slowly. "May I present *Whipfang,* legacy sword of House Sqaumata, claimed in victory by the law of blood."

Valerie wrapped her fingers around the grip, then offered her own sword, pommel first. "This is *Firebird,* a first-generation sword of Merchant House Merriweather, gifted to me by a dear friend."

Kai Nez plucked *Firebird* from her hand using only a few

fingers, then let the sword dangle from them, her eyes still on Valerie's face. "A brand new sword for the land's newest knight. How fitting. Have you *been* knighted yet?"

"No. I've been invited by King Logan to join his Knights at the Round Table," Valerie replied. "But the ceremony will take place once I officially accept."

Kai nodded, then whirled *Firebird* about, testing the balance. "I have to say I like the way she feels. A sword like this must come with a story worth a drink. I presume you'll stay and have one with me."

Whipfang lay heavy in Valerie's hands. It was ancient masterworked steel reforged through the ages. A line of blood-red thread was stitched through the handgrip. It made Valerie wonder how many lives had met their end on the edge of this blade. As her eyes roamed over the notches in the cross guard, she got the impression its current owner might be keeping a count. But it was a story she wasn't sure she wanted to know.

"I really need to be—"

"You!"

The shout came from the street.

Valerie turned to find the crowd around the steel cage clearing. A man of perhaps thirty stood beside the twisted bars, a sword in hand. With midnight black hair and eyes to match, he appeared to be a Native Avalonian. He wore jeans and a checked shirt with sleeves rolled to the elbows. His wrists bore a variety of bracelets, and a string of talismans hung from his neck.

"You killed my brother."

Kai Nez and the sheriff both turned to face this new threat.

"How on earth did you get a cutting blade inside the town walls, James Whitecar?" The sheriff's irritated tone cut through the other noise on the street.

"You can have it back once I've cut this hellspawn's murderous heart from her chest," the man replied. He pointed the blade toward Kai Nez. "You had no call to do what you did to him."

"All I did was give your brother a ride to town, James," Kai Nez replied. "And he was alive when I brought him in."

"Does he look alive to you?" Whitecar jabbed a finger toward the portable steel prison, his voice quaking with rage.

The man in the cage had in fact gone still.

"If your brother wanted a better class of transportation, he should have stolen a faster car."

The man in the street lifted his sword. "I'm calling you out, she-devil. Today I'll see your blood run in the street."

The crowd murmured, and more eyes fell on the bounty hunter.

Kai Nez turned to Valerie and held out a hand. "Looks like I'll be needing that back."

They exchanged swords again. Valerie kept *Firebird* unsheathed, wary of how the commotion in the street might play out. Kai Nez donned her gloves again, then lifted her sword, kissing the hilt at the crossbars. She whispered something inaudible to it, then strode calmly down the steps.

James Whitecar walked to the center of the street, distancing himself by a dozen paces, then pivoting to face Kai Nez.

"Are you just going to let this happen?" Valerie asked the sheriff.

Sheriff Trammel's eyes were still on Kai Nez. "She knows what she's doing. I doubt Whitecar ever picked up a sword before today."

A number of people on the porch began talking at once, and Valerie noted crown notes being brandished. A scrawny man with a wisp of a goatee nudged her arm. He was holding a notepad and a chewed-on nub of a pencil. "You want a number?"

Valerie studied him quizzically. "For what?"

"I say she does it in one cut," Trammel interjected. She pulled a gold fifty-crown coin from her pocket and flashed it at the man.

A flurry of activity followed as others rushed to get in on the action. The scrawny, pencil man scribbled frantically and accepted bets from a half dozen more citizens. He looked to Valerie once more, lifting his chin in an unspoken question, but she shook her head. She tore her eyes from the frantic scene around her and focused instead on the street.

A variety of other townsfolk were watching from a distance. Unlike the rabid group on the saloon porch, these faces looked solemn and wary. At one corner of the square, Valerie caught sight of the little girl, Clara, oblivious to the action and attempting to walk her new puppy on a length of twine. Leslie, her mother, dashed from a side street and scooped her up, hauling them both out of sight.

Kai Nez had handed off her hat, revealing a curtain of straight black hair that she took a moment to push away from her face. Her sword point was stuck in the dirt between two cobblestones, but when she finished running her fingers through her hair, she plucked the weapon from the ground and wiped the tip on her sleeve.

James Whitecar was twitching in anticipation, his shoulders flexing, feet unable to remain still. He shifted his weight side to side, his eyes boring into his opponent as if trying to bind her to him with his fury.

Kai Nez was statuesque in her stillness, a monument to calm, but Valerie noted the piercing intensity of her stare. There was something fierce and unholy about the woman's ability to shut out the clamor of the street—an ice-cold center to this roiling whirlwind of tension. A tension that threatened to ignite and incinerate the crowd around them.

There was no official to call a start, no seconds had been enlisted or boundaries set. It seemed the only check on the action was the internal dam holding back Whitecar's rage. The dam broke as Valerie watched, a primal scream erupting from the man's lips as he raised his sword and charged. His boots kicked up dirt as he ran, sword forward, a bull with its horns down, seeking to trample Kai Nez beneath heavy hooves.

But Kai Nez was moving too, sprinting, without even a flicker of hesitation. She didn't run as much as she flew, an arrow sprung from a bow, piercing the air in an unnaturally straight line. Her sword trailed behind, and her unbound hair lofted from her shoulders. For that moment, Kai Nez was fascinatingly beautiful.

Valerie was transfixed by the action. The crowd was unruly, loud, chaotic, but when Kai Nez's feet left the ground, the air went still, the crowd's breath held in unison—a collective symphony of silence. It was broken by the sound of steel against something distinctly not steel. A wet, warm sound, soft and viscous. It was followed by several quick thuds, Kai Nez's boots reintroducing her to the earth.

She didn't turn around. She stood in the center of the road and slowly raised her sword. She kissed the cross bars again, her fingers twisting around the crimson line in the grip, her lips caressing the metal slowly, almost indecently.

James Whitecar collapsed on his face in the dirt and didn't move again.

7

REPRIEVE

Valerie held a mostly-empty drink in her hand but hadn't taken so much as a sip. The glass of bourbon had been pressed into her palm sometime after the riotous commotion that had swept her into the tavern. She lost the majority of it while being jostled by chest-high elbows before ultimately becoming trapped in the corner near the piano. The waves of enthusiasm washing over the crowd seemed to crest ever higher inside the saloon. Valerie felt as though she was sloshing to and fro in a circumscribed sea, a tiny ship tossed about in an ever more crowded bottle.

It was impossible to absorb all of the clamor and energy of the townspeople after James Whitecar's efficient and bloody demise. Even if Valerie had been able to successfully lift her newly acquired drink to her lips while squeezed amid the press of humanity filling the saloon, she would presumably need to breathe first. It was a feat she hadn't attempted in close to half a minute. The last breaths she'd taken had smelt of unwashed bodies unconvincingly camouflaged by cheap cologne.

She was exhausted, her nerves frayed by both her lack of

sleep and the adrenaline-fueled peaks of the last twelve hours. She wanted nothing more than to crawl off to some dark place and recover. Her mind was threatening to take her there without her body if she didn't act soon. It was this state of mental revolt that caused her to not register the shouts of her name the first few times they fell on her ears. It was finally the shape of her name on the man's lips that she recognized, incisors biting into a lower lip, then a tongue flicking off them before the man's mouth formed the precursor to the hesitant smile that finished her name. Lay-dee Val-Er-EE.

The man was slender, clean-shaven, and actually clean, a fact she appreciated next as he pushed his way to her, and she finally let herself inhale. He had a dry, musty smell about him, the smell of an old library and desiccated books. He stood in sharp contrast to the turmoil around them, a hand held out politely, his mouth forming words again. This time he shouted to be heard. "Please come with me! Lord Hudson wishes to speak to you!"

Valerie didn't need a second invitation.

She abandoned her drink atop the piano, then followed the man as he forged his way onward. Her fingers grasped the folds at the back of his jacket, her lifeline to freedom. Valerie turned back only once, her head pulled around in curiosity, her gaze drawn like a magnet to the center of the room where Kai Nez was still surrounded by enthralled townsfolk.

Kai Nez wasn't pressed in upon by the crowd. To the contrary, she was being treated with a reverent awe. The only ones within arm's reach were her black-clad rider companions, the trusted disciples of this dark messiah. Kai Nez met Valerie's eyes as she left. Only for a moment, but the look was a statement worth a hundred words.

See this? See who I am? See what violence I can unleash?

In that moment Valerie thought she truly resembled a viper, but instead of falling victim to the rhythmic adulation of the crowd, it was Kai Nez who had put the rest of them in a trance.

Valerie broke eye contact only with effort, pulled away by her anonymous lifeline and towed into the daylight.

She breathed deeply outside, and the sunlight made her feel like she was waking from a dream.

"Please come this way," her companion said and gestured to a waiting automobile in the street.

Valerie didn't hesitate. There was something lustily attractive about the sight of the car's open rear passenger door and plush cushioned seat. It was safety, luxury, a door with a lock. She gave only a passing thought to the state of her clothes, slapping at the dust on her trousers and unbuckling her sword belt before climbing eagerly inside.

The door shut with a satisfying thud, cutting off the sounds of the outside world.

Valerie could breathe.

"It's a short drive," her savior said as he slid into the driver's seat and started the car.

Valerie didn't need it to be a short drive. She was moving again. Away from the bloodstains in the dirt outside the tavern. Toward somewhere she hoped would be a phone, a bath, and a path onward. She let her eyes close as the man drove.

Ten minutes later she opened them again, in time to witness the car pulling through an arched stone gate. She had missed whatever visual clues the driver must have given to pass within the walls because they were already inside the boundaries of Redrock Castle. This was a proper castle with stone walls and no sign of wooden logs, but the stone itself was true to its name—a dry, windswept, copper-colored sandstone. The castle had not been erected so much as carved, formed to fit the existing outcrops of stone that jutted from the earth at violent angles like so many sea creatures breaching the surface of a terrestrial sea.

Sandstone would have seemed a fragile base for a fortress had there not been so much of it. Valerie was also impressed by the beauty of the vista they had achieved. Sometime during the drive they had ascended at least a thousand feet, and now her passenger window offered a nearly panoramic view of the surrounding mountains and high plain.

The winding road that climbed ever higher was bringing her close to the central keep of the castle, a relatively low structure when compared to the natural rock features. It was surrounded by other long, stable-like buildings that she soon recognized as garages. Valerie hadn't seen many cars in town at all, but several of these garage doors stood open, revealing shining paint and polished chrome. There were utility vehicles and war cars but also highly-polished classic vehicles like a pair of matching Rockwell Falcons and a Westburg Boomerang. As they drove on, she also spotted luxury cars, limousines, and what must have been the prize of the showcase, a gold-tinted Monarch 8.

Even in her exhausted state, the sight of the cars roused her enough to realize that Lord Hudson was a very wealthy man.

She was relieved to find the driver of her vehicle didn't slow at the entrance to the main house. He continued on, winding around to a rear courtyard and what appeared to be a trio of guest cottages backed up against yet another red rock wall.

The driver sprung out of the car after parking and opened the door for her.

"Lord Hudson hopes you will make yourself comfortable. He knows you've had a tiring journey. You will find a closet at your disposal, and whatever amenities you wish for can be requested from the maids. They will hasten to assist you. Please rest and refresh yourself. His Lordship would be honored if you would join him this evening for supper. It will be served at sunset on the terrace."

The idea of a hot shower and change of clothes followed by a soft bed sounded rapturous. Valerie resisted the pull, however. "Do you have a telephone? Before I rest, I really need to make a call."

"Of course, my lady. Right this way."

She slung her sword belt over her shoulder and followed the driver past another cottage and into the extreme southern wing of the main house. A private room that smelled of wildflowers and old wood housed a sort of booth built into the wall. A small table and chair offered a place to sit, and the telephone hung within easy reach.

"I'll need a directory of road-train stations along the Queen's Highway."

"You'll find the directory in the drawer, just beneath the table," the driver said. "Will you need assistance returning to your cottage?"

"I can find my own way. Thank you," Valerie replied.

"Very well, then," the man said. He bowed and made a polite exit, closing the door behind him. Valerie searched for the drawer he mentioned and located the directory. It was the work of several minutes locating a map and the names of the proper stations, but she finally took the receiver in hand and dialed Hudsonville Station first.

A pleasant-sounding woman on the other end of the line greeted her.

"Yes. I was a passenger aboard the road train that was attacked last night, seeking word from other passengers I was traveling with."

In a series of calls and transfers, she was finally able to speak with a station attendant from the night before who informed her that Damon and Rico had left during the night in Damon's Vulcan, headed north. They had received no word from them since. Valerie called a few more places along the mountain route until someone finally was able to relay a message.

"A Vulcan? Yes. They came through this morning, said they were headed to a town called Rust Creek to meet a friend. I heard them talking to someone on the CB radio. Sounded like they were in a hurry."

Valerie's chest suddenly felt a thousand times lighter. She had to restrain herself from letting out a shriek of joy. Damon was on his way! He might already be in the village for all she knew. Her next call was to the communications operator in Rust Creek.

No. A Vulcan hadn't arrived yet. Yes, he would take a message and inform her as soon as the vehicle arrived. Valerie mentioned, for a second time, that she could be found at Redrock Castle with Lord Hudson. The man assured her again that he would pass along the message.

Valerie floated back to the cottage in a comfortable haze, the sort of blurry tiredness that left her feeling vaguely silly. She informed the servant attending her at the cottage that she would like to be awoken prior to sunset or in the event anyone called for her. The servant nodded fervently until Valerie felt assured that she had done all she could for the time being.

At the sight of the bed in the cottage, she was tempted to collapse face first into the pillows immediately, but she forced herself to shower first, rinsing a minor mudslide of dirt from her body and hair. After toweling off and dressing in a soft oversized shirt she discovered in a dresser, she noted someone had left a selection of crackers and cheeses on a table near her bed, along with what appeared to be fresh milk. She wolfed down several combinations of crackers and cheeses in a matter of minutes, crunching and drinking until the yawning emptiness of her stomach was replaced by a satisfied sense of impending peace.

The bed beckoned. She didn't bother to close the secondary curtains on the thinly veiled window, she simply burrowed beneath the covers and buried her head among the multitude of pillows.

Damon was on his way. She was safe. She had help. She could sleep.

But sleep didn't come immediately. Her eyelids were squeezed tight, but her mind still wrestled with the sights and sounds of her last twenty-four hours. Down in the village, two men lay dead, waiting for burial. A woman with a snake head on her sword was laughing, and somewhere in the mountains, a girl with kohl rimmed eyes was tearing down the road driving *her* car.

When Valerie did finally drift off to sleep, each one of the figures lingered in her mind and then haunted her dreams.

8

PITSTOP

Rico "Caliente" Cabrera wasn't able to hold it any longer.

"There's an outpost on the map. I don't think it's far. Maybe five miles," Damon said.

"I'm not going to make it," Rico groaned. "Just pull over."

This wasn't going to be pleasant. Rico knew that there were people in the world who relished being outdoors, existing far from civilization, seeing no one, and doing their business in the woods. He was not one of those people.

Rico enjoyed his privacy and preferred when it came with a roof, walls, and indoor plumbing. Would it be nice to have scented candles and perfumed air fresheners and a warm bidet? Of course it would. But he wasn't a diva. He had roughed it in public facilities plenty of times. But those were at least facilities.

The Vulcan's tires crunched gravel as the car rolled to a stop. Rico broke the seal on the passenger door with a subtle sucking sound. His feet landed in the gravel, and he was up and out of the car in an instant, his eyes already on the tree line.

"Hey. Don't forget this."

Rico turned to find Damon's muscled arm reaching across the passenger seat, a roll of toilet paper in his outstretched hand.

God, this was embarrassing. Of course it had to be Damon witnessing this, the sculpted demigod of sheer manliness, battle scars twisting in a web down his arm. Rico had no doubt that Damon had, at some time or another, done his business in the woods. He was that kind of guy. A man's man. But even more than that, Damon was the kind of guy who probably managed to somehow maintain his dignity in the process. The forest must thank him as though he had graced it with a favor.

Rico snatched the roll from Damon's hand, not making eye contact. Those gorgeous, slate-gray eyes were unbearable to look at as it was, he didn't need to deal with them now. It would just be rubbing salt in the wound.

"Watch out for poison oak," Damon shouted.

Rico swore inwardly. He hadn't even thought of that. Poisonous plants? The indignity of this wasn't enough? He supposed he also had to watch out for snakes and bears and wolves. He crept gingerly down the slope to where the trees had taken root. They were sparse here, not nearly the coverage he needed, so he waddled on. His gut clenched as he used the power of his mind to force his body to wait.

Wait wait wait.

His eyes roamed over each bush and bramble suspiciously. He didn't even recall what poison oak looked like. Had he ever known? Nothing here looked safe.

A bramble caught the leg of his pants, scratching at his calf and making him recoil. He dodged some sort of rodent hole and then a pile of animal droppings the size of bloated raisins. He looked at the pile only long enough to decide it had to have come from a small creature, then moved on. Perhaps it was a fluffy little rabbit. Some sort of miniature deer?

A squiggly branch in the grass made him start. If it had been a rattlesnake, he most certainly wouldn't have seen it in time. He would be dying a slow painful death right now.

He took a breath and focused.

The cluster of trees ahead looked promising. If he squinted, he could almost imagine them as a sort of structure. A tree house, the kind occupied by friendly elves or talking animals in storybooks. It wouldn't be the worst place in existence. He could do this.

When he reached the cluster of trees, he circled it once, examining the space from all angles. That knobby protrusion there could almost be a seat. The tree behind it could offer a little back support, couldn't it? He edged closer, then swatted at an iridescent, green beetle threatening to commandeer his spot.

"Shoo! Shoo!" He poked at the critter, first with a limp square of toilet paper, then with the stem end of a leaf. The beetle paused in its journey to wherever it was going, its antenna waving to and fro as it assessed this threat, then it slowly turned around and crept back the way it had come. Rico threw the leaf at it for good measure.

"Okay. This will all be over soon," he muttered. Unfastening his pants, he positioned himself on the makeshift seat and closed his eyes. He would imagine he was somewhere else. "I'll be at a palace soon," he said to no one in particular. "We'll pick up Valerie and be back on our way, and all of this will be just a bad memory that we will never speak of to anyone."

When he had completed the deed, he pushed himself off the tree knurl and hitched up his pants. He had used more of the toilet paper roll than had been strictly necessary, but one had to take the luxuries they could in these circumstances, few and far between though they may be. He was about to turn back the way he had come when he noted the burble in the distance. A stream. Some sort of waterfall. A place to rinse his hands would make this whole situation almost tolerable. He headed that direction.

It was a stream. Not just a rivulet of snowmelt either. The stream was wide enough to create a natural clearing between the trees. As Rico descended to the bank, he was met with rays of afternoon sun. He rested his roll of toilet paper carefully on a stone, then stooped to rinse his hands. The water was ice cold. He scrubbed at his fingers, then went so far as to rub his wet hands on the back of his neck. The sensation revived him and sent a pleasing chill across his skin. It was actually beautiful here. As the sunlight danced off the rippling water, he let a smile part his lips. Maybe he was outdoorsy after all.

"If I have to climb into this stinking getup one more time, I'm going to murder someone."

Rico froze.

The man speaking stood not more than a dozen feet away, his back to the stream, stripping out of a leather jacket bedecked with fringe. His dark hair was pulled into a tight braid that hung down his back. A raspy female voice came from just beyond a shrub on the same side of the stream as Rico. "If you'd bother to wash your clothes more than once a year, you wouldn't smell like the inside of a buffalo's ass." A lighter clicked closed, and a moment later Rico caught a whiff of cigarette smoke.

Through gaps in the branches of the shrub, Rico saw the woman stoop and splash her face, scrubbing at her cheeks with one hand while holding her cigarette aloft with the other. Her face ran with the remnants of war paint, and there were feathers and beads dangling from her hair.

But these people weren't Native Avalonians. The woman was a baked apple brown and her hair was black, but it wasn't a glossy natural black. Rico recognized the spotty, inconsistent hue of cheap hair dye. Her roots were actually a mousy brown tinged with a few strands of gray. Whoever the woman was, she needed a better stylist.

A third person stepped from behind a stand of trees and made his way to the stream. He was a thick-necked mountain of a man who pulled a dirty wig from his head and revealed a shiny dome of skull tattooed with various bent crosses and what might have been a dragon. When he reached the stream, he looked up and his eyes fell directly on Rico.

"Who the hell are you?"

The other two turned and located him as well. The first man's hand went immediately to a knife on his belt.

"Just . . . visiting," Rico managed.

The first two stared wide-eyed at Rico, then at each other. The man with the braid held up the jacket with the fringe and looked at his larger companion. "He's seen it all."

The scowl that the big man gave in return was all the response Rico needed to see. He shouldn't be here.

He spun in place, his shoes slipping off the rocks as he splashed through the shallow water.

"Get him!" the big man bellowed.

Rico launched himself up the low embankment, then broke into an all-out sprint.

"Damon!" He screamed the name as he ran, not daring to look back until he had crashed through fifty yards of brush and dodged two dozen trees. He'd gotten the jump on his pursuers, but they were coming after him. The woman with the dyed hair was closest. Rico was horrified to see that she was carrying a tomahawk in each hand.

Rico's sprint through the woods was powered by sheer adrenaline, but he soon realized he wasn't entirely sure which way he was headed. The ground here was too level. Hadn't the walk to the stream been entirely downhill? He swore and angled right, flying up the hillside with his legs already burning. His pursuers changed directions to cut him off, and the woman with the tomahawks was closing on him. The hillside ahead was strewn with rocks and was far steeper than the one he had come down. He was forced farther left.

"I'm not okay with this!" Rico shrieked as he ran. He never deliberately ran anywhere if he could help it, but now he thanked God that he'd spent the last ten years dancing. His legs pumped like pistons. "Come on, Rico," he admonished himself. "You didn't get out of Tidewater's backwash just to die here."

The woman with the tomahawks let out a shout and hurled one at him. Rico shrieked and dodged, the blade of the weapon sticking in the trunk of a tree only inches from his face. He swerved again but saw the second and third pursuers closing in from that side. His eyes went wide and he turned again, but his foot caught a root and he went sprawling, crashing through a tangle of brambles and shouting as he tried to regain his feet. The woman with the tomahawk retrieved her first weapon and had her arm cocked again. This time she was so close that Rico could see the crow's feet around her eyes and the gap in her front teeth.

He closed his eyes and held his arms over his face and head, waiting for the tomahawk to strike, but a familiar shout from his left made him look up again. Damon streaked past a tree and straight into the woman with the tomahawks. His raised elbow caught her under the chin, lifting her from her feet and sending her lofting backward until she crashed to the ground with a meaty thud.

Damon gripped a longsword in his other hand, and as he spun around to face the remaining men, he held it aloft in a front guard.

The bald man-mountain and his braided companion arrested their momentum and shifted wary glances from Damon to their fallen companion, and then to one another. The smaller man with the braid had only brought a knife to this fight and looked like he suddenly wanted to be someplace else. The big tattooed guy was better prepared. He carried a thick quarterstaff that could conceivably get the better of a longsword, but he was still sizing up Damon and seemed unsure.

"My friend has done you no harm," Damon said. "You'd be wise to remove yourselves and leave him in peace."

Rico climbed to his feet. The woman Damon had bowled over was stirring but was dazed and out of it. Rico spotted one of her tomahawks on the ground and quickly snatched it up. He couldn't locate the second one but hoped that meant she couldn't either.

"What are you doing in this forest, stranger?" the man with the quarterstaff said. He shifted positions as he spoke, angling toward his fallen companion.

"Just passing through. Tending to nature, and now we'll be on our way," Damon replied.

Big man sniffed and twisted the staff in his palms, moving to place himself between Damon and the unarmed woman. He extended a hand to her, and she climbed to her feet.

"We'll be going," Damon said, his sword still held at the ready. He gestured the way he had come and Rico wasted no time in scurrying past him. He noticed the woman was now eyeing something on the ground. As Damon backed away from the group and turned to follow Rico, the woman snatched her second tomahawk from the weeds. The big man with the staff was moving too.

"Damon, look out!" Rico shouted. Damon spun around just as the woman cocked her arm and threw. The clang of steel-on-steel rang through the trees as Damon's sword knocked the tomahawk from the air.

Damon hissed at Rico through bared teeth. "Run for the car! I'll handle this." He then charged the man with the staff who lunged forward with a roar.

Rico hesitated long enough to see the man's staff whirling in an arc toward Damon's head. Damon met the blow with the forte of his sword and sidestepped. "Go!" he shouted.

Rico ran. Slick leaves threatened to take his legs out from under him as he climbed. Water inside his one wet shoe still squished and spurted up his ankle. He broke the tree line to find that he was a hundred yards from the Vulcan.

But he wasn't alone.

The man with the braid had followed. His knife was in his hand, and he doggedly pursued Rico up the slope.

"Don't be locked, don't be locked," Rico prayed as he rushed across the last yards of scrub grass. He risked a glance over his shoulder and saw that the man with the knife was nearly on him.

He turned and hurled the tomahawk at the man's head, causing him to duck and throw an arm up. The tomahawk struck the man's forearm—only a glancing blow with the handle—but it gave Rico enough time to reach the passenger side of the car. The door handle moved. Not locked.

Rico flung the door open and scrambled inside, slamming it just in time to block the downward arc of his attacker's knife. Rico fumbled for the lock, slapping at it and pressing his palm over it to ensure it stayed in the locked position.

The man outside shouted and cursed.

Rico could see now that the braid in the man's hair was actually part of a wig. It had shifted during the run, giving him a sort of lopsided look. It did nothing to make him less terrifying. Rico checked the lock on the other door, then jolted as the man slammed himself against the window. The window was reinforced with wire and unlikely to shatter, but it was designed to withstand single strikes, not a repeated and sustained assault.

Rico rummaged frantically in the glovebox, displacing a ski mask, a lighter, and a flashlight.

There were no keys.

Rico realized his protection was also becoming his prison. If Damon didn't make it out of the woods soon, his options didn't look promising.

The lighter on the floor gave him pause. He spun around in the seat and reached for his tool bag. He unzipped the top and snatched the can of electrical contact cleaner from the inside pocket. Next, he scooped up the lighter from the floor, rolled the window down a crack and shouted at the man with the braid. "Hey, you brainless mudflap!"

The man froze, then immediately tried to jab his knife

through the gap in the window. Rico was ready. He flicked the lighter and sent a jet of fluid through the flame.

The stream of electrical contact cleaner erupted into a tongue of fire that shot out the window gap and engulfed the face of the man outside. He shrieked and fell away from the car, landing on his rear while swatting and swiping at his face. The wig ignited and he tore it from his head. He scrambled away from the car, only regaining his feet when he was half a dozen yards away.

"You tricky little bastard," the man said. "I'll fix you for that." He strode to the back of the car and jabbed his knife deep into the rear passenger tire. He crossed to the other side of the car and repeated the process with the other rear tire. He next reached up and tore at the radio antenna, wrenching it side to side until it snapped off in his hands. He used the antenna to hack wildly at the car. While it didn't do a lot of damage, it did make a lot of noise.

Rico was desperately trying to come up with another plan when the sound of an engine echoed from the hillside. The woman with the dyed hair came rocketing out of the trees on an all-terrain motorcycle. She spotted her companion and headed straight for him. "Get on!" she shouted. "That sword swinger stuck Wrecking Ball, and he's coming this way."

"He dead?" the man asked.

"Even if he ain't, I'm not going back for him. Get on."

"This little pit stain in the car saw us. Boss won't like him living to tell about it."

"He ain't seen nothing. Now get on, or you can face that death dealer on your own."

The man glanced down the hill and Rico was relieved to see that Damon was indeed coming up. He wasn't running, but he was moving quickly enough that the man with the knife thought better of staying.

The man muttered a few more curses, then strode forward and took one more stab at the car, this time sinking his knife into the left front tire. He next aimed the knife through the window. "I ain't done with you!" With one last glare at Rico, he climbed on the back of the bike, and the pair shot off down the road, a trail of dust and exhaust in their wake.

Damon reached the car twenty seconds later. He surveyed the flattened tires and swore. Rico climbed out and assessed the state of his friend. Damon didn't appear to be bleeding anywhere, but he moved slower than usual, and Rico thought he detected a hint of a limp.

"You okay?"

"I'd be better if we weren't stranded. I've got one spare. We could maybe stuff the others enough to roll if we take the time, but this trip just got a lot slower." He studied the stub of antenna remaining. "And it looks like we're not calling for help. Wherever Valerie is, let's hope she's safe. We won't be making Rust Creek tonight." He opened the trunk.

"You think those bikers will come back?" Rico asked.

Damon tossed him a tire iron. "Let's not stick around to find out."

9

SHAMAN

Dakota Wren pulled up to the circle of battered motorcoaches with a dozen pairs of eyes on her. The throaty rumble of the Guardian 770 was undoubtedly heard all across the clearing and had beckoned curious adults and children alike.

More than twenty motor rigs were scattered around the glade, and at the center, as always, was the sky blue behemoth of a motorcoach belonging to Chief Takawa.

Lanja and Sprocket were close on Dakota's bumper, each in trucks hauling the fuel tanks from their heist. They would let Dakota be the first to breach the circle. It had after all, been her idea.

The braves lingering around Chief Takawa's door looked shocked to see a war car in their midst. Just witnessing the confusion on their faces was worth the effort of the heist. Dakota let their stares linger on the Guardian for a few more seconds and left the engine running as she climbed out.

By now the rest of the camp had made an appearance.

Hammer Fist and Screaming Eagle moved toward her from

the shade of their trailer's canopy. They took in the remainder of Dakota's crew pulling up.

Hammer Fist was the best mechanic in the tribe. Chief Takawa had sent him east when he was young, and the rumor was that he had apprenticed at Rockwell Engineering as a war car builder. He had come home with skills that set the Black Hawk tribe ahead of its rivals in nearly every way. Of all the drivers in the village, Dakota knew that he would be one to appreciate the power and abilities of a Guardian 770.

Dakota expected to see admiration on his face, but his brow furrowed, and he hissed through his teeth.

"What have you done?"

Dakota gestured to the car. "What does it look like? I found us a weapon that's going to change everything."

"Stupid kid," Hammer Fist muttered. "Who'd you take it from? What have you gotten us into?"

Dakota frowned. "She won't be coming after us. We saw to that."

"She who?" Hammer Fist asked. "A knight? A noble? A car like this—" His gaze landed on the front grill where the bear claw emblem was. His eyes narrowed. "Is that whose I think it is?"

"It's *my* car now," Dakota said. "I dare anyone to say differently."

There had never been more than three war cars in the caravan since the time she joined. The drivers were heroes of the camp, champions of the tribe. Now she'd be one too, Hammer Fist be damned.

"I should've known letting you out of sight would do us no good." The gravelly voice came from behind her, and she knew it at once. She turned and found Chief Takawa standing on the steps of his motorcoach, both hands grasping the door posts.

The eyes of the crowd all fell on the chief.

Dakota took a few steps forward. "We brought gifts for the

tribe. Enough fuel to last us for a month. A war car to defend us. I struck a blow for the Black Hawks."

"You have gifted us trouble and violence, Dakota Wren," the chief said. "Your actions may yield worse in days to come."

"How many thefts and murders have been blamed on Black Hawk tribe in the last year?" Dakota asked. "We can barely move on the frontier without someone calling us thieves and accusing us of stealing cars or cattle. They blame us if we are innocent or guilty, so why not at least have the spoils to show for it?"

"You suggest we lower ourselves to the level of common thieves," Chief Takawa said. "Forsake our honor? For what? A few tanks of fuel and a car?"

"You act as though our honor has done us so much good," Dakota said. "What riches has our honor bestowed on us lately? We live on the run, unable to even settle in one place. Where are our crops? Where are our stores for the winter? Every day Hudson's men push us farther and farther into the mountains, and you do nothing? We're tired of doing nothing. Is that the legacy you want as chief?"

"My legacy will be watching my grandchildren grow to adulthood in peace," Chief Takawa said.

Dakota clenched her fists. "Your legacy will be cowardice and fear."

A collective gasp went up from the members of the tribe looking on. They murmured among themselves and many shook their heads.

Chief Takawa's expression hardened. "You are not yet a woman grown; therefore, I will forgive this insult only once. Your father had the ideas you have, and you know the pain it brought on your family. Go home to your mother and think hard on how she will survive without the protection of this tribe."

"You can't push her out, she's—"

"I'm not done speaking!" Chief Takawa roared.

Dakota clamped her mouth shut and squeezed her fists even tighter.

"You are forbidden from antagonizing the white men and their caravans again. When they come for you, we will explain that you are not a member of this tribe. Should you dishonor the tribe again, it will be true. You will no longer have a place among the Black Hawk people."

Dakota swallowed hard and scowled at the braves surrounding Takawa, but she kept her mouth shut.

"You will turn the car over to Hammer Fist. Perhaps he can strip it for parts we can use."

"No!" The word erupted from her lips. "It's mine!"

Takawa's eyes widened and his nostrils flared.

Dakota didn't wait for the reprimand. She spun on her heel and stormed back to the Guardian. She flung herself into the driver's seat and slammed the door before the chief's words could reach her. A few of the braves tried to get in front of the car to block her path but scattered again when the Guardian snarled its way toward them. There were some creatures you didn't want to be in front of when they were in a bad mood. This machine was one of them.

Dakota tore a semicircle of turf from the earth as she spun the Guardian around and rocketed away from the cluster of motor homes. Lanja and Sprocket both threw up their hands as she passed. She didn't need to hear the words they were speaking to know what they were saying. It was the same thing going through Dakota's head.

What the hell was she doing?

She ought to have simply stuck to the plan. The fuel heist would have been enough. She knew for a fact that members of the tribe had absconded with fuel from roadside stations before. Takawa had never kicked any of them out of the clan. To the Avalonian nobles, fuel was easily replaced. They often wouldn't even pursue fuel thieves. A few Black Hawk men had slept in cells for getting caught with a tank of stolen gas over the years, but none had received more than a sour look from the chief. Certainly not a lecture in front of the entire tribe.

Takawa had treated her like a child.

As if he could have braved the road train the way she had, snatching the tanker from under the white men's noses.

But she knew it wasn't the fuel he was upset about. It was the car.

This was all about the car.

Dakota felt the vibration of the engine through the steering wheel and in the shifter handle as she downshifted around a turn in the dirt road. She raced along the twisting mountain path and let herself melt into the rhythm of the engine's thrumming cylinders.

She hadn't been able to leave it. It had called to her and cast her under its spell again.

Change was coming as she predicted. A fork in the path of her destiny. Only now she didn't know where the path would lead or whether she even wanted to see.

The road straightened out, and Dakota spotted a blockage a quarter mile ahead. She decelerated as she approached the mule-drawn tinker cart belonging to the tribe shaman. He was stuck in a rut, the wheels of the cart buried in thick mud. Dakota could see, even at a distance, that the elderly animal was barely a match for the cart on a level path in dry conditions. It stood no chance of pulling the cart free on a muddy incline. She slowed the Guardian to a crawl.

"Young miss Wren," the old Shaman said as she pulled up. She didn't know how he always knew it was her when his eyes were cloudy white with cataracts. "Come to lend a hand then. And I thanked you sincerely, didn't I?"

He was once again narrating events as though he had already lived them and was simply telling the tale. Dakota wondered if he spoke this way to everyone he met or only to her. She left the engine running, not eager to have to hot wire the ignition manually again. The process was growing tedious.

"Ah. The roar of the bear," the old man said. "The woods and hills remembered its first visit to this place. But that was many years ago now, wasn't it?"

Dakota wasn't sure what to make of his words. She concentrated on the task at hand, popping the trunk to see if there was any towing gear to be had.

When she crossed to the back of the car and opened the trunk lid, she paused at the sight of the swords in the lid rack. "Whoa." Her fingertips traced the scabbards of the three blades.

"And where were you running to today, young Miss Wren? The tribe waited eagerly for your victory. They wait still."

"Chief Takawa will lead us nowhere," Dakota said. "I'll make my own path."

"You wished to choose your own destiny. You sensed the change coming. You knew its cause. But destiny came anyway."

Dakota thought about the feeling she had aboard the car hauler. The girl with the violent eyes. There had been chaos and change written across her face.

"What if I choose to not believe in destiny?" Dakota asked.

"Why should that matter, if destiny believes in you?"

Dakota rummaged around in the trunk and found a tether chain. There was an attachment hook on the back bumper ready to go. She marched her way over to the tinker cart and found the tow hook there. The old mule looked at her with an expression that looked like relief.

The act of pulling the cart out of the rut and onto firm ground took only a moment; the Guardian's powerful engine and wide rear tires made short work of it.

Dakota immediately set about unhooking the straps again.

"I owed you a debt of thanks," the shaman said. "I'm grateful that you accepted my payment in the form of friendly advice."

Dakota sighed. Were it up to her, she could do without the

advice, but it seemed the agreement was already arranged. She bundled the tow equipment into the trunk and shut the lid before turning to face the old shaman.

"And so I told you this," the old man said. "You cannot outrun the future in a car fueled by the past."

Dakota brushed the dirt off the palms of her gloves. "Watch out for more of those puddles. I don't expect I'll be back this way."

She turned and climbed into the car.

The old man's milky-white eyes fluttered in his eyelids. "Your mother made a roast prairie fowl for dinner tonight. There was once a path where you enjoyed it thoroughly."

"We're miles from her place. How would you know what she's cooking?"

"I love a good roast fowl," the old man said. "I can smell it from here. It's a shame you didn't invite me along."

"I'm not going home to my mother," Dakota said. "And she isn't expecting me."

"Seems to me you wanted to be in charge of your own destiny. Nothing is set, then."

"That's right," Dakota replied. "The signs aren't always right, you know."

"Then I shouldn't have told you to say hello to your mother for me."

"You didn't," Dakota answered. She shut the door and shifted into gear, rocketing away before the old man's words could rattle her any more than they already had.

She *was* in charge of her own destiny. This car was proof. She had done something completely unplanned, defied expectations. She wouldn't be made to be a pawn in the game of fate.

She slowed as she pulled up to the fork in the road. To the south lay Hudson lands, to the east the high plains. To the north was more of the mountain roads, the forest, and the smells and sounds of home.

A dozen miles of twisting mountain road would lead her to her mother. Her past.

Her fingers twitched on the steering wheel, her feet restless on the pedals. Her mind wrestled with the choice.

Who said she even had to choose? Any new future would still be there tomorrow, and she did love the way her mother roasted a prairie fowl.

But a nagging doubt in her mind objected. Fate was setting its snare, and she wouldn't play.

She turned the car south and headed for the unknown.

10

CASTLE REDROCK

Valerie Terravecchia woke to a knock at her door.

"Miss? His Lordship has sent me with a few items of clothing you might wish to try on."

The muffled female voice had a sense of urgency to it.

Valerie rubbed at her face and tried to orient herself to where she was. Judging by the dimming daylight outside, it was nearing sunset. She had slept for nearly four hours.

She was hardly refreshed. In some ways, she might even be more sluggish, but it had been enough rest to go on. Her growling stomach was a sign that her body had shifted to its next priority.

"Come in then," she said to the door.

A lady's maid entered, carrying an armful of clothing—primarily dresses from the look of it—and Valerie eyed them cautiously. The maid laid the clothing out across the bureau and stepped back, allowing Valerie to view them. She had no idea how the maid had managed to bring clothing her size when no one except the chauffeur had seen her come in, but each item was within range of something she could fit into.

"How formally does Lord Hudson expect his guests to dress for dinner?" Valerie asked.

"I presume anything here would be acceptable," the lady's maid replied.

Valerie skipped over the dresses and selected a soft black romper. With swishy black legs, it was close to being a dress but would allow her more flexibility if she needed it. She found a pair of comfortable black shoes in the closet to match and was dressed in a matter of minutes. Her face and hair took longer, as she had lines from the pillowcase on her cheeks, and her night of running through the wilderness had left her hair a tangle. She brushed it straight before tying it back with a silken purple scarf. It gave her a vaguely rakish look. She outlined her eyes and added a hint of color to her eyelids to accent the scarf, then decided she was presentable enough for the moment. It was time to see what the lord of this castle had to say.

She scooped up her badge from the nightstand and considered what to do with her sword. It was hardly an appropriate dinner accessory. She considered leaving it atop the bureau, but somehow it felt wrong to abandon the only piece of her life from home in this foreign and uncertain place. Finally, she decided to simply take it with her. If anyone asked, she would use it as an excuse to advertise the new forge Ann and Janet were starting. Since her victory in the king's tournament, the pair were already flooded with orders, but a few more never hurt.

Red Rock Castle was a meandering place. Entering the west wing of the main house, she tried several dead ends in her attempts to reach the terrace. She eventually located the stairwell that led to the upper level corridors. The interior decor was more rustic than the castles she had been to on the west coast. There were more hunting trophies on the wall than artwork or suits of armor, and it gave the place a casual appeal.

One theme she noted was a preponderance of framed newspaper articles, often the entire front pages from dates going back decades. The publication was called the Hudsonville Chronicle. Articles ranged in content from national news like the

Coronation of King Logan, to locally focused headlines: FLASH FLOOD WIPES OUT HOMESTEADERS, or APACHE TRIBE STRIKES AGAIN.

The articles featuring violence between colonials and local tribes were prominent, most especially in articles with recent dates. By the time she reached the dining room, Valerie suspected a person could be forgiven for thinking they were living in a war zone and not a country at peace.

She paused near the end of the hallway when she encountered a page from the newspaper with the headline: DISGRACED NOBLEWOMAN TRIUMPHS AT KING'S TOURNAMENT. There was a photo of her there, staring out from the page in black and white, a shot from when she had just completed the King's Tournament road race. The article highlighted the upset her victory had caused in noble circles but failed to mention her brother's murder at the hands of the Sterlings. Nothing in the article suggested she had entered the tournament seeking justice rather than glory. The omission left her feeling raw. Was this all that anyone outside Port Hyacinth knew of her?

Valerie entered the dining room and was met by a servant who guided her outdoors to her place on the terrace. The sunset was lighting up the sky in brilliant pinks and oranges. To her surprise, the table was only set for two. She wasn't familiar with Lord Hudson's history but presumed he would have some family or other local nobles in attendance. It seemed their dining experience would be much more intimate.

She took her seat and waited patiently, admiring the view. She accepted an offered glass of wine and smiled politely at the various servants stationed around the terrace. They left her in silence for what felt like several minutes before the doors from the dining room flew open, and a ruddy man in a stiff jacket pushed his way through. His hair was silver and thinning, but she suspected he wasn't much over fifty. "My deepest apologies for keeping you waiting, Lady Terravecchia. Please forgive my rudeness. You have come all this way."

Valerie rose.

"No no. Don't get up on my account. It is I who am late and should be minding my etiquette."

Valerie was already on her feet, however, so he approached and took her hand, bowing to brush it with a kiss.

Lord Hudson moved around the table, waiting for her to sit again before settling into his chair. "You honor me with your visit, unexpected though it might be. I heard about the incident on the train. A brazen attack. I'm thrilled to be able to hear a firsthand account of your part in the train's defense, as I understand you acted most bravely."

Valerie settled back into her chair. "Have you been in contact with the caravan? I was traveling with friends and am waiting for word."

"You've come to the right place," Lord Hudson said. "I'm a newsman. Communication is my business. You no doubt saw the papers on your walk in. I own a dozen long-range radio towers, the newspaper, and there is a telephone in every wing of this house. Nothing goes on in my district that I don't know about. You may not have thought that anyone this far east would have heard of your accomplishments in Port Hyacinth. You'd likely be right about the average yokel. But I followed the event closely myself."

Valerie nodded but pressed him further. "I've left word at the station in the village that I'm expecting friends. You would be informed if they arrived as well?"

"Of course. My people will assist you in any way we can. Have no fear. Now please, rest and eat. I understand you spent a night on the frontier, and you must be famished. I cannot have King Logan's next knight of the Round Table going hungry in my home."

She picked up a fork and considered her dinner salad. She

was indeed ravenous, but her hunger for information was gnawing at her more.

"My car was stolen from me by a young native warrior. She and her companions fled into the mountains. I need help going after them."

"I'm sure you must be furious to delay your arrival in Glastonbury Castle on account of such lawlessness. To have the king and queen awaiting your arrival, not to mention your fellow knights, it's no wonder that you wish to be back on your way as soon as possible. Have no fear, the House of Hudson will be your salvation."

"I very much appreciate any assistance you can lend," Valerie said as a servant placed a bowl of soup before her and inexplicably whisked away her untouched salad.

Lord Hudson reached across the corner of the table and rested his hand atop hers. "You will, of course, put in a good word for me at court, won't you? It's so rare that dignitaries, or even ambassadors, come out this way anymore, let alone a future member of the king's inner circle. They used to come in droves back in my great-grandfather's day. All wanting our oil contracts, you know. When that dried up, it was like they couldn't wait to be gone. Driven back east by the smell of greener pastures. But you! You will be right in the thick of it. The hub of it all. Words passed directly from your mouth to the king's ear."

"It's indeed an honor," Valerie said. "Of course, you have my gratitude for your hospitality, especially in this circumstance."

"You promise me now," Lord Hudson said, "You'll deliver a good word straight to the king, tell him of me?" His voice was almost plaintive, and Valerie felt as though the weight of his hand on hers was growing heavier. She pulled her hand away with a smile. "You have my promise. I'll give a faithful telling of your generosity."

"Splendid." Lord Hudson leaned back in his chair and smiled, his shoulders relaxed and his expression lightened. "A magnificent twist of fate, your arrival here. A most pleasant happenstance. I know the circumstances presented a detour on your path, but I think you will be most pleased with the outcome, even happy that these outlaws intervened. I'll tell you what I'll do. You no doubt passed my garages on the way in. You must have glimpsed some of the vehicles."

Valerie nodded. "It's an impressive collection." She sampled a spoonful of soup, lest the servants abscond with it, and relished the taste of warm broth and vegetables on her tongue.

Lord Hudson leaned in conspiratorially. "What say you to taking a stroll through my garages after dinner? I'll give you a personal tour. You can see the vehicles I have in reserve and I'll show you my collection of war cars. And, because I hold you in such high esteem, I'm going to let you *choose* one to take to Glastonbury Castle." He studied her face, clearly watching for her reaction to this news.

"That's . . . incredibly generous," Valerie said, "But—"

"Think nothing of it, my dear. To have the newest knight at the Round Table show up in one of *my* cars would be a tremendous honor. It would be my absolute pleasure."

"My lord, I'm afraid I can't accept. I mean to get my own car back as soon as possible."

"Perhaps you misunderstood," Lord Hudson said. "This won't be just a loan. I mean to *give* you the car. It'll be yours. A Boomerang perhaps, or a Rockwell Hurricane. You would own it free and clear. A gift."

Valerie worked to keep her voice steady and upbeat as she replied. "You are most generous, and as I said before, I am very grateful for your hospitality. What I could really use is your assistance with going after the brigands who took *my* car. It's a Guardian 770 that belonged to my father. It's very important to me that I get it back."

"Ah. A sentimental attachment." Lord Hudson spoke the words as though they left a bad taste in his mouth. "I understand.

I'm afraid these godless heathens tend to strip cars down and render them unrecognizable. It may already be too late to save your vehicle."

"Another reason I'd like to go after them as soon as possible. Surely you have other knights in your service who would be willing to accompany me in bringing the thieves to justice?"

Lord Hudson leaned back in his chair with a sour expression on his face, scowling at the servants as they replaced the soup course with a plate of what might have been venison or beef and baskets of warm bread. "Sir Everett Morningstar of the King's Fifth Regiment has not seen fit to station a garrison on this border. They have a garrison in Fleetwood, you know, and Cooper's Ferry, of all places, but they haven't deigned to station so much as a company in Hudsonville. We used to have one, of course, back when the oil fields needed protecting. Now all we have for protection here are the Rust Creek Regulars, and of course, Kai Nez and her Nightmare Nine."

Valerie leaned forward at this. "I met a bounty hunter named Kai Nez in the village. She's a road knight?"

"She wasn't knighted by me. I can't say who her mentor was. Someone long dead I imagine. But Kai Nez and her band of riders do keep the order in these parts. They provide protection to the peasant farmers and scare off bands of these ravaging natives. No one crosses her and lives long to tell about it, I can assure you."

"You're the lord of these lands. Does she swear fealty to you?"

"Of course she does. And she is paid handsomely for her services. But if these outlaws would stop challenging her and simply run away, I would pay much less in bounties each year. Unfortunately, Kai Nez is a necessary cost of doing business. One cannot own as many ranches and oil fields as I do and hope to keep them safe without someone willing to get their hands dirty."

"Was the stolen fuel tanker one of yours?"

"It was. Another loss that would make it seem obvious that we should have a garrison of troops stationed here. When you get to the king's court, I hope you will make him aware of the suffering you have endured at the hands of these savages. Sir Everett has been lulled into the belief that the tribes want peace and that the great border conflicts are over. He'll be this land's doom. Make no mistake. It won't be long before the natives amass enough stolen property to fuel and armor a real army. Sir Everett Morningstar will be resting on his haunches in Fleetwood or Mercy Garden while we're overrun."

"How far away is Sir Everett and the garrison at Fleetwood?"

"It's a two-day drive in the best of conditions. More if there is any manner of bad weather. Some roads are already washing out from spring floods. He's much too far to respond when we're in distress. This castle could be a smoldering ruin by the time he gets so much as a war car to us."

"I won't be able to wait for help from them," Valerie said. "I need to be after these thieves by first light at the latest. She already has too much of a head start. I suppose that means I'll need alternative help."

"It shall be as you wish, then." Lord Hudson leaned forward and picked up a bell from the table, then rang it. The servant Valerie recognized as the chauffeur appeared.

"Masterson, find Sheriff Trammel and Kai Nez. Tell Trammel to deputize the Nine to go after the road train thieves."

The man bowed to the lord, then vanished back through the doors.

"Why is Kai Nez's road gang called the Nightmare Nine?" Valerie asked. "I only counted six today."

"Who knows? I can't keep track of any of them," Lord Hudson said, slicing at his meat with apparent animosity. He stabbed a piece with a fork, then cast a critical eye on it as he held it up. His gaze shifted to her. "But as of first light, they have a new member."

11

FALSE STEP

The imprint of flames danced across Damon's eyes, even when he closed them.

There was nothing to be done. No one to be saved. The roof of the service station had already collapsed by the time he and Rico arrived. Acrid smoke now billowed from the ruin and lofted into the starry sky.

The sun had set as they limped the Vulcan the remaining miles to reach this place. The outpost on the map labeled 'Dempsey's Oasis' had promised relief and delivered none. Now the motorcycle tracks in the dirt left Damon feeling hollow.

He hadn't killed the tattooed man in the woods. He'd shown restraint. Mercy.

The riders had given these people none. He wanted to tell himself that the blackened wagon in the weeds was an antique, some collectible and not a true child's toy. Or that the family that had operated this establishment could have been away during the attack.

Perhaps they had survived.

But he lived with enough lies. He wouldn't tell himself another.

"What do we do?" Rico asked. He stood with one hand on the hood of the car, unwilling or unable to get any closer to the destruction.

Damon's fists clenched and unclenched. He forced down the fury that threatened to consume him.

"We go on."

It was nearly four in the morning when Damon rolled down his window to address the guard posted at the Rust Creek village wall. The man clinked as he walked, his armor loose and poorly fit to his spindly frame. He studied the car skeptically.

"What do you want?"

The man had reason to be suspicious. The Vulcan looked rough. The paint was scarred, the antenna missing, and two of the four tires were stuffed with hay raided from a farmer's field that they had passed along the way. It was a poor fix for the damage the knife had caused, but it was enough to keep the car rolling, albeit at a snail's pace. They had crawled on through the night, their only stop the burned outpost.

Damon attempted an expression that could be construed as pleasant.

"We've come to find a friend. We had word she came this way. Her name is Lady Valerie Terravecchia, and she'll be expecting us."

The man glanced toward a companion in the guard house. "What was that lady rider's name? Was it Terravecchia?"

Damon couldn't make out the other guard's response, but the one out his window grunted and shrugged.

"All non-residents have to check in with the sheriff. Weapons must be surrendered inside the walls. Pull inside while we search your vehicle." The guard gestured to his companion to open the gate. Once it was rolled aside, Damon pulled the Vulcan through. The gate groaned shut behind them.

The vehicle search was a tedious affair, a pair of sleepy local teenagers poked their heads into every compartment of the Vulcan, plucking out anything they deemed suspicious and trudging over to a surly older guard who sat in a chair and either accepted their findings or waved them off. Damon's three swords along with several knives and Rico's long-handled hammer were stacked at the guard's feet. The man had merely grunted at the rest of Rico's tools, and the teenage minions dumped them unceremoniously back into the trunk. If Rico could have inflicted pain with his eyes, Damon was sure the pair would have been impaled or possibly drawn and quartered.

"Do you have a maintenance shop in town?" Damon asked.

"Up the street, then take the first right. Won't be open yet, but you can leave your car there and walk the rest of the way to the sheriff's office. Wait on the porch till she calls you in. And don't go walkabout without Sheriff Trammel's say so." The man sniffed and wiped at his face with the back of his hand. "Get on now."

Damon and Rico exchanged a glance and climbed back into the car.

"These backwater watchmen always take themselves too seriously," Damon muttered after he closed the door. "Give them a little authority and they think they're the king's guard."

"At least Valerie made it through," Rico said. "We'll have one face that's happy to see us." He let out a yawn.

They followed the directions they'd been given, and the Vulcan's headlights soon illuminated a sign for a maintenance shop called "The Forge." Two crossed wrenches on a field of black indicated that the owner was a member of the mechanic's guild. "At least the car will be well taken care of," Damon said. "Why don't you stay here and rest. I'll visit the sheriff and satisfy whatever requirements there are for us to be here."

"I can come with—" Rico began to say, before another yawn cut him off.

"No need. I'll feel better knowing the car is in good hands, at least until the shop opens. I'll be back as soon as I can, and we'll get on with finding Val."

Rico nodded and fumbled for the seat-reclining mechanism. "I'd keep the radio on, but the antenna's busted."

"No worries. I'll be back shortly."

By the time Damon had gathered his jacket and shut the door, Rico was already reclined with his eyes closed.

Damon cut back along the side street they had come by and ventured onto the town's main road. The houses were dark, and only a few flickering lampposts lit the way. His eyelids were heavy, but he kept a watch for any kind of diner or bakery that might be open early. The thought of a cup of coffee was tantalizing, but it seemed even the bakeries were shuttered, if such a place even existed.

The village was quaint but lacked the charm of cleaner towns. Even in the dim light, he could tell the buildings were coated in road dust and waiting for a rinse. If it rained here, it wasn't often enough to manage the job.

He shrugged into his jacket and meandered down the center of the street.

There were a few vehicles parked along the road—a delivery van, several produce trucks, and one battered sedan—but nothing that could be construed as a vehicle of war. It was possible that the town's "no weapons" rule extended to cars as well. That or all the town's mobile armor was garaged behind the castle walls.

He walked until he reached a sort of town square. A shuttered saloon sat across from a squat, flat-topped building with bars on the windows. The sign labelling the building as the town jail hung at a slight angle, the post canted to one side as though someone had attempted to bowl it over but failed and gave up. Judging by the depth of the gouges in the wood, Damon suspected the vehicle used may have simply lacked the horsepower to get the job done. No one had bothered to straighten the post in any case, and in the dim light, it gave Damon the feeling that the axis of the world was not quite vertical or that he wasn't.

He acknowledged that the latter was possible.

An electric lamp was on somewhere inside the jail. It sent a solitary beam of light out the single windowpane, a six-inch-by-six-inch square of glass that was crisscrossed by steel and centered at eye-level in the door. The square of light illuminated a patch of dusty earth in the plaza. A figure crossed the lamplight, and a floorboard groaned.

Someone was clearly active on the other side of the door so Damon rapped on it with his knuckles—an authoritative summons. The beam of light broke again, and this time a silhouette of a head was framed in the window. A broad, wrinkled forehead and a pair of close-set eyes were visible. The eyes flicked up and down, sizing Damon up.

"What do you want?" A muffled female voice demanded.

"I was told by your village gate operator that I was to report to the sheriff."

"Why on earth would I want to see you at this hour? Go away and come back later."

"If you're the sheriff, I also need to report a crime," Damon said.

"I already know about the road train attack. It's been reported." The voice moved farther from the door.

Damon leaned close to the window and spoke louder. "There was another attack on the road south of here last night. A service station set on fire and destroyed. I saw the culprits."

His words brought a moment of silence, then the floorboards groaned again, and the face reappeared in the window. "You see them enough to identify them?"

"Yes."

The face disappeared from the window, but a bolt slid back, and the door opened a crack. "Wipe your boots. Don't need you tracking in any of that filth."

Damon dutifully scraped his boots against the bristled doormat, then pushed the door open and stepped inside.

The interior of the jailhouse office was lit by a single overhead lamp, and the sparse furniture cast deep shadows into the corners.

The sheriff herself took up a large portion of the front room. Damon wasn't sure he had ever met a woman quite so large. She was shuffling around the room in stocking feet, a nightgown, and a robe. The woman's hair hung loosely about her head, and something about it reminded Damon of the trailing moss that hung from trees. Not the color, though it did have a few silvery stands of gray among the brown, but rather the apparent lightness of it. It was the ethereal suggestion of hair rather than a reality. There was something thin and insubstantial about it, not something that could be said of the rest of the woman. The remainder of the sheriff's figure asserted its substantiveness with sheer volume. She didn't just exist inside the room, she defined it. Each item of furniture was spaced at a distance to accommodate the width of her, and it gave one the impression that the room would feel incomplete and spartan without her in it.

The sheriff buckled a tremendous belt around her waist and adjusted the handle of the knife that hung upon it. It seemed the knife belt was all that was necessary for her to transition from civilian to officer of the law. She even picked up a badge from her desk and pinned it to the front of her bathrobe to finish the look.

Damon glanced at the nameplate on the desk. "My apologies for the early hour, Sheriff Trammel. I've been driving all night and—"

"You turned your weapons in at the city wall?" the sheriff interjected.

"I did. You mentioned you already knew about the road train attack. Did a young woman from the train come through yesterday? She's a noblewoman who was traveling with our party. We're on our way—"

"Up at the castle. Lord Hudson is hosting her overnight."

"Oh, thank God," Damon muttered. The relief that flowed over him caused him to pause and physically press his fingers against his brow, pushing the stress he had built up away as he ran his hands over his forehead. "That's . . . wonderful news. We look forward to rejoining her and—"

"You said you had a crime to report," Sheriff Trammel said. "Take a seat." She gestured to a wooden chair across from the desk, then crossed her arms—an action that boosted her already abundant bosom and strained the buttons of her nightshirt.

"Yes. We ran into three riders on the mountain road south of here," Damon said, easing into the chair. "I believe they were responsible for an attack on a service station. We encountered them in the woods."

"Who is this 'we' you're referring to?" The sheriff crossed to her desk and picked up a notepad and pencil, licking her finger and flipping to a blank page.

"A companion I'm traveling with. A mechanic in the service of Lady Val—"

"Where is he now?"

"Minding the car. It's in need of repairs."

"Any others with you?"

"No. Just the two of us."

"Where did the incident occur?

"We were in the woods about five miles south of a service station called Dempsey's. We ran across two men and a woman wearing war paint."

The sheriff nodded. "We've had a great deal of trouble with natives lately. It was likely the local Black Hawk tribe. We've had word of raids all along the Queen's Highway."

Damon shook his head. "I believe they were meant to look like natives, but they were in the process of changing out of disguises when we found them."

The sheriff looked up sharply. "You can't be sure of that. It could be they were natives attempting to disguise themselves as citizens, and you simply caught them in the act."

"I'm not unaccustomed to interacting with Native Avalonian tribes," Damon said. "These riders weren't natives."

"Half-breeds then," Sheriff Trammel insisted, scribbling more notes. "These savages have been known to kidnap Avalonian women and hold them hostage, force them to raise their children. That's why you won't see me outside city walls without a contingent of swordsmen along."

Damon considered the tone of disdain in her voice. It was an attitude he had encountered in the borderlands in years past but was surprised to find it still existent here. He also found the sheer physics of anyone absconding with the sheriff dubious but opted not to argue.

"Whatever their heritage, I believe these three were likely responsible for the attack on the service station. They threatened my companion and damaged my car. I injured one of them during the attack, but the others escaped."

Sheriff Trammel gave him an appraising stare. "You injured one? How did that happen?"

"Just your usual dustup. Happened to get the better of him."

The sheriff was studying him more intently now. "What did you say your name was?"

"David," Damon lied. "David Benson."

"And your mechanic friend?" Her stare was insistent, her eyes boring into his with an intensity that seemed focused on his next words.

It gave him pause.

"It's . . . Cuidado. Richard Cuidado," Damon said. He shifted forward on his chair. "If Lady Terravecchia is up at the castle, I'll head that way now. We won't be lingering in town long."

"No. I'd like you to stay here until I've had a chance to ask your friend a few questions about the attack," Trammel said. "I'll need him to confirm the details you gave me."

"I'll go get him," Damon offered.

Trammel crossed the room and occupied the space between him and the door. "No need. I'll send someone." She pressed a button on the wall, and a buzzer sounded somewhere beyond a steel interior door. A few moments later, a man emerged, his hair sticking up at odd angles. He blinked at Damon and focused on the sheriff with half-lidded eyes. A badge clung precariously to his threadbare T-shirt, the weight of it causing his collar to skew to one side.

"Get down to The Forge. Fetch me back a fellow down there that just came into town this morning. Name of . . ." She squinted at her notes. "Richard Kwee-dah-doh."

"What's he coming in for?" the man asked.

"Doesn't matter. Just fetch him." The sheriff jerked a thumb toward the door.

The man hitched his suspender straps over his shoulders and took a sword and sword belt from a cabinet, tucking his shirt tail in before strapping it on. The sheriff held the door open for him. She was about to close it again when a sultry voice cut the air.

"I thought I saw a bit of trouble wander in here."

Sheriff Trammel opened the door again, and a woman in all black materialized from the darkness. She was wearing a longsword at her hip and an armored leather motorcycle jacket that adhered to her body like tar. Each step across the floorboards was a punctuation mark. A demand.

See. Me. Now.

She removed a short-brimmed cap, revealing a cascade of black hair.

Sheriff Trammel eased back from the door, leaving room for

the woman to pass. Trammel's lips parted, her pupils widened, and Damon thought she suddenly looked years younger. Gone was the steely-eyed officer of the law he had been dealing with a moment before. Gone too was the commanding presence that ordered the deputy out the door. This version of Trammel was somehow softened, childlike, awestruck. The transformation was so complete that it was almost as though he had only imagined the other version of her.

"Good morning, Kai," the sheriff murmured.

And it was her. Damon found himself staring at the slender figure and jagged hips of Kai Nez, the deadliest woman he had ever met in the flesh. He rose from his chair.

"Well, my, my. Damon Roark," Kai Nez said, casually crossing the floor until she was mere inches from him. "It's been a long time. I assumed you were dead by now."

"Thought the same thing about you," Damon replied.

"Don't sound so disappointed," she whispered, leaning close. She smelled of jasmine.

"You two know each other, then?" Sheriff Trammel shot Damon a sharp look. "He told me his name was Benson."

"I'm sure it might be today," Kai said, her eyes never leaving his. "People in our business do have a lot of names. What did they used to call you at Castle Breakwater? Saberhands? No. He was the one you killed. Oh yes, I remember. Bloodwalker. They said your boot prints stained their marble floors so red that they never came clean."

Kai Nez brushed her fingers down the arm of his jacket until they rested on his wrist. "Do you still have *my* scar? I still have yours."

Sheriff Trammel inhaled audibly, as though she was inflating herself for action. "An unregistered hired sword then, is it? Failed to mention that, I suppose?"

"I have another occupation now," Damon said. "I left that life behind. Shortens one's lifespan." He didn't break eye contact with Kai Nez.

Kai Nez addressed the sheriff in a voice that was nearly a purr. "I came to let you know that my crew is set per Lord Hudson's orders. We're headed north as soon as dawn breaks. Must get the jump on those nefarious train robbers." She addressed Damon. "Seems they stole a young lady's prized war car. She's quite fired up to get it back."

"Valerie," Damon said. "Is she going with you?"

"Will be soon enough," Kai Nez said. "Ohh, you're with her. Is *she* what made you leave the old life behind? Now that's sweet. You would make a cute couple. She seems a bit naive for one of yours, but then you always did have a bit of a thing for the pure ones, didn't you?"

Sheriff Trammel huffed again, and Kai Nez turned her attention back to her. "I'll be back soon, Cissy, baby." She ran a finger along Trammel's cheek. "You be good to my friend here. Make sure he gets some of that Rust Creek hospitality we all know and love."

The sheriff put a hand to her face where Kai's finger had been, then turned a wary eye on Damon. Kai Nez strode out the door and vanished around the corner.

A pale glow had lightened the pre-dawn sky and colored the street a mist gray.

"I'll have a word with Lady Terravecchia to let her know I'm here," Damon said, moving toward the door as well.

"In just a minute," the sheriff said. She slammed the door closed with one meaty arm and locked it. "I'll need a few more moments of your time."

"It sounds as though they're getting ready to leave in short order."

"I'll be sure to let them know to wait for you," Sheriff Trammel said. She gestured to the phone mounted behind her desk. "I have a direct line to the castle. Have a seat. This won't take but a minute." She gestured toward the chair.

Damon glanced at the door one more time, the muscles in his back twitching with tension. Kai Nez was a variable that he hadn't expected. A dangerous variable. But he still had options. Valerie was here in town. He'd be with her soon. They'd ditch this village in short order, and he'd have a sword back in his hands. Whatever small-town, political power trip Trammel was playing at would no longer be a bother to them.

He eased into the chair, forcing a polite smile back to his face. "What else can I help with?"

Sheriff Trammel settled into her own seat on the far side of the desk—a padded swivel chair that creaked as she edged forward to rest her elbows on the desk. "I'll be frank with you, Mr . . . Roark. It bothers me when a man is dishonest with a woman, especially an officer of the law."

Damon kept the amiable expression pinned to his face. "I understand your feelings on the subject. I did fail to mention that I've gone by several names over the years, as Kai pointed out. So it isn't so much dishonesty as it is a means of protection. I do go by David but you're welcome to call me whatever you please in the short time you know me. As I mentioned, I won't be in town long."

Sheriff Trammel leaned sideways and plucked her knife from her belt, grunting with relief when its handle was no longer pressing into her side. She set the knife gently on the desk, then used the tip of it to pry at a bit of food that had stuck in one of the crevices. "You say these riders you witnessed on the road, the ones you claim attacked you and your car . . . you could identify them for me if you saw their faces?"

"If they should happen to come into town while I'm still here, I'd be happy to do that for you," Damon replied.

"Anything else you want to tell me about why you're here? Any other business I should be made aware of?" The sheriff opened a desk drawer and moved a few items around, evidently in search of something.

"None that I can think of at the moment. Will that be all?" He pressed his palms to the arms of the chair in preparation of standing.

"Ah. There it is," Trammel muttered. She picked something up that appeared to be a button of some kind. Damon recognized it as a remote switch. A remote for what?

She mashed the button.

The floor fell out from under Damon's chair and he was pitched violently backward. The jolt of the drop caused his stomach to go into his mouth. He tumbled through a narrow hole made by the sudden appearance of the trapdoor, plummeting at least ten feet before slamming into an earthen floor.

His palms stung. His ribs ached. But the shock of the impact receded quickly from his mind as he gasped for air and struggled to get his next breath. He coughed and wheezed. His mouth tasted of blood.

When he finally got a lungful of air, he rolled over onto his back and stared up at the illuminated square of light in the floor that he had fallen through. It was now a ceiling far out of reach. The wooden chair he had been sitting in was still bolted to the trapdoor and hung at a strange angle, making the experience that much more surreal. Sheriff Trammel's bulbous form slowly appeared at one edge of the hole. She peered down at him, her face lit from only one side, the other cast in shadow.

"I'm the law in this town, Mr. Roark. I don't abide liars, and I won't abide no hired sword swingers either. A man with your kind of past has no place in Rust Creek. While you're down there, I hope you think long and hard about the sins you've committed and square yourself with the justice you've got coming to you."

Damon struggled to an elbow, trying to find his voice. He had bitten his tongue in the fall, and he was forced to spit a mouthful of blood before he could speak.

"Valerie Terravecchia," he finally managed. "She's the king's justice. Knight Warden of the West. She's the authority here."

"Not yet, she ain't," Trammel replied. "But I'll be sure to tell her you said hello if she comes looking." She mashed the button on the remote again and the trap door swung shut, the chair once again arcing upward and leaving Damon to be swallowed by the darkness.

12

FORGE

R ico woke to a tap tap tap on the passenger door window. He inclined his head and blinked away the haze of sleep, noting the shadowed figure outside. He sat up, rolling down the window just a crack.

"Yeah?"

"If you're here for repairs, that's fine, but you're blocking my doors. Gotta move this thing." The request was punctuated by another couple of taps, this time on the roof.

The speaker moved off, and as he crossed into the overhead light from the pedestrian doorway, Rico could get a look at him. He was a barrel-chested man, maybe forty-five, with a beard down to his chest and a shaved head that glistened in the light. He pulled a heavy set of keys from a studded belt and unlocked the armor-plated door, then let himself in.

Rico unlocked the car and eased out of the passenger seat into the predawn chill. He yawned and stretched, then ambled over to the lit doorway. He leaned on the doorframe and called into the vacant office. "You have any particular place you want it?"

A voice came from the back, from what Rico guessed was the

parts room. "Gimme just a second, and I'll have the rolling doors up. Pull into bay three."

Rico pushed off the doorframe and wandered around to the driver's side of the Vulcan before sliding inside and fishing the keys from the cupholder. The Vulcan complained a few times, but then started with a grumble.

The garage doors opened with a rattle of chains, and light flooded the pavement of the parking lot. The first thing that caught his eye was the charred frame of a disassembled electric motorcycle, but it didn't keep his attention long. Rico pulled into bay three and discovered he was parking alongside a partially restored Rockwell Spitfire. The old war car had temporary rims and a primer spotted paint job, but it was clear that a lot of love had gone into straightening the lines of the body and grinding away any hint of corrosion. Rico killed the engine on the Vulcan and kept his eyes on the Spitfire as he climbed out.

"Hot damn, is that a '57 autostick?"

The big man with the beard grunted and took a few steps closer.

Rico pushed his hands into his pockets but ducked low to inspect the interior. "Factory armament dash, race-grade speed shifter. Is that the original roll cage?"

"Had to do a welded sleeve repair on the rear overhead rail, but otherwise it's the stock configuration race seat."

Rico studied the cage. "Slick work. If you hadn't told me, I doubt I could have spotted the repair."

The man lifted his chin in acknowledgement of the compliment, then strode around to the front of the Vulcan.

"Your Vulcan just in for tires, or does she have other problems too?"

Rico leaned in the window and popped the hood latch. "Tires for sure but it could also use tuning for altitude. This higher elevation has been hell on the fuel control." He raised the hood and let the man have a look. The Vulcan's engine said more just sitting there than Rico could possibly have elaborated with words. Its beefy Magnum cylinders and race grade turbocharger said power, performance, and full-throttle rage. It was an engine that belonged in a showroom, not in a primer gray, middle-of-the-road, highway cruiser.

"Damn. That's some sleeper," the big man muttered. "What's your name, kid?"

"Rico."

"I'm Sal. You need anything? Cup of coffee?"

Rico ran a hand through his hair. "I could use a visit to the head if you don't mind. It's been a night."

"Through there," Sal said. "Make yourself at home. You mind if I poke around and have a look at what else you have under here?"

"Be my guest," Rico said, reaching into the back seat and pulling his duffel bag free. "It's not actually mine. It's my friend's car. I just work on it."

"Not a bad gig either way," Sal said, his eyes never leaving the engine.

Rico wandered past a tire balancer and an air compressor, then found the door leading to the bathroom. It wasn't much, but after his recent experience in the woods, the sight of indoor plumbing felt like living in the lap of luxury. He dumped his bag on the counter near the sink and took a look at himself in the mirror. The night had taken its toll. The dark circles under his eyes said the catnap in the car wasn't going to cut it. He set to work splashing his face and trying to wake up.

A new voice out in the garage made him stop.

"Wow, what you got there, Sal? No, don't tell me. It's a . . . Titan, right?"

Rico cocked an eyebrow. What kind of idiot mistook a Spitfire for a Titan? He shook his head.

"Can I help you with something?" Sal's voice carried through from the garage. Whoever the guest was, Sal didn't sound pleased about the visit.

The other voice took on a serious tone. "Could be. You seen a new guy hanging around? Somebody that goes by the name Richard Kwee-da-doh? The sheriff says I'm supposed to fetch him."

"He done something wrong?"

"Dunno," the man said. "Trammel just said fetch him. You seen him or what?"

Rico cracked the door and peered out. Sal had his arms crossed, surveying the spindly newcomer. "You have a description?"

"I don't know. Some guy who looks like he's called Kwee-da-doh, I guess. I'm thinking he sounds like some kind of Spaniard?"

Kwee-da-doh.

Cuidado? Rico eased the door closed again.

He stared at his reflection in the mirror, then started rummaging in his bag.

"This car come in recently? What's this one, a Champ? It's a Champ, right?"

"You know a lot about cars," Sal said.

"Well, I mostly know bikes," the man admitted, missing the sarcasm in Sal's tone. "But I been around to the races a few times." He launched into a recitation of all the racers he had seen in person at the track.

Rico located his black dress, matching pumps, and makeup kit, then opened a tube of eyeliner and set to work fast.

He didn't have time to run a razor over his face, but he'd never had much growth there anyway. In the dim light of the garage, he doubted it would be a problem. He applied a little color to his lips, then stuffed inserts into the built-in bra cups of the dress, pressing them together until he was satisfied with the shape. Finally, he pulled the wig from his bag, adjusted it atop his head, then gave his curls a bounce or two before taking a deep breath and stepping out of the bathroom.

The scrawny stranger standing between the cars in the garage looked like his clothes were stolen from a man twice his size. His suspenders held up the waist of sagging pants that might have once belonged to a suit. Wrinkled and frayed, they no longer looked appropriate for any formal occasion, but they looked equally out of place with his cuffs dragging along the oily floor of the automotive shop. Rico knew he had little to criticize while wearing a dress that was far more appropriate for a night out than an early morning at the garage, but something about the man's vacant stare suggested that he wouldn't know the difference.

"Good morning, boys." Rico dangled his bag from his elbow and affixed his best showtime smile to his face.

Sal was staring now too, his eyebrows lofting toward his non-existent hairline.

"Sorry. I didn't know you had company," the man in the suspenders said.

"Just on my way out," Rico said. "Sal, honey, are you going to be my hero and give me a ride home or should I walk it?"

"I can drive you. Pretty sure Billy here was just leaving," Sal said. "He's on some kind of manhunt."

"Oh my. No one dangerous, I hope?"

Billy of the Saggy Suspenders blinked and nodded. "No. Just some new guy in town I'm supposed to find. You haven't seen someone hanging around outside here have you, uh, miss ..."

"Esme. Esme Mercedes de la Vega. I'll certainly come find you if I see something suspicious. It all sounds perfectly thrilling."

Billy nodded, gripping the tarnished hilt of the sword at his hip. "Right then. Just . . . carry on, I suppose. He eyed Rico's legs, and Rico was grateful for having waxed them prior to the trip. He rummaged in his bag and found his lipstick again, making a show of reapplying it in the Spitfire's side-view mirror. When he finally turned around, the inquisitor had walked on.

He found Sal staring at him from across the hood of the Spitfire.

"I've seen my share of unexpected things in my day. But you coming out of that bathroom wearing that dress rates right up with the best of them."

"I hope I haven't harmed your reputation or put you out."

"You have to have a clean reputation first if you want to get it besmirched. I suspect we're safe on that account," Sal said. "Just so long as you aren't making me a party to some deed I'd rather not be involved with. What's this fella he come looking for done that's got Sheriff Trammel's attention?"

"I wish I knew."

"I've dealt with enough Spaniards over the years to know 'cuidado' means to be careful. You've got someone looking out for you, it seems."

"He is," Rico replied. "But I need to find out why. Will the car be safe here? Once I find my friend, I can bring you some money for the repairs."

"Likely to take me a couple days, as backed up as I am. But I'll get her fixed up for you."

"Thanks. I owe you one. I'd be willing to come back and help out too. I've got my tools in the trunk and can lend a hand if you're busy."

"Suspect you could," Sal replied. "When you find your friend, come back around, and we'll see what we can do."

Rico nodded and slung his bag over his shoulder.

"And if you're looking to avoid friends of Trammel's, I'd steer clear of the boarding house over the saloon. You'd be better off with Leslie next door at the mercantile. She's got a couple of rooms upstairs she lets out to the right folk."

"Will she take me like this?" Rico asked.

"It's a hell of a dress." Sal gave him a wink.

Rico's smile was the real thing now. He nodded to the mechanic and walked out the door with an extra swing in his hips. He realized he wasn't regretting the need for a return trip. He looked forward to it now. He only turned once to look back, and Sal was still watching. He raised a few fingers in a casual salute. Rico smiled and sashayed on, his smile only fading once he reached the main street.

He focused on the task at hand.

Damon hadn't come back, and his cryptic warning message was all Rico had to go on. He would have to move carefully from here. Rust Creek was clearly full of surprises, and it was time to be on guard for the next one.

13

POSSE

The roar of the motorcycles cluttering up the courtyard of Redrock Castle threatened to wake every resident inside the walls. At least three of the bikes in Kai Nez's posse lacked any mufflers worth speaking of and the rest hit similar decibel levels every time the riders revved their engines.

"I guess we won't be sneaking up on anyone today," Valerie said. "I suspect they can hear us coming from the other side of the valley."

Lord Hudson stood beside her, surveying the group of rough-looking men and women Kai Nez had assembled. "I think her strategy relies more on intimidation than stealth," he shouted to be heard over the noise.

Valerie had to admit that the group was intimidating. Six of the riders she had seen before, Kai Nez and the group she had ridden into town with the previous day, but there were a few other riders she was seeing for the first time. The new riders were clearly cut from the same cloth—leather armor, steely gazes, and each carrying more weapons than could possibly be employed by one person.

Lord Hudson gestured to the motorcycle to Valerie's left. "I hope you will find the Wanderer comfortable. It's served me well on trips into the hill country."

The twin cylinder trail bike did indeed look comfortable. It was a bit tall for Valerie and she imagined she would be on her tiptoes at every stop, but she was grateful to have a ride that seemed less likely to catch fire than her last borrowed mount.

"I'm grateful for your generosity, Lord Hudson. I hope to return it to you in short order once the villain who took my car is apprehended." She fidgeted with the straps of the borrowed helmet she had in her hands. "Did any word come in for me overnight? Anyone new in the village that was looking for me?"

"No word yet," Lord Hudson replied. "But the moment I have it, I will let your companions know to wait for you."

Valerie frowned. She would have liked to contact Damon prior to departing again, but she didn't feel comfortable delaying the entire party of riders indefinitely while they waited.

"Godspeed and happy hunting," Lord Hudson said. "Once you have your car, we can open a celebratory bottle of wine. I do have a few Terravecchia vintages in my cellar." He gave her a knowing wink.

After Lord Hudson had departed, Valerie double-checked the gear strapped to the back of the bike, then mounted the seat of the Wanderer. Other than *Firebird*, her trusted longsword, her gear was all borrowed from Lord Hudson's supplies or provided by other riders. Kai Nez had loaned her a helmet. She didn't like starting the trip already in the bounty hunter's debt, but she also wasn't about to go into a possible battle unprepared.

Kai Nez was conferring with some of her men, but when the conversation was over, she wheeled her motorcycle over to Valerie. The bounty hunter rode a custom beast of a chopper with high handlebars and a sloped, predatory front fork. The strange, twisted steel cage Valerie had seen before was disassembled into several pieces and protruded from a specialized rack at the back of the bike and gave the vague impression of dragon wings. The bike menaced its environment with its sheer existence.

Kai Nez pulled up next to Valerie and fixed her with those intense, jade green eyes.

"Ready to ride?"

"I'm ready to get back what's mine," Valerie replied.

Kai Nez grinned and revved her engine. "Okay, City Law. Let's see what you've got." She let off the clutch and laid down a patch of rubber with her rear tire before racing off in a cloud of smoke. The rest of the posse whooped and followed, gunning their throttles and tearing out of the courtyard in a wave of sheer noise. The percussion of engines backfiring and exhaust pipes popping flames filled the roadways, echoing from the walls of houses and empty market stalls. Valerie shifted into gear and joined the throng, following the pack of riders out the main gate and onto the open road. From there the group picked up speed. Riders streaked past Valerie with shouts of jubilation, a pack of Hell's own furies unleashed upon the world.

Valerie flipped her visor down and rolled on the throttle as she endeavored to keep up.

The group eventually settled into a cohesive unit, Kai Nez and a rider with an axe across his back were the heart of the group. The other riders formed up based on that position, some ahead, some behind, but never out of sight of the woman with the viper sword.

The pack took the mountain roads, avoiding the village of Rust Creek and heading north. After riding about ten miles, they encountered another motorcycle on the side of the road and the man and woman aboard it were familiar to the group. Kai Nez and the rest of her crew hailed the duo and encircled them to share news. Val couldn't hear much, but from their body language the two were aggravated.

"What's that about?" Valerie asked, addressing a biker idling beside her.

"A couple of regulars in the Nine." The man sniffed and seemed to feel no further explanation was necessary.

The new additions stayed mounted on the same bike and joined the hunting party. The woman who sat in back had died black hair that flew like a flag from the back of her head. She wore no helmet and must have made a habit of it because her skin was a dark leathery brown. She cast a few suspicious glances in Valerie's direction before managing to light a cigarette as they rode, leaving a trail of smoke in their wake.

They rolled onto the high prairie, the winding rural road rising and falling with the undulating hills. Cutting north past cattle ranches and fenced farmer's fields, they continued on into the open frontier. A herd of buffalo a thousand animals strong was grazing in the prairie and eyed their approach warily. They must have been well enough accustomed to the sound of riders that they didn't immediately move off. A few of the calves shifted closer to their mothers and the entire herd kept an eye on the riders' progress, but as the riders moved north, they were soon back among the trees. A river cut across their path running from the mountains in the north and joined a secondary stream from the northeast. A covered stone bridge crossed the river and the engine noise from the motorcycles echoed along the ceiling and carried across the river in all directions.

The party made several stops along the route. Once to inquire from the bridge guard whether her car had passed through. Another stop was a local farmer who sent his children scurrying back into the house at their approach. He met Kai Nez at the gate of his driveway. A wrapped bundle was passed through the gate and Kai Nez handed it off to another rider. Valerie had a hard time making out what was being said and was tired of feeling left out of the loop so she let her bike idle, climbed off and joined the group at the gate. The farmer rubbed his jaw as she approached.

Kai Nez welcomed her with a smile. "Able here says he knows where your car went."

The farmer licked his lips and stuffed his hands into his pockets. "Just heard it from one of my boys. They were up playing in the hills this morning before breakfast. Said they saw a native girl driving a black war car. Disappeared up the mountain. A while later the girl came back down on a motorcycle. Figured it for foolishness but they were insistent they were telling the truth."

"Thank those boys for us, Able," Kai Nez said.

Valerie and Kai Nez walked back to the bikes.

"This is the edge of tribal lands," Kai Nez explained. She pointed northwest to the mountains. "Our thief is banking on the idea that we won't chase her across the border. She'll trust that she's safe."

"Isn't she?" Valerie asked. In her experience, the king's justice only extended to the borders of Avalonian lands. Sovereign borders of tribal lands weren't meant to be encroached upon.

"A lot of trees look the same," Kai Nez replied. "And besides, we now have a credible witness saying he saw the car. We have justification to pursue her across the border."

"It's hearsay from some kids we haven't even spoken to."

"You want your car back, or not?"

Valerie frowned but climbed back aboard her borrowed bike.

They rolled on and were met by another member of their group.

The scout had discovered tracks. A single rider had passed through aboard a motorcycle not long ago.

There was some debate about whether the tires appeared to be native or from an imperial manufacturer.

"We split up from here," Kai ordered. "Lynx and Whiplash will take groups northeast and northwest. Bone Saw is with me and I'll take City Law as well. I'll need her to identify the thief.

Let's fan out. If anyone flushes a target, you know what to do. We'll watch for your signals. Let's roll out."

The more boisterous of the crew let out whoops and battle cries, then gunned their throttles and tore off into the trees. Valerie wondered how one could even navigate the forest on motorcycles but when they rolled onward, she found the wood was in fact riddled with trails. Some were clearly made by animals, but the one Kai Nez followed had been worn down by many a rider, a path that led right into the heart of the forest.

Valerie had ridden trails on motorcycles with her father and brother as a child and was comfortable enough aboard a trail bike, but this forest was unfamiliar, its gullies and culverts requiring her full attention to keep from steering into a tree or tipping the bike into a stream. The company she was with also kept up a much faster pace than any she had attempted before. She found herself falling farther and farther behind despite her best efforts.

The riders grew quieter as they fanned out, though Valerie could still make out the echoes from other engines far to their right and left. It was as though the entire forest was invaded. Flocks of startled birds wheeled overhead, and must have had a stunning view of the posse as it swarmed like a wolf pack through the forest.

It was only a matter of minutes until someone shouted. A signal had been spotted. A flare shot into the sky to the north and a blast of horns erupted from several bikes to the northwest.

Valerie's adrenaline was already pumping but her heartbeat accelerated even more as she broke out of the trees and took in the view ahead. A half dozen riders were streaking out of the trees to the west side of a clearing, in pursuit of a single rider that was fleeing uphill on what appeared to be a single engine trail bike. The race was an uneven match, the high-powered engines of Kai Nez's gang were running down their quarry quickly, but Valerie saw that the girl astride the little trail bike wasn't going to give in easily. She was headed for a rocky canyon, no doubt hoping to lose her pursuers among the boulders. The girl's shoulders were bare. Her back was arched, and she stood on the pedals with knees bent to absorb the shocks from the uneven terrain. The girl's silky black hair lofted behind her, every muscle straining as though she was part of the machine.

Even at this distance, Valerie could tell it was the same girl who had stolen her car.

She knew they needed to run her down to discover the car's whereabouts, but there was a part of Valerie that felt an unexplainable twinge of hope that the girl would escape. There was something about the way she rode, the sheer determination of her stance atop the bike, that resembled the elegance of a deer.

But the wolf pack on her heels was closing fast.

The girl gained the canyon, navigating a series of hairpin turns that led her higher and higher up the rocks. She was more goat now than deer, forcing her narrow motorcycle along trails that looked barely wide enough to fit her tires. Here's where the advantage shifted. Several of the riders in pursuit were forced to sheer away from the direct chase and search for alternative routes up the rocky hillside.

The busty rider Valerie had heard called Lynx was riding a powerful trail bike that was lean and fast, unencumbered by the saddlebags and weapons racks that enlarged the other bikes. She shot up the hill on the fugitive's tail, forcing her ever higher.

"This way! We'll flank her from the other side!" someone shouted, and a trio of men veered into the woods to the northwest.

Valerie followed the path of Kai Nez. Due to the extra gear aboard her bike, the bounty hunter was forced to take a wider and slower route along a river that cut through the canyon. Valerie caught up to her on the path and stayed close on her trail, a maneuver that made Kai Nez accelerate faster.

They left the riverbank and cut up an animal trail likely carved by bison or elk, losing sight of their quarry until they had crested the hill. When the trail leveled out, it was clear that the native girl was attempting to flee toward a wooden footbridge that spanned a mountain waterfall. She was almost to it when Lynx caught her. The warrior woman swerved into the path of the native girl, lashing out with her sword and forcing the girl to abandon the route and circle back.

There was nowhere to run. Riders appeared from every direction. Valerie finally had a good look at the rider's face. She had those high cheekbones and her black-rimmed eyes looked as though they could eviscerate her enemies. On this bike, with her jagged hair flying every direction, she seemed even more like a wild creature, unbridled and untamed, an element of nature set loose upon the frontier.

The cloud of dust grew as riders with weapons circled, closing the noose around their quarry. The girl saw the trap for what it was and made one last desperate bid for freedom, gunning her throttle and shooting straight for Lynx, feinting to one side, then swerving hard to cut across and just miss the warrior woman's front wheel. Lynx lashed out with her sword and the girl ducked, flattening herself to the frame of her bike as Lynx's sword took the rear-view mirror off her handlebars. The tip of the blade still found flesh.

Valerie gasped.

The girl shrieked and lost control of the bike. It slid out from under her and slammed into rocks to the left of the wooden footbridge. The girl rolled after it, tumbling across the ground in a cloud of dust and uprooted turf. The fall should have been the end of her flight, but the girl was back on her feet as soon as she found them. She staggered once, then tried to run, struggling on what looked like a twisted ankle. She let out a shout of pain, but reached the footbridge, scrambling onto it.

Her success was to no avail. The riders Valerie had seen sheer off earlier had somehow found their way around the falls and now emerged from the woods on the far side. The sight of them made the girl pause.

Kai Nez's riders had all stopped their pursuit, cutting off escape but allowing room for Valerie and Kai Nez to approach. "Looks like the end of the road, little hawk," Kai Nez said.

"What do you want?" the girl shouted.

"I'm guessing you know or you wouldn't have run!" Kai Nez turned to Valerie. "You said you could identify the one who took your car. This her?"

Valerie's heart was still pounding from the chase, and the sight of the blood flowing from the cut on the girl's shoulder blade was making her queasy. The words finally made it from her throat. "Yes. That's her."

"Splendid," Kai Nez purred. She cut the engine on her bike and dismounted, then drew her sword. She strode forward a few feet to square off with the girl on the bridge. "You going to come easy or do you plan to come hard?"

The girl straightened, clenching her jaw. Then she pulled a knife from a sheath at her back.

"I hoped you'd say that." Kai smiled, but she lowered her sword and turned to Valerie. "This one's all yours, City Law." She stood aside and left a path for Valerie.

Valerie pressed the kill switch on her handlebars, then dismounted the bike. She readjusted her scabbard around her waist and drew *Firebird*.

The girl's expression hardened as their eyes met.

Valerie cleared her throat and focused on the girl's face. She was so young. Somehow, she had expected a hardened criminal. The closer she got, she realized that for all her fierce looks and 'don't mess with me' attitude, this girl was practically a kid.

"Listen, you tell me what you did with my car, and we can see to that cut. You need help. If you let it go untended, you might be signing your own death sentence. This doesn't have to end badly."

"Get bent, Sunshine Sally. I don't need you blowing smoke up my ass. You want to get cut, you just keep coming."

Several laughs erupted from the Nightmare Nine. They seemed to be enjoying the standoff. A few leaned close to one another, passing comments.

"Maybe this one's got too much spirit for you!" The taunt came from one of Kai Nez's captains.

Kai Nez gestured to her bike. "Get the rack, Bone Saw. We may have to drag her back by her toes."

The big man moved to the tail of the motorcycle and began offloading the strange cage contraption.

The girl's eyes widened at the sight of it.

"We aren't going to use that," Valerie said. "It'll kill her."

"She looks pretty sprightly yet," Lynx commented. "I'd put even odds on her making it back alive. If she don't bleed to death first."

The girl with the knife still held her ground, but Valerie could tell that her resolve was wavering.

Valerie took a few steps closer and dropped her voice till only the girl could hear her. "Hey. Look at me." The girl focused on her warily. "You don't want to end up in that cage. I've seen what it does to people. If you tell me where my car is. I promise you'll be treated fairly."

"You're just going to kill me anyway," the girl said. "I know what your people do to car thieves. I might as well die right here."

"I'm not going to let anyone kill you," Valerie said. "But the only way you get back to town safely is with me. So tell me where the car is. You take me to it and we'll ride back together. We'll treat that wound and I'll make sure you have a chance to tell your side of this. Lower the knife."

The girl seemed on the edge of agreeing. Valerie sheathed *Firebird*.

"Hey, Bone Saw!" Valerie shouted. "I saw you had some cuffs in your gear. Bring them for me, will you?"

Bone Saw gave a quick look to Kai Nez, then pulled the handcuffs from his belt clip and tossed them to Valerie. She caught them and dangled them toward the girl with the knife. "We put these on you, you can ride on the back of my bike."

The girl looked around the ring of warriors with weapons, then finally lowered her knife. She turned the handle over and held it out to Valerie. Valerie extended a hand and took the knife, tucking it behind her back and into her belt.

"She's going to double-cross you," Kai Nez said. "Sure as she's breathing. We're putting her in the cage."

"We're not putting anyone in that death trap," Valerie said, her blood rising. "She's a thief but she's going to cooperate." She eased closer to the girl and gestured for her to turn and face the railing of the bridge. The girl dutifully shifted her feet and stared over the edge of the bridge to the frothing water below.

Valerie winced at the sight of the girl's shoulder wound. She had just tightened one cuff on the girl's wrist when Kai Nez's voice cut through her like ice. "Bone Saw, relieve City Law of her charge. It's time to end this kiddie show."

The big man immediately strode onto the bridge and made straight for them. He put a rough hand on the girl's upper arm.

"No!" Valerie slapped at his forearm, causing him to recoil in surprise. His eyes narrowed and he extended his hand again, this time grasping the native girl by the hair.

"Let go of her!" Valerie shouted. Bone Saw outweighed her by 150 pounds and there was no way she was going to win a game of tug-o-war, so she did the only thing she could think of and slapped the free end of the handcuffs over her own wrist just as Bone Saw pulled the native girl away. The native girl shouted. Bone Saw jolted to a stop when he felt the resistance. He looked back to find Valerie holding up her wrist.

"Listen, Dump Truck, she's not going in that cage unless you plan to put me in too." She snatched her badge from her belt and held it up in his face. "And that wouldn't be a good idea."

Bone Saw grunted and scowled as he stared her down, then turned to Kai Nez.

The bounty hunter crossed her arms. "Looks like City Law is pulling rank, fellas. I guess she doesn't need our help anymore." She jerked her head to the side. Bone Saw grunted again and released his grip on the native girl.

Valerie exhaled, relieved that the monster of a man had stood down. It was a small victory, but it felt good. She relaxed her shoulders and turned to address her captive, but at that moment, the girl grasped Valerie's wrist and lifted her arm, spinning herself under it and shifting behind Valerie's back. Valerie found herself struggling with her handcuffed wrist pinned behind her own back. The next moment she froze as cold steel pressed against her neck. The girl had retrieved the knife from Valerie's belt and was now pressing it to her throat.

"Nobody moves or this chick dies!"

Kai Nez was grinning.

"I knew I liked this one," she said. "It's going to be fun watching her spin." She had sheathed *Whipfang* during the conversation, but drew it again. She started walking toward them.

"I'm not messing around!" the girl hissed. "Tell her to stop!" She pressed the knife into Valerie's skin.

"I think she means it!" Valerie shouted. With her arm pinned painfully behind her back she could think of no way out of the hold.

Kai Nez kept coming.

The girl yanked on Valerie's arm, pulling her back against the railing of the bridge and using her as a shield. Kai Nez held *Whipfang* aloft, its point forward, and Valerie had the realization that her body wasn't going to be a deterrent to the bounty hunter running the girl through. The girl must have felt the same way, because her grip suddenly shifted, wrapping her elbow around

Valerie's throat. The girl's mouth was next to her ear. "I guess you're coming too!"

Valerie realized what was going to happen a moment too late. The girl hauled back on her neck and they both went over backwards, toppling over the railing and plummeting from the bridge.

14

RUST CREEK

Damon's eyes were open, but it didn't matter. Black was black and the darkness around him was complete.

Eyes open. Eyes shut. No difference.

He had slept fitfully for what he imagined was a couple of hours. After his initial fall, his blind search of the space had left him little else for options. There was a rounded wall that encircled three sides of his enclosure. The fourth had an alcove that he had explored with some hope of it leading somewhere, but only discovered a foul-smelling bucket, a short passage, and impassable metal bars at the end. There was a space beyond the bars but his outstretched arm only found a void. Somewhere he could hear water trickling, though it was out of reach and of no use to his current thirst.

He'd made a few attempts at climbing the chinks in the walls in order to reach the trap door, but after several falls, he quit trying.

He had to conserve his energy for whatever was next.

There had been no further sign of Trammel. The hole in the ceiling, once shut, had sealed his prison cell completely. Not so much as a sliver of light penetrated from above and he had little hope that the sound of his shouts traversed the trapdoor either. The efficiency of his imprisonment, along with the smells from the bucket, made him believe that he was far from the first person to be trapped here.

As falls go, he had survived this one mostly intact. His ribs were sore and the initial impact had left him struggling for air, but after testing his various joints and moving his arms and legs, he could find no significant breaks or strains.

Mostly he was angry.

Angry that no one could hear him.

Angry at himself for falling into this trap.

Angry about failing to reach Valerie.

Angry for failing to see a way out.

He did an inventory of his pockets. He had a wallet, a few loose coins, and a pen knife. The little folding knife wasn't much of a weapon. The blade was only a couple of inches long, certainly nothing fearful, but it might come in handy.

He returned to the gate at the end of the hallway, and slumped back to the floor, but he couldn't stay completely idle. His fingers probed the bars until he found the lock mechanism. It was nearly out of reach against the left wall. He tried working the tip of his pen knife into the lock but it was no use. He measured the slot at the bottom of the bars designed for a tray of food, going so far as to lie on the ground and test its height with his head. It was too narrow by at least an inch. Even if he squeezed his head through, the rest of his body would be too big to get under. The hinges to the gate weren't in reach. There would be no breaking out this way.

Damon sniffed the air. It smelled damp down here. More than could be said of the rest of the town anyway. It wasn't necessarily a good thing. It left him feeling chilled and liable to rot if he was left here too long.

Hours passed in slow monotony. He drifted in and out of sleep until roused by a clatter somewhere in the bowels of the dark. A light flicked on, illuminating the passage and revealing it to be a juncture of other passages. The rock had been hewn carefully and shored up with timbers. It was then that he realized what this was.

He was in a mine.

Footfalls sounded along the illuminated passage and soon a figure with an oil lantern emerged. Trammel.

She had changed out of her bathrobe and was now wearing an armored mail shirt that hung to her swollen knees. A sword was slung at her belt. She plodded toward him carrying a broad plate filled with small sandwiches. "Step back from the bars," she commanded. "You give me any kind of trouble and I dump this right on the ground for the rats."

Damon sized her up. She didn't seem to be carrying any keys. It made any hope of a physical confrontation useless. Even if she were to get in range and he somehow bested her—strangulation till she blacked out perhaps—it would serve no purpose without a means of escape.

He backed away from the bars.

"That's using your head," Trammel said. "You've worked it out. My rules down here. Really simple. You do what I say or you starve." She set the lantern and plate of sandwiches down and shifted her grip on the little jug of water.

"What do you want with me?" Damon asked. "I've broken no law."

"And that's where we disagree," Trammel said. "Now take off your shirt and turn out your pockets."

Damon frowned, then rummaged in his pockets, revealing the wallet and coins. "It's not much, but if there was some sort of fine I need to pay . . ."

"Toss them on the ground out here. Shirt and boots."

Damon grudgingly removed them, tossing each item through the bars.

"Jacket too."

Damon retrieved the jacket he had balled up to use as a pillow and tossed that through the bars as well. The sheriff inspected one of his boots with her foot, mashing on it with her own boot. Satisfied that they didn't contain anything illicit, she took a step closer. "All right. Those pockets had better be empty. Pull them out all the way." Damon dutifully tugged on each pocket lining until they were hanging out.

"Okay. Back up now. You know I have to take precautions. You're a sword swinger. Death Dealer. The kind of man this town doesn't need. The kind of man that's been nothing but trouble for us."

"So let me go," Damon said. "Show me to the gate and I'll be on my way. I'll be some other town's problem."

"Could be that's what we do," Trammel said. "But I want to know a few things about you. I'm gonna ask you some questions. But every lie you tell me, the less food you get. I call this the plate of truth."

Damon took a step closer. "What do you want to know?"

"Why are you here in Rust Creek?"

"I came to find a friend. I'm escorting her east to Glastonbury castle. She's been invited by the king."

Trammel locked eyes with him, then popped one of the sandwich triangles into her mouth. The bacon and lettuce crunched between her teeth, then vanished down her gullet in a matter of seconds. She licked her lips. "Let's try again. Why did you come here?"

Damon narrowed his eyes. "I've come to meet with Lady Valerie Terravecchia, an invitee of King Logan to his Knights of the Round Table. We were passengers aboard a road train. I'm escorting her east to Glastonbury Castle."

Trammel scrunched up her face, then picked up another piece of sandwich. It likewise disappeared, but not before a trickle of tomato juice dribbled down her chins. She wiped at it with the back of her hand.

"Why are you here, sword swinger?"

Damon shifted his feet, his mind racing to try to figure out what she was after.

"Look, I'm here to help Valerie Terravecchia retrieve a war car, stolen by natives."

When the next sandwich triangle crunched between her teeth, he lost some of his composure. "I'm telling you the truth! What else do you want?"

"I see that this is going to take a while," Trammel said with her mouth still full. "If you're not ready to be honest with me, then you won't be getting any of this for now." She wagged the last triangle at him, dislodging a piece of lettuce that fluttered to the floor. "Think hard about how you want this to go next time. I'll see you tomorrow."

"Wait. Tomorrow?" Damon lunged forward.

Trammel's hand went to the hilt of her sword. "Don't test me. You think those bars are to keep me safe? They're to keep *you* safe from me." She crammed the last bit of sandwich into her cheek and crunched down on it, then stooped to scoop up the lantern. "I was feeling generous today. If you don't learn to tell the truth soon, you'll see me in a worse mood."

She then turned her back on him, lumbered slowly around the corner and was lost to sight.

Damon moved to the bars, watching and waiting. Then the light went out, returning him to the darkness.

When he was sure Trammel was gone, he crept cautiously to the filth bucket, tilted it back on its edge with one finger and felt around the hollow he had made beneath. He retrieved his pen knife, slipping it back into his pocket. Then he waited.

～

Rico didn't think much of the town of Rust Creek. In his observation so far, he had seen little that would be of interest to a deliberate visitor—if this town even had those.

His walk down the covered walkways of the main street had revealed a rather uninspired place, more of its buildings standing vacant than were occupied. It still had the basic necessities of any town of its size. There was a schoolhouse, a mercantile, a feed store and cattle market, a produce market, and of course the automotive repair shop he had just left. The barber shop and the bath house showed a splash of creativity with their red and blue signage. They at least had the nerve to use a color palate that wasn't brown. Though it was possible that the other shops and stores were simply covered in so much dust and dirt that their original colors were indiscernible.

The building Rico currently had his attention on was the local jail. In a place of prominence in what could possibly be considered the village square, it sat opposite a saloon and intimidated its surroundings with red stone walls and a rusted iron door of almost the same color. Everything about the jail looked heavy. Solid. Immovable. So too did the woman who emerged from the jail and made her way across the street. Rico lingered near a bench on the porch of the produce market and watched as the woman in the mail shirt and oversized coat took the steps of the saloon one foot at a time, a seemingly permanent scowl stamped upon her face.

It wasn't the manner or even the size of the woman that made Rico hesitant to approach.

There were rules to this game. Rules to being a man dressed in women's clothing in a strange town. Even if Damon hadn't passed along the cryptic message of caution, "cuidado," Rico would have taken this step carefully.

No laws in the Kingdom of Avalon forbid people like him from being citizens, but there were other laws to consider. Regional magistrates. Territorial Lords. Local sheriffs. Each had their own circles of power, and appealing to a higher one could be a difficult and sometimes counterproductive solution.

Damon had advised caution.

So Rico watched. He waited. Then he moved slowly to the window of the saloon. As he suspected, it was mostly deserted at this hour, but a few men were lingering on stools, their hats in their hands, seemingly waiting for something. They kept casting glances toward a corner. Rico pretended to be checking his hair in the reflection of the window, and caught a glimpse of the sheriff in the corner booth. She was unloading notebooks and ledgers from her coat's deep pockets.

Rico was considering whether to enter the saloon when a figure on a motorcycle turned the corner of the street. He was hunched over a custom bobber that was moving at a veritable crawl. Even with his odd posture, Rico instantly recognized the tattooed bald man as one of the group he and Damon had run into in the woods—Wrecking Ball. This surly rider had a pale and bloodless look to him, even in the early morning sunlight. To Rico's horror, he pulled directly up to the saloon and parked his bike.

Rico turned his back to the man and pretended to rummage through his bag for something. He kept one eye on the man's reflection in the glass. The big biker groaned as he climbed off the bobber and limped forward, clomping up the steps with one arm cradling the other. It seemed that in addition to whatever was bothering his leg, his left arm also hung limp and bloody. He had made some manner of bandage for his shoulder.

To Rico's relief, Wrecking Ball was clearly not in the mood to pay attention to anything else. He pushed his way through the doors to the saloon with only a passing glance at Rico.

It was the shouting that began afterward that riveted Rico's attention. It was mostly swearing at first. Some man was bearing the brunt of Wrecking Ball's anger for occupying a spot he shouldn't. Rico angled himself toward the window again for a better look. It was the sheriff's booth that was the location of the scuffle. One of the men he had seen waiting patiently earlier was being evicted from the booth. Wrecking Ball may have been injured but he was clearly hale enough to badger this other man into submission. The displaced patron was thrown bodily to the floor in a manner that would have better befitted a sack of potatoes.

The man cursed and spat, but he picked himself up and shuffled off through the doors, shoving them open and escaping with whatever remained of his dignity.

"What are you looking at?" He demanded of Rico when he caught him staring. But the question needed no reply. The man lurched off the porch, battered the dirt from his hat, then reaffixed it to the top of his head before sulking off.

Rico knew he couldn't keep lingering outside the window any longer. His presence hadn't drawn as much attention as Wrecking Ball's entrance had warranted, but as the situation inside settled down, he caught a few more glances through the window from the men inside.

He considered withdrawing, but he wasn't going to learn anything about what happened to Damon that way. He took a deep breath, ran one hand over his wig, then strode into the saloon.

He kept his eyes fixed on a particular stool at the bar as he walked in. His gaze didn't wander anywhere near the corner where the sheriff and Wrecking Ball were in heated conversation. He instead focused on his desired seat, not letting the stares of anyone in the room slow him down.

The bartender was standing with his hands on his hips at one end of the bar, but reluctantly diverted his attention from the conversation in order to come serve him.

"What'll it be, miss?"

"Just a cup of coffee please," Rico said. He received a few more curious glances while he crossed his legs on the seat and tried to think what possible reason someone named Esme Mercedes de la Vega could have for being here.

He had chosen his seat for one reason—its proximity to the mirror behind the bar. From his new vantage point he had a clear view of the Sheriff's reflection, albeit a reflection surrounded by a wall of liquor bottles. He couldn't hear everything going on in the booth, since the sheriff wasn't blustering as loudly as her companion, but he hoped to make up what he missed by reading the sheriff's lips.

Rico picked up a discarded newspaper someone had left on the bar and pretended to read the help wanted section as he watched the conversation in the mirror.

Wrecking Ball was describing the encounter with Damon in the woods, though his version included a great many wounds inflicted on his adversaries that Rico knew weren't true.

The sheriff seemed like she wasn't buying it either. She must have already met Damon by now.

Rico struggled to make out the majority of the sheriff's words, but the name "Valerie Terravecchia" made him perk his ears. He reminded himself that Esme wouldn't know a thing about any Valerie Terravecchia and relaxed his posture, but he listened intently anyway.

" . . . Up at the castle. Lord Hudson will see to her."

Wrecking Ball finally lowered his voice and whispered something Rico couldn't hear. He found himself leaning closer to the reflection in the mirror, though logically he knew it made no sense.

"What's your name, pretty lady?" A man slid onto the stool next to him, blocking the view of the sheriff's booth.

Rico cursed under his breath and laid the newspaper back on the bar top.

What was his story? The first thing that came to mind was a character from a stage play he had written years ago. A traveling merchant's daughter escaped from an unwanted betrothal and fleeing across the frontier for a fresh start. He dug deep and sank into character.

Esme Mercedes de la Vega pivoted slowly and unsheathed a winning smile. "Why hello, there! You sneak-ed up on me." Rico decided at the last second that English wasn't going to be Esme's first language. He bopped the man's nose playfully. It was not a nose that one would suspect received a lot of bopping. The man was immediately taken by surprise.

He may have been a farmer or a rancher. He wasn't especially handsome, but neither was he awful to look at. He reminded Rico of his kindly old employer at a car garage that . . . Esme definitely didn't ever work at. He forced himself to focus.

"Enchanted to meet you, señor . . ."

"Ah, you're from down south, then," the man replied. "That explains it. I heard you Spanish women don't do all the tweezing and waxing and such the women up here do."

Esme kept a winning smile on her face while Rico did a rapid inventory of his body. His underarms surely weren't in view, though they did feel prickly. He rubbed a palm over his knee.

Nothing there to warrant suspicion.

He supposed his eyebrows were bolder than this guy might be used to, but a bold brow was in on the west coast. Hadn't these people gotten the update? Damon was right. This really was a backwater.

And who was this guy to criticize? He had a veritable hair forest growing from the lobes of his ears, and *his* eyebrows could make a yeti feel underprepared for winter.

He glanced at the booth where the sheriff and Wrecking Ball were still whispering.

"Gonna be a long wait for the good sheriff today, if that's what you're here for," the man said.

Esme gave him a casual smile and tossed a breezy hand in the air. "I have nowhere to be and now there's good company. No more am I in a hurry."

"New in town, huh?" the man inquired. "You another one that was held up on that road train? Saw one of your lot come in yesterday. Girl on a motorcycle. Some kinda noblewoman."

Rico tried not to look as interested as he was. "Have you seen anyone today? A man? There were people on the train I traveled with. I hoped to find them."

"Ain't seen nobody today, and I been here since Virgil opened the place a half hour ago. If your friends are here, they ain't come in yet."

"You didn't tell me your name," Rico said, fixing the man with his most fascinated expression.

"Name's Walt. And I'd bet you're the best looking thing that's come into town since the rush ended."

"The rush?"

"Sure. The oil rush. Rust Creek used to be someplace. Back in them days, they say you couldn't wave a stick without hitting someone that was rich as a duke or as pretty as a princess. Course the oil all got pumped up, and they moved the highway. Between the droughts and raiders, it's a wonder anyone's left in this town."

"Is that why you're here?" Esme asked. "You need the sheriff to protect your land from raiders?"

"Well, that ain't nothing a pretty lady like you ought to worry about," Walt said. "Thing is, I already pay for protection. Kai Nez and her regulators guard us plenty. Only with things being what they are, I'm a little shy on the payment this month. Come to see if the sheriff here will cut me a break."

"She does not have the face of someone who cuts people breaks," Rico said, casting another glance toward the back booth.

"See, that's where I have this figured out." Walt leaned in conspiratorially. "All you gotta do is blame your troubles on the natives. Sheriff Trammel may hate a man coming in short on his dues, but she hates them local red-skinned tribes more. All you gotta do is say you had your crop burned or your cattle stolen and them nomad savages is the ones that did it, and she'll let you off another month."

"Did the natives really steal your cattle?" Esme asked.

"Not yet, they ain't. But I bet they's fixin' to. That's why I ain't even raising cattle no more. Sold what I had and now I've got plans to cash in down at the River Boat. They've got a chance down there where you can win ten times the money you put down. A hundred times even. I tell you what. My luck's gonna change. I feel like you're lucky too. All them other big shot river gamblers got themselves pretty ladies on their arms. If you want to, you could be mine."

"You're trying to get a trophy gal and you haven't even won anything yet?" Rico tried to keep the sarcasm out of Esme's voice.

"Sure. Because if you want to be my lady now, before I got all that money, I know I can trust you for when I'm rich, you get me?"

"You have this all figured out, don't you?"

Walt's gaze drifted to the stairwell door. "You staying upstairs in the hotel? If you like, we could go up to your room and get to know each other a little." He pressed a hand to her thigh in a manner that he must have imagined was sensual.

It gave Rico a chill. He picked up Walt's hand and placed it back in the man's own lap for him. "I think your sheriff is looking for you."

Walt turned and found that Sheriff Trammel had risen from her booth and was lumbering over to the bar with a scowl on her face. She set her empty coffee cup on the bar and faced off with Walt.

"You're late on your payment again, Slonaker. That's two months in a row. What did I tell you would happen if you were late again?"

Walt blanched. "Now sheriff, I've been meaning to see you sooner. It's them native raiders, they been, well . . . raiding again. Cleaned me out for all I got."

"And yet Wrecking Ball says he saw you down at the river boat three nights in a row last week. You mean to say that the raiders got to you before you went on that losing streak that cost you your protection dues?"

"Uh . . . well, it might have been after."

"Walt, what you're going to do is walk across the street, head over to the stocks, and you're going to put your neck and arms in, and you're going to stay there until I've got time to come lock you up."

Walt balked. He glanced at Rico sheepishly, then held up his palms to the sheriff. "Now let's talk this thing out, can't we?"

"I told you the next time you came in short I was putting you in the stocks. You calling me a liar, Walter?"

"No. Of course not, but you want me to put *myself* in? What kind of man puts his own self on display for a mockery and don't even have no one making him do it?"

"You put yourself in this situation. So you can put yourself in the stocks. I'll be along to lock you up eventually."

"How long have I got to be in there for? You know I can't pay you nothing if I'm . . ." But he trailed off under the continued scrutiny of the sheriff. He bunched the brim of his hat together, cast another sheepish look at Rico, then slouched off through the front door.

The doors had just finished closing when the sheriff addressed Rico. "And who might you be?"

Rico put a hand to his chin and swallowed. "I'm Esme Mercedes de la Vega," he murmured. He attempted to recall the backstory he had conjured for himself.

Escaped fiancée. Seeking a new life.

No one in their right mind would want to start over here.

He hadn't even been asked any questions, but he could already feel himself sweating. This woman was going to see right through him.

His mouth opened but no words came out. The sheriff continued to stare him down with suspicion.

"I've come to town looking for . . . uh, looking for . . ." His eyes fell on the help wanted section of the newspaper.

The sheriff narrowed her eyes.

"A job," he finally managed.

The sheriff picked up the paper and studied the job offers. "Were you planning to apply for the mason's guild apprenticeship, or the maid position up at the castle?"

"Still deciding," Rico said with a nervous laugh.

The sheriff didn't smile.

"Of course, the maid position," Rico added.

"Dressed pretty fancy for a scullery maid. You plan to scrub pots and kettles in that dress?"

"It's said that you should dress for the job you want," Rico said. "Perhaps when they see me, they'll see other potential."

"I suspect they'll see something all right," the sheriff said. "Best get on up to the castle then, eh? Lord Hudson's kitchen staff gets an early start."

Rico paid for his coffee, fishing coins from his bag with trembling fingers, then slid off the stool and walked to the door as calmly as he could manage. He felt Trammel's eyes on him the entire way. When he was outside, he finally took a deep breath. His eyes strayed to the stocks outside the jail where Walt had dutifully installed himself with his neck and both arms hung through the holes. He gazed forlornly at Rico.

Rico averted his eyes, cast one last glance back at the saloon, then fled back the way he had come.

What on earth had become of Damon?

15

PLUNGE

Dakota hit the water first, her arm still locked around the road knight's neck. Once they were under, she released her grip. This greenhorn warrior was no longer the threat. The fall from the bridge to the river wasn't the problem either.

It was the next drop that would determine her fate.

Dakota gained the surface and took a gulp of air just as the rush of the river propelled her and her involuntary companion over the edge of the falls. She braced herself and tried to get her feet under her, but then they fell, plummeting the fifty feet to the foaming and frothing pool below.

Her stomach was in her chest as she fell. Wind and her own wet hair slapped at her face. She tucked her feet up, mentally preparing to strike a rock and be killed, or careen off one to drown, paralyzed at the bottom of the river.

But her feet broke the water's surface cleanly. She went under in a rush of noise and brilliant-white foam. Her feet hit the river bottom, hard, but not hard enough to break her. She compressed into a ball, the energy of her fall dissipating in the omnipresent bubbles.

Her left wrist jerked to one side, a reminder that she hadn't fallen alone.

If the other girl had struck a rock or been knocked unconscious during the fall, the dead weight might drown her before she could even make the surface.

The current was already moving them, pushing down and out, forcing them under the turbulent waves. Her knee struck a stone and she winced. An eruption of bubbles left her mouth.

Up. She had to get to air. A jerk on her left wrist let her know that the other girl was alive. Alive and swimming. They both broke the surface at the same time, but facing opposite directions.

During the scuffle on the bridge, this road knight had handcuffed herself to her wrist, but had done so in a hurry, attaching Dakota's left wrist to her left arm. When they had been facing the same direction, one behind the other—Dakota's arm behind her back—it had been a logical move. Now it was a big problem. With arms extended in front of themselves, each of them was facing opposite directions.

"Are you crazy?" Valerie shouted. "You could have killed us!"

That was obvious. Maybe she wasn't as clever as she looked.

"You're not taking me in!" Dakota shouted back.

She had lost her knife in the fall, otherwise she would have a quick way of shutting this girl up.

"Let me loose!" She yanked on the handcuffs. Valerie yanked back and they both sank underwater.

That's when Dakota caught the glint of silver. The sword. The Terravecchia girl still had it sheathed at her waist. Dakota lunged for the hilt with her free hand, her fingers wrapping around the grip. Valerie clamped a hand over her wrist, pinning the sword hilt in place, and the pair thrashed and kicked as they struggled for control. They sank further, their feet soon scraping the floor of the riverbed. Dakota jerked at the sword and attempted to push off Valerie's chest with her handcuffed hand, but it was no use. This girl was a match for her in strength, and it seemed she wasn't in any hurry to get back to the surface.

Dakota's lungs burned. She fought with the sword hilt a little longer, then gave up, releasing her grip on the sword and pushing off the floor of the riverbed in a bid for air. She didn't make it. Her wrist held her down. She turned to find the determined face of her captor staring back at her through the turbulent water. Valerie had planted her feet against a stone in the riverbed and was using the current against her. She didn't seem like she was even concerned about drowning. How did she still have air?

Dakota suddenly realized the trouble she was in. If she didn't do something soon, this girl was going to drown her.

Her chest ached. It felt like her very veins were on fire. Her vision was beginning to narrow and there were flecks of light dancing through the water that she was pretty certain weren't really there.

Valerie raised a hand and proceeded to use a manner of sign language.

You.

Stop.

She tilted her head, then ran a finger across her throat. The message was pretty clear.

Or else.

Dakota nodded frantically. Her jaw was clamped shut but it was all she could do to keep from opening her mouth and swallowing this entire river. She just needed something in her lungs. Valerie gestured toward her once more, this time pointing two fingers.

I'm watching you.

Yes. Whatever. Dakota didn't care. She just needed air. Right now. She kicked desperately for the surface and this time she rose, Valerie kicking off from the riverbed and rising with her.

Dakota gasped and gulped at the air, coughing and sputtering. She tread water and saw that they were now a long way downstream from the falls. The river was slowing but they were back under cover of the forest. Evergreen boughs only allowed periodic glimpses of the sky. Spruce and fir, aspen and pine. They smelled better than she had ever remembered.

It was loud here. Her hearing seemed amplified with the rush of oxygen back to her brain. She looked around and saw that her captor was swimming for the bank nearest them. Valerie gained her footing, then yanked Dakota toward her. Dakota struggled to get her feet under her, obligated as she was to back up to the riverbank. She walked at an angle till she could get her free hand into the wet earth as well, then finally crawled out of the water and onto the muddy embankment.

She panted for several more seconds as she worked to catch her breath. Looking back along the route they had come, she could just make out the base of the falls. A chill ran up her spine. It was a wonder they had survived. At the time, facing that viper sword and a dozen soldiers, it had seemed like a reasonable escape plan. Looking at it now, she doubted she would ever try her luck again.

She turned to look at the girl at the other end of her handcuffs. "You going to let me out of this thing or what?" Dakota lifted her wrist.

"I would," Valerie replied. "Except you knocked us off the bridge before I could get the key. It's still up there." She tilted her chin toward the falls. "So we'll wait here until the rest of the group finds us. You can sit there quietly and this will be over soon."

Dakota muttered and stood.

"What are you doing?" Valerie asked, forced to stand too in order to remain on guard.

"I'm not going back with that snake demon." Dakota would have thought this was obvious based on her most recent actions, but apparently this girl wasn't getting it. Maybe the cold from the river had dulled her wits.

Another chill rushed over Dakota's skin, leaving gooseflesh in its wake.

"She's not my favorite person either but we don't have much choice," Valerie replied. "I've got no ride or handcuff keys without them, and you're in no position to go anywhere."

Dakota leered at her. "You want to bet?" She took a step closer, attempting to stare down her captor. The girl's face was blurrier than she recalled.

The blurry face looked unimpressed.

"You're losing a lot of blood. You need help. If you stay calm, I'll try to help you."

Dakota could feel the warmth wicking out of her shoulder. It throbbed, her skin pulsing. She couldn't see the wound but the waistband of her jeans was soaked red and she was certainly lightheaded. She reached her free hand up over her shoulder and winced as she touched the cut. Her fingers came away bloody and warm. The scent was of metal. The girl wasn't lying. She didn't have a lot of time.

"They're just going to kill me anyway," she murmured.

"I'm not going to let that happen," Valerie replied.

"That demon is going to kill you too," Dakota said. "You know she is."

Valerie didn't respond. She merely stared at the blood trickling down Dakota's elbow. Eventually she met Dakota's eyes again. "You're going to bleed to death if you don't get some help. Come on. We're going back." She jerked on her wrist and turned back toward the waterfall.

Dakota stood her ground. "No."

Valerie sighed and yanked on the handcuffs again.

Dakota yanked back this time and took a swing with her other hand, her fist connecting with Valerie's cheek.

Valerie reeled, but rallied with a punch of her own. Dakota instinctively brought her hand up to block the blow but couldn't because of the handcuffs. Valerie's fist struck her, followed by a jab from her elbow.

Dakota shrieked and tried to sweep the legs out from under the girl, but she stood her ground, pivoting and catching hold of her wrist before flinging her to the mud.

Dakota landed with a thud on her back. She grit her teeth from the pain.

"We're going . . . back," Valerie snarled. She glared down at Dakota from above.

"I'll take you to the car," Dakota panted. "It's not far from here."

Valerie canted her head to one side, clearly resistant to listening to another argument, but Dakota knew she had her attention.

"If you don't take me back to that snake woman, I'll take you to the car. Otherwise we'll both die on this river and you know it."

"You don't know that she wants to kill me. And even if she did *want* to, that doesn't mean she'll try anything. I'm an officer of the law."

"You think that matters out here?" Dakota asked, gesturing to the shifting boughs of the trees overhead. The wind was rustling the leaves—whispering its secrets. The spirits were near again. She could hear them on the wind. "I don't know why she wants to kill you. I don't know how she'll do it. But that woman wants you dead. You know she does."

"And I'm supposed to believe you *don't* want me dead?" Valerie asked. "Why should I trust you?"

"Because I know who you are," Dakota muttered. "And I know the spirit you're chasing."

"I'm not chasing spirits," Valerie said. She set her jaw and heaved on Dakota's arm, pulling her to her feet.

"You chase the bear. You're wearing his sign." Dakota's gaze settled on the saturated symbol on the back of her captor's jacket.

The wine-red bear paw. Five claw marks spread out across her shoulders. "And I know where to find him."

Valerie met her eye again.

"There's a hunting cabin. If we go north." Dakota pointed through the trees. "You take me there, and I'll show you the one you're looking for. And I'll take you to the car."

"What do you mean exactly? What bear spirit?"

The girl's face was getting blurry again. Dakota swayed to one side. The earth swayed. But then she felt an arm around her waist, steadying her.

Her captor's voice was now right in her ear. "North. How far?"

Dakota whispered only a little louder than the wind. "Till we make it."

16

PRISONER

Valerie struggled to keep her prisoner on her feet as they made their way through the deep woods. The girl was getting delirious but was still moving.

They had made it perhaps a quarter of a mile, but they weren't going to make it much farther if the girl kept losing blood. Valerie stopped to rest, leaving her captive against a tree, then shrugged her free arm out of her jacket. With her wrist still handcuffed, there was no way to get it all the way off, but she turned the sleeve inside out, rotating the jacket and sliding it up the other girl's arm.

Valerie removed her T-shirt. It was still soaking wet and not the cleanest, but she had no better options. With it dangling from her wrist, she drew her sword and sliced through it, severing it in two. She sheathed the sword and then stripped the shirt into a makeshift bandage, tying it around the girl's neck and armpit to cover her bloody shoulder blade. The girl groaned but took it, her eyes still closed. Valerie brought their conjoined wrists up so she could keep pressure on the wound with that hand while she unbuckled her belt with the other. Her sword and scabbard fell to the ground as she freed the belt, and her captive's eyes fluttered open momentarily at the sound.

"Don't even think about it," Valerie said.

She then looped the belt under the girl's armpit, and used it to secure the bandage over the wound. Due to the awkward way they were conjoined at the wrist, the jacket was upside down and inside out now. There was nothing to be done about that, but she pushed the sleeve up the rest of the way and slung the jacket over the girl's shoulders. It might help keep her a little warmer.

It was an ungainly and unattractive solution, leaving her captive looking like a hunchback, but she hoped it would stop the flow of blood for now.

Valerie shivered as she picked up her sword and slung her captive's arm over her shoulder. She held the girl's wrist, keeping the crook of her elbow over her neck. It wasn't the best position for the girl's shoulder wound, but it was the only method she had found to keep them both facing the same direction while walking. She slung her free arm around the girl's waist, simultaneously retaining her sword and trying to keep her captive upright.

"I need you to tell me if we're close," Valerie said.

The girl's eyes fluttered open. "Keep going. Just keep going."

"You have to keep talking," Valerie said. "Don't pass out on me."

The girl moaned in response.

"What's your name?" Valerie asked. "You can at least tell me that."

"Go to hell."

Valerie continued to struggle uphill. "Your mother must not have liked you much to name you that."

"My mother . . . is . . . a fighter," the girl murmured. "She'd fight you. She'd fight . . ." Her voice trailed off.

"She the one who taught *you* to fight?" Valerie asked, grunting as she pulled the girl over a fallen tree limb. "Because if so, I'm not scared."

"My mother . . . would hate you," the girl said. "If you were her daughter, she would tell no one. She would tell you to go get water from the river. Then she would move."

Valerie paused, considering the girl in her arms. She shook her head, then kept going. "You're lucky you have a mom who fights for you. I wish I had that."

"You would have died in the first week if you were born out here. You're a city girl. Soft. The Black Hawk tribe only keeps warriors."

"Sorry I don't live up to your standards," Valerie muttered. "But that's fine by me. Once I get my car back, you can have this place all to yourself. Every. Last. Bit." She kicked a stone out of her way and hauled her captive onward. Her back was sore, and the metal handcuff bit into her wrist.

She glanced back the way they had come, listening for the sound of engines. Had Kai Nez and the rest of the posse even looked for her? They may simply have assumed she was dead. Not an illogical supposition, but she would have hoped they would have at least checked and not left her drowned body for the vultures.

"It's there," her captive murmured.

Valerie looked up the hill and could just make out the silhouette of a building through the trees. Another hundred yards and they'd reach it. She tightened her grip on the girl and climbed on, this time with renewed energy. They broke out of the trees twenty yards from the log cabin. It was an old building, bedecked with lichen, and the wood was stained from years of rain and snow. There was a log pile and old axe and a separate shed that looked like it might be big enough to house a car. Valerie vowed to check. There were several trail bikes scattered around the weedy clearing. Some were propped on kickstands and one leaned precariously against a porch support. The front porch was littered with fishing poles, a half-barrel of arrows, and a number of animal skins hung on the wall.

"You know who this cabin belongs to?" Valerie asked. Whoever it was, it looked like they had been here recently.

The girl's head was beginning to loll.

"Hey. Stay awake, you hear me?" Valerie said, giving the girl a shake.

"Garage," the girl muttered. "In the garage."

Valerie headed that way, dragging her captive to the door, then propping her up with her shoulder while she tried to get the door open. She finally managed it, then caught the lethargic girl before she could collapse. The inside of the garage was dusty and dim, but the light from the doorway was enough to illuminate a workbench, several wall racks of tools, and a vehicle parked at the center, covered in tarps. The shape of the vehicle gave Valerie a thrill of hope. She could see nothing of the car itself, but it had familiar lines and a bold profile, even under wraps.

But revealing the car would have to wait. Something more necessary caught her eye. She struggled across the garage, set her sword on the workbench, then stretched to grab the bolt cutters hanging from the hook. She had just gotten her hands on them when the girl next to her collapsed, causing Valerie to stumble to her knees in her efforts to catch her.

The girl landed in her lap, moaning in pain.

"Hey. You can't give up now," Valerie said. "We've almost got this." She got her legs under her and heaved, lifting the girl back to her feet. They were facing each other now and the girl was draped over her, as though to give her a hug. Her chin rested on Valerie's shoulder, though their left arms were still joined in front of them.

Valerie twisted and reached for the bolt cutters, this time successfully removing them from the hook.

The thought occurred to her that she could cut her wrist loose, leave this girl here, and be gone with the car. No one would ever be the wiser. As tempting as the thought was, she knew she couldn't do it. She grunted and got a better grip on the girl, then carried her back out the door, across the weedy turf of the yard, and up the porch steps. A porch swing hung from chains in the ceiling. She had intended to get the girl all the way inside to a bed, but this was going to have to do for now. She maneuvered the girl onto the swing, laying her face down so her left arm hung to the floor.

"We're almost free," she muttered. "Then I'll get you some help." She positioned the bolt cutters on the porch next to their conjoined wrists, prying them open with her knee and one good hand. She slid the jaws over the handcuff links and got ready to cut, one side of the cutters pinned against the boards of the porch. With a groan and grunt, she pressed hard on the handle. The jaws bit the links, and the handcuffs snapped apart.

"Finally," Valerie muttered.

The girl's eyes fluttered open. She looked at Valerie and gave a wan smile. "My name is Dakota."

"You're welcome, Dakota," Valerie said. "Now you're free."

"You're not going to be too happy with me," Dakota murmured. She trailed off with something Valerie couldn't hear.

Valerie leaned close till their faces were mere inches apart. "What?"

The girl squinted through her dark lashes. "Now you're ... my ... prisoner."

Valerie rocked back on her heels, trying to decipher the girls' words. She was clearly delirious.

But then she heard the footfalls.

She turned slowly to find the figures of four teenage natives making a semicircle on the lawn. One was a girl with a bow. The arrow was nocked and aimed right at her.

Valerie's hand went involuntarily to her hip, but her fingers found nothing. Her sword was still in the garage on the workbench where she'd left it.

"If she's dead, you can bet you will be too." The speaker was the guy in the middle of the group. He likely wasn't more than nineteen or twenty, but his lean, pock-marked face had sharp eyes that reminded her of a falcon or an eagle. He had a long knife in his hand and wore boots that laced all the way to his knees.

"She's not dead," Valerie said. "But she needs help. Right away. Clean water. Stitches. A doctor if you have one."

The man with the knife gestured to one of his companions, and the lanky teenage boy rushed to the front steps of the cabin, keeping a wary eye on Valerie. She recognized him as the same one she had knocked to the ground and stolen the Troublemaker from. He clearly recognized her, too, because he gave her a wide berth.

"You're the ones who robbed the train," Valerie said.

"Ain't none of us ever took nothing that wasn't ours to begin with," the girl with the bow said.

"Quiet!" the man with the knife shouted, "while I think what to do with her."

"Let me shoot her and you can figure what to do with the body," the girl hissed. She had a hard, unsympathetic look to her; the tattoos running down her bow arm were a tangle of thorny vines and withered flowers. There was something about her eyes that made Valerie certain she wasn't afraid to use the bow to kill.

"That doesn't sound like something an innocent person who never robbed anybody says." Valerie put her hands up but slowly rose to her feet. "You don't want to get into more trouble than you already are."

"Only one in trouble here is you." This came from the other native, a handsome teen of maybe seventeen. He was athletic and lean with his hair shaved into a mohawk. He seemed to be having trouble keeping his eyes off her damp figure. His attention made her wish she was standing there in something other than her athletic bra.

The lanky boy reemerged from inside the cabin with a bucket of water, several rags, and a battered medical kit. He stood uncertainly in the doorway. The man with the knife gestured for Valerie to step aside. The teen with the mohawk joined the lanky boy, and the two examined the wounded girl.

Dakota.

Valerie wasn't sure why, but she felt suddenly possessive of the girl's health. She'd gone to a lot of effort to keep her alive. It felt somehow wrong to quit now.

"The wound will need washing. That dressing wasn't clean."

The boy with the mohawk unbuckled the belt and held up her tattered, bloodstained T-shirt. He examined it, then tossed it aside.

"Get inside," the man with the knife said. "Keep your hands up and don't try anything."

"If you give me back my car, I'll be gone and you'll never see me again."

"Shut up and do what I tell you."

The teen with the mohawk looked up from where he was working on Dakota. "We're going to have to cauterize this wound right away, Sprocket."

"Why the hell you telling this girl my name, numb nuts," Sprocket said.

"Oh, sorry," the teen with the mohawk mumbled. "But . . . it's not like that's your real name, right?"

"Just shut up about it!" The man called Sprocket turned his focus back to Valerie. "Now you're going to open that door real slow. Then I want you to step aside while I come up there. You move too quick and you get an arrow in the gut. Ain't that right?" He shouted this last to the girl with the bow.

"She may get one anyway if she keeps eye-ballin' me like that."

Valerie calmly averted her eyes and focused on the door.

First rule of a knife fight was to run. First rule when facing a bow and arrow was to find cover. As the door yawned open, she made a quick inventory of what she could see inside. Cots, blankets, a rough-hewn dining table. She considered simply bolting in and locking the door, but it was a standoff she wouldn't be able to manage long if there was no other way out. Not unless she could find a weapon. They hadn't shot her yet, which means they may be considering some use for her, but she wasn't sure she wanted to find out what that was.

If she could somehow make the garage, that would be a different matter. There were tools and weapons aplenty. She had a spare key to the Guardian hidden underneath the car in a spot only she knew. If she made it inside the car, there was nothing this crew would be able to do to stop her blasting out of there.

"Hey, get a fire going and put some steel in it. Get it good and hot." Sprocket was talking to the lanky kid again. "And fetch me some rope."

Valerie continued to scan her options inside. She needed a shield. Pot lids and skillets weren't going to cut it.

The clock was ticking. If they got her inside and tied up, it was going to be all over. There was a hallway. Bathroom. The hallway wall was illuminated by daylight.

A back door.

That was going to have to work.

Sprocket turned to her again and waved the knife. "Okay, nice and easy. In we go." He stepped onto the porch.

The girl with the bow let the arrowhead wander. She was aimed more to one side, waiting for Sprocket to clear the shot.

Human shield. Not the worst plan.

Valerie took a step toward him and lashed out with a kick to the man's knife hand, her boot connecting with his fingers and sending the knife soaring upward and embedding itself in the wooden ceiling to the porch. Valerie and Sprocket both stared up at the quivering knife for half an instant. Surprisingly, it was staying up there.

Sprocket lowered his open-mouthed stare toward Valerie, but by this time she was already spinning into a kick, planting her boot squarely into his chest and sending him flailing backward toward the girl with the bow. Valerie didn't wait to see what would happen next. She instead turned and sprinted through the cabin. She knocked over a kitchen chair in her flight, ran down the short hallway, and crashed through the partly open back door.

Garage.

She rushed to the right. She had only seconds to beat the others there. Would they know where she was headed? The kid wouldn't be the threat. It was that bow.

As if on cue, the girl with the bow sprinted around the corner of the cabin. She raised it, drawing the arrow back. Valerie dove and rolled as the girl released. The arrow whizzed high and wide to embed itself in the wood planks of the garage wall.

That was all she needed. By the time the girl could pull another arrow from her quiver and nock it, Valerie was through the side door of the garage. She slammed it shut behind her, scrambling to find the lock on the latch. She swept items from the neighboring bench to the floor behind the door for good measure. Cans of motor oil, a small toolbox. Anything that would make the door harder to get through. Then she rushed for her sword. *Firebird* was where she left it. She snatched up the scabbard, then rushed around the driver's side of the tarp-covered car.

Almost there. Uncover the car. Grab the key. Bust out of here.

She tore at the tarps, unleashing a cloud of dust in the process.

Dust?

She coughed and yanked the last of the covers away, revealing the distinctive shape of the Guardian 770.

It *was* a Guardian.

A Guardian without windows. Without interior. Without an engine.

It wasn't her car.

Valerie dropped the armful of tarps to the floor.

This really wasn't her day.

17

INCOGNITO

R ico had a plan. But every once in a while, a plan requires a little shopping.

He pushed through the door of the mercantile and scanned the assorted shelves.

"Hello. Can I help you?"

Rico looked up to find the proprietor of the mercantile watching him from a counter at the back of the store.

"Yes. I'm looking for any women's clothing you might have?"

The woman nodded, then gestured toward the right-hand wall. "We have some dresses and church wear, and down at the end you might find a few things for everyday wear. Local seamstress named Mrs. Staub sells them on consignment."

Rico wandered to the racks she indicated and browsed the options. The fabrics were mostly calico and wool, dyed a variety of simple colors and stitched with sturdy seams.

"You must be new in town," the proprietor said. "We don't get too many fresh faces these days."

A yip from a dog echoed from somewhere upstairs.

"The guild mechanic next door said you rent rooms," Rico said. "Is that true?"

"I think I could find you something," the woman replied. "As long as you don't mind animals. My daughter has been saving all summer for a dog and finally got her wish."

"Assuming it's friendly," Rico said.

"Friendliest face you're likely to find in Rust Creek." The proprietor put out a hand. "But I'll try to compete. I'm Leslie."

Rico shook her hand. "Esme."

"Are you visiting or planning to stay a while?"

"Saw an advertisement for a maid position up at the castle. Might try for it."

Leslie's face darkened. "You're applying to work for Lord Hudson?"

"You don't think it's a good idea?"

"Not my place to speak of the lord," the woman said, quickly averting her eyes and examining the clothes Rico had selected. "You'll want these taken in, I presume? I can let Mrs. Staub know your measurements."

Rico studied her face. The woman's sincerity seemed genuine. He decided to take a chance.

"Listen, a friend of mine came through town yesterday. I think she's staying up at the castle. Did you happen to run into her?"

"Would she have been carrying a sword? Pretty girl but looking a little roughed up?"

"Sounds right."

"She came in yesterday, dropped off the dog for my daughter. Came by way of a mutual friend. Last I heard she went up to the castle."

Rico nodded. "I'm looking for another friend too. A man. Tall, good-looking guy with a bunch of scars down his arms. He was supposed to be meeting the sheriff, but now I can't find him. Any chance you've seen him?"

"Hasn't been in here." She moved to the clothing display and plucked a simple gray dress from the rack. "This will be the look Lord Hudson will be going for up there. You can change in back if you like. I'll see about fixing you up a room for when you get back."

Rico fumbled for his wallet and extracted several bills. "Thank you for the help. If either of my friends happen to come in, will you tell them I was looking for them and where I went?"

"Happy to," Leslie replied. "You be careful out there, all right? This town gets rough, especially after dark."

"Thanks. I appreciate the advice."

Rico changed into the new dress in the washroom and did his best to tidy Esme's appearance. He touched up the make-up he had done in a rush that morning and put several hairpins in the wig to style it into a more professional look. The dress was snug but comfortable. He left the duffel bag with his remaining clothing items with Leslie and took only a small purse with him for his trek to the castle.

The afternoon sun was still bright as he made the climb to Redrock Castle, and Rico was regretting not having eaten anything for lunch. It hadn't looked far, but the twists and turns in the road were deceptive. He was forced to pause frequently and cool off so as not to arrive at the castle dripping with sweat. He was catching his breath in the shade of a fir tree when the sound of a motor reached him. He peered down the path he had come by and moved toward the road, thinking he might catch a lift the rest of the way up the hill, but when he saw the vehicle, he quickly ducked back behind the trunk of the fir.

Sheriff Trammel was aboard a three-wheeled motorcycle that revved at high RPM as it strained its way up the hill. Trammel's head was thrown back, her thin hair trailing in the wind and her jowls shaking from the vibrations of the motorbike. She passed by without noticing Rico, and the sound of the engine was soon lost in the wind. All that lingered was a faint hint of exhaust and the slightest scent of pickled onions.

Rico waited another minute to see if any more riders were following, but the road remained silent and he continued on.

When he finally reached the outer walls of the castle, he showed a copy of the help wanted ad to the guard and was shown to the servants' entrance by a bored-looking man-at-arms. Rico's mouth fell open as they passed a series of garages, some of them with bay doors open revealing roadsters and war cars the likes of which he had never seen. Whoever this Lord Hudson was, he had excellent taste in cars. He caught a glimpse of a mechanic working on a monstrous black beast of a machine in one of the bays. It had to be twice the size of an average war car, but as soon as the mechanic spotted him, he rolled the door closed.

As the guard rapped on the door of the servants' entrance, Rico tried to recall Esme's backstory.

Her fiancé had been a card player. He gambled away their future. They'd fled the loan sharks back east looking for a new life. Where was he now? Stampede of buffalo did him in? No. Better keep it simple. Hit by a train.

The door swung open, and a gruff-looking doorman admitted them. The man-at-arms explained their business, and Rico was led through a series of winding corridors to a sitting area.

"Lord Hudson prefers to interview the potential staff himself these days," the doorman explained. "You'll wait here till he has time for you. We'll send someone round with some tea and biscuits while you wait." The doorman vanished, leaving Rico alone in the spacious sitting room.

He settled into an armchair so plush that he sank several inches. When the tea tray arrived, he waited politely for the servants to leave, then wolfed down the little vanilla cookies they had left before dabbing up the crumbs with a finger. The tea was mild and summery. He drank two cups as he waited, but before long, it grew cold. He climbed out of the armchair and studied the room.

Bookshelves lined one wall, but others were adorned with

hunting trophies, and one held a large map. He studied the line that defined the border of Hudson lands. Beyond them, the territory of the Black Hawk tribe was annotated with the words, "Savage lands." The map had symbols for rivers and bridges and a multitude of strange marks dotting the mountainside and clustered more densely near the border. Rico had to consult the legend to figure out that these symbols represented oil wells.

Rico studied the map with curiosity, then continued his perusal of the shelves and furniture, eventually making his way to the wall farthest from where he entered. A second door stood slightly ajar, and he could make out voices from somewhere beyond. One of the voices he recognized as Sheriff Trammel. He stood near the crack to listen.

"Gave his name as Benson, but Kai Nez says his name was Roark. Damon Roark."

Rico perked his ears at the sound of Damon's name and eased the door open farther. The door led to an interior hallway, and the voices were coming from another room a short distance along it. Light from the second room spilled onto the hallway rug.

"We can't have anyone else nosing around and stirring up questions. If this Roark swears he could identify the riders, that's a liability." The second voice belonged to a man. He spoke smoothly with a soothing voice that was measured and calm. "It can't be reported in any other township."

Trammel spoke again. "He says it was him and another man. Someone by the name of Cuidado. We've had no sign of him yet, but I've got a few men looking around town."

"Get more. We can't have this person loose and unaccounted for. You have the Roark fellow contained?"

"Dropped him into one of the mine cells, out of sight. Won't no one hear from him again if we don't want."

"Good to hear that old mine still has its uses." Someone clinked a bottle neck to a glass, and the sound was followed by the subtle sloshing of liquid. "The loss of the Terravecchia girl is a shame. I would have liked to have her on our side of things. She could have been an asset to our cause at court. Still, she might be yet. When King Logan gets word that his new champion was killed by a Black Hawk, our case will be made. It won't just be frontier homesteads getting burned and the fuel supplies being siphoned off, we'll have something that affects him personally. If that doesn't get the regiment stationed here again, I don't know what will."

Rico's breath was caught in his chest. Valerie dead? He put a hand to his mouth to stifle a cry.

"I don't mind her being knocked off a bridge," Trammel said. "But it would be a lot more convincing if we had a body. Kai Nez says her boys didn't find one."

"Those rough riders are a pack of wild dogs. They might be fierce but I'm doubtful of their attention to detail. That's why I'm counting on you to deploy them judiciously and follow up on their work. Our case is far stronger if we can prove the Terravecchia girl is dead. If she isn't, you'd better finish the job on her return."

"If she comes crawling back out of those woods, we'll give her a warm welcome."

It wasn't sure then.

The thought gave Rico a glimmer of hope.

A chair scraped the floor, followed by footsteps. "I knew I could count on you, Cecily. You're a true professional. Now, if you'll excuse me, I believe I have a young woman waiting for me down the hall."

Rico backpedaled frantically, suddenly realizing how far down the hallway he had traveled while listening to the conversation. He scrambled back through the doorway just as the man's shadow hit the rug in the hallway. Rico closed the door to where he'd found it and raced back to the armchair on the far side of the room. He threw himself into the chair and tried to control his breathing.

Just be calm. Be calm. Esme. His name was Esme.

When the door to the hallway swung open, a graceful, well-dressed man presented himself and appraised him from a distance. Rico rose and curtsied. "Your Lordship, it's an honor."

"Indeed it must be," Lord Hudson said. He smiled. "Now why don't you tell me *all* about yourself."

18

GHOST

S unset lit the clouds above the little cabin in hues of golden orange and satiny pink over a backdrop of a deepening blue sky. Any other time, Valerie would be appreciating such a sight, but at the moment, sitting on the rough boards of the cabin's front porch, bound at the wrists and ankles, she was far too uncomfortable.

To make matters worse, a veritable cloud of mosquitoes had materialized from the woods and were now gorging themselves, flitting about her bare shoulders, midriff, and even her face. She had tried to shake them away at first, twitching and jerking around on the porch, but it was no good. Her hands, in addition to being bound together, were also tied via a length of rope to one of the vertical roof supports. Her captors had considered gagging her as well, but ultimately left her while they sought refuge from the mosquitos by hovering around the smoky bonfire in the clearing.

After discovering that the car in the garage wasn't hers, there had been no other option but to surrender. A brief negotiation of terms shouted through the chinks in the wall had involved her promising not to try to kill them, then she had opened the main garage door to find not one, but three bows drawn with arrows pointed her direction. Even the lanky kid she had knocked off the bike had one, though the pretty boy with the mohawk had opted to arm himself with the wood cutting axe.

These were far from professional soldiers, but she was outnumbered, and the odds of winning a fight against the entire bunch were too long to consider. Now all that was left was to see what would become of her.

She discovered that her captors' indecision on the subject was due to the fact that Dakota was still unconscious. She had been awake briefly—painfully awake as her ragtag bunch of wannabe doctors cauterized her shoulder wound with a red hot knife.

Valerie still had the lingering scent of burning flesh in her nostrils.

But Dakota had passed out after the event. Her crew had cleaned her up, bandaged her, and placed her on one of the beds in the cabin. If Valerie angled herself the right way, she could make out Dakota's limp arm dangling off the edge of the bed. Though in the fading light, even that was growing difficult to see.

Somehow, despite being unconscious, it seemed Dakota was still the leader of this group, and they struggled to make decisions on their own. Sprocket, the likely next-in-command, had ordered the pretty boy with the mohawk away, sending him into the woods on a motorbike. Valerie had the impression it was to retrieve someone specific. Valerie hoped it was a doctor or someone familiar with battlefield wounds because she had her doubts about the attention they had given Dakota. She even had her doubts about the group's ability to manage a bonfire. They had burned far too much wood already, creating a blaze that was bigger and hotter than anything they could have had a use for. While Valerie appreciated that the occasional plume of smoke would drift her way and temporarily discourage the mosquitos, she was sure, now, that this bunch of teenagers was far from an organized gang.

They were punks.

Troublemakers.

It was true they had managed to hijack a fuel tanker, but it was clear they weren't indiscriminate killers. The only one that concerned her was the girl with the thorn tattoos. At the moment, she seemed content to obey Sprocket's orders, but she cast occasional glances at Valerie that were as prickly as the vines entwined down her arm. The girl had claimed Valerie's sword and was currently wearing it around her waist.

Valerie let her eyes wander to the garage.

The sight of the partially constructed Guardian had left her with more questions. Had Dakota stolen her car because she thought it was easier than restoring that old wreck?

She couldn't entirely fault the logic there. But there had been something more. There was something else to Dakota. Valerie felt a familiarity that she just couldn't shake. Of all the cars to find a body for and try to restore, why a Guardian?

She wondered where Damon was. Was he still searching for her? He must have made Rust Creek by now. Lord Hudson would have told him where she'd gone. They were, no doubt, in contact with Kai Nez and her riders by radio. She assumed that the group would have continued down the shoreline, discovered the area where she had emerged from the river, and would have trailed them. The trail couldn't have been that difficult to follow. She hadn't made any effort to conceal it. Still, without dogs or a trained tracker, it was possible they had missed it. Or perhaps they assumed no one could have survived the plunge over the falls and hadn't even bothered to look.

If they had, wouldn't they have been here by now? She scanned the trees, listening for any sign of movement. The night only answered with the trill of crickets and the distant hoot of an owl. Another mosquito buzzed in her ear, and she jerked against her bonds trying to swat at it.

"Hey! Keep it down!" Sprocket shouted.

"You could have the decency to give me a shirt or a blanket or something," Valerie called back. "I'm getting eaten alive over here."

"Little rich girl needs a blanket," Thorn Tattoo said. "Poor baby. Her delicate noble skin can't handle a few bug bites."

Valerie scowled at her, but it only seemed to amuse the girl.

"You untie me, we'll see how tough you really are," Valerie said.

It was a useless taunt. These teenagers had all the power. There was no need for them to prove anything to her.

But the girl rose from beside the fire, her eyes glinting.

Valerie had struck a nerve.

Maybe it was the boredom of the hours on the porch. Maybe she just craved something for her muscles to do. Either way, she didn't leave it alone.

"You think you're tough, huh?" Valerie said. "Just because you live out here and fancy yourself some kind of outlaw? If you're so badass, why do you need these dudes to keep you safe?"

The girl with the thorn tattoos nodded and flexed her knuckles. "Okay, okay. Let's see what you got, little princess. Achak, cut her loose."

That was easy.

The lanky boy looked unsure.

"Don't be ridiculous," Sprocket said, walking up behind her. "Just leave it till he gets here. He won't like it if you let her get away."

"You don't think I could take her? Screw you. Achak, cut her loose!"

The boy called Achak looked to Sprocket. Valerie only then noticed the fine line of hair on the boy's upper lip that he had obviously intended to be a mustache. It looked like it was about ten years from growing in fully. His assertiveness must have been a late arrival too.

"Nevermind. I'll do it." The tattooed girl stepped over to

Achak and plucked the knife he was wearing from his waist. His objection was unintelligible.

She headed straight for Valerie, brandishing the knife and pressing it to her throat. "You want to talk trash about me? I could cut you right now. Don't think I wouldn't. But it's going to be fun taking you down." She moved around to Valerie's back and began sawing at the ropes.

"Lanja! Stop it!" Sprocket said. "You're being ridiculous." But he didn't move to restrain her.

The cords broke loose.

Valerie was tempted to try to wrestle her sword away from the girl and take them all on, but there was a stronger part of her that wanted to see this through. She rubbed her wrists and simply walked toward the fire. Not rushing, not trying to escape. She took a position on a level patch of ground and turned around.

The tattooed girl, Lanja, unbuckled the sword belt and handed it to Achak along with his knife. She stepped off the porch and cracked her neck, pressing on her jaw with one palm. Then she stretched and took a few steps closer. "When I knock you out, you won't wake up till next week."

Valerie took the fighting stance she had been practicing all week with Damon. It felt good to stretch out. "You sure talk a lot."

Lanja glared at her and moved in. She stopped before she got in range, however, hesitating and trying to circle.

Valerie flexed her back and circled too. The opening came a moment later. Lanja looked to be leaving her back exposed. Valerie lunged forward, stepping into a roundhouse kick. But Lanja lunged forward too, her fist jabbing straight for Valerie's neck. Had Valerie not pivoted at the last second, the punch would have caught her under the jaw and possibly laid her out. As it was, the punch still grazed her, forcing her to duck away quickly to recover.

This girl wasn't untrained.

Valerie shifted her stance and moved into *Plunging Panther*, a form she had learned recently that was designed for a street fight. Lanja shifted too. Her pose took the form of *Hidden Fist,* a position Valerie had seen in books but had yet to master. Where had she learned that?

They danced around each other, trading blows, but neither landing anything decisive. Valerie tried her best combinations, but Lanja was always just a little faster, her feet and fists moving in a blur in the firelight and dancing around so much it made Valerie dizzy.

Valerie was thinking of going for a grappling move instead, some way to force this girl to the ground, when a pair of headlights illuminated the yard, bathing the cabin and the entire clearing with light.

Valerie took her eyes off her opponent long enough to see the rusty frame of an old Lockley Sidewinder pulling into the driveway. The engine was throaty and raw. Way more power than a stock Sidewinder would dream of. She caught a glimpse of a face behind the wheel. It almost looked like—

Valerie's legs went out from under her and she landed on her back with a thud.

Lanja stepped forward and loomed over her. "I told you I'd put you on your ass."

But Valerie was no longer paying attention to the scrappy girl with the bad attitude. She tilted her head up, viewing an upside-down world and the person stepping out of the car. A boot crunched gravel. Then another. A cane followed as the man pushed himself out of the driver's seat. She was vaguely aware of the kid with the mohawk climbing out of the passenger side of the Sidewinder, but her eyes were riveted to the bearded face and bushy eyebrows of the man with the cane. He wore a duster coat that hung to his knees. Thick and barrel-chested, he was an imposing figure, but his face was the puzzle that Valerie's mind was trying to solve.

His eyes were on the cabin. "Where is she?"

That voice. Unmistakable. But impossible.

Valerie rolled over, unable to handle this upside-down world a moment longer. She half expected that when she righted herself, this apparition would disappear, or at least resolve itself into a form her mind could comprehend.

But as she got to her knees, the man turned toward her, and their eyes met. His beard was grayer, his hairline receding, but there could be no mistaking it.

She was looking at her dad.

19

WOUNDED

H enry Terravecchia II was a dead man. At least that's what the courts had decided. Valerie had been there the day the lawyer showed up at the house with the death certificate. They had never found a body, but three years of no contact had let everyone in the family assume the worst.

Sir Henry was a road knight. A legend. But in New Avalon, legends meet violent ends.

As the years rolled on, Valerie had made her peace with it. It was decided. He was gone.

That was why her mind rejected this new apparition before her.

It was a ghost. A wraith.

But the tricks of firelight and darkness couldn't explain away the tangible reality before her.

Ghosts don't drive cars.

The only answer her brain would accept was that this was a man who looked incredibly *like* her father. A doppelgänger. An anomaly. He couldn't be her *real* father because that would mean Henry Terravecchia II was a liar.

The man hadn't been focused on her when she was on the

ground. His gaze had lingered on the cabin. But when she rolled over to her stomach and their eyes met, their focus became riveted to one another, a bond of rapt attention.

It was clear that he hadn't expected her here. She knew the look of shock well enough. It was the same feeling that had her frozen in place. They stared. They didn't flinch.

It was Lanja who broke the spell.

"This one attacked us. She's trouble, but I put her in her place."

She gave Valerie a kick in the ribs that caught her by surprise.

"Don't!"

Lanja was now the one who froze. It seems there was more she had planned to say, but her mouth hung in limbo, midway to forming a sound.

"You won't touch her again." It wasn't a suggestion. The man who looked like her father spoke calmly, but his tone left no room for argument. His words were a statement of fact, inflexible as a mountain.

Lanja took a step back.

"Valerie?"

Valerie climbed to her feet, only vaguely aware of the bruising from Lanja. Her body was existing in a different time. Lanja. The cabin. The events of her day. Those were all cares of the present, but she was looking through a window to the past.

"I don't know what you are," Valerie said. Her vision was blurry. Her eyes filled with unbidden tears. It was as though she didn't know how to control her body. This couldn't be real. How was she supposed to deal with a crack in the world?

Nothing made sense.

If she was dreaming, it was like no dream she had ever had.

A part of her wanted to run to him, throw her arms around him to prove he was real.

A part of her wanted to scream.

The wound she thought long healed was torn open and it was as raw and angry as ever.

"You have questions," the man said, "and I'm going to answer them. But right now, I need to check on a girl that's hurt in that cabin."

A girl that's hurt.

Valerie knew what he meant. He meant the kind of wound that was healed with bandages and medicine. A wound of flesh and blood and bone. Not the kind of wound she bore. A wound of grief, and loss, and rage.

She rose to her feet but remained frozen in place as he walked closer. Step-by-step he came into clearer focus.

He was a man who looked like her father. Talked like her father.

He didn't walk like her father.

He limped. He hobbled. The ankle of one foot didn't move in a natural way.

He passed by without pausing and walked up the steps of the cabin.

Clomp. Clomp. Clomp.

Not the footsteps of a ghost, but those of a man.

Flesh. Bone. Blood.

Her blood.

Her father.

He had walked away.

The truth crashed over her like a wave, the weight of it crushing the air from her lungs. He had left her. Left her family, her brother, their home. He had been alive all this time. Years. Years upon years. And he hadn't come home.

She gasped for air like a fish flopping on a dock. Painfully. Uselessly.

The legacy. The legend. It was all a lie.

Standing outside the cabin, arms bare in the evening wind, her hair smelling of smoke and ash, she had a sudden vision of a redwood tree on her family's property that she used to play in with her brother. The tree had been struck by lightning, gutted by fire, hollowed and blackened. It hadn't died. Its branches still grew leaves high overhead. It had survived to stretch for the sky with its peers but had never truly healed.

She was that tree.

She knew she showed signs of life on the outside, but her insides were empty, her core gone.

There would be no recovery. No bandage could mend the chasm that yawned open in her soul.

This moment was her lightning bolt, the fire that would consume her from the inside.

Her dad wasn't dead. He left.

She started walking. Slowly. Mindlessly. Without a destination.

Lanja laid a hand on her. She attempted to hold her back. Valerie spun and struck her, knocking her backward into the dirt. The tattooed girl stared up at her from the weeds, wide-eyed, her hand going to her cheek.

Valerie didn't know what it was that made the girl stay down this time. Maybe something in her eyes betrayed the fire consuming her soul. This girl was smart enough to not want to get burned.

Valerie looked to Sprocket and the other two boys. They didn't move to stop her either. They watched. Were they waiting for her to combust?

Valerie returned her eyes to the path ahead. The path to nowhere. And she started walking.

∾

Dakota woke to the touch of a hand on her shoulder. She flinched and blinked in the dim light of the cabin and took in the shape of Henry silhouetted against the faint backdrop of flickering firelight.

"You," she muttered. "Did Takawa send you?"

"One of these halfwits you call friends had enough sense to get help," Henry said. "What have you done?"

Dakota lifted herself to an elbow to see him better. Her back ached.

"Wait. Let me take a look." Henry unwrapped the bandage around her shoulder and inspected the wound. He sniffed the air, then gently covered it back up. He placed the back of his hand against her forehead. "I'm taking you to your mother. She'll sort this better than I will. Get up. We need to get going. I'll need to summon the council."

Dakota sat the rest of the way up. "I'm okay. We're handling it. You don't even know what happened."

"You've kicked a hornet's nest like you can't possibly imagine," Henry said. "You've defied Chief Takawa, endangered yourself and your family, and for what? To prove something to these troublemakers you hang around with?"

"We're doing something real," Dakota argued. "We're doing what Takawa and the rest of the tribe are too scared to do. We're fighting back."

"You almost got yourself killed," Henry said. "And of all the people to have brought into this, you picked her. You picked my daughter."

"I didn't *know* she was on the train. I only saw the car. How was I supposed to know she was going to jump onto it like a lunatic?"

"It's true then. You stole the Guardian."

"It was *your* car. I thought someone else had it. How was I supposed to know she was the one traveling with it?"

"You don't know what you've done." He turned his back on

her and moved to the standing wardrobe, pulling open the door and rifling through the clothing hanging inside.

"I did it for you," she said. "I thought you would *want* me to."

Henry paused in his perusal of the wardrobe's contents. "Things are going to be more complicated now. Gather your things."

Dakota rose slowly and winced as she stretched her aching back.

Henry pulled a sweatshirt and a jacket from hangers in the wardrobe.

"I don't need a jacket," Dakota said.

Henry closed the wardrobe doors. "It isn't for you."

She followed him outside. Henry paused when he reached the bottom of the steps, searching the yard.

"Where did she go?"

Achak pointed toward the road. Henry muttered something Dakota couldn't hear and started toward the car. But he paused near Lanja.

"Is that hers?" He pointed to the sword slung at her hip.

"It's mine now," Lanja said.

"The hell it is," Henry replied. He took a step toward Lanja and held out a hand. She glared back at him, and for a moment, Dakota thought she was going to refuse, but Lanja broke eye contact and swore, unbuckling the sword belt and tossing it to Henry's feet.

Henry arched an eyebrow, but he used the end of his cane to hook the sword belt and first lift, then toss the scabbard to himself. He caught it in the same hand as his cane, managing both with one hand and his armful of clothing in the other. He made a show of walking the rest of the way to the car without the cane.

Dakota shook her head at Lanja—a warning not to press her luck.

Sprocket was staring. Questioning. But she didn't have time to justify her leaving to all of them. She had started this, she needed to finish it.

~

Valerie had walked about an eighth of a mile before the sound of the engine caught up with her. The glow of headlights stretched her shadow for fifty yards until it vanished into the woods. She stopped walking but wasn't willing to turn around.

The engine idled.

A car door opened and closed.

Boots scraped dirt—that strange limping pace that was so unlike the man she knew. His shadow stretched out alongside hers. Waiting.

"I brought you something to wear. You're cold."

She was cold. The fire inside her was out. It had left her hollow.

"I don't need your help."

"A lot of that going around tonight."

She turned. He was close. A few feet. She could smell him now. He smelled the same. Like leather and gasoline and hard work.

Like a vineyard after the rain.

Like a thousand hours of training together in the yard and Sunday drives along the coast with the sea breeze coming through the windows.

Like home.

But that was just her memory of him.

This man was a stranger.

"If you get in the car, we can talk on the way." He held out a sweatshirt.

She took it. There was no alternative. They both knew it.

He nodded and walked to the passenger door, opening it before continuing around the back of the car and making his way to the driver's side again.

Valerie slipped into the sweatshirt without much in the way of conscious thought. Her body acted out the movements while her mind still dealt with the unreality of this place. She walked to the side of the car and peered into the back seat.

She was back there. Dakota. The thief.

Dakota cocked an eyebrow.

What was her role in this?

Another question Valerie wasn't entirely sure she wanted the answer to. She climbed into the car, discovering *Firebird* had been clipped into the ceiling sword rack. She studied the sword, then the man at the wheel for a long moment, before settling her gaze on the road out the windshield. She slammed the car door.

"Where are we going?"

It didn't really matter, but her words had an effect. Her father's jaw worked as he chewed on whatever words he was pondering. There was a gulf of distance between their seats that stretched for years—a chasm of unknown depth. She had made the first step toward bridging it.

"I'll take you to where the answers are."

20

KAI

Footsteps on stone and the flickering of lantern light brought Damon to wakefulness. He had drifted off again, somewhere in the endless black that hid day from night. He had the feeling it ought to be late evening by now but had no reference.

He pushed himself away from the wall, the cold of the stones still clinging to the muscles in his back, and faced the opening to his cell as the light drew nearer.

He readied himself to face his captor again, but when the lantern appeared around the corner of the tunnel, it wasn't Sheriff Trammel carrying it.

It was Kai Nez.

A sly smile broke the corners of the sword fighter's lips as she approached. She sauntered forward with her usual ease, the lantern hanging casually beside one leg. Her viper sword hung beside the other.

"This certainly is a sight," Kai said. "Someone finally got the better of Damon Roark. Always thought I'd be the only one to manage that."

"So far, this sheriff of yours has less charm than a bull with its balls in a noose," Damon replied. "I'm surprised she hasn't seen through you yet."

"Oh, Cissy's a push-over if you know what she likes. Sadly for you, that doesn't include half-naked men. Though I'm not opposed to this view." Kai Nez's eyes roamed over Damon's exposed torso.

Damon gripped the bars that divided them. "What kind of game is she playing with me? I've done nothing to deserve this."

"Haven't you? I have a hard time believing this is your first time behind bars. Not to say I don't think you put on a good show. You play the highborn noble well. You've even convinced your pretty young protégé that she's safe with you. But she's not all that clever, is she?"

"Where's Valerie?" Damon snarled. "If you've caught her up in your schemes . . ."

"Our king's precious new Knight of the Round Table? Who am I to influence someone like that? Surely a lowly bounty hunter couldn't dream of harming her. Besides, she's more than capable of getting herself killed all on her own."

Damon could barely contain his fury. "What have you done to her?"

"Why would you suspect me, my darling Damon? We used to be on the same side." Her fingers extended toward his face and brushed the edge of his jaw. He pulled away. Kai Nez smirked. "Don't pretend you've forgotten all the good times we had together. I know those nights were nothing if not memorable. You'll find things easier now if you decide to play nice."

"I don't plan to be kept as a pet," Damon said. "Whatever you and Trammel are after, I'm not interested."

Kai Nez rested a hand on the pommel of her sword. "The way Cissy's been talking, this could be a brief pit stop on your journey, or it could be the end of the road. It's really up to you."

"I said I'd get lost as soon as I found Valerie," Damon said. "I don't care what you're up to here."

"And that's what I told her." Kai Nez slowly unzipped her motorcycle jacket almost to her navel, revealing the fact that she wasn't wearing a shirt beneath. She then reached into the interior breast pocket and removed a folded slip of paper, holding it up for Damon. "All I need from you is a signature on your statement."

Damon averted his eyes from her surplus of exposed skin and snatched the document from her hands. He unfolded it and squinted in the dim lantern light to make out what it said. It was an account of the events involving the Dempsey service station fire.

"This isn't what I told her," Damon said. "It wasn't natives. This is wrong."

"But *is* it?" Kai Nez replied. She held out a pen.

Damon closed his eyes. So that's what they were after. When he reopened them, Kai Nez still hadn't zipped up her jacket. She leaned forward to put a hand on the bars, granting him even more of a view, all while watching him with an amused smile on her lips. "Seeing the picture now?"

"What did these natives do to you?"

"They didn't do much of anything. That's the problem. Place is getting downright dull."

Damon handed the paper back through the bars. "I'm not interested in being a party to whatever this is."

"Thought you might say that. Still riding that high horse. I'd guess that means you'll be extending your stay at Trammel's little bed and breakfast. You find it that enjoyable?"

"I have a few complaints to file with the management. Can't say I'll be recommending it."

Kai Nez eased closer to the bars. "If you want a place with a bed, I'll let you visit mine. You can trade these bars for some handcuffs." Her words came out as a purr.

Damon flashed a hand through the bars and gripped her belt,

then slammed her up against the bars. "This isn't a game you want to play with me."

Kai Nez laughed, then ran her fingers along her jaw where it had struck the bars. Her tongue flicked at the corner of her mouth. "I knew you liked it rough."

But the next moment Damon felt the prick of cold steel against his abdomen. He looked down to find the tip of her dagger pressed to his skin. He released her belt and backed away a step.

Kai Nez backed up too, languidly checking the tip of her dagger before sheathing it again. She picked up the lantern and moved toward the tunnel. "I'll tell Cissy you want to amend your statement about the service station fire. Could be she just heard you wrong. But you may want to rethink my offer about the accommodations. She can be a bit forgetful when it comes to the complimentary breakfast."

"You didn't tell me where Valerie is," Damon said. "What have you done with her?"

"Your girlfriend took a tumble down Canyon Falls this morning. Doubt she survived the plunge. But if she did, she's a captive of the natives by now. Sad turn of events. But she *is* the law. These things happen in the line of duty."

Damon set his jaw and tried to hold back his rage. He clenched the bars again. "You'd better pray she's alive, Kai. If she isn't, I'm holding you to blame."

Kai Nez zipped her motorcycle jacket up to her neck. "If she does come back, I'll be sure to give her a warm welcome." Then she blew out the lantern. Everything vanished into blackness and the sound of her footsteps slowly diminished down the tunnel.

Damon slunk slowly back into his cell, then retrieved his penknife from his pocket again. He felt the blade. The tip was now broken and the blade already dulled, but he clamped the knife between his teeth and found the handholds he had carved in the wall. He climbed. One step, then another. He felt for the chink in the stones he had last been working on, then pulled the knife from his teeth. His muscles strained to keep him balanced as he got back to work, angrily chipping away at the mortar in the dark.

~

Rico got the job as a maid. Well, Esme had gotten the job because of what he thought was some of the greatest acting he had ever done. She'd been modest, sympathetic, and even managed a few tears when recounting the loss of her fiancé to that horrible train.

Lord Hudson had believed him. Believed his experience, his sincerity, and even his gender.

And now he had no idea what to do next.

The staff had started him right away and kept him busy all evening, changing sheets, organizing closets, cleaning the tea service he'd used earlier. He'd even been asked to draw a bath for a woman being entertained by Lord Hudson this evening. All night, he had tried to work out what to do about the information he now had regarding his friends.

Damon was a prisoner, Valerie was gone, lost and likely dead in the woods. It hadn't taken much acting to bring himself to tears during the interview. He was on the edge of tears again now just thinking about it. How on earth was he supposed to help them? He racked his brain as he folded the last of the laundry he'd been assigned.

"Good gracious. You're still here?" Rico turned to find Matilde, the head housemaid, standing in the doorway of the laundry. "You should have been done and gone hours ago. Don't you know anything?"

Rico folded his hands and bowed his head.

"Oh, come along. You can walk back to the village with me." Matilde waved him over.

As they traversed the bewildering corridors of the castle, he had no recollection of which wing he had first entered. But ultimately, as Matilde led him along a carpeted hallway, Rico glanced through a doorway and recognized the map on the wall of the room he had first interviewed in.

The map.

Sheriff Trammel had said Damon was being kept in a mine. A mine ought to be on the map.

As he continued down the hallway, he pretended to stumble, knocking into a table and sending a trio of flower vases crashing to the floor. They shattered in a spray of water and glass.

"What on earth!" Matilde stared in shock. "What have you done, you clumsy, foolish girl!"

"I'm so sorry," Rico stammered. "It was an accident!"

"Don't move. Don't touch another thing! I need to get this cleaned up." Matilde hiked up her dress and walked carefully backward. "I'll fetch the towels and brooms. Don't you move. Of all the ridiculous idiots . . ." She continued to mutter and swear as she disappeared around the corner.

Rico raced back to the room with the maps. He scanned the one on the wall and searched the legend for symbols that might indicate a mine. There was nothing. Rico swore. But then he noted the open doorway that led to Lord Hudson's private office. He crept into the hallway and worked his way to the office door. Peering carefully around the corner he found it empty. But on the broad desk sat a number of documents, including several maps. Rico rushed to examine them. Somewhere this mine they were referring to must be marked.

He scanned the maps on Hudson's desk and found one that had been marked by hand. The Black Hawk territory was dotted with symbols he couldn't identify that looked vaguely like tiny horse heads. Where had he seen those before? But closer to Rust Creek, there were several symbols of crossed pickaxes. The mine.

There were multiple entrances, one just between the castle and the village. Not far. Rico extracted the map from the pile of documents, folding it and stuffing it down his dress. He hastily rearranged the remaining items and dashed back to the hallway where he'd broken the vases, resuming his place just as Matilde reappeared in the corridor.

"Let me help you. Perhaps the towels," he offered. Matilde considered him skeptically. "I think you've done quite enough for one day. You can get yourself home on your own while I deal with your mess. I'll speak to his lordship about this tomorrow, and we'll determine if you need bother returning. Now get along, and don't touch a single thing on your way out."

"Yes, ma'am," Rico replied. He stepped over the mess as best he could and walked stiffly away, doing his best not to let the map in his dress crinkle and give him away. When he looked back, Matilde had her head down, focused on picking up glass from the floor.

Rico pushed through the door at the end of the servant's corridor and walked as hastily as he could manage without raising suspicion. Once he was through the tower gate and out of sight of the castle guards, he broke into a run down the hill.

For the first time all night, a twinge of hope surged in his chest. He'd found a clue. He had a map.

And now he had a plan.

21

OUTSIDER

Despite the promise of answers, the drive through the woods was mostly wordless. Only the engine dared break the silence, humming beneath the hood—a song with a melody that Valerie knew.

There was so much of the past layered over this present. So much was the same. Her father in the driver's seat, a country road at night, headlights illuminating ancient trees that rose up and vanished again like ghosts into the night. Only she was no longer twelve years old. And he was no longer the solid rock that she had built the foundation of her life upon.

The legend of Henry Terravecchia II had shaped so much of her world. It was a legacy of honor. Knight. Champion. Hero. A name that transcended that of mere mortals.

Now he was a stranger, more mystery than myth.

"There're a few tools in the glove box. Maybe something you can use to get that cuff off," her father said. He nodded toward the half of a handcuff still dangling from Valerie's wrist. She opened the glove box and found a multi-tool, a few screwdrivers, and several other odds and ends like spark plugs and a gapping tool.

She used a punch on the multi-tool, and after a few attempts at the latch of her handcuff, she was able to spring the release. She caught Dakota watching her from the back seat. Valerie offered the tool to her, and Dakota snatched it out of her palm. A few seconds later, the other half of the cuffs likewise fell to the floor.

Dakota didn't bother to pass the multitool forward again.

Valerie had forgotten to check if it contained a knife.

As the Sidewinder wound its way northwest through the hills via a winding, forest road, Valerie watched her father from the corner of her eye. She could sense the tension of his movements, the way he stomped the clutch pedal, the force of his grip as he downshifted in the turns and roared back out. He was driving like a man running away from a place as much as he was driving to somewhere else.

The car finally slowed when they reached a clearing. A homestead.

A long aluminum motorcoach sat in the center of the glade. Once shiny, the rain had since stained its sides, and a number of tomato vines twisted and climbed their way up the rear ladder. The vehicle sat on blocks, leveled and anchored to its weedy bed.

Despite its immobility and weather-beaten exterior, the little motorhome looked homey. A warm glow emanated from the interior windows, and a small fire was burning in a pit out front. A picnic table was positioned in a place of prominence under a sun-faded awning.

As the headlights of the Sidewinder swept over the yard, Valerie noted a few other outbuildings. A shed. A latrine. Her father angled the car toward a larger structure that looked like a garage.

The door to the motorcoach opened, and a woman appeared in the doorway, backlit by lantern light. She was a Native Avalonian with deep-black hair pulled back in a simple ponytail. She wore blue jeans and a flannel shirt with the sleeves rolled to the elbows. A speckled cattle dog wriggled past her legs and leapt to the ground. It sprinted the distance to the car, and by the time they stopped, the animal was at the driver's door, its hind end wriggling as its tail whipped back and forth in a frenzy.

Henry Terravecchia had barely opened the door when he was assaulted by the wet nose and nuzzling face of the dog. He pushed the animal away and struggled to rise. Valerie opened her door as well and was instantly met by the enthusiastic canine. It snuffed and snorted as it investigated the scent of her legs and boots. It became even more excited when it noted Dakota.

"Cisco. Get back!" Her father's voice boomed from the other side of the car. The dog retreated to the front of the car, clearly ecstatic to be in the company of its master.

It was only after Valerie had stood aside and made room for Dakota to climb out of the back seat that she had a good look at the woman in the motorcoach. She had stepped down to the makeshift patio, viewing the scene with a frown, her hands perched on her hips. Her gaze fell on Dakota and her brows knit.

Dakota, for her part, looked unenthusiastic about being there. She didn't meet the woman's gaze.

Even in the dim light, Valerie couldn't help but notice the resemblance between them. Mother and daughter. Had to be. The look that passed between the woman and Valerie's father was unmistakable. Intimate. Knowing. A simple glance that revealed a secret language of shared experience. The kind of communication that only came from years of reading one another's body language.

Valerie didn't need to ask. She knew that this woman was more to her father than some passing acquaintance. The motorcoach, the dog, even the way her father had parked the car, spoke volumes—more than anything that could have been explained in words. This was his place. His life. His home.

And what did that make her?

Valerie stood frozen next to the car. She was suddenly even more out of place, a stranger amid so much unspoken familiarity.

There was a sense of the bizarre to her existence. Up was down and inside was out. This situation somehow made her uncomfortable in her own skin.

There was some vague relief in the fact that Dakota looked uncomfortable too. But it was for a different reason. The girl clearly belonged here. This was her history, her story.

A deep well of resentment was growing inside Valerie.

In the missing years, her father had become a stranger, Dakota had been there with him. There for every passing season. Living the relationship that ought to have been hers. Another daughter. Her replacement?

Valerie found herself studying this native girl—assessing her. Of course she was strong. Of course she could fight. How could a child raised by Henry Terravecchia turn out any other way. But there was more to her. A toughness that Valerie hadn't ever acquired from her father's training. It was only the crushing absence of him and the crucible she had been through in the past few months that had finally hardened her.

Dakota was pretty, too, underneath the snarling exterior, the piercings, and the overwhelming black eyeshadow. There was no denying it. Her natural beauty was all the more obvious by her rejecting it.

Beautiful, tough, a fighter. She was the daughter Henry had always wanted.

"You're injured," the woman with the ponytail said. She glanced from Dakota to Valerie. "From her?"

"No," Dakota declared. It was a declaration of defiance. No, Valerie hadn't hurt her. That would have been an admission of defeat, something this girl was incapable of.

"Go inside. I'll tend to it."

Dakota looked as though she might object, but something in her mother's stare made her change her mind. She cast a quick glance at Valerie, all daggers and mistrust, then vanished inside the motorcoach.

"Winona, this is Valerie." Her father's voice was formal, careful. It was a statement of fact that left his emotions out of it.

"You are welcome here," Winona said, though her tone was far from warm. Valerie had the sense that there was simply no alternative. Custom demanded it.

Winona turned to Henry. "What will you do now?" Again, the words hid the other questions that lay beneath the surface. They were plain enough to Valerie anyway. *What is she doing here? What have you done? How do you expect me to deal with this?*

Her father must have read the subtext as well. His voice dropped. "We'll discuss it privately. For now, we need to arrange a place for her to stay."

"I'm not staying," Valerie said. "I need to get back. I have people looking for me."

Her father's jaw clenched. He sighed through his nose. "I can't take you back tonight. We'll need to address what has happened with Chief Takawa. He'll decide how to proceed."

"I'm not waiting for some tribal council pow wow," Valerie said. "I have friends. They'll be worried."

"And I'll do my best to return you to them as soon as I can," her father said. "But things are beyond my control here."

Valerie studied him, this stranger who used to be her father. There was so much unsaid between them that they may as well have been on opposite sides of a mountain. It was too much. There was nowhere to even begin.

The exertion of the day weighed her down. She was emotionally exhausted. Some part of her wanted to stay, to unravel this puzzle, but the rest of her wanted to flee. This was too strange, too foreign, too much to process.

Her father was alive, living in the woods with a new family. A wife. A daughter. A dog. He had abandoned her. He had abandoned her brother. Their entire life. And it was all more than she could handle.

She needed to escape, to go back to normal. Damon. Rico. Back to where things made sense.

"I can't stay here," she repeated.

"You can't leave."

Another statement of fact.

If he wasn't going to take her, there was nowhere to go. She didn't know the roads. She could wander mostly south and perhaps find her way, but it was too far to travel on foot. And at night without a vehicle, she could quickly fall prey to wolves or mountain lions.

She had a sword but it was useless.

Even if she thought it was possible, there was no world where she could threaten her own father with a weapon and demand he take her back.

"It'll be okay," he said. "I promise."

A promise. From a man she no longer knew.

He took a step closer. She could feel he was trying to bridge the chasm again, reaching out.

Part of her wanted to let go. Forget her anger and her inhibitions and simply go to him. Touch him. Put her arms around him. Prove that he was real. She took a step closer.

"Dad!"

The shout from the motorcoach made her turn. A little boy stood in the doorway, perhaps all of five years old, his eyes wide, and a grin spreading across his face. He leapt from the steps and landed on the run, sprinting the few yards to her father's position before wrapping both arms around the big man's waist. Henry Terravecchia was caught off-guard. He attempted to regain equilibrium after this assault of affection.

Then the boy looked at her.

Valerie balked.

The boy had thick brown hair and freckles from the sun, but his features were familiar. It was a face she had never seen before but knew intimately. The shape of his eyes, the playful quirk of his lips, the dimple in one cheek. She was looking at a younger version of her older brother Henry.

The boy looked at her. Curious.

It jolted a flash of memory from her brain. She and her brother playing in the vineyards. Him popping out from behind the vines to scare her. Laughing. That smile. Those eyes.

It was too much.

Valerie turned away. She stared at the tufts of grass and weeds that fought for life amid the tire tracks, not seeing them so much as trying to unsee all that she had in her mind. She pressed her palms to her eyes and set her jaw, trying to force down the other memories that came unbidden. Henry lying in her arms, blood wicking through the fibers of his shirt and soaking her hands. His last word: Valerie.

She had avenged his death, but it didn't bring him back. Another part of her heart was now buried in her family's plot alongside her mother.

Now this.

"We have another bed, in the garage," her father said. His uneven footsteps came closer. A hand rested on her shoulder, and she immediately flinched, shrugging away from him.

A chill ran down her spine. The touch of a ghost.

"Don't." The word came from somewhere raw and sore inside her. She couldn't let him back. Not when what he did had changed everything. The lie that had changed everything.

"I understand that this will take time to get used to," he said.

"I'll take her." Winona stepped past them both and led the way toward the garage. She paused only once, her eyes meeting Valerie's.

Valerie followed, not questioning how this woman had become her better option.

The door of the garage swung open to reveal a workspace that, in itself, was familiar. The way the tools on the walls were organized, the layout of the ramps and toolboxes. No matter where she looked, she couldn't escape the signs of her father's presence. She knew them too well.

There was a cot, a sink, and even a small shower with its own water barrel perched above it on a shelf.

A number of newspaper clippings from the Hudson Tribune hung in rough frames on one wall. Valerie read one of the headlines. "Henry Terravecchia III wins regional longsword championship."

Her stomach twisted in her gut.

"The garage has electric light. Batteries are over there," Winona said. "But try not to leave them on all night. You'll have to use the toilet in the latrine out back, but you can make yourself comfortable in here and have your own space. I suspect you might want some of that right now."

Winona's voice was calm. Soothing even. But there was also a firmness beneath the surface of her words and a steely look in her eyes that spoke of unquestionable nerve. She knew without asking that this woman had seen her share of trouble in her life, and Valerie showing up here likely didn't rank very high on that list.

Winona moved toward the door. Her fingers found the handle.

"Am I a prisoner?" Valerie wasn't sure what made her voice the thought out loud, but it was out of her mouth even before the question was fully formed in her mind.

"You are our guest. For tonight," Winona said. "I don't know what you'll be tomorrow."

An honest answer.

"Thank you," Valerie said.

Winona nodded and moved to the door.

"How old is he?" Valerie asked. "Your little boy."

Winona stood stock still, her eyes on a point somewhere outside. "His name is Mato, and he'll be six in the fall." Then she stepped out into the darkness and closed the door.

22

TAKAWA

Valerie woke to the sound of strange voices. Men talking in low tones somewhere in the yard.

Night had passed. Dawn light crept through the crevices of the wood-framed garage. There were motors running outside, and a faint smell of exhaust. She listened but couldn't identify any of the engines. Whoever was out there, it wasn't Kai Nez and her Nightmare Nine. If it were, the tone of the distant conversation wouldn't be so mild.

She had slept like the dead—dreamless, or with dreams she couldn't recall. Perhaps her consciousness had too many memories to sort through awake to manage them in her sleep. She did feel rested. There was a clarity to her mind now, a focus she had lacked the night before, overwhelmed as she had been by the sheer audacity of her new reality.

The morning is for making new plans.

The mantra had been her father's and had seen her through many rough mornings. But could it possibly see her through this?

She rose from her cot and splashed her face in the gravity-fed sink, washing away the residue of salty tear tracks that had dried on her cheeks overnight. She stared at her face in the mirror, breathing slowly and trying to recognize the girl in her reflection. The foundation of her past had been plowed up and broken to pieces. What did that leave her to stand on?

The girl staring back at her wasn't new, but she had lost something. Something she knew she would miss.

Valerie noted the pile of clothes someone had left on the narrow countertop. They were neatly folded: a clean pair of jeans, a worn-in T-shirt, and a flannel overshirt not unlike the one Winona had been wearing the night before. There were socks and undergarments too. A kindness.

She availed herself of the shower, rinsing away the previous day's filth. The water was cold, pricking her skin with gooseflesh and sending chills down her body when she first stepped in, but it brought her to a state of alertness unrivaled by any cup of coffee. When she toweled off and slid into the fresh clothing, she found them a close enough fit that she could almost convince herself that she was in her own jeans. There was a patch on the back pocket and the denim felt as though it had been hand-washed a hundred times over stones. Winona, if that was indeed whose clothes she was in, was at least a woman who knew what it was to be comfortable.

Her boots had dried out overnight but still had a lingering scent of river water. Valerie laced them up, then moved to the door to figure out what the commotion was outside. *Firebird* leaned against the doorframe. She picked it up by its scabbard and cracked the door.

Motorcoaches. At least ten of the big mechanized houses filled the clearing. The ones running were only a small fraction of the entire group. How she had managed to sleep through the arrival of these machines was a mystery. A half dozen trucks and cars also dotted the meadow. These were not your standard road cars. Every vehicle was lifted. Knobby tires and all-terrain suspension were a given. Several vehicles were armored. While nothing in sight resembled a factory-built war car, the amount of custom modification was impressive. The largest of the vehicles was parked at the center of the group, a sort of rolling fortress painted an optimistic sky blue. She counted six axles and at least eighteen tires.

The caravan boasted twenty vehicles not counting the smattering of motorbikes also in attendance.

The number of people in the group was less obvious. The window shades on many of the rolling motorcoaches were still down, their residents not yet awake. The cluster of men who were visible were Native Avalonian braves. They stood around the ashes of the previous night's fire, voices low and casting occasional glances at the garage. One of the men noted her peering out the door and lifted his chin, signaling the rest of the half dozen men. More faces turned her way. One belonged to her father.

Valerie pushed her way through the door and stepped into the daylight. She was conscious of the weapon in her hand, noting that none of the braves around the remains of the fire appeared to be armed. Several pairs of eyes found *Firebird* as well, though she kept a casual grip on it and did her best not to give away the tension she felt in her muscles.

The braves around the fire spread out and left room for her approach. The man at the center of the group remained still and focused his gaze on her. He had deep crow's feet at the corners of his eyes, and his black hair was streaked with gray, but he was fit and strong. If Valerie had to guess, he might be a decade older than her father, but it was hard to say. He had a number of necklaces and talismans around his neck, symbols of power. A black feather hung among them and several of what appeared to be tiny talons. She found his continued stare unnerving.

Her father's voice broke the silence. "Chief Takawa, may I present to you, Lady Valerie Terravecchia. My daughter."

"She rises from her bed with a sword in her hand," Chief Takawa said, watching her approach. "And the death of her enemies is in her eyes." He glanced at her sword, then turned back to Henry. "Is this how you see fit to manage a prisoner on tribal lands?"

"Valerie is our guest."

"This is Black Hawk land," Takawa replied. "The welcoming of guests is my business." He took a step toward Valerie. "You've been the talk of the territory, Lady Terravecchia, and an uninvited guest on this mountain. By what authority have you come here?"

"I came to collect what's mine," Valerie said, sizing up the chief and his group of warriors. "I was robbed."

Chief Takawa addressed Henry again. "Where is Dakota Wren? Have you managed to keep *her* contained, or has she been left to wander unattended as well?"

"I'm capable of minding myself." The voice came from the motorcoach, and Dakota pushed open the screen door. She descended the steps and strode toward the group. She had a bandage plastered to one shoulder, but her skin tone was much improved overnight. Her face was defiant, and if she was feeling weak from her wound, it didn't show.

Takawa regarded her coolly. "I doubt the time since our last meeting was sufficient for you to develop a sense of responsibility or regret, but perhaps you have had time to reconsider your words?"

Dakota's lip curled, and Valerie felt a sudden apprehension about what the girl might say, but Dakota seemed to choke down whatever reply was on the tip of her tongue and instead gave a curt bow. "I was . . . agitated . . . yesterday. Please forgive my offensive words." She kept her head down.

Takawa nodded. "I'm happy to see that you've come to your senses. You made serious accusations. I will not be called a coward in front of my own braves. You think me old and toothless, but you will see I have fangs yet. Where is the car?"

Dakota looked up, her eyes narrowing. "I won't let you strip it for parts."

"It is not yours to decide," Takawa replied. "That car is the fruit of your crime and will be destroyed."

"No!" Valerie and Dakota both shouted the word simultaneously. The response had come unbidden from Valerie's mouth. If you had asked her a moment earlier, she wouldn't have been able to explain her feelings on the subject. There were so many emotions tied up in her relationship with the Guardian that she didn't know how to begin to unravel them.

She certainly didn't know how to feel about her father. She was hurt and furious, frustrated and confused.

The Guardian was tied up in all of that, an object wrapped in the pain and bitterness of the past, but the idea of someone taking it from her again would be like losing a limb. The car was more than just a gift from her father. How many hours had she spent with Damon and Rico prepping it for the King's Tournament, and again for this trip. It was more than a car. It had been her lifeline. It was the rock she had rebuilt her life upon.

Takawa turned his intense eyes on her. "You came to this territory uninvited, armed for war. My people witnessed your riders leaving the mountain, fleeing back across the border before our wrath could pursue them. What right have you to speak?"

"The war car is mine," Valerie said. "My invitation to your land was from her the night she stole it."

"That car is a weapon of war," Takawa replied. "The kind of weapon your people have used for many decades in forcing my people from their lands. The kind of weapon you may yet use against us should I return it to you."

"She attacked a road train on treaty lands. I was only passing through."

"You are too young perhaps," Takawa said. "Too young to know how many treaties were written in Black Hawk blood. But we haven't forgotten. Dakota Wren behaves like an obstinate child, but she is right to refocus our eyes on the wrongs enacted on our people. Long have I prayed for peace, but the winds of war have returned. You rode them here." Takawa turned to Henry. "What say you, Orso Nero? Your child claims the war car is hers, but it bears your crest."

"I gifted the car to Valerie in my absence," her father replied. His eyes met hers. "I make no claim to it."

"But now you harbor two lawbreakers under your roof. Both lay claim to the car. How would you settle this?"

Henry glanced from one girl to the other.

Valerie couldn't understand how it was even a decision. The car was hers. Dakota was a thief. What more could be discussed?

But Dakota stood defiant, glaring at him. It wasn't a look of supplication or pleading. It was a demand.

Henry scratched at his chin. "I say we let them drive for it."

Valerie blinked. What?

Takawa nodded slowly. "You think we should let the fates decide. The spirit of victory will choose the path."

"I'm not agreeing to this," Dakota said.

"She has no legal right to it," Valerie objected.

"Actually, she does," Henry explained. "Black Hawk law treats weapons and articles of war as property that can be commandeered in battle. On their land, it's their rules."

"Sneaking aboard a train in the dark during peacetime isn't the same as taking a weapon in a battle," Valerie argued. "Where's the honor in that?"

Dakota addressed Henry. "Who gets to drive it?"

Henry appraised her. "You will. Valerie can drive the Sidewinder. If she beats you, you give her the car. You beat her, you can keep it and she calls off the law." He turned to Valerie. "What do you say?"

Valerie glared at him. She wasn't even going to be able to drive her own car? If she had been angry with him before, this only stoked the fire. Could there be a more obvious declaration of his loyalty? Dakota was his chosen daughter, and she was just in the way.

It didn't matter. Not now. She didn't need him. She only needed to get off this mountain. If that meant trouncing this punk girl in a car race? Fine. That's what she'd do.

She locked eyes with Dakota.

"Where's the starting line?"

The racetrack was an unpaved path, little more than a dirt road cut through the trees, but it was wider than any road had a need to be and filled with equally unnecessary hairpin turns, humps and bumps. Valerie recognized it as a rally course.

She had accompanied her father to enough events as a kid to know the ins and outs of the various types of races. Rally racing had been one of her favorites. It wasn't just about top speed. It was a race for control. Control of your car, control of the terrain, control of your mind. Only this time she wouldn't just be racing a clock.

"You should take the car around the track. Learn the course." Her father held out a notebook with ragged pages. The cover looked as though it had been left out in the rain.

She snatched it from his hand. It was full of hand-written notes on each element of the track.

"Dakota will know this course backward and forward, but with a simultaneous start, you'll be able to stay with her. Try to either stay out front or get ahead of her prior to the stone bridge; otherwise, there's no room."

On the drive to the track, he had tried to offer a few bits of advice, but Valerie had left him in silence. Whatever fragments of the bridge that they had tried to reconstruct between them were now burned and charred. The gulf yawned wide again. He had made his choice, so let him stew in it. Some last-minute track advice wasn't going to make a difference.

Valerie opened the hood of the Sidewinder and studied the

engine. It had guts. She could admit that. Heavy duty engine mounts rivaled those on her war car. The tires had plenty of tread and were arguably better suited to the conditions than the Guardian, which was still sporting multi-terrain tires on the rear and street tires up front. A peek under the fenders revealed a beefed-up suspension and custom brake lines.

"Is there a skid plate under the oil pan?"

"About a quarter of an inch thick," her father replied. "Racing mud flaps. Protective screen over the radiator. Should handle whatever debris you kick up."

She nodded. Considering the Sidewinder's custom features, she had to acknowledge that this was the better rally car.

The problem would come with the Guardian's raw power and the simultaneous start. The heavier frame and armor would be a disadvantage in speed but a menace when it came to collisions. If the girl had any kind of skill, Dakota could smash and bash the Sidewinder off the road or simply push through it on a straightaway. The Guardian also came with an armament dashboard—a battering ram, tire cutters, and it even had a newly installed flamethrower that she prayed Dakota wouldn't know how to operate.

The Sidewinder was basically a roll cage with an engine. It was at least a powerful engine, and the frame looked solid enough to take a few hits.

"You remember your left foot braking?"

Valerie fixed him with an icy glare.

"I'm just asking. It's been a while since we've practiced."

"You think?"

Her father put his hands in his pockets. "I know this isn't exactly the time and place, but I don't know how much more time we have together. I wanted to say that I'm happy to see you. I've missed you."

"You don't—" Valerie bunched a fist and held it up before

209

pointing a finger at him. "You don't get to say that." The words came through her teeth.

"I don't blame you for being angry. I would be too. I know you must think that—"

His voice was drowned out as a familiar roar echoed through the woods—the Guardian, retrieved from whatever hiding place Dakota had stashed it in. It hadn't taken her long. It must've been close. Likely somewhere Valerie almost could have reached on foot had she known where to look. The thought only made her more irritable.

She turned back to her father.

"If you had missed me, you knew where to find me. You had your chance." She climbed into the Sidewinder and slammed the door. She cranked the ignition, and the Sidewinder came to life. She pulled away, only daring one glance in the rear-view mirror. Her father stood leaning on his cane, a diminished shadow of the man she remembered. The pain was evident on his face.

He earned that. She refused to feel sorry for him.

Dakota watched the Sidewinder vanish down the track and into the woods in a cloud of dust.

Her competition.

She downshifted as she pulled the Guardian into the place Valerie had vacated. Henry lingered nearby as she shut off the ignition and climbed out.

"What did you tell her?" Dakota asked. "You giving her advice on how to beat me?"

"What makes you think she needs it?" Henry asked.

Dakota appraised him skeptically.

Henry's eyes fell to the car between them, and his fingers stretched for the hood. He pressed his palm to the warm metal.

"Does it look the same as you remember?"

He nodded. "It's always been the same. You can overhaul the engine, change the paint, modify the armaments. Doesn't matter. It's the same heart that beats inside this car. I used to think it was the real heartbeat that kept me alive."

"Then why did you give it to *her*?"

"If you don't know the answer to that, I won't explain it to you."

Dakota pulled her driving gloves from her back pocket and started putting them on. "Why don't you just say it out loud. I know you loved them more than you'll ever love us. Not like it's a secret."

Henry's head jerked sharply upward. He glared at her with a look that was at once angry and hurt. But his expression shifted, and he turned away. "You think you've got it all figured out now, huh?"

"I know mom only ever felt sorry for you because you were crippled. If you think she loves you the way she loved my dad, you're crazy."

Henry adjusted his grip on the cane and straightened. "Winona made up her own mind. So did your father."

"Just because he wasn't born rich like you doesn't mean he didn't deserve better. If he'd had a car like this, you can bet things would have been different. Hudson never would have caught him. That's for sure."

Henry sighed, then moved to a tree stump before easing himself down. He let his cane lean against the wood as he pulled his pant leg up to his knee. Dakota watched him adjust the straps on the prosthetic leg where it met the stump of his shin. She knew the device pained him, but she refused to help. Not this time.

"One day, maybe you'll understand what it is to have a child,"

Henry said. He retightened the strap around his artificial calf. "And the things we do for them." He sighed. "It may be true that if your dad wasn't born where and when he was, he never would have taken to stealing cars. I never would have been called out here to catch him. I'd have never met your mother. All sorts of things never would have happened. But that's 'back then' and 'what ifs.' We've got the here-and-now on our hands, and they come with enough trouble of their own.

"It could be that you following him down that road is the legacy he would have wanted for you. You know better than me what he was like. But what I saw was a man trying to make a better life for his family. And I have serious doubts that he'd have wanted you jacking cars from road trains just to prove something to yourself about what you think his legacy was, or thinking somehow it will make Hudson pay for what happened."

The woods were beginning to fill with ambient voices. Engines. Music. The members of the tribe that had come to watch the dispute get settled were getting boisterous.

Henry pulled the pant leg back down around his prosthesis and rose to his feet with assistance from his cane.

"I hope you have a nice speech like that ready for *her* when I get done winning this race," Dakota said, tilting her head toward the track. She moved back to the open driver's door.

"Like I said. You should worry about the here-and-now. Mind the transition out of third gear. It used to stick a bit when you try to upshift in a turn. Never could figure out why."

"I don't need you to tell me how to drive," Dakota said. She climbed into the driver's seat and slammed the door.

Henry nodded slowly, then shuffled off toward the makeshift stands that were filling with a smattering of spectators.

Several minutes later, the Sidewinder reappeared from the woods after completing the circuit. Valerie had finished her scouting of the track. Dakota doubted she had seen all of it, but enough to get the idea of what they were racing on.

Valerie positioned the Sidewinder on the starting line.

Dakota restarted the Guardian, and its engine growled as she roared past the stands where Henry and Chief Takawa were sitting. She turned a hard 180 degrees in the road amid a cloud of dust before rolling back to the start.

They'd see soon enough. This was about more than just a property dispute. This was about setting things right. Things that had been unbalanced and wrong for nearly as long as she could remember.

The tribe would see. Henry would see. Then she would take this car and make Lord Hudson pay too. Him and every road knight and motor warrior he sent after her. This car was going to change everything. She could feel it.

When she pulled up next to the Sidewinder, she only needed one look at the girl in the other vehicle. They locked eyes and sized each other up one last time. Vibration from the Guardian's engine thrummed through her body, pulsing every time she pressed the gas pedal. The tachometer jumped. The beast snarled. It wanted to run, pounce, hunt down and devour every curve of the road and any obstacle in its path.

The girl next to her broke eye contact first, focusing on the track ahead.

Chief Takawa shouted something, and Hammer Fist took a position near the front of the cars. He was shouting things too, but Dakota tuned him out. She knew the rules. She didn't need another lecture.

There was only one rule that mattered.

Win.

Hammer Fist raised his arms. The engines revved.

His arms dropped and Dakota floored the accelerator.

The race was on.

23

RALLY

Valerie launched off the line in a cloud of dust, desperate to get in front of the Guardian. If she could stay ahead, she could win this thing.

Time slowed as she tightened her grip on the wheel with her left hand and shifted with her right.

The world dissolved into engine noise, tires on dirt, and the Black Hawk spectators vanishing in her rear-view mirror.

The Guardian roared beside her. The black beast kept pace. There was something surreal about looking out the window and seeing her own car racing along next to her. In the last few months, it had become a part of her, as essential as breathing. Suddenly it was as though her heart was beating a lane away.

She wanted it back.

She refused to entertain the thought of any other result to this matchup.

Her focus narrowed. They had both come off the line well, now there was only the road ahead.

Despite her anger with her father, Valerie had taken the time to read his notes on the track as she drove the reconnaissance lap. It wasn't the whole rally course but rather a shorter circuit built into it for races such as this, and short or not, it still had its hazards: steep hills, hairpin turns, streams and ditches, and even a single lane, arched bridge that only one car could pass at a time. It had been too much to memorize completely, but she had learned what she could from her dad's handwritten notes. The rest she would have to figure out on the fly.

And flying is what they were doing now.

They tore into the first turn doing sixty miles per hour, and she took the lead by a car length. The Sidewinder was lighter, quicker to accelerate. She just needed to stay out of reach. A hard swipe from the war car could send her careening into the trees. This race would be over before it began.

But it looked like Dakota was racing straight up. Valerie glanced in the side-view mirror and caught a glimpse of the massive intake of the Guardian's turbocharger snorting like a frothing racehorse. She upshifted as she got onto the next stretch of road and tried to remember what was next. A wrong move now might see the war car plowing clean through her.

She came out the next curve with a pendulum turn, the rear end of the Sidewinder fishtailing across the loose surface of the road. Straightening the wheel, she got on the gas again, both feet working as she pumped the brake and accelerator around the next turn. Her ears were straining, listening to the engine, shifting cleanly with the transmission based on the sound and not even using the clutch. Every one of her senses was on alert. She gained another car length on the Guardian. She could still make out Dakota in the rear-view mirror, her eyes blazing with fury as she worked to run her down.

This was a contest of more than just speed. The Sidewinder had an edge in acceleration and maneuverability, but Dakota had an intimate knowledge of the course coupled with the Guardian's raw power.

One mistake and this could be over.

The Sidewinder launched over the next hill, and all four

wheels came off the ground. It was a matter of inches but enough to press her into the seat cushion as the wheels touched ground again. The car's suspension took the jump in stride, but there was barely enough time for the tires to gain traction before she was into the next turn.

She took the curve and immediately cranked the wheel to navigate another.

She was going too fast.

Trees whipped past in a blur. Then there was the Guardian, looming, gaining on her in the rear-view mirror. Dakota was coming on strong, heedless of the upcoming curve. The Guardian's front ram brushed her bumper, nudging her and threatening to dislodge the traction of her rear wheels.

If she spun off into the trees at this speed, she might not walk away.

Valerie noted a sign on one of the trees as they flew past. They were halfway around the course.

She steered hard into the turn, both feet working to keep the wheels on the road. Another pendulum turn, then a second as they rounded another hairpin. The Guardian was a dark blur dancing back and forth across her mirror. Sunlight flashed from the windshield, and the world behind them went gray with dust.

Valerie came out of the next turn with only two wheels on the ground.

By the time she got the car back under control, Dakota was making her move. She'd read the turn better, cut the corners cleaner, now she pulled alongside with a quarter mile of open road ahead. Valerie floored the accelerator, but the Guardian slammed into her driver's side, forcing her toward a runoff ditch. She wrestled the wheel but it was no use, there was no way she could muscle the war car out of the way.

The Guardian hit her again and she fishtailed, falling back and forced to brake to keep from losing control. She caught a glimpse of Dakota's jubilant face as the war car rocketed ahead.

Valerie regained control of the Sidewinder and raced to catch back up. She caught the Guardian at the next curve, but before she could make a move to pass, an eruption of silver shot from the projectile ports at the back of the war car and showered her hood with two-inch balls of spikes. Two of the spike balls hit with enough velocity to embed themselves in the windshield glass.

"Oh, you little brat," Valerie muttered. But she counted herself lucky that Dakota had mistimed the shot. None of the spikes had landed in the road for her tires to find. Staying close on the Guardian's bumper had saved her. But Dakota playing with the armament dashboard wasn't good news. If she found more weapons, things could go wrong for her quickly.

Valerie swung left and tried to get around the Guardian, but Dakota swerved too, blocking her path. The front fender of the Sidewinder scraped the back fender of the Guardian, but Valerie was forced to fall back again when the spikes welded to the Guardian's lug nuts tore through her front fender.

How was she supposed to get around again in one piece? They swung into another curve, and she spied the little stone bridge in the distance. She recalled her father's advice. If she was going to pass, she was running out of time.

She spotted several of the Black Hawk cars amid the trees, members of the tribe standing atop them, watching them race toward the finish.

She had to make a move.

Valerie let the rpms redline before shifting, swinging wider this time, taking the Sidewinder almost to the extreme left edge of the road. Dakota swung left too, as expected, using the Guardian as a battering ram to force her off the road, but Valerie was already braking hard with her left foot as she accelerated with the right, cutting to the opposite side of the road with millimeters between her bumper and the rear end of the Guardian. By the time Dakota caught the move, Valerie's foot was off the brake, and she was racing forward. The Sidewinder pulled alongside the Guardian, then leapt ahead. The Guardian clipped her rear end with its ram, but the glancing blow wasn't enough to knock her off track.

The stone bridge was coming way too fast.

What the hell. It wasn't her car.

Valerie pressed the accelerator to the floor and hit the incline of the arched bridge doing eighty miles per hour. The Sidewinder went airborne, and this time it wasn't a matter of inches. The car rocketed off the bridge and soared. Valerie's heart went into her mouth as the Sidewinder tore through the air. The car cleared seventy-five feet before slamming back to the earth and bottoming out hard against the road. The car bounced once but kept going.

Valerie kept her speed up and dared a look in the rear-view mirror. Dakota had been forced to slow coming over the bridge, and while she was still coming, she was now a dozen car lengths back.

"Yes!" Valerie shouted. She tore around the next curve and caught sight of the finish line. More spectators lined the road now. Some of the children must have seen the jump because they were cheering.

Valerie kept her focus. A quarter mile. Eighth of a mile. She was going to make it.

"Yes, yes, yes!" Valerie shouted as she flashed through the finish line. Her father was there near one of the benches. He was on his feet. So was Takawa. It was only when she glanced in the rear-view mirror that she realized something was wrong.

There was no Guardian.

Valerie brought the Sidewinder to a skidding stop in the middle of the road amid a cloud of dust, turning ninety degrees in the process. With the car canted sideways, she had a clear view of the last section of track before the finish.

The Guardian was sitting in the road, a quarter mile back, still running as evidenced by the waves of heat coming off the hood and the exhaust smoke from the tailpipes, but the girl behind the wheel was just staring.

"What the hell?" Valerie muttered.

Then the Guardian lurched into motion. Not forward, but into reverse. The car accelerated backward, then was cranked hard into a turn before the wheels spun forward again, kicking up twin rooster tails of dirt and gravel as it accelerated back the way they had come.

"You have got to be kidding me!" Valerie shouted. She shifted into gear and stomped the accelerator, her tires spinning briefly before gaining traction and launching her back down the track. The entire crowd was on its feet now, but there was only one person Valerie cared about, and she was on the run.

24

THE OLD MINE

Rico was at the door of Rust Creek's only guild mechanic just after dawn. His raps on the door were met by a surly and irritable Sal. The big man's growl of greeting softened when he saw who was knocking.

"Your car's not done yet. I got the tires done, but I'm still working on the radio antenna."

"Don't worry about that. As long as it drives. I've got an emergency. And I need a favor."

Sal drove the Vulcan out the town gate while the tower guards were still sleepy and less than inquisitive.

Just out of sight of town, he popped open the trunk, and Rico climbed out.

"I hope you know what you're doing," Sal said. "They've been snooping around the garage, wondering if you've been back."

"Then they'll know you drove the car out this morning. Will you be in danger?"

Sal shook his head. "Those jackasses don't know a Vulcan from a Merlin. I'll tell them one of the other cars on the lot was yours and you haven't been back for it."

"Don't do anything that'll get you in trouble. You're one of the only nice people I've met in this town, and I'd feel awful if I was the reason you got in trouble."

"Some things are worth a little risk," Sal said. "Keeps me young."

"Thank you." Rico put his hands on Sal's shoulders, extended on his toes, and gave the big man a quick kiss on the cheek. "I owe you one."

Sal blushed a little. Clearing his throat, he nodded. He gave a quick wave as he backed away, then retraced their path up the road toward town.

Rico noticed he was smiling.

Climbing back into the Vulcan, Rico drove roughly a mile down the road, then hid the car behind a stand of thick trees not far off the road. Once safely out of sight, he removed his dress and wig and changed into trousers and a T-shirt.

He retrieved a flashlight, compass, and a few tools from the Vulcan's trunk, then set off into the woods, the map in his hand giving him confidence.

His confidence faded as the hours slipped by, and he still hadn't located an entrance to the old mine. The woods were full of brambles and briars, and the steep inclines and challenging rock formations made maneuvering difficult. The sun was high in the sky, and his canteen was empty by the time he came across a partially buried metal track that had been laid along a dirt path. He followed the track into a culvert, and there at the bottom, he discovered a boarded up entrance.

"Now we're talking," he muttered.

He set to work with a stubby pry bar, tearing away the boards. It was only when the opening yawned wide in front of him that he hesitated. It was a dark hole full of creepy crawly things he was about to disturb. But he thought of Valerie and Damon, summoned his courage, and forged ahead, kicking a few rocks ahead of him to warn any snakes of his approach.

"I'm coming in," he said to the darkness. "And I promise I taste terrible. You don't bite me and I don't bother you, okay?"

It was cool inside the old mine. The sweat he had accumulated on the hike now chilled his skin. It smelled old down here—stagnant and dead. The occasional pile of animal droppings or discarded snakeskin reminded him that he wasn't alone. The squeak of bats set his teeth on edge when he discovered a colony of them nesting up an air shaft. He held his nose and stepped cautiously around the mound of guano beneath them. He hurried on and checked his compass often, taking passages that led generally east, the direction of town. He took care to mark his path periodically, chiseling notches in support beams and scratching arrows in the dirt with his heel to guide him on the way back. It would do no good to locate Damon but get them lost in the mine on the way out.

His path was not always direct. On several occasions, he encountered tunnels that were blocked, and more than a few that led nowhere. But after nearly an hour underground, he discovered a tunnel that ran due east and before long ran into a perpendicular corridor marked with footprints that looked recent. The footprints showed travel in both directions. He chose the right-hand route.

He moved cautiously, doing his best to quiet his breathing, listening for any sign of trouble. He covered the beam of his flashlight with his hand, limiting the light but allowing enough to make progress.

A rhythmic scraping sound made him stop. He stood against one tunnel wall and listened. It sounded as though someone was chiseling at a stone with a spoon. Then came a clattering of something falling, followed by a slew of curses.

"Use your damn head, idiot. Drop that one more time, and we're never getting up this wall."

The voice caused a thrill of elation in Rico. It was Damon. He unleashed the full beam of his flashlight and dashed forward, ascending a small rise and erupting into a chamber containing two jail cells. In the left-hand cell, bare-chested and pale, Damon stood, blinking, at the base of one wall. He had his hand over his face, squinting and blocking the light.

"Who's there?"

"Damon! I'm so happy you're alive!"

"Rico? Good God, is that you?" Damon rushed to the bars.

Rico raced to him and put a hand out to his but balked at the sight of his friend. Damon's fingertips and toes were bloody and covered in dirt. His chest and abdomen were scratched and red, and his lips were dry.

"Are you okay? What have they done to you?"

Damon clenched the bars. "Valerie. Is there any word? Have you seen her?"

Rico shook his head. "I only know she left town and is somewhere in the woods. Damon, they're planning to kill her. I was up at the Castle. Lord Hudson wants her gone."

"I figured as much," Damon growled. "Kai Nez, an old competitor of mine, rode out with her. She said Valerie fell into a river at a place called Canyon Falls. You have to find her before someone else does."

"How do I get you out?" Rico said. He scanned the bars that kept Damon captive. The entire wall of bars was a door, but the hinges were covered with heavy steel guards bolted to the stone. The lock side had a massive padlock on it, and there was no way he could bust it with the tools he'd brought. He needed a key.

"Don't worry about me," Damon replied. "If you can get out of town, I want you to find Valerie and get her far away from here. Don't come back for me. Her safety is all that matters."

"I can't leave you here," Rico said.

"You don't have a choice. If Valerie's alive, she could be headed back to town right now with no idea what she's walking into. Someone has to warn her. And they're hunting you too.

They're trying to pin the service station fire on the natives, and you and I are loose ends."

"Where's the key?" Rico asked. "If I can get you out, we can find Valerie together."

"No. I won't have you going up against Trammel and Kai Nez alone," Damon said. "Trammel could show up any time. They'll toss you in one of these cells or just get rid of us both. Your being loose is probably the only reason I'm still alive. You've got to get out of here."

The flashlight started to flicker.

No. This was too soon.

"Is that water?"

Damon was staring at the canteen on Rico's belt and licking his cracked lips. Rico swore. Why hadn't he saved some?

"It's empty. I'm sorry. But I have some tools. A few things in my bag." He located the little pry bar and a few other odds and ends he had brought along and held them out.

Damon extended a hand for the pry bar. His palm was blistered and raw. "Yes. This will help. I won't be able to hide much else." He gripped Rico's forearm. "It's good to see you, my friend. Now please go, before they catch you. Find Valerie. Get her out of here."

"I'll get you help too," Rico said. "I promise."

"Just warn Valerie what they're planning. But don't tell her I'm down here or let her come back for me. You need to get her to the king."

"She'll see right through me. You know she will, and she'll want to come straight back."

"Kai Nez is a stone-cold killer. Valerie's good, but she's no match for her. If she comes back here, she'll die. Promise me you won't let her come back."

"I'll try."

Damon squeezed his hand. "Now go. Hurry."

The flashlight flickered again. Rico swallowed hard and

released Damon's hand. He backed away slowly, Damon's pale figure receding into the darkness. He turned and hurried back along the tunnel.

The flashlight continued to flicker. When he reached a long straight stretch of tunnel, he turned the light off to conserve the battery, feeling his way through the dark and only turning the light on in bursts to save it. Following his own trail, his return trip was much faster than his journey in. He finally spotted daylight ahead and breathed a sigh of relief when he stepped out into the fresh air. The sun had faded however. Clouds were rolling in and obscuring the sky. He backtracked hurriedly through the woods, making his way back to the Vulcan.

By the time he climbed into the driver's seat, he was soaked with sweat and out of breath. He studied the darkening horizon with a growing sense of dread but forced himself to focus on his task. He fumbled with the map and searched it for any sign of the location Damon had spoken of. Finally he located it. *Canyon Falls.* He started the car and shifted into gear, only pausing once with his eyes on the rear-view mirror. "Hang in there, Damon. I'll get you help. Somehow."

Thunder rumbled in the distance. Rico pulled out of the trees and back onto the road, the Vulcan's engine answering the distant thunder with a roar of its own.

25

FATHERS

D akota kept her foot on the gas as she tore off the track and onto the access road. This wasn't the plan. This wasn't how this day was supposed to go. The sight of the finish line—with Henry, Chief Takawa, and most of the tribe lined up to witness her defeat—*cheering* for Valerie—was too much. That was no path for her.

But where else would she go?

When she looked in the rear-view mirror, she flinched. The Lockley Sidewinder was back, coming on fast. What the hell. Didn't this girl ever let up?

Dakota clenched the steering wheel and upshifted. She wiped at her cheeks, clearing the tears that welled unbidden from her eyes.

"Don't you dare lose it," she admonished herself. She caught a glimpse of herself in the reflective glare from the engine instruments. Her eyeliner was smeared and she looked a mess.

Out the window, the world was growing darker as storm clouds rolled in from the east.

It only made her more resolved. There was no going back for her. Not now. Not ever.

~

Valerie rode the Guardian's bumper for a half mile before backing off. It was a one lane road with no room to pass, and her shouts out the window had done nothing to convince Dakota to slow her flight. She was low on options.

The Sidewinder had proved itself a match for the Guardian in speed but stopping the war car was another thing entirely. Even if she managed to pass it, she might as well hurl the car in front of a train for all the good it would do.

This confrontation had gone from a sprint to an endurance race—a game of attrition with no finish line in sight.

Where on earth was she headed?

The dirt road wound its way over the mountainside, dipping through culverts and rising over hills. They crossed one stream, then another, heading vaguely southeast but without an obvious destination.

Valerie eyed the building clouds out the window, then checked the fuel gauge. The needle sat at a quarter of a tank.

How much fuel had been in the Guardian last time she checked? Half a tank? Less? She had no way of knowing if Dakota had found a way to refuel, but the ground they covered till now must have taken a toll.

As the drive wore on, she wondered if Dakota even knew where they were headed. But finally the Guardian turned down a side road and then a dirt driveway that led to a house.

Part of a house.

The wood frame was weather worn and dingy. There was a roof over only part of the structure, and the bones of the walls were up, but the house had never been completed. A few tools were still scattered around the site as though the builders might wander back one day and pick up where they left off. But the tools were rusty, and the rafters were entangled with twisting vines.

The Guardian idled in the driveway. Valerie parked the Sidewinder a few car lengths behind it and got out.

There was no sign of motion in the war car, but she approached cautiously, moving around the passenger side and leaning low to peer inside.

Dakota had her head against the headrest while staring vacantly out the windshield.

Valerie rapped on the passenger window with a knuckle.

The native girl turned languidly to observe her.

Valerie pointed to the lock and jiggled the door handle.

Dakota narrowed her eyes briefly, but then leaned across the car and unlocked the door. Then she slumped back in her seat.

The new door seals made a sucking sound as Valerie pried open the door. She considered the girl in the driver's seat for another moment, then slid into the passenger seat next to her. She let the door hang open.

They sat in silence for over a minute, just staring out the windshield at the old house and the bees working frantically over the wildflowers that had invaded the yard. A breeze was kicking up, a sign of the changing weather, but the bees seemed determined to press their luck.

It was Dakota who finally broke the silence, but her gaze was focused on some non-existent horizon.

"He said he was going to fix it up for us one day. It was going to be a surprise for my mom." She rested an elbow on the window frame and let her fingers rest in her hair just above her forehead. "I was the only one who knew the secret. Right up until the day they caught him."

"You're talking about your dad? Your real dad?" Valerie asked.

"He never finished anything in his damn life," Dakota said. "So I don't know why I thought he would finish this. I believed it though. I used to daydream all the time about what it would be like to live here. To have a view of the valley that was always this good." She cocked the rear-view mirror.

Valerie shifted in her seat till she could look out the rear window. Sure enough, from where the Guardian was parked, you could see all the way down the valley.

"What happened to him?" Valerie asked.

"You mean the first time they caught him stealing cars? Or the second time?" There was a tinge of resignation in her tone that betrayed her usual toughness. "Well, the first time he got caught by Sir Rupert Longletter and Sir Henry Terravecchia II." She uttered each name carefully, precisely, as if they were sharp objects that might cut her if mishandled.

Valerie processed what she was saying. Her father had been one of the men who captured Dakota's dad?

She had memories of Sir Rupert as well. He was a brutish, intimidating man who had caused her to hide behind her mother's skirts as a child. As she grew older, she had grown bolder, sometimes laughing and joking with the knights her father had invited to visit their home. She and her brother had once even orchestrated a mock joust for the knights' entertainment. Despite her antics, Sir Rupert had never warmed to her, or she to him. While her mother had never spoken ill of the man, she had always been careful to spirit her brother and her away in the evenings, especially when the knights were drinking.

"My father was meeting with Sir Rupert the last time I saw him," Valerie said. "Going off to hunt outlaws."

"They caught my dad near the river. Right down there by the creek," Dakota said, nodding out the passenger window. "I was with him. We'd just finished washing up and were headed up here for lunch when he saw Sir Rupert's war car in the drive. He told me to hide so I did." Dakota's gaze still had a far-off quality, looking into the past more than the present.

"They arrested him?" Valerie asked.

"Henry wanted to arrest him, but Sir Rupert said my dad was too dangerous. Too much of a threat to put in the car. He said he would execute him instead."

"A field execution? On Tribal Land?"

"My father was an outcast from the tribe. The knights even had an arrest warrant co-signed by the tribal council. That's what they said anyway. They had him tied up on the lawn and were set to execute him. Sir Rupert wanted Henry to do it, and I think he was going to until I came out from behind the wood pile. I ran up and threw myself between Henry and my dad. I said I didn't care if he killed me, but to leave my dad alone."

"What did he do?" Valerie asked, finding herself riveted by Dakota's account.

"Sir Rupert pulled me away and wanted Henry to go ahead with it, but Henry objected. He said he wouldn't execute a man in front of his child."

Valerie felt a hint of relief at that. The Henry Terravecchia she knew would certainly never have stood for such a thing.

"But then the two of them argued. Sir Rupert claimed that, as a senior knight, he could have Henry stripped of his title for disobeying an order, but Henry still refused. Sir Rupert decided to do it himself and would have cut my dad down right then, but Henry got in the way. They pushed and shoved each other. My dad kept telling me to run, get away, but I couldn't leave him. Sir Rupert was in a rage. He swung at Henry with his sword, and they started dueling. It all happened so fast I don't know exactly what happened, but Sir Rupert cut Henry's leg, and it looked like it was over, but when he came for my dad, I wouldn't get out of the way. My dad was yelling, telling me to run. I was crying and screaming. It was a nightmare. Sir Rupert raised his sword, and I knew from his face that he was going to kill both of us."

Valerie found herself holding her breath. "What happened?"

"Henry," Dakota said. "The sword never fell because Henry

took Sir Rupert's head off. I had my eyes closed but I still remember the way it sounded when it hit the ground."

"My God," Valerie muttered. She stared out the window, the scene painted in her mind.

"I remember we all just stared at each other," Dakota said. "Until Henry fell over. He was bleeding badly from his leg wound, but he handed me his dagger, told me to cut my dad loose. I was shaking so much, I could barely hold it at first."

Dakota sighed and ran her hand over her face. "I wanted to run. If it hadn't been for my dad, I would have just run away as fast as I could and never looked back. But my dad made me help Henry. We tied up his leg to stop the bleeding, but there was no way he could walk or drive. We put him in Sir Rupert's car. Dad made me sit and watch him while he put Sir Rupert in the trunk. All the way back to the motorcoach, I could hear his head rolling around back there."

"How old were you?" Valerie asked.

"Ten."

"I can't imagine how that made you feel."

Dakota shook her head. "I don't think there is any age that would have made it any better."

"What happened after?"

"It was a mess," Dakota said. "My dad dropped me off at the motorcoach. Henry was passed out. We thought he was going to die from the blood loss. If it hadn't been for my mother being a healer, I think he would have. Dad got rid of the car. I helped him push it into the lake. Then we took off. Hid in the mountains."

"You took my dad with you?"

"I wanted to leave him somewhere because he terrified me, but my dad said we owed him a debt and couldn't just leave him to die. He lost the leg though. Mom couldn't save it, and they had to take it off. He was laid up in the motorcoach for weeks, in and out of fevers. They put him in my bed, and I slept with them."

Dakota fidgeted with her nails.

"Then one day dad went on a run for supplies and didn't come back. We found out later that he'd been caught with a gang of his old friends stealing cars from Lord Hudson's land. They didn't even bother with a trial. They hung him on the spot."

Valerie studied the girl's downcast eyes and distracted expression.

"I'm so sorry."

Dakota picked at her nails some more. "Shouldn't be. Not your problem." She shook herself from wherever her mind had been and focused on the view out the window. "And that was that. Dad was gone, and we were worse off than ever. Good story, huh?"

"Your story's far from over. What are you, sixteen?"

"Oh yeah? You see a happily ever after in my future somewhere? You think it's all going to turn around from here? Glad you can feel good about that."

"That's not what I'm saying," Valerie argued. "I'm just saying your life's not over yet."

"You know, when I saw this car sitting on the trailer that night, I *felt* like something was going to change. It was the first time in forever when I thought something was finally going my way. Turns out, I'm just deluded. Same as everyone else on this mountain."

"If it makes you feel any better, I've been deluded too. I thought I had a dad who would have cared about me enough to tell me he's been *alive* the last six years. I guess I was fooling myself."

Dakota nodded slowly, then pulled the keys from the ignition and offered them to Valerie. "You'll be needing these."

Valerie took the keys, and the two of them climbed out of the car. Valerie retrieved her sword from the Sidewinder, along with its ignition keys. She met Dakota at the front of the Guardian and tossed the keys to her.

"I thought for sure I had you," Dakota said. "Especially in this car."

Valerie stared at the Guardian, the intimidating black snarl of its intake, the aggressive posture of its fenders. Then her eyes fell on the Terravecchia crest mounted to the front grill. It made her frown.

She drew her sword, wedging *Firebird*'s blade tip behind the chrome emblem. It was a brief test of strength between the car and the sword, metal against metal, but then the emblem broke free, snapping cleanly off its mounting points. Valerie bent over and scooped it from the dirt where it had landed. She turned it over in her palm, considering the bear paw symbol, then handed the emblem to Dakota.

"Here. If you wanted to be a part of the legend, I think that's all that's left. The last Terravecchia that really loved me was my brother. And he died in my arms two months ago, killed in a duel protecting our family's honor. You can tell my dad *that's* what's left of Il Orso Nero's legacy."

Dakota held the emblem carefully, as though it might suddenly burn her. A few drops of rain made solitary plonking sounds as they bounced off the metal surfaces of the cars.

Dakota brushed the hair out of her eyes. "Where are you headed?"

"Back to the friends I can count on. The ones who *always* have my back. You should get yourself some." Valerie walked around the side of the Guardian and climbed into the driver's seat as more rain drops thudded across the windshield. She started the engine and took one last look at Dakota, who was standing like a statue in the yard of the old house. Something about the girl seemed temporary. Valerie had the feeling that she might just fade away into the woods once she looked away—dissolved by the rain or vanished like a bad dream. She slammed the door.

She shifted into reverse, and the Guardian burst backward a dozen yards. Then she slammed it back into first, tearing a semicircle in the dirt as she tore away. She never looked back.

26

REVELATION

D akota pulled up to her parent's motorcoach in a steady drizzle of rain. Even Cisco, their cattle dog, had opted to stay indoors. Dakota spotted him pushing up the blinds in a corner window of the old vehicle. She pulled into the separate garage and parked the Sidewinder. She shut the car off, then climbed out, pulling the chain for one of the bare, overhead bulbs before making her way over to the extra fuel cans. She picked up one, then another, shaking the contents till she found a container that was mostly full.

Moving around the far side of the car, she popped open the fuel door and located a funnel. As she stood listening to the gurgle of gasoline sloshing its way into the tank, her eyes wandered. They landed on an unusual lump of fabric resting atop one of the toolboxes.

When the fuel can was empty, she carried it over to the toolbox and rested it next to the odd lump.

Then she recognized it as the jacket Valerie had put around her when she was wounded in the woods. Winona had washed it and left it here, clearly hoping Valerie would be back to claim it.

Dakota slowly unfolded the jacket, noting the bear paw emblem emblazoned across the back.

For most of her life, the Terravecchia crest had been a symbol she resented. Il Orso Nero wasn't a legend to her, he was the man who had replaced her father. The symbol was that of the family who had everything she never did. Honor. Reputation. Money. She had imagined Henry Terravecchia's children growing up in a shining castle, never knowing a struggle in their lives. She had loved hating them. But even so, she hadn't been able to resist the pull of that car.

Had she stolen it to hurt them, or was it to be more like them? She wanted it to be hate, but now that illusion was shattered. She owed her life to a Terravecchia, not once but twice now. And this time it felt different.

Dakota slipped her arms into the jacket. She moved to the mirror by the washroom and studied her reflection. Did she look anything like one of them? She pictured Valerie arriving at Glastonbury Castle and meeting the king, being formally inducted into the Knights of the Round Table. A road knight with a badge and the authority of the king's inner circle. Dakota felt the lump in her jeans pocket and fished out the silver emblem Valerie had pried off the front of the Guardian. She held it up and imagined herself in the role. Knight Warden of the West.

"It's a good look, isn't it?"

Dakota whirled around to find Henry in the doorway, watching. She quickly shoved the chrome emblem into the inside breast pocket of the jacket, hiding it from view. "I was just messing around." She started to take off the jacket.

"Don't. It suits you," Henry said, taking a few steps forward.

She let her arms relax.

Henry scratched at his beard. "I've tried to never push any of my family history on you, but one of the things I love about that emblem you're wearing is what it stands for. The words of the Terravecchia House are *Rimani sempre nobile di cuore*. It emphasizes that nobility doesn't come from a name or a lineage. It comes from the heart."

"Nobility like hers," Dakota said, fingering the fabric of the jacket.

"And like yours," Henry replied.

Dakota looked up and met his eyes. His expression was sincere, kind. She realized it had been a long time since she had looked him in the eyes.

"The courage you've seen in Valerie is courage I see in you too. She may have grown up with the motto and the name, but you've lived it. I saw it the first day I met you. The day you came running out of the woods to throw yourself in front of a sword to save your father. That was as noble an act as I've ever witnessed. And you were capable of that at ten years old."

"A whole lot of good it did," Dakota said. "He got himself killed just the same. What was the point?"

"I think you know why it matters," Henry said. "In your heart."

Dakota looked at the ground. "If you're right, then why am I still so angry about it?"

"No one ever said being noble is the same as being a saint. I'm sure you could ask Valerie. She's as angry as I've ever seen her, and I know her brother will be just as furious when he finds out I'm alive." Henry moved to the Sidewinder, idly brushing water droplets from the paint.

Dakota looked up but bit her lip. He didn't know. Could she really be the one to tell him? If not, would it be worse to keep it from him?

"Valerie wanted me to tell you . . ." Dakota began, but when Henry turned his attention back to her, her courage failed.

"Tell me what?"

Dakota shifted her feet. "Your son . . ."

Henry moved closer.

"She wanted me to tell you that he's . . . that he's . . ."

Henry's face darkened. "That he's what?" He loomed over her now, his gaze boring into her.

"There was a matter of honor. Someone he had to duel."

Henry's expression twisted. His upper lip quivered. "Who?"

"She didn't say. Only that . . ."

Henry's hands locked on her shoulders, and his voice came out as a growl. "Tell me."

"She said he died in her arms. A couple months ago."

The pressure from Henry's hands on her made her wince. He flinched, noticing her pain, then released her. He backed up one step, then another. His eyes roamed to the yellowed newspaper clippings on the walls, then came back to hers, but this time they were wild, burning through her. "Are you sure she . . ." but his voice trailed away. He pushed his palm up over his mouth, then backed into the wall, knocking a shower of tools loose from their hooks. "I wasn't there. I should have been there."

Dakota felt suddenly like she might need to catch him, prevent him from collapsing to the floor, but Henry rallied, his eyes focusing on the car. He stumbled around the rear of the Sidewinder and rushed for the driver's door.

"Wait! Where are you going?" But Dakota was too late. Henry flung open the door, slid inside, and slammed it behind him. Her calls to him were drowned out by the Sidewinder's engine as it thundered to life. Henry slammed the car into reverse and launched backward into the rain. Dakota ran after him, but he cranked the wheel hard and spun around. The rear tires churned mud and flung it toward the garage. Dakota ducked out of the way and noted with frustration how similar his method of exiting a conversation was to Valerie's. She was tired of watching members of this family take off and leave her, but especially Henry. Where was he going?

Her fury melted into concern. He clearly wasn't in a good state of mind. Nothing good could possibly come of it.

Her mind flashed back to the last time she had seen her own

father, the car door slamming, him racing off to join friends for the car heist he'd never return from. It *felt* like this. Even the sound of the wind through the trees seemed to be echoing that hateful day.

She stared at the motorcoach and the steady glow of the light inside. Her mother would be inside with Mato. Cisco, the dog, still watched her from the window. The ones left behind.

She was tired of being one of the left behind. She wouldn't do it again. Ignoring the rain, she walked back into the garage, retrieved a pair of riding goggles, and climbed aboard Henry's trail bike. The motorcycle was tall for her—she couldn't stand flat-footed while seated, but she would manage. She kickstarted the bike angrily. When the motor finally caught, it sent a plume of exhaust jetting to the back of the garage. She lowered the goggles over her eyes. The tachometer needle spiked as she revved the engine and let off the clutch. She rocketed out of the garage, ignoring the stinging droplets of rain that assaulted her skin. The rain seemed to come twice as fast as she flew down the trail, her headlight carving a path through the night.

She looked back only once. Cisco was barking madly in the window of the motorcoach. Then even his warning faded into the night.

27

BURNT

The wipers worked overtime on the Guardian's windshield as the rain came down in a torrent. The sky had opened up and was making the roads a muddy soup. Stands of trees overhanging the road offered intermittent protection, just long enough for Valerie to try to get her bearings before driving into the next onslaught.

Valerie couldn't be sure if it was the way the tree limbs bent and swayed in the wind or the continual pelting of the rain, but she thought everything outside looked different. She didn't recognize this stretch of road or the woods that it ran through. As she had feared, the gas gauge on the Guardian showed even less fuel than had been in the Sidewinder, a situation that must not have concerned Dakota during her flight up this mountain.

A steady drip drip drip was coming through the slim, puncture hole in the Guardian's ceiling armor. The rhythmic sound was a ticking clock in the back of Valerie's mind, a reminder that her situation was growing pressing.

As she wandered around one bend after another, she could barely get a sense of which direction this road was even heading. Without the sun or stars overhead to guide her, she was disoriented. She made it another quarter mile before reaching a curve that offered a view of the valley below. Getting out of the car, she braved a drenching by the rain for the opportunity to see where she was headed.

Valerie stood at the edge of the muddy road and peered through the rain, one hand shielding her eyes. The clouds obscured the distant mountaintops, and there was no sign of civilization.

Except . . .

Was it?

Yes. A blinking light. Blue. Green. White.

And that looked like the top of a windmill.

Valerie squinted through the rain, but she was sure now. Looking between the hills, she could make out the metal structure and whirring mismatched blades of the windmill flashing beneath the beacon.

Fiddlestick's Garage.

She was surprised she had come this far south, but it was the best sign she could hope for other than a village. It was hard to know if the fuel trucks had returned and if J.J. could even help her, but the alternative might be driving around in the forest until she ran out of gas.

Valerie dashed back to the car and climbed in, easing the Guardian down the mountain, coasting as often as she could and making all the turns that seemed like they would lead toward the garage. The needle on the gas gauge was dipping into the reserve when she crested the last hill, but she breathed easier when she saw the beacon flashing ahead.

Then her breath caught completely.

The tire wall that had shielded Fiddlestick's garage was in ruin. Piles of tires lay strewn all about the area. Some were smoking in spite of the rain. The scent of rubber smoke grew thicker as she approached. The tall windmill was still standing, the whirring blades still powering the light, but not much else of the compound was intact. Fire had ravaged the buildings, leaving burnt shells of cars scattered around the perimeter of the smoldering foundations.

Valerie's headlights swept over the ruins as she pulled through what used to be the front gate and spotted the shape of a dog darting into the night. She climbed out of the car and walked through puddles dark with ash as she surveyed the wreckage. Near the spot where the front door of the service station had been, she found the remains of the Troublemaker 100 she had left with J.J. The hole in the tank was patched. He had fixed it. The rest of the bike hadn't faired too badly in the fire, but the front and rear tires were both punctured with arrows. The arrows were clean and untouched by the flames. The black feathers of the flights were still glossy. Looking around the ruin that was the rest of the station, it was clear they were left on purpose. A sign.

But Valerie had been with the Black Hawks all day. Nearly the entire tribe had been in attendance of the rally race that afternoon. What cause would they have had to attack Fiddlestick's?

It made no sense.

Something stirred in the wreckage to her left, causing her to jolt. It was only then that she saw a pair of amber eyes peering at her from beneath some fallen sheets of corrugated tin. She squatted to get a better look, and the ball of fur came out from under the tin, whimpering.

It was Peaches. J.J. Fiddlestick's littlest dog. The bedraggled animal slunk up to Valerie, shivering in the rain. She scooped it up and held its soggy, quivering form to her chest. Then she moved to the fallen sheet of corrugated tin, tapping it first to check its temperature. Finding it cool enough to touch, she tipped the sheet metal away and discovered what she feared she would, the partially blackened body of J.J. Fiddlestick lying dead on the concrete. He was wearing mechanic's coveralls with a bloody slash across the chest. His eyes were open, staring vacantly in the direction where the back wall once stood. Valerie followed his gaze to the little cemetery at the rear of the compound and the small gravestones still visible among the wreckage.

Valerie couldn't tell which droplets on her cheeks were rain and which were tears. She blinked and wiped at her face. Then she noticed the forms of a few more dogs in the darkness, watching her.

"I'll find who did this," she said, not sure if she was speaking to J.J. or the animals.

The dogs merely watched.

She set Peaches down again so she could lift J.J.'s arms. She dragged the body of her friend through the rain to the rear of the compound and rested him near the tombstone that read, "Tommy."

She didn't have any true digging implements, but the ground was softened by the rain, so she fashioned a makeshift shovel from a piece of angle iron and set to work digging.

The hole didn't end up nearly as deep as she would have liked, but with blistered, muddy hands she pulled J.J.'s body in and stood over him for a few minutes. The rain had settled to a steady drizzle, but she was soaked through. Water ran down her forehead and dripped from the end of her nose, falling to the mud next to J.J.'s new grave. Words were difficult, but she felt she ought to say something.

"I hope wherever you're going, you've got someone waiting at the end of the road," she began. "I'm sure they'll be happy to see you. Thanks for making my road a little easier. I won't forget it."

With that, she began to gently pile the dirt back over him. A half dozen soggy dogs watched from the perimeter of the little cemetery. She had nearly finished and was looking around for something that might be useable as a grave marker when the revving of an engine made her look up. Not far down the road, a lone rider sat astride a motorcycle. The bike's single headlight flicked on.

How long had they been watching? Valerie moved instinctively toward the front of the compound where she had left the Guardian, quickening her pace as she went.

As she walked, she kept her eyes on the rider. The headlight blinked again. Once. Twice. A third time.

Valerie looked down the stretch of road and caught the moment when several more headlights blinked on in that direction. More riders. More headlights. Three. Five. Seven now.

More engines revved.

The twilight air suddenly came alive with noise: the high-pitched whine of motors screaming, calling to the rest of the pack. She never saw the signal, but suddenly the lights darted into motion. A wave of noise closed in on her. Valerie ran, sprinting the last few yards to the Guardian. She flung open the door, but before she could leap inside, a dirty ball of fur shot beneath her legs and launched itself into the car and across to the passenger seat. Valerie slid into the driver's side and slammed the door, paying no attention to the little dog that began yapping continuously at the approaching lights. Valerie grabbed at the roof lever and slammed the protective windshield grate into place, then repeated the process for the windows. She then twisted the ignition key, and the Guardian's engine let out its signature snarl. She shifted into reverse and launched the car back toward the road just as the phalanx of riders closed in.

They were helmeted, masked. Some wore wild spikes and mohawks affixed to their helmets. The Guardian's armor was struck several times in quick succession by some manner of weapon. She spotted riders with flails and lances, some had crossbows. Nothing her car couldn't handle, but she had to stay moving. Bad things happened to war cars sitting still.

She shifted into gear, and the rear tires squealed as she launched the car forward again. The engine snarled. She raced directly toward a pair of riders headed for her on the highway, and they wisely veered to either side to yield the road. In this fight, she was a lion and they were merely hyenas. But there were a lot of them.

Valerie took a deep breath and tried to focus. First rule of a road fight, keep moving. Second rule, protect your tires. Her hands flew over the armament controls. She cranked the handle for the tire shields, extending the fender armor to offer greater protection. The tires themselves were heavily reinforced with wire and should be able to withstand almost anything except heavy road spikes, but she wasn't taking any chances. She checked her mirrors. The pack of riders was forming up behind her. Maybe they just meant to run her off and wouldn't pursue.

But as she watched, the headlights grew brighter. They were definitely giving chase.

"Fine. You want to play? Let's play," Valerie said. She pressed in the clutch, then cranked hard on the wheel and applied the parking brake at the same time, torquing the car into a 180-degree turn over the wet asphalt. The dog yelped as it was pinned to the passenger door.

She shifted back into first and blasted back toward the oncoming riders. She deployed the spikes on her front ram, but the motorbikes scattered wildly as she plowed through, some of them launching themselves off the berms to either side of the road and soaring yards into the air. One unlucky rider didn't get out of the way in time, and her ram clipped the rear tire of his bike as he tried to get clear. The bike came unfixed from the pavement and went twirling off the road, its rider launched airborne into the weeds. Once she was through the entire pack, Valerie executed another 180. This time she ended up with a dog in her lap as Peaches scrambled for something to hold on to. "These bastards want more, we'll give them more. What do you say?" Valerie muttered.

The dog was uncharacteristically silent. Valerie let herself smile at the sight of the various riders working to get their bikes back onto the road. Her smile faded when a pair of headlights appeared over the nearest hill. As the lights drew closer, she realized this wasn't two more riders. It was a Republic Hellcat. The heavily armored war truck was churning out a plume of black smoke as it hurtled toward her. At a glance, she could see a spike ram twice the depth of her own, flame ports and a ballista turret.

Valerie swore. Then she jammed the Guardian into reverse, racing backward along the rain-slicked road before flicking the wheel hard and hurling the car into an aggressive J-turn, shifting directly into second gear as she came out. She stomped the accelerator and rocketed away, her eyes in the rear-view. The Hellcat was gaining on her. The bikes came racing out of the brush, too, speeding after her. Valerie upshifted and felt the turbocharger kick into full boost as she flattened the accelerator. The Guardian ate up the ground, the Hellcat falling away in her mirror.

One look at the fuel needle dancing precariously in the red made her set her jaw. She had no idea how she'd get out of this. But whatever she came up with, it had to be soon.

28

CONFESSION

It had been six long years since Henry Terravecchia II had been anywhere near civilization, and certainly not to Rust Creek, but as he pulled up to the guard tower near the village gate, he knew it was time. The wipers flicked rain from his windscreen but could do nothing about the tears in his eyes. He'd barely been able to see for the last few miles. But this was the end of the road.

No more running.

No more hiding from what he'd done.

He'd abandoned his family and left his son to fend for himself against the kinds of people he should have known would prey on him. His daughter had fought and nearly died to protect the family name he had given her, but what had he done to help? He'd given them a sword and a car and thought fate would be kind.

Fate was not kind.

And he'd been a fool. He was a fool to think he could simply run from what he'd done, pretend it would go away. It seems he had lost far more than his leg the day Sir Rupert had cut him. He'd lost his courage.

He didn't regret killing Rupert. If he hadn't, Dakota wouldn't be alive today. Dakota, with all her wild ideas, her defiant eyes, and smart mouth. She couldn't see it, but he loved her for every bit of who she was. He saw so much of her mother in her.

He felt another twinge of pain when he thought of Winona. Right now, she would be caring for Mato. Mato, who never knew anything of his father's shame. Mato, who might now be the one to grow up without a father.

But Henry wouldn't live another day in hiding. He had done what he'd done, and it was time to face it. Valerie had shown more courage in just this day than he'd felt in a lifetime. She'd been there when her brother died, fought to avenge him. All while he'd been hiding and living a life of delusion in the woods.

The guards approached the Sidewinder, appraising it cautiously.

No. He hadn't brought any weapons. They were welcome to search it.

He stood in the rain, leaning on his cane as they rummaged quickly through the vehicle.

"What's your business in Rust Creek?" the chief guard asked.

"I've come to see the sheriff."

They let him through, free to meander through village streets for the first time in half a decade. He located the local jail in the village square, its solid proportions seeming to fit his imagination of it perfectly. It was the kind of place one goes when deserving punishment, a force both immovable and unforgiving.

He left the keys to the Sidewinder in the ignition and stood in the street staring at the jail. But his courage failed again. His hands trembled. He strode into the saloon instead. He dripped his way to the bar and slapped a few soggy bills on the bar top.

"Whiskey," he muttered, when the barman showed interest.

The shot went down fast. He held the glass out again. The barman cocked an eyebrow but tipped the bottle again.

Henry glanced around the saloon. Shadowed faces leered at

him. Mean, hard looks from desperate men. The kind of men he used to make it his business to put away. Maybe some of them were here. Now he was more like one of them than ever before.

He ordered another drink, slid more bills across the bar top.

Valerie and Henry. His children. He'd been such a fool to think that a legacy would protect them. A family name and a grand motto. *Rimani sempre nobile di cuore.* The words he'd said to Dakota came back to him. What had *his* heart been revealed to be? Certainly nothing noble.

The warmth of the whiskey coursing down his throat soon made its effects felt. The coward's substitute for courage. He pushed himself away from the bar, snatching up his cane.

A pair of brutes rose from a table and sauntered into his path. They were feeling their youth, stirring for a fight. He knew the type. What would be the first move? A shove? Kick his cane out from under him? Perhaps they'd bother with a perceived insult. Some offense he'd committed by existing in their presence.

One of the young idiots had a sloppy grin on his face as he stepped in for the confrontation. A shove. Unimaginative.

The brute's hands never came close. Henry knocked the thug's arm aside with a flash of his cane, connecting with the elbow first, then bringing the weighted head of his cane around in a whirl to crack the man across the skull. The second brute's eyes widened as his friend hit the floor—put there by a leg sweep that came so fast there was barely enough time for anyone to see it. Henry brandished the cane at him, and the man backed away, palms raised.

Several chairs scraped the floor as patrons rose. Henry knew he'd kicked a hornet's nest, but he didn't hesitate as he shoved his way through the doors and back into the rain.

He stomped down the steps of the saloon and limped across the muddy street before climbing the steps to the jail. He could feel the eyes of men on him as he rapped on the door with the end of his cane, but no one crossed the street to drag him back.

Henry cast one glance at the saloon, where a half dozen men were standing on the porch, watching. One of them was the brute he'd put on his back. Afraid to get wet. More tough-guy cowards. He would have enjoyed hurting their feelings.

When the door swung open, he was met with a view of a sheriff that didn't match his imagination at all. In fact, he doubted he ever would have dreamed up the woman standing before him. She was the kind of person with dimensions you might suspect existed somewhere in the world but never thought you'd encounter in the flesh. A horizontal giant. She peered at him with close-set eyes that narrowed even further the longer she glared at him. In a way, she matched the jailhouse perfectly, immovable and unforgiving. She scanned the scene behind him, then her eyes came back to his.

"What do you want?"

Henry took a deep breath and rested his cane against the doorframe. "I've come to confess to a killing. I'm turning myself in."

～

Damon clung precariously to the top of his cell for the fifth time in as many hours. Each attempt at the trap door had ended in a fall. His back was bruised, his muscles stiff. The beds of his fingernails bled.

The haze in his mind signaled that his faculties were growing weak again. His lips were dry and his tongue felt like he'd been licking hot concrete. This last climb had been excruciatingly slow. Only the force of his desire to reach Valerie had kept him going. The memory of her face, her smile. The idea of losing her when they'd only just found the way to be together.

But for all of his determination and efforts to get up the wall, he had to admit failure.

It was too far.

He'd reached the trap door, whittled away at the wood around the hinges with the stubby pry bar he'd received from Rico, but he'd been foiled. Probing the trap door mechanism in the dark, he'd determined how it worked, but opening the door required triggering two separate spring-loaded lock pins, and he could only reach one at a time. Even if he could release one, he could only barely hold it in place with the pry bar while he maneuvered to release the other. With his pry bar hand pressing hard against the pin on one side and legs quivering with the effort to keep himself balanced in the footholds, his other arm was too short by a matter of several inches.

He couldn't reach the other pin.

Muttering every curse he knew, he tried keeping his balance with one hand and foot this time while stretching upward with his toes to reach the other pin, but his other foot slipped from the foothold, he lost his grip on the door mechanism, and he fell, thudding to the cell floor with a groan. The pry bar clattered off the stones with a clank and the sharp ring of steel.

This time he didn't move. He simply lay breathing, watching his last hope die somewhere overhead in the blackness.

He was still lying there several moments later when he heard a loud clunk, then a beam of light shot into the space past his cell bars. Someone shouted. This was followed by a *whomp*, as someone fell through the ceiling into the next cell over and hit the floor with an all-too-familiar thud. A chorus of moaning ensued.

Then Damon heard the voice that haunted his nightmares, Sheriff Trammel. She shouted down the hole. "This is what we do with killers in Rust Creek. At least till we can find someone to man the gallows. Don't get comfortable. I suspect we'll have a nice crowd for a hanging in the morning once this weather clears. You won't be staying long."

Damon rolled over and crawled to the bars at the entrance of his cell. He tried to peer out, but there was nothing to see of the cell beside him.

Someone else had fallen through Trammel's trap door. Now he understood why the two seats at her desk had been spaced so far apart. It hadn't been to accommodate her girth as much as it was to allow for each chair to drop someone into a separate cell.

The moaning and groaning continued in the neighboring cell, but Damon waited until he heard the solid click of the trapdoor being reset before he spoke.

"Hey! You okay over there?" His voice sounded strange to his own ears, raspy and dry.

The groaning stopped. Then a gruff voice replied, "No. Can't say as I am."

When no explanation followed, Damon tried again. "Take it easy. Not much call to move around anyway. There's no way out of these cells that I can see, other than the way you came in. There might be a way to trigger the door, but only if you're good at climbing. You, by chance, fit enough for that?"

"Definitely not," the voice replied. "I expected to be spending the night in a cell. I didn't expect this."

"I think these are the cells for the ones she's ashamed of."

"Suppose it serves me right," the other man said. "I've had it coming."

"No one deserves this mockery of justice," Damon replied, slumping with his back against the bars. "Locked up with no trial, no witnesses. This Trammel is as crooked as they come. I don't know what you've done, but if you're looking for justice, you'll find none here." Damon coughed, then gave the new guy a few minutes of silence before he spoke again. "You got a name?"

"I've had a few. All of them sullied beyond recognition," the voice replied.

Damon nodded. "Time for a new one then. Been there a few times. I'm Damon."

After a long pause, the voice replied, "Henry."

"Good to meet you, Henry," Damon said, feeling the dryness in his throat. The sudden presence of another person had him feeling loopy. He hadn't fully recognized the effect that hours upon hours of darkness had wrought on his mental state. Between that and the dehydration, he suspected his brain was in revolt. He touched his dry lips with his fingertips. "I don't suspect I'll be in much longer than you. Haven't had a drop of water in a couple of days. That'll get me before long."

"Did you say days?" The voice came from a bit closer now. Damon heard a scraping noise, then clothing against stone. Soon he could hear the man's breathing from only feet away. "Here. It's not much to offer a man, but it's wet. Can you reach that?"

Damon stretched an arm through the bars and felt the darkness in the direction of the neighboring cell. His fingertips brushed something damp.

"That's my handkerchief, you feel it?"

Damon stretched again and this time was able to grab it. The handkerchief was soaked through.

"It's raining buckets out there, and that was in my pocket. Couldn't help but get soaked."

Damon already had the handkerchief in his mouth, sucking the water from it.

"It's good. It helps," Damon said when he finally gave the fabric a break. "Thank you." He continued to suck on various corners of the handkerchief as he sat there.

"You've been here days?" Henry asked. "Anyone else know you're down here?"

Damon paused to consider his words. Was there any way someone knew he'd been visited by Rico? Was this an elaborate ruse to get him to talk? He couldn't imagine how but spoke cautiously anyway. "I think there might be if I'm lucky. Not sure yet what good it'll do."

"It's better than what I did, then," Henry replied. "Should have thought this through better. I deserve to be judged for what I've done, but swinging in the gallows tomorrow wasn't the end I had in mind. What's this sheriff like to talk with? Any chance I can get her to see reason?"

"About as much chance as her squeezing through these bars to give you a sloppy kiss."

"Then I guess that's that," Henry said. He sighed and went silent.

Damon let his mind wander to Valerie and the dangers she must be facing on the frontier. The temporary high that had come with having the stranger to talk to was fading. It wouldn't be long till they were both dead anyway. He tried to hold out hope that wherever Valerie was, she was at least alive and headed somewhere far from this place. He muttered a prayer to the darkness. Only the silence answered.

29

AMBUSH

Before Rico crossed the old river bridge that divided Hudson lands from the native territory, he had nearly stopped. The bridge was a symbol, a warning that this was far more dangerous a journey than he had ever attempted on his own before. His stomach roiled, and the nerves made him sweat, even in the damp chill of the rainy twilight. But he had come this far. There was no turning back.

He thought of Damon's pale face behind the bars of his cell. For the first time in Rico's memory, he'd looked frail and weak. He wasn't sure how much longer he'd last in there. If Valerie was still alive, they needed her now.

He followed the mountain road, leaning forward to squint through the windshield and the onslaught of rain, occasionally referring to the map he had purloined from Lord Hudson. Unsurprisingly, the roads behind the border of Hudson's lands weren't well marked or sometimes not marked at all. But there were guideposts, natural features of the land that Rico used as reference. That mountain pass, that river, a strange formation of rock labelled Big Horn. He noted each landmark as he passed and checked it against the map. His finger found Canyon Falls. He was getting closer.

He first attributed the movement in his rear-view mirror to a shadow or trick of the light. Each time he looked back, he found it gone. But then he slowed and rolled down the window to listen. There was a definite sound in the woods, a higher pitched popping and ticking that sounded nothing like the Vulcan. Rico came to a stop and let the engine idle. Whatever was behind him paused too, then the sound was parallel to him. Finally a shape descended the hill from ahead and to the right, emerging from the woods to stop directly in the road ahead. It was a Native Avalonian girl on a motorbike. Young, but warlike. There was something ferocious about her eyes even behind the riding goggles. Wet hair clung to her forehead and cheeks. To his surprise, she was wearing the canvas jacket with the bear claw logo he had stitched for Valerie. Had she taken it from her body? Rico switched off the headlights, raised his hands from the wheel and held them up to show they were away from any armament controls. He then leaned toward the open window.

"I'm here to talk! And we don't have much time!"

The girl climbed off her bike and strode over to his window. "Who are you? What do you want?"

Rico shrunk away from the window just a little. "I'm looking for a friend. A knight of the kingdom. Knight Warden of the West, technically—"

"Valerie," the native girl said.

"Yes!" Rico exclaimed. "You know her? Is she alive?"

"What do you want with her?"

"She's in danger. She can't go back to Rust Creek. Lord Hudson and someone named Kai Nez plan to kill her. I don't know what they're—" But the rest of the words died in his throat as the girl reached through the window and unlocked the door. The next moment she had the door open and was yanking on his arm.

"Hey, what are you—" Rico shouted, but by then he was being pulled from the car. How was this girl so strong? He found himself sprawled in the mud, staring wide-eyed as she climbed into the Vulcan and slammed the door. She tossed his map out the window and turned the window crank, shutting out the rain.

"Hey! I thought you were going to help me!" Rico scrambled to his feet. "Where is Valerie? Have you seen her?"

But the native girl put the Vulcan in reverse and rolled backward, not paying him the least bit of attention. She sped down the lane, turned the car hard up an embankment, then tore off, back down the road he had come by. Rico was left watching the taillights of the Vulcan vanish in the drizzling rain.

He swore and plucked his soggy map from a puddle.

Did that mean she knew where Valerie was, or was she still out here somewhere?

Rico turned and eyed the still-idling motorcycle that the native girl had left running in the road. He set his jaw. He still had promises to keep, and one carjacking wasn't going to be enough to stop him.

Valerie kept her eyes on the road. The rear-view mirror glowed brightly as the Hellcat pursued her down the mountain, relentless in the chase. She was lighter, faster, but she was driving unknown roads, running on fumes, and fleeing a multitude of assailants. She'd counted at least seven bikes. She was sure one had been demolished, but were there more?

The answer came in the form of headlights ahead of her on the road. Two bikes, one on either side of the highway, their brights on, blinding her. Valerie squinted and tried to see the road beyond. Tire spikes perhaps? She slowed to a stop. The road still looked clear. The bikes weren't blocking her path. They must have learned that lesson. But there had to be a reason for their positioning beyond blinding her and ruining her night vision.

Something wasn't right. She could feel it in her gut.

One look in her rear-view mirror showed that she was running out of time to make a move. She either turned now and took her chances against the Hellcat or forged ahead.

The little dog on the seat next to her was whining and looked like it had wet itself.

"I wasn't a good bet, dog. I think you're better off taking your chances back home." She reached over and scooped the animal up, then opened her door and deposited him on the wet asphalt. The dog immediately took off toward the woods at the side of the road. It never looked back.

Smart dog.

Valerie watched it disappear into the darkness, then her hand moved to the shifter. The lights of the Hellcat were getting closer. She scanned the armament dashboard. She wasn't entirely out of options. Rolling forward, she gathered speed, drawing nearer to the two motorbikes and their blinding headlamps. They weren't the only ones who could light things up. Valerie twisted the knob for the Guardian's fuel oil valves and depressed the trigger on the shifter. Two white-hot jets of fire shot from the fenders. Valerie directed the twin flame-throwers to either side of the road, engulfing the two motorbikes as the riders dove for cover.

But that's when she saw the wire.

She slammed on the brakes, but the wet roads made it impossible to stop in time. A heavy-duty steel cable had been strung from tree to tree across the road, and the Guardian hit it hard. The cable glanced off the car's sloped hood but caught the intake for the supercharger, slamming Valerie forward in her harness and then wrenching the car sideways as the rear end came loose.

Something snapped free from the intake, and the cable

ricocheted off the windshield as the Guardian plowed onward, tires screaming on the asphalt. The cable had failed to stop her, but as Valerie got her eyes back on the road and straightened the vehicle out, she could tell the Guardian was wounded. The engine was shaking, hammering and vibrating against its mounts. The trap had been poorly set, the height of the cable too high, but it had done enough. As the tachometer needle shot toward the red, Valerie upshifted and tried to gain ground, but the motor groaned, gasping for air and unable to maintain power.

"Come on, come on!" she shouted, desperate to stay moving. But as the engine shrieked beneath the hood, she lost more and more speed. She downshifted, trying desperately to coax the car into a gear that would keep her on the road.

That's when she noticed the gas gauge needle had pegged all the way to empty. The engine gave one last gasp, and the car ground to a stop.

Valerie glanced at the rear-view mirror and saw the glow of the Hellcat's lights bearing down on her and the wild eyes of Kai Nez behind the wheel. There was no time to escape. She barely had time to screw the valve closed on the fuel oil lines and grip the steering wheel before the impact.

The world outside tipped on its end. The view out the windshield was suddenly pavement and darkness as the Hellcat's ram pushed under the Guardian's rear bumper and launched it forward, propelled up and over from the impact. The Guardian landed on its roof and slid, the screaming of metal on asphalt changing to the scraping of earth as it shot off the road and across the shoulder. Valerie was pinned in her seat by her five-point harness but felt like a pinball just the same. A second impact came as the Hellcat hit the Guardian again, this time the inverted front end. The two metal rams sparked against one another as the big truck pushed the vehicle over the edge of the embankment.

Valerie's world went sideways. The Guardian tipped and rolled, crashing down the hillside faster and faster as it picked up speed. Valerie's head struck something hard as the roof caved in around her roll cage. Stars erupted in her vision even after she clamped her eyes shut. Glass exploded around her. The Guardian kept rolling, impact after impact, for what felt like an eternity, but finally slammed into the earth with a WHUMP of finality—water, mud, and engine oil splattering the inside of the car with viscous sludge.

Valerie tasted blood in her mouth. Her vision swam and her hands were numb. The world flickered and faded as she struggled to maintain consciousness.

One of the windshield wipers was still attempting to move, a crippled half-length of arm twitching across two inches of the metal grating. The glass was gone.

This small motion was mesmerizing. An electric motor somewhere under the dash still held out hope of life. It strained to do its duty even when the rest of the vehicle lay in ruin.

She looked up the hillside, past the twitching wiper blade.

The car had landed right-side up, its broken chassis angled slightly upward, offering her a view of the slope she had just rolled down. The engine had stopped, but there was a steady, rushing sound. It took her a while to realize that it was flowing water. She had landed in some manner of stream or runoff ditch. Even now, the water was rising up past her seat, pouring into the car from somewhere behind her and slowly filling the interior in its effort to escape downhill. The water chilled her but kept her alert.

Outside, over the gurgling and gushing noises of the stream, she could make out voices. Shapes moved on top of the hill, dark figures silhouetted against a barely lighter sky.

"She has to be dead, ain't she?" a man asked.

"You'll find out. Fetch me the body," a woman replied. "Drag her back to town in the cage."

That voice. A cold steady calm. The voice of the viper.

Valerie blinked as blood dripped into her eyes. She reached a hand up, felt the wet on her fingers. Warm. Dark.

Then she blinked again, and the figures atop the hill were gone. Engines revved. Headlight beams sliced the darkness, sweeping across the sky. They turned. Valerie's vision went dark, her neck muscles succumbing to gravity, but she jolted upright again. No. This was important. She had to stay awake.

Why was it so important? She longed to fade into the darkness.

But then she saw the shadow. The figure moved cautiously down the hill. He was testing each step lest he tumble down face first. She vaguely recognized the shape of him, as if from another lifetime. They had met before. Where?

The man made steady progress down the hill while Valerie's mind wrestled with his memory. She saw him on a bridge. Hauling on Dakota's arm, trying to tear her away.

Bone Saw.

That was his name.

And he was coming to kill her.

That thought finally sharpened her focus. He was coming to kill her.

Valerie looked down to find that water was now up to her ribs. Her legs were numb with cold, but she could still move them. She tested each foot, then brought her hands to her chest, running her fingers down the straps of her shoulder harness, feeling for the center buckle underwater. She fumbled for the latch, but her fingers were stiff and uncooperative.

Bone Saw was only a dozen yards away, head down and watching his feet. She wasn't sure if he would be able to see her through the busted windshield grating when he looked up, but she knew there was no way she was going to get out of this car without him noticing. She didn't even know if she could walk, let alone outrun him. Her eyes found the hilt of her sword still clipped into the ceiling rack. *Firebird.*

She reached for the handle, her arm a lead weight. Her numb fingers refused to cooperate. Why wouldn't they close around the grip?

She forced herself to tune out Bone Saw's approach, and the steadily rising water in the car, and focused all of her attention on the sword.

Her fingers hovered next to the handle.

Now close.

She hooked her numb hand around the hilt and pulled. The sword fell from the rack with a splash, disappearing under the water.

No!

Bone Saw stopped moving. His silhouette was frozen against the hillside.

"Oh ho, still kicking around in there, are we?" His voice was calm, almost amused. He continued his descent, his hand going to his hip and removing a long knife from his belt. Even in the dim light, Valerie recognized the glint of steel.

She fished in the water beside her, frantically feeling for *Firebird*.

"I'd kind of hoped we'd have a chance to tussle again," Bone Saw said. He was at the front end of the car now and waded slowly into the water. The rushing flood rose to his thighs. He planted a hand on the Guardian's crumpled fender and steadied himself as he moved. Valerie's breathing came in ragged gulps as she struggled with the harness. She gave up on it and went back to fishing through the water beside her for the sword. Where had it gone?

The metal window grating blocked Bone Saw from reaching in, but he peered through one of the holes and grinned at her. "I guess I should have brought a can opener." He sheathed his knife again, and his thick fingers laced through the holes in the driver's side window. He tugged at it, yanking harder and harder. To Valerie's horror, the grate came away. Several of the mounting points had been damaged in the crash, and their failure enabled Bone Saw to peel one side of the window screen away and tear it from the window.

Now, nothing stood between them but the cold night air.

Bone Saw pulled the knife from his belt again. "Let's see what we can do about getting you out of there."

"Get the hell away from me!" Valerie shrieked. Tears flowed unbidden from her eyes. Her lips trembled.

"Now we can do this the easy way, or we can do it the fun way," Bone Saw said. "Easy way is I slit your throat right now, then I cut you out after. Part of me would prefer that. But another part of me is thinking that since you're still alive, maybe we have some fun before we get to the messy part. You stay real still, and I'll cut those straps first and get you out of that tin can. We can go from there. Which is it going to be?"

Valerie was ready to opt for the quick death, but at that moment the fingers of her right hand rested on the unmistakable curve of *Firebird*'s scabbard. She stiffened.

Bone Saw nodded, mistaking her lack of motion for agreement. "Okay then. Glad to see you've got a little sense in you." He eased himself closer to the car.

Valerie let her body go limp—all that he could see of it, in any case. Beneath the surface of the water, she lifted the scabbard of the sword ever so slightly, letting it slide down her palm until she felt the crossbars of the hilt. She eased the tip of the scabbard over the center column of the car, grateful that it cleared the shifter without protruding from the water, then she rested the end of the scabbard between her feet, clamping it there to get some leverage to pull the blade free.

Bone Saw reached through the window, dipping the tip of his knife under the left shoulder strap of her harness. As he sawed at it, Valerie worked to get *Firebird* firmly in hand. She finally got her fingers to grip the handle, then pulled at the bottom of the scabbard with her feet, gently easing the blade out. Each motion was so slow she wanted to scream.

Her left shoulder strap fell away, and Bone Saw reached across her chest to the other shoulder. The knife passed a fraction of an inch from Valerie's throat, and she froze, her eyes on his, watching to see if he would change his mind.

But Bone Saw seemed to be enjoying himself. Valerie had his stinking breath in her face as he sawed through the right shoulder strap. When it fell away, he lingered, his broad nose a fraction of an inch from hers.

"Now, let's see if we can find that lap belt," he said. And his smirk spread into a leering grin as he plunged his meaty hand into the water, pressing it to her stomach and running it down to her waist.

Valerie's anger consumed her fear. "Find something you like?" she muttered.

Bone Saw twisted his face toward hers, grinning, but before he could respond, she flung her head forward and smashed his nose with her forehead.

Bone Saw recoiled, smacking the back of his head on the windowsill, then roared as he yanked his hand from the water and felt his nose. "Why, you tricky little whore. You'll bleed for that."

"No. You will," Valerie said. The scabbard fell away from the tip of *Firebird* and she brought it from the water, ramming it through the big man's throat.

Bone Saw's eyes went wide and he flailed back, his head slamming against the window frame once more before he flung himself backward and out of sight. A great thrashing sound followed, along with a gurgling cough, and Valerie caught one more glimpse of the man, the knife now fallen from his grasp, both hands held to his throat. He reeled in the waist high water, slipped, and went down with a splash. A moment later, a thud signaled that the current had swept him against the rear of the

Guardian, but then the water pushed him on, and the world outside grew quiet.

Valerie stared at the rear-view mirror with her breath coming fast, focused on the back end of the car and the water rushing over it. When a minute had gone by with no sign of Bone Saw, she finally lowered the sword from where it had been frozen, its reddened tip guarding the open window.

She could barely feel her body anymore and knew there was no chance she was going to be able to get her belt off to crawl out the window.

The steadily rising flood would claim her. If not, there would no doubt be more of Kai Nez's hoods to finish her off. But at least she'd taken one of them with her.

It wasn't the end to this trip she'd imagined. And not the way she thought she'd go out. But when she leaned back against the head restraint, she thought she could almost see her brother's face, like a reflection on the water.

He was waiting.

The water was nearly up to her chin now. She found the Guardian's steering wheel with her free hand and made her fingers tighten around it.

Valerie let a smile turn up the corners of her lips. Not many could say they died behind the wheel of a Guardian 770. If she had to go, this would be the way she'd be remembered. She closed her eyes. She could live with that.

30

RIVERBANK

I f it hadn't been for the bike parked alone at the side of the road, Dakota wouldn't have seen the signs. She'd followed the Guardian's tire tracks down the mountain as far as the burned out service station but had lost the trail on the old paved highway. But now there was this. The motorcycle at the side of the road had a cage attached to the back. The cage Kai Nez had threatened to drag her back to town in.

Dakota shut off the Vulcan and climbed out.

The rain had slowed to a steady drizzle, but the embankment at the side of the road was slick and treacherous. Dakota noted the gouges in the asphalt where something big had slid off the edge of the road and through the mud. She stepped cautiously to the precipice and peered into the ravine.

A torrent of flood water had washed down the mountain, and it now crashed over rocks and fallen tree trunks at the base of the hill. A cluster of limbs and branches had clogged a portion of the flow, damming the culvert and causing the water to back up. A dark figure was floating in the water, pressed against the obstruction. Dakota squinted to make out the shape. It was a body, a man, face down in the water. The rider? How had he gotten there?

And then she saw the darker shape in the water. It was the crushing black of a void but still slick and glossy in the turbulent water. Even in its ruined state, it looked like a monstrous sea creature surfacing to devour prey. The Guardian.

Valerie.

Dakota hurried to the part of the embankment where the car had gone over and clambered down the hill. The footing was precarious, and it took her several minutes to descend the slope, progressing mostly by feel. She finally reached the Guardian and took her jacket off, hanging it on a tree limb before braving the rushing water. The Guardian's crumpled fender provided a handhold as she slid cautiously into the current. It was cold, and her feet slipped several times on the rocks beneath her, but she grasped the remnants of the mirror and pulled herself to the Guardian's window. Water was up to her chest.

The window grating on the car was gone, and Valerie's head was just visible above the torrent. She appeared to be unconscious or worse. The water covered her chin and mouth and was a fraction of an inch from submerging her nose as well. Dakota reached through the window to rouse her.

"Valerie! Can you hear me? Wake up!"

No response. Valerie's head dipped, submerging her face.

"No, no!" Dakota shouted and pressed Valerie's head back against the restraint.

She had to act quickly. She reached through the window and tried to hoist Valerie from the seat, but something held her fast. Severed ends of the shoulder harness floated limply in the water. There had to be something else. Dakota leaned into the window and plunged her head and arms under the water, feeling her way down Valerie's body to her hips where the lap belt still held her tight. She fought with the latch, holding her breath and refusing to come up until she had it loose. Finally the clasp released and Valerie's legs rose from the seat. Dakota got her arms under Valerie's and pulled, the girl's head lolling onto her shoulder.

"Come on, you know you're too damn stubborn to die on me," Dakota grunted as she dragged Valerie's limp form out of the window and into the swelling torrent. She nearly went under when Valerie's full weight was on her, but she regained her footing and staggered step-by-step to the embankment. Looking up the hill, she knew there was no way she'd be able to haul Valerie back up that distance. She yanked her jacket from the tree limb she'd hung it on and slung it around Valerie's shoulders. She then dragged the girl a dozen yards to an overhang of the embankment where a previous flood had eroded the earth beneath the roots of an enormous pine. The soil under the exposed tree roots was still dry. Dakota laid Valerie on the ground and dragged her under the overhang. She tilted her head and held her ear close to Valerie's mouth. She felt the soft touch of her breath. Still alive.

Alive but cold.

Dakota tucked the jacket around Valerie, the only item even vaguely close to being dry. Then she studied the swollen stream. The rain was letting up, but that didn't mean there wouldn't be more water coming down from the mountain. She'd need to stay vigilant. She considered climbing the hill and going for help, but there was no one nearby. It would take her an hour to get to any settlement or village she knew. She didn't trust leaving Valerie that long. The girl was shivering as it was. Dakota got on the ground and laid next to her, propping Valerie's head on her shoulder and doing her best to warm her with whatever body heat she had.

Valerie moaned and her eyes fluttered.

"Hey. I've got you," Dakota said. "It's going to be okay."

"Where . . . where did . . ." But Valerie's voice trailed off as her eyes closed again.

What had she been asking? Where had she come from? Where did the others go?

"I'm going to stay right here, okay?" Dakota said. "When you're ready, I'll get us some help."

Valerie's eyes fluttered open again. "If I die . . . I want you to know . . . I don't hate you, even though you stole my car."

Dakota looked out toward the wreck of the Guardian. "Maybe now you're thinking you should have let me keep it, huh?"

Valerie let out a hint of a chuckle that turned into a cough and a groan. "Don't make me laugh. It hurts too much."

"You still think you're the better driver?" Dakota squeezed Valerie's shoulder tighter, trying to stop the shivers running along her body.

"I know I'm the better driver," Valerie said. "But I think . . . I think maybe you're the better sister."

Dakota didn't have a response to that. Even if she had, when she looked down at Valerie again, she saw that she was asleep.

Dakota affixed the jacket over both of them, holding Valerie's head tightly against her chest. She stared out at the darkness and listened to the gurgle of the stream while she pondered that word: sister.

The dawn light was late to the culvert where Dakota and Valerie had outlasted the night, but the clouds had moved on, and Dakota could glimpse sunlight on the mountaintops. Valerie was still asleep, and she didn't want to disturb her, so she crawled from under the roots of the old pine and looked around on her own.

The stream, which had been a rushing torrent the night before, had subsided to a quiet trickle that burbled gently over the rocks. A few birds were awake in the trees, and their trilling calls to one another were echoed from around the hills.

The Guardian rested with its front end still angled slightly upward as if it might start and climb its way up the hill, but the body of the car was a crumpled ruin. The roll down the hill had pushed in the roof panels and shattered every window. The slope of the rear window frame was now concave. One of the rear wheels was affixed at a strange angle, snapped loose from its axle but still pinned beneath the car.

Dakota moved closer and looked inside. It was a wonder Valerie had survived. Had it not been for the roll cage and restraining harness, she would have undoubtedly been pulped by the hammering the car had taken. The interior still had a foot of standing water inside. A glint of steel caught Dakota's eye, however, and she reached inside to pull Valerie's sword from the water.

It was a thing of beauty. Dakota had never seen a sword with so many colors evident in the blade. It was as though it still held the fire that forged it trapped within the metal. As she moved the blade through the light, she could almost see the flames dancing. She fished around and located the scabbard as well, then carried both as she made her way back to Valerie.

Valerie was awake. She watched her approach with her brow furrowed.

"Hey," Dakota said. "How are you feeling?"

But Valerie's eyes never left the sword.

"I think I killed a man last night."

Dakota turned and looked downstream. She could no longer see the figure she had spotted the night before. Hours of flotsam piling into the dam had hidden the corpse from view.

"Yeah, I think you did too." She turned back to Valerie. "But I'm guessing he had it coming."

"I've never killed anyone before," Valerie muttered.

Dakota shook the scabbard in her hand, emptying out any remaining water, then slid the sword back into it. She offered the hilt to Valerie. "You're a knight, right? I'm guessing you got into the wrong business if you didn't think you'd run into a few people that needed killing."

Valerie accepted the sword. "No. I knew it. And he deserved it. Still, feels different somehow."

"If you didn't feel anything, I'm guessing that would be worse," Dakota replied. "Do you think you can stand? If he had places to be, people might start wondering why he isn't there this morning, and my guess is they'll come looking. We can't stay here."

Valerie rolled over and attempted to get to her feet. Dakota stepped forward, pulling on Valerie's arm and helping her right herself. Valerie winced but was able to stand.

Dakota attempted to move but Valerie was still frozen, staring at the battered remains of the Guardian.

"Yeah," Dakota said. "We're going to need to get you a new car, but lucky for you, I found us a ride. It's just up that hill." She pointed.

Valerie lifted her chin and stared at the rocky slope. She took one more look at the Guardian, then set her jaw and started putting one foot in front of the other, leaning heavily on Dakota for support.

Navigating the still-slippery hillside took the better part of fifteen minutes, moving slowly, giving Valerie time to maintain her balance. By the end of it, she seemed to have regained some of her stability. Finally, they climbed the last remaining yards and stood on the dirt shoulder of the road, a dozen yards from where the lone motorcycle still sat.

"We're going to have to figure out what to do with this piece of garbage," Dakota said. "We can't leave it here."

But Valerie was transfixed, not by the sight of the motorcycle, but by the car parked beyond it.

"Where did you get *that*?" She staggered forward unassisted. Dakota was forced to chase after her.

"That Vulcan? I jacked it from some guy who came up the mountain looking for you."

"He was looking for me? Where? Was it Damon?"

"Damon? I don't know. I never asked his name."

"What did he look like? Was he tall, really annoyingly good-looking? Scars down his arms?"

"I guess he was good-looking if you're into that. Not tall though. Kind of fragile but with a sweet face. He was sort of pretty if you don't mind the shrieking and all the, 'hey, that's my car' stuff."

"Fragile? I don't think we're talking about the same—wait, was he Spanish, and short but with, like, killer eyelashes?"

"Yes." Dakota pointed a finger at her. "He did have pretty eyes. They were a little wide and terrified, but he had super good lashes."

"Rico," Valerie muttered. "What did you do to him?" Her eyes were suddenly on fire. The wild, violent look Dakota had witnessed the first time they'd met aboard the train.

"I didn't do anything to him. I mean, I took the car, but I didn't hurt him or anything."

"Take me there," Valerie said. "Wherever you left him." She immediately started limping for the car.

"Okay," Dakota murmured. "Hang on. I'll be right there." She walked over to the bike, studied it briefly, then climbed onto it and started it up. The weird cage made an unholy sound as it rolled along behind her, but it left distinctive marks on the pavement, clear evidence that it had moved. She rolled downhill in the direction of Rust Creek, but at the next bend, she aimed the bike toward the edge of the road and leapt off. The bike stayed upright, maintaining its course until it plummeted over the edge of the ravine. The cage flew into the air and disappeared after it, crashing down the hill. The repetitive sound of metal crunching on stone sent a flock of birds streaming from the trees.

Dakota walked to the edge, saw that both the bike and the cage were sufficiently destroyed—and not poorly hidden in the shrubbery—then turned with a satisfied smile. She brushed away the tire marks in the dirt that showed the bike and cage had left the road. When she was happy with the results, she made her way back up the hill.

The Vulcan's driver's door was hanging open, and the engine was running. Dakota slid into the seat and found Valerie clenching her sword on the passenger side.

"Evidence destroyed," Dakota said. "With any luck, they'll see the bike moved, you gone, and assume he left with you in the cage. Won't buy us a lot of time, but let's hope enough to throw them off looking for you by yourself."

"I need to find my friend. Did he say anything about someone else? No one else was with him? Did he say the name Damon at all?"

"We weren't super chatty." Dakota shifted into gear. "Never saw anyone else. He did say he was trying to warn you though. That's why I didn't hit him with the car when I was leaving."

"Let's just get back to where you left him and hope no one else found him first."

Dakota eased the clutch out and relished the way the Vulcan accelerated. "Is this his car?"

"It's Damon's," Valerie replied.

"Well, this Damon is a guy I'd like to meet. He knows how to build a sweet ride."

Valerie's attention was out the window, however, and as fast as Dakota drove, it looked like Valerie wished it was faster.

They were nearly back to the spot where she had hijacked the car when the sound of motorcycle engines echoed from somewhere behind them.

Valerie flinched in the passenger seat, twisting to look behind them. "Step on it! It could be Kai Nez!"

But Dakota let off the gas. She recognized the sound of the bikes.

"What are you doing?" Valerie exclaimed. "Drive!"

"It's not them," Dakota said. "It's friends."

And sure enough, three trail bikes came racing around the

bend. Lanja, Achak, and Sprocket were flying along the road. They slowed as they approached the Vulcan, wary and eyeing it skeptically. Dakota let the engine idle and opened her window. She stuck her head out and waved them on. "Hey! It's me!"

The motors on the bikes popped and whined as the three riders shot forward again, encircling the car. Sprocket pulled alongside the Vulcan, his face flushed.

"We've been looking for you everywhere," he blurted out. "Word just came from town, the whole place is churning with trouble."

He leaned down and spotted Valerie. "What's she doing here?"

"Don't worry about it," Dakota said. "What kind of trouble?"

Sprocket's face grew serious. "They've got Henry. The Sheriff's planning to execute him for murder."

"What?" Dakota exclaimed.

"Yeah. Him and some other dude I never heard of named Roark. They hang at noon."

31

RESCUE PARTY

V alerie pushed her door open and limped around the back of the Vulcan. When she reached the driver's side, she squeezed between Sprocket's motorcycle and the car and pulled the door handle. "Get out. I need the car."

Dakota looked up at her with a confused expression. "What? Can you even drive? You're in no state to be doing anything."

She wasn't wrong. Valerie ached in places she didn't know she had. Her muscles were bruised, especially where she'd slammed into the restraining harness, and there was a distinct possibility that the reason it hurt so much to cough was a broken rib. Maybe more than one.

She didn't care. Her head was fuzzy, and she could feel her pulse in her temples, but there was no way she could sit by and let anyone else control her next destination. She was headed to town. Nothing was going to stop her.

Dakota looked to Sprocket. "There was a guy in this car when I found it. I ditched him in the woods a couple miles up this road. He's probably on Henry's bike. Make sure he's okay."

"What are you going to do?"

"What do you think?" Dakota looked at Valerie, then slid across to the passenger seat.

Valerie eased herself behind the wheel. "You don't have to come with me."

"The hell I don't. He's my dad too."

Valerie nodded. For all the anger she'd felt regarding her father's betrayal, nothing changed the fact that he was family. He was still her dad. No one was going to hurt him while she still breathed.

Sprocket was still lingering by the door. The girl, Lanja, that Valerie had fought at the cabin was still watching through the front windshield, her expression as hard as ever.

"How do you expect to go up against the Nine?" Sprocket asked. "You got a plan?"

"It's eight now," Valerie said. "Maybe less."

"Still too many for you to take on."

"Tell the kid on the bike back there to get out of my way."

"Achak!" Sprocket shouted and waved an arm. "Go find the dude from this car. Takawa will know what to do with him."

As soon as the boy was clear, Valerie hit the accelerator and flew into reverse for a dozen yards. She cranked the wheel and turned around, racing back down the road the way they had come. When she checked the mirror a half minute later, she was surprised to see Sprocket and Lanja tailing them.

"What the hell are they doing?" Valerie asked.

Dakota checked the mirror. "You know how you told me yesterday that I needed to find some friends that always have my back? I've already got 'em."

~

Damon lay on the floor in the front passage of his cell. He'd

275

taken to staying close to the bars because from there he could hear the breathing of the man next to him.

Henry.

They had talked some, but Damon's throbbing head and dry mouth made it less than pleasant to do at length. Still, it was something to have another soul in the darkness, at least for awhile.

He had no concept of the hours anymore. The beating of his own heart was an inconsistent timekeeper. He noticed his heartbeat had sped up of late, straining with the dehydration slowly turning his blood to sludge. His gut was a cavern of cravings. Hunger had come and gone, but it was the thirst that persisted.

He resisted the urge to lick the stones of his cell again. The last time they had offered a tantalizing coolness to his tongue, but despite the storm supposedly pouring rain outside, they remained frustratingly dry.

"You still alive over there?" The voice came from someplace in the void that seemed almost near enough to touch.

"Mmmhmm," Damon managed.

"Seems you were right about these cells. Did another tour of mine. Nothing to be gained except by climbing. You got up there? You must be some kind of spider."

"Did me no good," Damon rasped. "The catches on the trap door are too far apart. Can't reach 'em. If you were over here climbing too, maybe you could lend me a hand. Otherwise, I'm done. The only way we're getting out is Trammel dragging us out."

Damon rolled over and faced the wall.

After a long pause, the man in the other cell spoke again. "Pity I can't lend you a hand. But how about a foot?" Something clunked against the bars near Damon's head. He sat up and extended his fingers. They met a solid object, curved to hold it, and discovered he was touching a foot. Not a living, warm foot but a hard, inflexible one. The man in the other cell released his grip on the object, and Damon dragged it into the cell with him. The artificial leg that attached to the foot ended at a place for a knee. There were a few straps as well. In total, it was over a foot and a half long.

Damon measured it again with his outstretched fingers, then allowed himself a smile.

~

A mile outside of Rust Creek, Valerie pulled over and climbed out of the Vulcan. She rolled her head around her neck, trying to loosen the stiffness in her muscles, then peered up at the sun. It had made a reappearance and was perhaps an hour away from its zenith. Not much time left.

She pulled the trunk release lever and moved haltingly to the back of the car. As the trunk lid yawned wide, she saw that the rack had been stripped of its weapons. A pair of Damon's swords had previously occupied the rack, but their absence didn't reduce her enthusiasm. She pushed Rico's toolbox aside and dumped the other luggage on the ground, then started tugging on the carpet of the trunk's floor.

"What are you looking for?" Dakota asked, appearing at the side of the car.

"Damon never shows all his cards at once. I'm sure he's got something for us in here if I look hard enough." She managed to get the carpet loose, then felt her way around the floor. Slipping her fingers down a barely visible crevice near the trunk latch, she found a groove and a slider that might be a lock. She shifted it to the opposite side of the groove, and the floor of the trunk popped loose. "Okay. Now we're getting somewhere."

By this time Lanja and Sprocket had caught up and were

idling behind them, their faces curious. Valerie pulled the floor hatch up and revealed a hidden compartment beneath.

"Damn," Dakota muttered.

Inside the compartment was a neatly organized stash of weapons: several swords, two round shields, two unstrung bows, and four quivers of arrows. There were a few clothing items as well: armored gloves, a helm, a mail shirt and one metal breastplate with a leather back.

"If we're going up against the Nightmare Nine, we'll need to be ready." Valerie offered one of the swords to Dakota, who nodded and accepted it. The breastplate and helm were sized for a man, so Valerie offered them to Sprocket. Lanja claimed a bow and two quivers of arrows. Valerie took a pair of armored gloves and retained a shield, but the rest she doled out, helping Dakota into the mail shirt. Sprocket figured out a way to secure the second shield to the front of his handlebars, offering a sort of protective screen. It wasn't much, but better than nothing. Lanja stashed her bike in the woods, then climbed onto Sprocket's motorcycle with her back to his and her feet on pegs jutting out from his rear wheel, an act she did with so much ease that Valerie was certain they were well practiced at it. From that position, Lanja would be able to twist and use the bow while in motion.

"That gate stands open most of the day, but I'm guessing they'll rush to get it closed as soon as they see us coming. When I go over that hill there, I'll have to be on the gas the whole way. Be sure to keep up."

"What happens if they get the gate closed before you can hit it?" Sprocket asked.

"Then this is a short fight," Valerie said. "It's about a quarter mile to the gate from cover. This car on this terrain? I'd need ten to twelve seconds. If I'm already up to speed by the time I clear cover, I can cut that to eight, but I'll need someone spotting to give me a signal and let me know the guards are as far as we can get them from the doors."

"I can spot from the tree line," Lanja said.

Valerie located a pair of binoculars in Damon's kit and tossed them to her.

"You sure you can fight?" Dakota asked. Valerie noted the concern on her face.

"I'm not at my best, but I'm not dead. That's the only thing that would stop me from going through with this."

Dakota nodded.

Valerie took the time to stretch, flexing her muscles and attempting to work out the worst of the damage from the crash. Her neck and back remained sore, but she was pleased to find that her arms and legs had their full range of motion. Her head had stopped pounding, and her vision was clear. As she finished stretching, Dakota held out the jacket Rico had decorated for her.

"You should be the one wearing this," Dakota said. "Let them know who they're messing with."

Valerie accepted the jacket and slipped it on. It wasn't much in the way of protection, but it felt right.

"All right. Let's go get Dad."

32

ASSAULT

First rule of a drag race? Nail the launch.

Valerie and Dakota sat side by side in the Vulcan with the engine running, Valerie's foot hovering over the accelerator. Her eyes were fixed on the figure of Lanja, who had crept to the edge of the trees and was peering down the road to the perimeter gate of Rust Creek.

The advantage they had was that this was not a proper castle gate. There would be no moat or drawbridge to deal with. The wooden wall of the village was sturdy, however, made of thick tree trunks sunk deep into the earth. While the gate itself was weaker, once closed it would have enough strength to stop them and possibly flatten them both against the inside of the windshield grate. In her already sore state, the idea of colliding headfirst with a closed gate did nothing for her.

But the other advantage they had was that the guards at the village wall weren't professional soldiers. They were villagers not accustomed to being attacked in broad daylight and certainly not by a solitary vehicle driven by a fugitive. She had the element of surprise. She also had over four hundred horsepower of snarling engine under the hood. And unlike the Guardian, which could be heard a mile away when the engine spooled up, the Vulcan's power came out in a lower tone, a purr more than roar. It was a monster, but a predator of stealth. With its understated gray exterior and subtle sound, the guards might not spot it coming till it was too late.

At least that was her hope.

Lanja's hand went up, but it wavered for the third time in the last ten minutes. Then she went still, her back straightening. She'd seen something. Lanja's hand flew down and she turned, waving Valerie on.

Valerie launched the Vulcan forward, the beast leaping cleanly off the line. It accelerated fast, a cheetah on the move. The tree line approached, last chance to stop, but Lanja kept waving, her binoculars still trained over the hill.

The Vulcan shot out of the shadow of the trees doing sixty-five miles an hour. In seconds it was eighty, eighty-five, ninety.

Valerie kept her eyes glued to the road ahead but Dakota's were on the gate.

"Still okay, still not looking . . ." she muttered. "Damn, I think one sees us."

But by then they'd covered over a third of the distance. Valerie pressed the accelerator down as far as it would go and the Vulcan's speedometer leapt past a hundred. The needle hit 105, 110. When she saw 115, she stopped watching it and fixed her eyes on the gate. Men were scrambling in every direction. Their mouths were moving, shouting to get a man with a produce cart clear of the gate. That must be the opening Lanja had spotted. With the cart in the way, there was no way for them to get the gate shut. Though now it was in her way too.

"They're closing. It's closing!" Dakota shouted.

The produce cart was inside and the guards were working to get the doors shut.

One looked up in alarm as an arrow embedded itself in the wooden planks of the gate. Valerie glanced in the rear-view. The shot had come from Lanja, standing aback Sprocket's motorcycle. It hadn't hit anyone, but the shot itself must have been close to a hundred yards.

It did its job. The men pushing the gate had hesitated.

There was no turning back. Valerie clenched her jaw and held on.

Figures scattered as the Vulcan hurtled through the gate. The gap was so narrow that the gate sheared both mirrors from the side of the car in an instant. But they were through.

Valerie hit the brakes, and the tires screamed as they came sliding to a stop two hundred feet beyond the gate. The shock on the guards' faces would have been humorous in any other situation. As it was, Valerie was only grateful that they were too stunned to move. Sprocket and Lanja shot through the still-open gate and raced to join them. Only then did a pair of the guards resume their positions, pressing to get the gate closed. The only problem was that some were now running the other way, escaping out the gate and fleeing from this sudden invasion. Lanja hastened their exit by loosing several more arrows in their direction.

They'd made it into town.

Valerie leapt out of the car, fastening *Firebird*'s scabbard to her belt. Dakota slid over to take the wheel of the Vulcan. She then tossed Valerie her shield.

"Eyes out for trouble. Let's get to the square." Valerie leapt onto the back of the Vulcan, gripping the rear window armor and giving the roof a few taps to signal Dakota. She rode the rest of the way through the village that way, feeling a vague sense of déjà vu from the last time she'd been atop a car with Dakota driving. She was at least comforted that this time Dakota wouldn't be deliberately hurling her off.

The faces of villagers turned in shock as Valerie and these

three Native Avalonians cruised down the center of their main street. No one moved to stop them, but Valerie knew the path wouldn't remain unobstructed for long.

Sure enough, when they rounded the final curve toward the square, they were met with the sight of a half dozen riders mounted on motorcycles. The faces were ones she recognized from the posse she'd ridden out of town with. Turk, Whiplash, Lynx. She couldn't recall the others' names.

Gallows had been erected in the center of the square directly between the jail and the saloon. Valerie was relieved to see that the nooses dangling from it still hung empty. A crowd had gathered—villagers of all ages and genders—but it was primarily unarmed men.

The riders facing them in the street were armed to the teeth.

Behind the six riders, a sort of dais had been raised that held seats for a select few. One of them was Lord Hudson. A gleaming, pearl-white war car from his collection was parked next to the dais. Hudson rose at their approach, his head at a level with Valerie's, and they stared at one another over the heads of the crowd.

Dakota brought the Vulcan to a stop, engine idling with a throaty rumble.

Lord Hudson spoke at a volume that carried across the square. "King Logan's wayward knight returns. What a pleasure it is to see you again, Lady Terravecchia. I presume you've come to join the festivities. We're about to have a spectacle."

"I didn't come to witness any more of your games," Valerie shouted. "I'm here to settle the score."

"Looking to level the scales of justice? You'll find no finer exhibition of justice on these lands. Or perhaps you haven't heard. We caught ourselves a murderer." Lord Hudson smiled. "But where is my head? Of course you must know. There's a family relationship. Your long-lost father. Perhaps you should be the one to set him swinging and prove to the kingdom which side of the law you're really on."

Valerie drew her badge from her pocket and brandished it. "I demand you release Henry Terravecchia into my custody now. Whatever crimes he's committed will be dealt with by a fair Avalonian court, not this mockery of justice you've concocted."

"I'm afraid we're going to disagree with your authority here, Miss Terravecchia. I know you're awfully proud of that shiny new badge. But we're a long way from Glastonbury Castle. We haven't seen a king's representative in ages. Do you know what we've done in the many years of our neglect? We've established our own law. Frontier law. Because when savages terrorize the countryside and threaten these fine people, it isn't the king's soldiers who can protect them, it's my men. They are the only justice that matters in these parts, and I count more of them than you."

"You'll count fewer if they don't stand down."

A cold laugh rang out, causing many in the crowd to turn.

Kai Nez stepped off the porch of the saloon and into the daylight. One of her gloved hands was resting on the pommel of *Whipfang*, her fingers drumming against the handle.

"You have to give her credit for guts. I didn't think she had this in her." Kai Nez strode coolly across the square, villagers giving her a wide berth. She stopped in the midst of her riders and smiled up at Valerie. "You do strike a lovely pose up there. Now I see why your boyfriend was so smitten."

Valerie bared her teeth. "Where is he? Where's Damon?"

"Don't worry. He'll make an appearance. Sheriff Trammel's been keeping him safe for you." Kai Nez squinted up at her. "Hudson's got a point, you know. You're outnumbered. The sad little crew you brought along isn't cut out for this. There's no way you win this fight." Her voice was still calm, as soothing as a lullaby. "Now why don't you come on down before you hurt yourself."

Valerie cast a glance at Sprocket and Lanja. Lanja had an arrow nocked on her bow and a look of grim determination on her face. Sprocket less so. He was putting on a brave face, but she couldn't tell if the shaking in his arms was from the motorcycle or his nerves. She suspected both.

Dakota chose that moment to rev the engine on the Vulcan. The vibration of the motor pulsed through Valerie's body, breaking the spell of the bounty hunter's soothing words.

Valerie drew her sword. "This is only going to end one way, Kai. And you know it." She jumped down from the car and held her shield in front of her.

Kai Nez smiled. But she didn't draw her weapon, she raised her hand instead, and when she snapped her fingers, the six riders on the bikes drew theirs.

Valerie found herself staring at a half dozen faces snarling with hate. Maces. Swords. Hundreds of pounds of mobile steel. But the Vulcan growled beside her, and when the wave of riders shot forward, Valerie raised her sword.

<><><>

Sheriff Cecily Trammel plodded down the last creaking steps to the old mine and lumbered through the narrow tunnel. A set of keys jangled at her hip. Her longsword hung at the other. She held the lantern aloft when she reached the final chamber, illuminating the two cells. Had she been wanting to, she could have made her deputy move these two up to the regular cells in anticipation of their trip to the gallows, but something tickled her about leaving them in the dark right to the end. They'd have one last glimpse of sunshine on the way to the gallows, but it would shine only on their failures.

She found that poetic.

"All right, you murderous scumbags. Lady justice is calling your names. We'll do this one at a time and stretch the show out for the crowd. Who wants to be the lucky—" but she paused midway through her sentence, because only one of the men in the cells was visible. Henry Terravecchia was standing at the bars of his cell squinting at her from beneath bushy brows. He was missing the lower half of one leg, and he was smiling.

"What in the hell happened to you?" Trammel said. "Your leg. It's—"

"The rats down here are ravenous," Henry said. He looped his arms through the bars. "Mighty pleased to see you, sheriff. Even a miserable hellspawn like yourself has to have a virtue or two over them beasties."

Sheriff Trammel blinked at the place his leg ought to be. He'd had two when he came down here, hadn't he? There was no way that rats could've—

At that moment, something big slammed into the wall of the second cell, and a beam of light shot from the ceiling as though heaven itself had opened up.

A man's shadow obscured the rectangle of light on the floor. Trammel nearly fell over herself to reach the bars as she tried to see the top of the cell beyond the gateway. The shadow on the floor vanished.

"No! No no no!" Trammel fumbled with her keys, attempting to jam them into the lock at the side of the cell but then thought better of it and abandoned them, drawing her sword instead as she turned to rush back the way she came.

"No one escapes!" she shouted. "No one!"

She made the run down the tunnel faster than she had ever done in her life. By the time she reached the stairs, her breath was coming hard and fast. She struggled up the stairs one at a time, shouting for her deputy whenever she could spare a breath. But wherever that lazy sod was, he didn't answer her shouts. Trammel huffed and puffed up the last of the stairs and plowed through the doorway, slamming it against the interior wall. She wheezed as she thundered down the last hallway. Only one more door barred her path to her office. She opened this one slowly, her sword at the ready.

Her office looked normal. Chairs where they should be, trapdoors shut, the main entrance door closed. It was only when she turned toward her desk that she stopped. Damon Roark was seated in her rolling desk chair, guzzling water from a huge jar she had been drinking from that morning. Rivulets of water leaked past his mouth and down his chin in his haste to drink. He held up his index finger toward her as if requesting her to wait.

The arrogant fool hadn't escaped when he had the chance. Stupid move.

Trammel crossed to the center of the room, barring any path to the exit.

"I don't know how you got up here, swordslinger, but you made your last mistake."

Roark looked pale and exhausted, his days of isolation showing on his face. Trammel smiled. She'd enjoy cutting him down.

Damon set the empty water jar down and eyed a sandwich tray on the corner of her desk. She'd requested that Billy, the deputy, bring her one while she was downstairs. If that was here, what on earth had happened to—

But then she saw the boots jutting out from beyond her desk. Her deputy was lying prone on the floor. It was hard to say if he was dead or knocked-out, but he certainly wasn't moving. Roark had bested him?

Trammel took a step back toward the door. Perhaps she ought to enlist the help of the Nine. Kai Nez and her gang were waiting in the square, not to mention dozens of townsfolk. She didn't have to wrangle this renegade on her own. He didn't appear to be armed. After days in the hole, he had to be weak, but why not enlist a few more hands? She took another step backward. But then she froze. Damon picked up her sandwich, and with his eyes locked on hers, took a leisurely bite.

Cecily Trammel felt her blood begin to boil. It wasn't the fact that he was eating her food, it was the *way* he was eating it. It was impertinent, taunting. His slate-gray eyes never left hers as he shoved the wedge of tuna melt deep into his mouth. Melted cheese oozed from his lips. There was something indecent about it. Sacrilegious. He bit off a huge mouthful and chewed. Loudly. He had no hesitancy, but neither was he rushing. She could almost have forgiven a ravenous devouring of food from a man who had been deprived of it for days. She could forgive an animal need. But the way he swallowed, stared at her, and took another sensuous bite left it abundantly clear. He was not eating the sandwich because he was hungry. He was eating the sandwich because it was *her* sandwich. And *that* she would not tolerate. She strode forward, longsword raised above her head. She would cleave through him like a sirloin. She didn't care that the desk stood between them. If she had to, she'd hack through that too.

A guttural roar erupted from her throat. She picked up speed as she charged and swung. But at the moment her sword should have been cleaving through his skull, Damon shot to one side, rolling away in the office chair. Trammel thudded into her desk, her stomach rolls impacting the oak and bringing her to a sudden stop.

She turned to glare at Roark, but he was six feet away, still chewing. He swallowed, then held something up in his right hand. It was small. A trigger button from her desk drawer. The remote for—

The two trap doors swung open simultaneously, the chairs in front of her desk vanishing in an instant through the floor. Trammel looked down and gasped, finding herself teetering on the thin strip of floor that divided the two trap doors. The solitary floor beam was perhaps eight inches wide but seemed suddenly like a sliver. She'd never been on this side of the desk when the doors dropped before, and the view down the two gaping holes made her instantly drop her sword to the desk and grab for its surface. She flattened her palms against the wood, determined to keep her balance.

"Trouble with your footing?" Damon said, with his mouth partially full. He swallowed, then leaned forward and retrieved something from the floor. "I can help with that." When he rose, it was to hurl something big. The object flew at her, and Trammel barely had time to recognize it as a foot. A foot striking her squarely in the face. Trammel shrieked and let go of the desk as the force of the kick in the face from this flying foot sent her reeling backward. Only, when she stepped backward, there was no step. Her boots found nothing but open air, and she plummeted into the hole the trap door had made in the floor.

Cecily Trammel had watched many men fall through this floor. She knew what was coming—the long drop to the stone cell far below had been a source of infinite pleasure for her to watch. She'd witnessed men breaking ankles, ribs, occasionally their skulls on impact. This time, the event unfolded as though time had slowed. She waited to hit the floor, for the shattering of bones and thud of her flesh on stone. But what she felt was a tremendous pressure, a squeezing, and her momentum was suddenly arrested. She looked up to find that she had fallen only a few feet. Her legs and waist had vanished through the floor and her shoulders were pinned in place next to her ears, arms extended above her head. But she was no longer falling. She was stuck.

She looked up. Damon was leaning over her desk, observing her, mouth frozen midway through chewing another bite of her sandwich. "Well, damn. Didn't see that coming." He picked up her longsword from the desk, turned it around, and pointed the tip at her face. "Now, you be good and don't go anywhere. I have some people who will want a word with you."

"You get her?" The shout came from the trap door opening beside her.

"I'll be right down, Henry!" Damon shouted. He polished off

the last of the tuna melt and winked at her. "Thanks for the sandwich. Gotta go."

Trammel tried to scream and kick, but the motion only caused her to slip farther down the hole. She froze, wedged tight with her legs dangling. Damon rushed out the door.

33

SHOWDOWN

Valerie stood her ground. The roar of engines around her was deafening, but she refused to be intimidated. Motorcycles flew at her from every angle, a mace blow glancing off her shield, a sword thrust parried by her own. It was like fighting inside a hurricane. Everywhere she looked, the street was filled with racing machines, dust, and imminent death.

Dakota was one of the blurs whipping around the square. The Vulcan had plowed through the incoming wave of riders and was now on the warpath, pursuing whichever members of the Nightmare Nine were in range. Arrows flew from the back of Sprocket's motorcycle as he and Lanja hurtled around the perimeter, pursued by several other riders.

The townsfolk scattered, but many remained in view, cowering behind shop windows and concrete barriers. Valerie tucked and rolled to avoid the incoming sword blow from a woman on a passing bike and came up running. Kai Nez hadn't moved from her position near the gallows. She watched with a detached, disinterested gaze and hadn't even drawn her sword.

Valerie sprinted at her.

The roar of an engine stopped her short as a pair of bikes

screamed toward her with a chain held taut between them. Valerie changed direction and rushed to the edge of the street, leaping over a barrier before the bikers with the chain could take her head off. The riders whooped and hollered as they circled. Another of the Nine was off his bike and strode toward Valerie across the plank sidewalk. Wrecking Ball. That was his name. He wielded a war hammer with a head the size of a brick. A blow from the iron hammer pulverized a chunk of the concrete barrier directly behind Valerie as she ducked and dodged. She quickly found her footing and launched a counterattack. *Firebird* danced through the air, a brilliant flash of color and light, feinting one way and another before slicing across the warrior's leg just above the knee. He roared and went down, clutching his leg.

Valerie had no time to relish her victory because an arrow embedded itself in the boards near her feet. She looked up to find one of Hudson's archers nocking another arrow atop the jailhouse.

"Lanja! Look high!" she shouted, as Sprocket and Lanja flashed past. The Avalonian native caught her gesture and looked, then sent an arrow flying at the roof. The archer on top of the jail ducked out of sight. Things were getting more serious.

"Leave him to me!" Lanja shouted, leaping from the back of the motorcycle and sprinting up a set of stairs at the side of the town bakery.

Valerie kept her shield up and eyed the door to the jail. There was a Lockley Sidewinder parked outside. Her father was in there somewhere. She leapt off the wooden sidewalk and sprinted toward the jail.

The archer peeked his head from concealment, noted her running, and loosed an arrow. Valerie blocked it with her shield. She had made it roughly halfway across the square when she was broadsided by a biker who came in so fast she couldn't get clear. His mace struck her shield so hard that she was sent tumbling backward, her feet flying over her head before she crashed to the dirt. The shield came loose from her arm and rolled several yards as she attempted to get back to her feet.

She realized to her horror that she was no longer holding her sword. She scrambled to locate *Firebird*, then spotted it on the ground, in the opposite direction from her shield.

Whiplash had stopped, climbing off his bike to come back and finish her off. He pulled another weapon from his saddlebags. A wicked-looking flail. The spiked ball dangled at the end of a two-foot chain, and he whirled it over his head before rushing toward her. Valerie dove for her shield, rolling over top of it and bringing it up with both hands just in time to stop the biker's flail from crushing her chest. The spiked ball buried itself in the wood of the shield so deeply that when he yanked his arm back, he wrenched the shield from her hands as well. Her only defense went clattering to the street as the big man tossed the flail aside. He gripped his mace with both hands and raised it high over his head, a scowl spreading across his face as he swung at her.

Valerie wanted to close her eyes and scream, but before she could do either, the man and his mace vanished, displaced by the car that came plowing through him. Valerie scrambled backward on her hands and witnessed her attacker sailing through the saloon window in a shower of glass.

Dakota was in the driver's seat of the Vulcan, looking across the car at her.

"Hey! You good?"

Valerie could only nod, using all of her focus to catch her breath. She clambered to her feet, slapped the side of the Vulcan a couple of times, then rushed to pick up her sword.

~

Inside the Vulcan, Dakota shifted into reverse and twisted to check her path. That's when she spotted the movement near the gallows. Lord Hudson had descended from his place in the spectator seat and was headed for his car, a pearl-white Continental Commander. For the briefest moment, his eyes met hers.

Her father's killer.

Dakota felt the anger grow white-hot inside her. How many years had she dreamed of one day meeting the man who had ordered her father's death and what she would say to him.

A life lost, a father gone, lives ruined.

Her dad had been a thief. A thief doing what he had to, to get by, and some days she hated him for leaving her just as much as she hated Hudson for executing him. But now, staring at the man who had ended his life, she knew she couldn't let him simply drive away. Someone had to hold him accountable.

Hudson climbed behind the wheel of his car and slammed the door. Dakota whipped the Vulcan around and aimed straight for him. Their eyes met again across the plaza, and he must have known. He must have seen.

The Commander's tires smoked as Lord Hudson launched into the street. Dakota launched, too, and tightened her grip on the Vulcan's steering wheel, upshifting and bracing for a possible head-to-head collision. But almost as soon as the Commander was moving, the car swerved, angling toward a side street and heading uphill—the route to the castle.

Dakota took a glance in the rear-view mirror and saw Valerie with her sword back in hand. A pang of doubt crossed her mind. Valerie needed her. This fight wasn't over. But then she saw the brake lights of the Commander flash as it turned north toward the castle. Dakota clenched her jaw, shifted gears, and followed.

~

As the Vulcan tore out of the plaza, Valerie turned in place, analyzing the remaining threats in the square.

The street had cleared. Any villagers who weren't hiding indoors were keeping their distance. At least three of the six riders she'd initially faced off against were down: one wounded by her own sword, the second put through the saloon window by the Vulcan, and a third lay motionless on the opposite side of the street punctured by two of Lanja's arrows. But there was no sign of Sprocket and the other bikers. Somehow, in the melee and chaos, she'd lost sight of them. The sound of motorcycle engines still echoed along the village streets, but the fight had expanded farther from the square.

She checked the top of the jail. The archer was no longer visible. Was he still up there?

The only constant in the chaos had been Kai Nez. The bounty hunter stood staring at her from across the plaza. Valerie dusted herself off and moved into the center of the street. Kai Nez moved too. She strode across the cobblestones at a pace that matched Valerie's, then stood opposite her, separated by a distance of fifty feet.

"Looks like it's down to the main event," Kai Nez said. "I hoped we'd get to do this."

A shout came from on top of the bakery. "You want me to drop her?"

Valerie looked up to find Lanja with her bow bent, an arrow aimed at Kai Nez.

Valerie turned her attention to the bounty hunter. "Surrender now and we'll let you live."

Kai Nez laughed. "Poor little City Law. Do you think you've won? Where did you learn to count?"

The sound of engines grew louder and two motorcycles roared around the corner, one of them dragging something behind it. It was Sprocket, bound at the wrists and hauled along the ground, the steel chest plate making a horrific grinding sound as he skidded across the stones. The armor had protected him somewhat, and he was alive, but his forearms and shins were bloody and raw.

"Sprocket!" Lanja shouted from the rooftop and turned, aiming her bow toward the rider dragging Sprocket. But another woman stepped out from under the shadow of the barber shop roof and fired a bow of her own. The arrow struck Lanja in the side, and she screamed, tumbling from her perch on the roof and disappearing over the ridge line.

"No!" Valerie shouted.

"You want me to put *her* down?" The woman with the bow had fitted another arrow to the string and now aimed at Valerie, echoing Lanja's words from moments before.

Kai Nez was smiling. "No need, Lynx. City Law needs a minute to come to terms with her failure."

Lynx relaxed her bowstring and lowered the bow.

"This must have been a real education for you," Kai Nez said, sizing Valerie up. I have to give you credit for coming back. That took guts. It was stupid. Useless. But you've made a fair showing of yourself. A worthy competitor."

"Why are you doing this?" Valerie asked. "What's in it for you?"

Kai Nez cocked her head. "Seriously? I get paid. You think there's some elaborate motive? But I do admit, the job comes with its perks. Every once in a while, I get to cut down an arrogant upstart who thinks waving a sword around is all it takes to be a killer. Sometimes they wave badges."

Valerie reached into her pants pocket and removed her badge, studying the now dingy emblem of the crown and cross of Avalon. She dropped it to the street. "You're right. I won't need a badge for this. Just the sword."

She raised *Firebird* to a front guard.

Kai Nez smiled and took off her hat, tossing it to the ground.

Her raven hair fell to her shoulders, and her eyes brightened. She drew *Whipfang* from its scabbard, and the sunlight danced down the blade. She leaned forward into a sprinter's crouch, the sword concealed behind her.

Valerie had seen this play out. She knew the deadly stakes. Her mind flashed back to the outlaw and his brother, James Whitecar, that Kai Nez had left to die in the street.

Villagers were creeping slowly from their hiding places—eyes watching from porches and doorways. A muttering came from the stoop of the saloon, bills changing hands, betting on the outcome. How many blows would it take for Kai to cut her down?

Valerie flexed her sword arm.

Kai Nez was a statue.

The midday sun beat down on the cobblestones and the heat rose, but it was nothing like the inferno inside Valerie. This would end now. She clenched her jaw and sprang into a run. Kai Nez broke free too, flying across the ground, her trajectory as true as an arrow. Forty feet. Thirty. Her boots pounded a rhythm across the stones. Twenty feet, ten. Kai Nez leapt, soaring through the air, *Whipfang* flashing in the sun. Valerie leapt too . . . and swung.

34

VIPER BITE

I t had taken Damon longer than he expected to retrieve Henry from the cell below the jail. The path through the tunnels to the cells was poorly marked, and while Trammel had helpfully left the keys, Henry himself was moving slowly. Even with his leg reattached, he hobbled up the stairs, leaning on Damon for support. Damon retrieved another longsword from the jail's armory and gave it to Henry to lean on.

The sword did something to the man. With it in his hands, he looked different, more complete, and Damon had the strange feeling that he'd met him before. There was something about the shape of his eyes and the quirk of his mouth that was so familiar. But he didn't have time to muse on the subject as they navigated their way past the shrieking upper torso of Sheriff Trammel, still wedged in the hole in the floor. They ignored her ranting and moved to the exit door.

"Things might get hairy out here," Damon said, "but we'll get to your car and go from there."

Henry jingled the keys he'd retrieved from Trammel's desk. "I'll be the wheelman."

But when Damon swung open the door, the vision of the street in front of the jail was nothing like he expected. The gallows and spectator seats stood vacant, and while there were people rimming the street, not a single eye was on the jail. Bodies lay strewn around the square, including an archer lying dead on his face between the jail and the Sidewinder. And every face in the town was watching two figures facing off in the center of the street.

"Valerie!"

The exclamation had been on the tip of Damon's tongue, but it wasn't him who spoke it. He turned to find Henry pushing past him, his eyes wide and his attention fused to the girl in the street.

The realization hit Damon then like a freight train. Henry was *the* Henry. Valerie's father, Il Orso Nero.

The revelation had no time to be sufficiently processed in his mind because his attention was once again commandeered by the action in the street. Kai Nez and Valerie both had swords drawn, and they lunged toward each other like wildcats.

"No!" Damon shouted and raced forward himself, but there was no amount of speed he could employ that would get him to Valerie in time. The two women streaked toward one another on a collision course, and all he could do was watch.

Kai Nez, the deadliest woman he had ever known, flew into the air and deployed one of her signature moves, *Twisting Viper*. She had invented it, perfected it. And as Damon watched in horror, *Whipfang* completed its transition from one of Kai Nez's hands to the other, passing behind her back and around to move across her body from left to right. As the two women met in the air, the blade went cleanly under Valerie's thrust, slicing across her chest in a powerful slash.

The two women hit the ground, Valerie spinning as she fell, her jacket fluttering around her, crumpling to a heap and rolling over in the dirt. Kai Nez landed on her feet.

The crowd on the stoop of the saloon erupted into cheers, though many of the other villagers remained silent. A hundred pairs of eyes were still riveted to the fighters. Kai Nez turned, slowly, and caught Damon's eye. A playful smile flickered at the corner of her mouth, and she started to lift her sword in a salute. But partway up, her arm wavered. *Whipfang* tumbled from her fingertips and clattered to the stones. Kai Nez's smile faded as she looked down to find the hilt of a sword protruding from her chest. Her other hand felt for the handle, and she attempted to pull *Firebird* from between her ribs. The effort was too great and she collapsed, first to her knees, then to her side. She lay still in the street.

Damon sprinted for Valerie. When he reached her, he grabbed her shoulder and she moaned. He rolled her onto her back and gawked at the vicious cut that had slashed a tremendous rip in her jacket. But Valerie opened her eyes and blinked at him.

"Damon!" Her arms shot to his neck, and she pulled him to her. "Oh my God, I was so worried."

"*You* were worried?" Damon exclaimed. "Kai—she cut you. Right across the chest."

Valerie released her grip on him, then looked down to her torn jacket. It was indeed slashed in a way that ought to have cut her in two. Blood wicked into her shirt from beneath her left breast where something had cut her, but when she pulled the jacket aside, she could tell that the wound was superficial, a graze across her ribs. Something had prevented her from being cleaved.

That's when a fold of the severed jacket fell open and something heavy fell to the stones. Damon picked it up. He recognized it as the bear claw emblem from the front grill of the Guardian. It had a gash directly across the center from Kai's sword. He handed the emblem to Valerie. "How did that . . ."

"Dakota," Valerie whispered, taking the emblem from him

and regarding the slash across the center. She pulled open the jacket to reveal the inside pocket where the emblem had been hiding. Her eyes grew wide, and she scanned the plaza. "Dakota. We have to find her."

Damon pulled Valerie to her feet. But that's when he saw a woman with a bow raised. The arrowhead was oscillating between him and Valerie.

"Better make a good choice," a voice said. Damon turned to find Henry stepping in front of them, blocking the woman's shot. "You get one arrow, then bum leg or not, I'm coming for you."

"Me too," Damon said, raising his sword. "And I'm faster."

The woman with the bow wavered, her expression growing more frustrated. Her eyes flicked to one side, to the still form of Kai Nez lying dead in the street.

"Hell with this," the woman said and tossed her bow to the ground. She backed away a few steps toward the shade of the saloon. Damon turned to check the rest of the square. Two bikers sat on their motorcycles a dozen yards away, watching. He recognized them as the pair he and Rico had encountered in the woods. Tomahawks and the one who'd worn the fake braid.

"You again," Damon snarled. He took several strides in their direction, his sword raised. The duo on the bikes blanched.

"Why'd it have to be this guy?" Tomahawks muttered. Her companion hastily detached a tow chain from his bike and throttled up. The pair of them left smoking rubber in their wake as they gunned their bikes and streaked out of the plaza.

Valerie rushed to the aid of the man they had left behind. He was in rough shape. Abrasions marked his arms and legs as well as a few cuts on his face. But despite his pain, the first words out of his mouth were "Where's Dakota?"

Henry bent slowly to one knee, resting a hand on the young man's shoulder. With his other hand, he held the car keys out to Valerie. "I'll see to him. Go. Find her."

Valerie took the keys from her father, looked Damon in the eye, then sprinted toward the Lockley Sidewinder parked outside the jail.

Damon walked to the fallen form of Kai Nez, pulled *Firebird* from her chest, and followed.

35

SURROUNDED

Lord Hudson drove like a sissy. Dakota hadn't expected that running a Continental Commander off the road would be simple, but less than a quarter mile from his castle gates, she'd caught him. The sound of metal scraping metal had caused him to panic. Maybe he was so worried about marring his pearl paint job that it had affected his driving. Either way, when Dakota brought the Vulcan past him and slammed over hard, the Commander left the road with little resistance. The unfortunate element had been that the Vulcan's front fender lodged into the Commander's wheel well, and both cars ended up in a tangled heap in the ditch.

Hudson's door popped open, and he sprinted from the car.

Damn. This guy did have a few surprises.

Dakota clambered out the passenger side of the Vulcan, sword in hand, and gave chase. The castle walls loomed overhead as she ran him down.

"Help! Help me!" the lord shouted. Helmeted heads appeared on the battlements. Startled cries erupted from overhead. A moment later, an arrow whizzed past Dakota, burying itself almost to the flights in the soft earth. But the soggy ground made it hard going for Lord Hudson as well, and Dakota was right on top of him. She leapt, tackling him to the ground and foiling the archers' attempts to shoot her. Dakota hadn't thought much beyond this moment, but the look of terror on Hudson's face as he rolled over was sheer bliss.

"Stop! Don't you know who I am?" he shouted.

"You know who I am?" Dakota replied and slugged him in the nose. "That's for my father!"

Hudson shielded his face from any more blows and scrambled back to his feet. But they were up against the castle walls now with nowhere to run. "You're a lunatic. A *dead* lunatic. I hope you've enjoyed this little stunt because it's the last thing you'll ever do."

A contingent of a dozen armed soldiers came trooping out of the castle gate, spears and shields at the ready.

Dakota swore and brandished her sword, then leapt behind Hudson, pressing the blade to his throat. She pulled her knife as well, holding that to his ribs. "If I go, you go with me." She backed them up till they were in the very shadow of the battlements. Any archers would have an even harder time hitting her from this angle. But as the soldiers fanned out, they cut off her only escape route.

"I'd say we have a checkmate, you stupid savage," Hudson said.

"Call them off," Dakota said. "Order them back inside."

"And lose my only leverage? You must be insane."

"Call. Them. Off," Dakota hissed, pressing the sword to his throat till his neck bled.

"Okay, okay!" Hudson shouted. "Let's not be hasty. I'm sure there is some sort of arrangement we can come to." He held up his hands, stopping the approach of his soldiers. The captain of the guard made a fist, and the men beside him froze.

"Now send them off," Dakota said, her heart pounding so loudly she could barely hear herself think.

"This doesn't end well for you," Lord Hudson said. "If you kill me, they'll cut you down in moments. Is your hatred of me so strong that you're willing to die for it?"

"They'll kill me either way. I'm just getting warmed up for the mess it's going to make when I take your head off."

Hudson swallowed and licked his lips. "Okay. Perhaps something else. A car. We can get you a car."

"Yes," Dakota exclaimed, seizing on the idea. "Tell them to bring me one. We both get in, we get away from here, and I'll kill you somewhere nicer."

"A tempting proposition. Forgive me if I don't leap at the chance."

The sound of an engine came from the road. Dakota looked up as the Sidewinder appeared around the corner. She let out a sigh of relief. "Nevermind. Looks like I have a ride."

The contingent of soldiers quickly shifted positions, a handful of them turning to face the new threat.

The car stopped, a door opened, and Valerie stepped out, her eyes flashing to the battlements where no doubt the archers were training arrows at her. She remained behind the door. A tall, distractingly handsome man stepped from the passenger side, mirroring her.

"Well, well," Lord Hudson said. "I'm surprised to see you still alive, Lady Terravecchia. Does this mean our legendary Kai Nez has finally met her equal? My money was on her killing you in one stroke."

"Not for lack of trying," Valerie replied. "Your Nightmare Nine are done. Your death grip on this community is at an end."

"You're still outnumbered by my count," Lord Hudson replied.

"A lot of people relying on math today," Valerie said. "Ask Kai Nez how that worked for her."

But another half dozen of Hudson's soldiers were hastening belatedly from the castle. Most were armed with spears and pikes. They took a position around Valerie and the Sidewinder and slowly pressed in.

"You were saying?" Lord Hudson taunted.

Dakota's heart sank. But there was still one chance of beating these numbers.

"If you let them go," Dakota said. "I'll let you loose and turn myself in."

"No!" Valerie shouted.

Lord Hudson sneered. "Am I supposed to take you at your word?" He flinched as Dakota prodded his side with her knife. "Okay! Let me go. I promise they'll leave these grounds unmolested. We'll settle our scores another day. But that is my final offer."

"Swear it on your life," Dakota said.

"I *swear* it," Hudson replied.

Valerie met Dakota's eye, shaking her head.

Dakota pushed Hudson forward a few steps and released him. "Now let them go."

But no sooner was Hudson clear, then he backed toward his castle and shouted to the soldiers, "Kill them! Kill them all!"

The captain of the guard flinched, seeming unsure.

Dakota sprinted toward her sister.

"You hear me?" Hudson shouted. "If any of you want to work another day in your lives, kill them!" Dakota was only halfway to the car when a soldier near her lashed out with a pike. Dakota screamed and parried the blow with her sword but just barely. Another soldier lunged forward, attempting to skewer her, but suddenly Valerie was there, knocking the man back and hacking at him with her sword. "Get away from her!"

A few curses came from the man beside the Vulcan, but in a flash, he was there too, abandoning the safety of the car to come to their aid. Dakota noted the ribbons of scars on his muscular arms as he lined up next to her. This must be the friend Valerie seemed obsessed with talking about. Damon. As he menaced the soldiers with his sword, she understood why.

The three of them stood back to back, swords raised, surrounded by at least a dozen soldiers. Damon parried a few thrusts from the men on his side and drove them back with a series of whirlwind attacks. But all around them, the circle of soldiers tightened. Dakota bumped into Valerie, and the sudden contact triggered a flood of emotions.

"I'm sorry I got you into this," she stammered. "You were right. Maybe I should have appreciated how much life I had left to live."

"Probably a bit less now than we'd imagined," Valerie replied, keeping her guard up.

One of the soldiers made a move, and suddenly they were all fighting for their lives, swords flashing and parrying strikes from the spears. A spear tip sliced across Dakota's shoulder, and she cried out. Then they were overwhelmed. Weapons pressed in from every side.

But Dakota's cry was answered.

From the road, a blast of horns drowned out the noise of the fight. The soldiers backed off as a monstrous sky-blue motorcoach, its war turrets bristling with archers, motored up to the fray. It was followed by a dozen more coaches. Cars and motorcycles swarmed the hillside as well, each one carrying multiple Black Hawk braves. Atop the lead motorcoach, Chief Takawa rode next to a young man Dakota had seen only once before. The pretty, young Spaniard with the killer eyelashes. He'd come back, and he'd brought the entire tribe.

36

REBUILT

"The king will hear of this," Lord Hudson shouted. "This is treason!"

Hudson's men had laid down their weapons. With the majority of its men-at-arms surrounded outside the castle walls, Redrock Castle surrendered.

The Black Hawk tribe made quick work of disarming any remaining soldiers inside the castle, a number that was surprisingly low. It seemed the pitiful wages Hudson offered had inspired few to work for him, and those who did had no qualms about retiring from their positions immediately.

Lord Hudson fumed and spat as he was led to meet Chief Takawa for a discussion of terms.

Valerie accompanied him, keeping a wary eye on the lord, though as soon as Rico had climbed down from the motorcoach, they rushed into each other's arms.

"God it's good to see you," Valerie exclaimed. "How on earth did you end up with the Black Hawks?"

"Long story," Rico said. "How much time have you got?"

"Your friend came to us with disturbing news," Chief Takawa

said. "A shocking betrayal of the treaty of peace we've held with this man." He gestured to Lord Hudson.

"You have nothing on me," Lord Hudson spat. "It's you who have broken the treaty, bringing armed men to overtake my lands. The king will send his entire army for this and wipe your insignificant tribe from the map."

"This map?" Chief Takawa asked. He held up a battered and disheveled map of the territory. "Imagine how shocked I was to find that an Avalonian lord had a map of Black Hawk land, already surveyed for its oil deposits."

Hudson blanched. "Where did you get that?"

"You've been invading our territory for years, noting its riches, then instigating acts of war on your own people to blame on us," Takawa said. "We have witnesses of your evil. Men of integrity and honor. They will testify to your king of your betrayal." He gestured to Rico and Damon.

Hudson's eyes narrowed as he studied Rico's face. "Wait a minute. The maid?"

Rico mimed a kiss, then narrowed his eyes.

"I promised I would send word of you to King Logan," Valerie said. "You've ensured that. But I don't think you'll like what his response will be."

"And I do thank you for the map," Chief Takawa said. "There has been such a shortage of fuel of late that I'm pleased the Black Hawk tribe will now be able to supply it. The Kingdom of New Avalon and the Black Hawk people will once again have a thriving commerce."

Lord Hudson was practically foaming at the mouth by the time the braves dragged him away, but his grumblings grew ever quieter as his figure diminished down the hill.

Valerie faced Chief Takawa. "This only works if your braves continue to abide by the treaty. We'll need to prove to King Logan that the only offenses that occurred were on the part of Hudson's thugs."

"And what about the ones that weren't?" Dakota said. Valerie turned and found her with eyes downcast. "The road train attack was on me."

"We'll have to explain that and make amends. The fuel tanker will certainly have to be compensated for. You already gave the car back, but that's a bit of a moot point now. Not sure how the king will respond to the crime itself."

Dakota nodded but looked glum.

"The fact that you helped bring a much bigger criminal to justice has to count for something. I'll be able to speak to King Logan personally when I get to Glastonbury Castle. He's a good man. He's sure to listen." She turned to Damon. "Speaking of good men . . ." But Damon didn't say a word. He simply stepped forward and took her in his arms, then kissed her, his grip on her firm and strong. It was exactly the way she'd hoped the conversation would go.

Valerie found her father seated in a wooden chair on the front steps of the jailhouse. He had his chair leaned back and was keeping a wary eye on the saloon across the street, a bare sword laid across his lap.

"Any trouble?" Valerie asked.

"None to speak of, but I thought I'd at least see it coming if there was." He reached into his shirt pocket and removed something, then held it out for Valerie. It was her badge. The finish was scuffed and dirty, and the shine was gone, but the crown and cross still stood in sharp relief. "Found this in the street. Figured you might need it back."

Valerie accepted the badge. "Not entirely sure I deserve to keep wearing it."

"No leadership without sacrifice. Isn't that what it means? He who wears a crown must also accept the cross."

"Lord Hudson's arguments aren't completely wrong. I did lead a native insurrection on Avalonian land. Do you think the king will still want me as a knight at the Round Table?"

"I suspect there's only one way to find out for sure. You'll have to ask him."

Valerie wiped the dust and dirt from the badge and clipped it to her belt. "I guess it's one mess at a time. Any sign of Sheriff Trammel?"

"Technically still in her office. I suspect you'll find her attentive and eager to cooperate," he said. He reached back and grasped the handle of the door, pushing it open for Valerie to peer inside.

"Oh my," Valerie said. "I see what you mean."

By evening, every person in the village was talking about the arrest of Lord Hudson. As much as Valerie was tempted to drop Sheriff Trammel into the same pit she'd used on Damon, she resisted the urge, and had a trio of strong men hoist her from the hole in the floor and put her in a regular cell next to Hudson.

Tensions in the village were high with the Black Hawk tribe camped directly outside the village walls, and Valerie kept an eye out for trouble, but it seemed everyone had seen enough violence for one day, and no one was in the mood to start more.

The worst casualty they'd suffered was Lanja, who had been pierced with an arrow and had also fallen ten feet from the roof. Miraculously, she hadn't died. She did have a punctured lung and a broken wrist, but the town doctor said she ought to pull through. Sprocket stayed by her side all night, declining a bed of his own. The doctor was kept busy with her many patients, some of them former members of the Nightmare Nine.

In all, three of the biker gang had been pronounced dead. The following morning, the mortician could be observed carving the names "Whiplash" and "Stucky" into headstones. A third was reserved for Kai Nez.

The search was on for Cinco and Turk, the two riders who

had escaped town. Damon identified them as the pair he had encountered in the woods with Rico. Valerie posted "WANTED" notices but suspected the duo would be long gone by now.

Word was dispatched to Sir Everett Morningstar and the garrison at Fleetwood of the need for support, but it would be two days till the peacekeeping company would arrive.

It was two days Valerie spent reassuring villagers and taking their testimonies. It seemed that with Kai Nez dead and their lord in jail, the locals were more than happy to unburden themselves of their grievances. Valerie felt more exhausted and sore from the hours writing down their complaints than she had been from the Guardian crash.

The loss of the car still grieved her, but on the morning of the second day after the battle, she was summoned from the jail to find a caravan of vehicles streaming into the square. One of the Black Hawk motorcoaches was towing a fuel tanker. The same fuel tanker that had been stolen from the road train. Dakota was aboard the motorcoach and descended to meet Valerie.

"It's been refilled," she said, striding forward to meet Valerie. "If they want interest, Chief Takawa said he's willing to pay it and take it out of my earnings later."

"You a full-fledged member of the tribe again?" Valerie asked.

"Says I'm still trouble," Dakota replied. "But they aren't kicking me out. Seems there's going to be a need for a lot more communication with the Kingdom, and they need the drivers. And a few warriors to help guard the eventual caravans. He thought I might have a few ideas about increasing security."

Valerie smiled at the irony. "Good decision."

"I have something else for you," Dakota said, waving her toward the back of the caravan. "A present. Come on."

Valerie followed her sister past a second motorcoach pulling a trailer. Atop the trailer was a car with a familiar shape covered in a tarp. Dakota unfastened the cords and pulled away the tarp, revealing the motor-less and windowless Guardian 770 that

Valerie had seen in the garage at the cabin. "I know it's not complete, but I took the local guild mechanic and your friend Rico out to your car, and they are towing it back with a wrecker. They think that with a little time, they can salvage enough of it to combine with this one and get you back on the road."

"You're giving me your car?" Valerie asked, emotion raw in her voice.

"Damon told me how much you wanted to roll up to the Round Table in your Guardian. Rico said by the time we're done, all it will need is a bear claw emblem for the front. I told them I knew someone who had one."

Valerie couldn't control the smile that spread across her face. She admired the bold lines and rugged form of the Guardian body, her fingers twitching at the sight of the steering wheel. Then she turned and wrapped her arms around Dakota. "Thank you."

Valerie served in the role of substitute sheriff only long enough for Sir Everett Morningstar to arrive in Rust Creek with his company of soldiers. Morningstar was a stern man, prone to stroking his chin and nodding contemplatively, but he was reasonable and patient in hearing testimonies. During his occupation of Redrock Castle, a great many more maps and surveys of the Black Hawk land were discovered, along with receipts for payments to Kai Nez and her band of riders that coincided with dates of attacks on local settlements. Hudson denied trying to reignite a war with the Black Hawks, insisting that the natives were to blame for every attack. But faced with the prospect of many years of jailhouse rations, Sheriff Trammel sold him out, confessing the entirety of their dealings to Sir Everett in a bid for leniency.

Valerie was happy to let the events play out without her. She spent the majority of the days in Sal's garage with Damon, Rico, her father, and Dakota. And also Peaches. When Sal and Rico had returned to salvage the Guardian, they'd found the bedraggled dog barking and defending the wreck. "Darn runt wouldn't stop yapping till I put it in the truck," Sal said. But he had obviously made a friend. When they'd returned to the shop, the dog followed him around the garage like a shadow. It seemed to be a situation they were both happy with.

Sal had managed to get his hands on a windshield and windows and did much of the welding repairs the war car needed while they combined efforts on rebuilding the engine and drivetrain. In a matter of a few short weeks, they had a running Guardian. While the body was dotted with primer and the seats still smelled vaguely of river water, the car had a bear claw emblem on the front and sounded meaner than ever. Looking back on the experience of rebuilding the car, Valerie decided they were some of the best weeks of her life.

"You ready to get back on the road?" Damon asked one evening after they'd finished signing their final testimonies for Sir Everett. They were holding hands while sitting together on the trunk lid of the Guardian. "Summer's almost over. You have a king and queen waiting."

Down the street, Valerie's half-brother, Mato, was kicking a ball with some of the village kids, her dad, and Winona looking on.

Valerie studied the fading twilight sky and nodded. "I suppose so. This trip hasn't gone quite the way I expected, but I think it's time to get to the end."

"You're nervous?"

"A little. The last of the Black Hawks are packing up tonight, heading back to their territory in the morning. Winona and Dakota plan to go with them."

"But not Henry," Damon concluded.

"Dad still feels compelled to face up to what happened with

Sir Rupert all those years ago. He wants to go with me to Glastonbury Castle and confess it to the king himself."

"You're worried he'll be punished?"

"I don't know what I'm worried about exactly. His case is strong. He did what he did to save Dakota, and the king should side with him in the end. But then what? Does he stay here with Winona and Mato? Does he go home to Briar Valley and our lands? For the last six years, I've wanted him back, wished he could be a part of my life again. Now I see the life he's made here, and I'm torn. The last couple of weeks we've all been together with no reason to choose. But if the king does clear his name, what will he decide then?"

Damon squeezed her hand and peered down the road to where Henry had his arm around Winona, laughing at the antics of the kids in the street. "There's a lot of road between here and Glastonbury," he said. "You should ask him."

The ball got loose from the kids and came bouncing in their direction. Mato chased after it but slowed to a stop when he got close. He peered up at them wide-eyed.

Valerie slid off the trunk of the Guardian and retrieved the errant ball. She brought it over to him. Valerie had suspected it was Damon the little boy was intimidated by, but as she got close, Mato backed up a step. "It's all right. Here you go," Valerie said, bending to a knee and offering the ball.

Mato continued to stare. "Are you on our side now?"

"We're all on the same side. But especially yours. You know who I am?"

"You're a knight."

"Almost. But more importantly, I'm your big sister. How do you feel about that?"

The little boy cocked his head. "Are you bigger than Dakota?"

"I'm older, if that counts."

"So . . . you can tell her what to do?"

"I don't know if I'd get far with that."

"But if you're older, and you're on my side, then she can't tell me what to do anymore, right?"

"How about you just listen to your mama and stay out of trouble. Then I think you'll be fine."

Mato stepped forward and claimed the ball, but before he turned to go, he lunged forward and gave her a quick hug, wrapping one arm around her neck. The next moment, he was dashing back down the street to rejoin his friends.

Damon was smiling as she turned around. "Be careful. Next thing you know he'll be stowing away in your luggage.

Valerie climbed back onto the trunk lid next to him. "Wouldn't be the worst thing. I'm starting to like that little guy. You're still coming with me, right?"

"Rico and I can follow in the Vulcan. Need to check on a few things at the train depot in Hudsonville, make sure the Blackbird and all our other gear made it onward, but I don't suspect we'll be more than a half day behind you."

"I'll drive extra slowly so you have time to catch up."

"You? Slow?" Damon cocked an eyebrow.

"There aren't a lot of things worth waiting around for, but you're one." She ran her hand up his arm, stroking the line of a scar that crossed his wrist. "Are you okay? I saw that cell Trammel had you in. I can't imagine what days in there must have felt like."

"The only part I couldn't stand was not knowing if you were safe. The rest was minor." Damon eased closer and put his arm around her. Valerie nestled into his shoulder. An owl swooped overhead and disappeared toward the prairie.

"When I was standing in the street, facing down Kai Nez, I had your voice in my head the whole time. Our training. But if it hadn't been for pure luck and Dakota leaving that emblem in the jacket pocket, I'd be dead."

"There's always going to be someone better, someone faster. There's no way to train for every adversary. But you're still here. I have to think there's a reason."

"Because maybe the kingdom still needs me? Like it's fate?"

"I don't know if I believe in fate," he said. "But I'm starting to believe in love."

Valerie pivoted to face him, locking her eyes to his. "Love. Now that's a conversation we've never had."

"Sure we have. You must not have been listening."

"I'm listening now," Valerie whispered.

He leaned over, his lips barely brushing hers, the smile still lingering on his face. Valerie's lips quirked too but then she couldn't resist any longer. She pressed her mouth to his and her hands found their way up his chest. She felt her body melt into his. A few moments later she pulled back. "Wait. What were we talking about?"

Damon grinned and threaded his fingers through her hair before pulling her back to him. "You're lucky I don't mind repeating myself."

37

ROUND TABLE

The wind played with Valerie's hair as she drove, windows down and one arm extended to the summer sun. For the last seventeen hundred miles, her home had been the open road. In the passenger seat, her father rested, eyes closed—not asleep —but listening to the hum of the engine and the sound of tires on pavement.

The Guardian made the drive in excellent time, Valerie's lead foot having been restored once she sighted Damon and the Vulcan in her rear-view mirror near Cooperstown.

The first few hundred miles had felt tense, her father and the hurt of his absence weighing down the car. But as the miles rolled on, Valerie let herself be consumed by the scents and sounds of the road, burning fuel, rubber on pavement, and the distinctive combination of her father and the Guardian's leather seats. These were the same sense memories she'd relived for years, when her father was in the driver's seat, and they'd spent hours in the winding hills of Briar Valley, exploring the vineyards, then rolling west to the coast or north to the redwood forests.

The sights out the window were different now. Plains stretching to an untouchable horizon, followed by miles of farmland, lakes, and forests. They camped under the stars, and little-by-little the words came easier. Fond recollections of her mother, her brother, and their time spent together slowly spilled out. The names still stung her lips, the memories bringing heartache with the smiles, but saying them aloud felt like exhaling after having held her breath for weeks.

Henry was more reserved than he'd been in her youth, growing more somber the farther east they traveled, but the gulf between them had narrowed. When they crossed the River Easton, she stretched a hand out to his, clasping it firmly. His eyes opened, and he turned to regard her. He then surveyed the road ahead.

"We're getting close. Over that next hill we'll have a view of the city." He straightened up to sit taller in his seat.

"You've been this way before?"

"Many years ago. But it's not a sight you forget."

When the Guardian crested the hill, she released her father's hand and downshifted, slowing and then easing to a stop. He was right. She'd never seen a city so beautiful. The woodlands faded, and several miles of low grassy hills met another fork of the river. Arched bridges connected to the gleaming white walls of the city, and the spires of Abbeys and Universities stretched for the sky beyond. Above them all, on the highest of the hills adjoining the harbor, sat Glastonbury Castle. Even from this distance, Valerie could catch the glint of sunlight on stained glass, and she imagined that she could almost hear the cracking and snapping of the banners as they streamed in the ocean breeze.

A jewel by the sea. Poets and songwriters had penned verse after verse attempting to capture the beauty before her, but now Valerie realized all of them had failed.

Her heart sped as she admired the glittering harbor.

"Have you ever seen anything so stunning?" Valerie asked.

"It has its appeal," Henry said. "But it's no Briar Valley."

Valerie smiled. "I guess we have high standards."

Henry's face darkened. "I know there isn't much road left, and I still owe you more of an apology than I've managed to put into words these last few days."

Valerie shifted into neutral and let her foot off the clutch. "Hard for one road trip to fill in for six years."

"I'm not sure what the king is going to say about what I've done. I suspect it'll be a while till I get any kind of resolution from the law, but I don't want you to have to wait that long. What I did was meant to protect you—save you the shame of a family reputation in ruins. but I know I should have come clean sooner. Come home. Faced it together. If I had, Henry would still be—" He ran a hand across his mouth, unable to finish the words.

Valerie gripped the steering wheel and clenched her jaw. But her shoulders relaxed as she took in her father's downcast face. "You saved Dakota," Valerie said. "That's not nothing."

"Not enough," he murmured.

"I don't know what happens from here, either."

Valerie thought about home, the vineyards, and Lady Charlotte. How would she handle the news that her husband was still alive but living with another family? If she knew Charlotte at all, that was going to be a trainwreck. She'd want a divorce. She'd want the land. She'd want it all. Still, when it all went down, Valerie knew which side she'd be on.

She reached for her father and gripped his hand again. "I don't know what's going to happen, but I'll be there when it does."

Henry turned and met her eyes, then nodded, grasping her hand with both of his.

Valerie squeezed once more, then released him and shifted into gear.

Near the outskirts of the city, they encountered checkpoint after checkpoint of imperial soldiers, but displaying her badge earned her deep bows or rigid salutes from every one of them. She spotted Damon and Rico in the Vulcan not far behind and claimed them as part of her entourage. The soldiers didn't salute the Vulcan but waved them on without hassle. Her arrival was heralded from checkpoint to checkpoint, and by the time she had entered the city proper, word must have spread that the king's newest knight had arrived. Thrilled citizens waved and cheered at the sight of the Guardian, and little children raced along behind the car shouting and whooping, attracting the attention of every set of ears for miles around.

Valerie found herself more and more distracted by the cars they passed. Knights of every rank and station seemed to drive war cars here. Vehicles so beautiful and deadly she could barely take her eyes off them. When they reached the castle gates, a vehicle marshal directed them onward.

"Lady Terravecchia, His Majesty King Logan has been alerted to your arrival and wishes to see you at once. Take the Boulevard of Lords to the Avenue of Arthur. That will take you all the way to the Courtyard of the Round Table. Sir Henry will need to disembark at the Gate of Galahad but will be able to wait in the citizen balconies. Only Round Table Knights are permitted to enter the courtyard."

"Don't worry, I know my place," Henry said.

The marshal nodded and waved them on.

The Boulevard of Lords was a tree-lined lane that wound past towering monuments to knights and nobles of the past. A couple of cars passed them heading the opposite direction, and Valerie was once again left staring at the pristine paint jobs and mirror-finish chrome. Dappled sunlight danced across the primer-speckled hood of the Guardian as they drove, and the apprehension knotted in her stomach the farther they went.

"This is the honor of a lifetime," Henry said. "By your expression, we could be headed for a funeral."

"When I set out on this trip, I thought I'd be showing up a little differently," Valerie said.

"Perhaps without a father in your custody for murder?"

"I certainly didn't see that coming. But I thought I'd *feel* differently too. And I thought for sure my car would look the part."

When they reached the Gate of Galahad, she slowed to a stop. Several members of the king's guard were on hand to accompany her father. She stared at the closed portcullis that marked the entrance to the next courtyard and tightened her grip on the steering wheel. "You really think I belong here?"

Henry paused with the door open and one hand on the roof handle. "I don't think King Logan invited you because he liked your car." He extended a hand to hers and squeezed it again. "But this is a choice that's still up to you. Whatever you decide, I'll be waiting for you on the other side."

"Thanks, Dad," she said.

He climbed out of the car, retrieved his cane, and closed the door. A last knock on the roof of the car signaled his departure, and she watched the king's guard escort him toward some stairs in her side-view mirror.

The groan of the portcullis being raised could be heard over the sound of the Guardian's throaty rumble. She waited till a guard signaled her to proceed before passing through.

She had seen paintings of the Courtyard of the Round Table in schoolbooks as a child, but nothing compared to the real thing. A circular wall rimmed a symmetrical plaza with paved paths radiating from the center like spokes. She drove the perimeter road that hugged the wall, passing segments of beautifully manicured lawn between each spoke of the circle. The history books showed previous incarnations of the Round Table as an indoor surface of painted wood, but the table at Glastonbury Castle was outdoors and made of polished black-and-white marble. The table was divided into thirteen segments with a low-backed stone bench for each knight to sit upon. The table and benches were covered by an open pavilion to keep the sun and rain off and behind each bench was a black marble parking slab for the war car of the knight in that seat.

As Valerie drove the perimeter of the circle, she passed more thin driving lanes leading to each parking slab. Beside each glistening war car a banner snapped in the breeze, displaying the house colors of the knight parked there.

Never in her life had she seen anything as glorious as that circle of cars. There were Monarchs, Avengers, and even a Gallant Constellation polished to shine as brightly as the sun.

The war cars of the knights of the Round Table.

And as she rounded the far side of the circle, the knights were there, dressed in their full driving armor and standing sentry in front of an open parking space. The black marble parking slab was slick and polished. The poles for house banners stood bare, but King Logan himself stood at the end of the space. He met her eyes.

It had been months since she'd last seen him, and at their parting, his mood had been jovial. He was deadly serious now. Not even a hint of a smile was evident in his gaze.

She turned onto the spoke of the lane that led to the open space, driving three quarters of the distance and stopping, as encroaching any closer to the king seemed unwise. Valerie shut off the Guardian's engine and climbed out of the car. She wished she had dressed more appropriately for the occasion. Her own driving armor was in the trunk. It was a patchwork gleaned from other drivers, but anything would have been better than the blue jeans and T-shirt she was in now. It was too late for changing. She moved around to the front of the car and bent to one knee, bowing before the king.

"Stand, Valerie Terravecchia, and keep your head raised," King Logan said. "We all meet as equals at this table."

Valerie rose and let her eyes meet the king's again. The other knights were staring as well. Nine men and two women. She knew most of their names by heart. It would be difficult to find a collection of persons in the kingdom more talked about than this one.

"I've invited you here to consider a sacred duty. It is the task of this assembly to protect the Realm, serve in its betterment, and guide it into the future. It is a task that requires men and women of the highest integrity. You have proven your courage in battle, your prowess in a war car, and your skill with a sword. What we ask now is the desire of your heart. Do you wish to serve as a knight at this table?"

"Your Majesty, it would be a tremendous honor to be a member of this company. If you still think I'm the one for the job." The king studied her face, and Valerie kept her expression neutral, despite the spike of adrenaline coursing through her.

"What say these knights?" the king asked.

Sir Gabriel, an imposing man wearing the yellow and black of House Stewart, stepped forward. His helm and colors reminded Valerie of a wasp. "Troublesome rumors preceded your arrival, Lady Terravecchia. It has been said that Sir Henry, your father, has come to this castle to confess to serious crimes. It raises questions as to whether the House of Terravecchia is still worthy of a place at this table."

"She brought her father in her custody," another knight said. Valerie recognized her as Dame Sabine of the House of Mambwe. "And one does not bear the dishonor of their entire house on one's shoulders, if such dishonor exists."

"And what of the accusations from Lord Hudson that she inspired revolt and revolution among the Black Hawk people?" Sir Gabriel's words were daggers. "Is it not treasonous to aid in the overthrow of an Avalonian castle without a directive from the king?"

"Would you like to respond?" King Logan asked.

Valerie nodded. "Sir Gabriel, Redrock Castle was only held by the Black Hawks for a matter of days until Sir Everett

Morningstar could take possession of it. And Lord Hudson is a snake."

"An unfair comparison," a voice said. "For the snake."

Valerie recognized the speaker as another knight named Sir Oberon and noted belatedly that the sigil of his house was a serpent. But the handsome knight had the hint of a smile on his lips.

"What has become of your war car, Lady Terravecchia?" King Logan said. "I see some changes since last we parted."

"The road was long and treacherous, Your Majesty. I'm afraid the car and I are both worse for the mileage."

"I may choose to disagree," the king replied. "When I left you in Briar Valley, you were a warrior champion who had survived a tremendous ordeal, but one that had been fought within the bounds of tournament rules. The girl I saw then was brave, and virtuous, but untested beyond the bounds of the arena. I see a *woman* before me now, and you are no longer untested, though your challenges are far from complete. Your quest to join us here will be the first of many if you join this company. I, for one, welcome the woman you have become and would be honored to fight beside you." He drew his sword. "I will ask again of this company. If you deem Lady Valerie Terravecchia worthy of a place at this table, lift your swords and so declare it."

Dame Sabine was the first to draw her sword, followed by Sir Oberon. They both shouted "Aye!" Then, one after another, eight other swords were drawn. Lastly, Sir Gabriel put a hand to the hilt of his sword. Valerie held her breath. Then the blade sang as it was drawn from its scabbard. Sir Gabriel held it aloft with the others. "Aye."

She couldn't stop the smile that spread across her face.

"And now," the king said. "Lady Valerie, should you choose to join this table as an equal member, you may kneel."

Valerie stepped forward and sank to her knees on the edge of the black marble, her heart swelling in her chest.

"Valerie Terravecchia, do you swear to remain loyal to your king, uphold the laws of this kingdom, defend the weak, speak the truth, act bravely and with honor, and forever champion that which is good and just?"

"I swear it, Your Majesty."

The flat of the king's sword touched each of her shoulders in turn.

"Then rise, *Dame* Valerie Terravecchia, Knight of the Round Table."

A round of applause and thunderous cheering erupted from behind her. As Valerie climbed to her feet, she turned and found that the perimeter balcony held spectators. Damon, Rico, and her father were all smiling broadly. A beautiful woman was standing beside Damon, also applauding. Valerie was shocked to recognize her as Queen Kimiko.

When she turned to face King Logan again, she found him smiling too.

"You'll have to suffer through a public ceremony as well, I'm afraid—banquets full of pomp and circumstance. But the deed is done. For now, go get your car and your sword." He winked at her.

Valerie backed up slowly, then turned and walked to the Guardian. As she slid into the driver's seat, the twelve knights melted away from the parking space, giving her room, but she noted someone had affixed Terravecchia House banners to the sigil poles. The Guardian's guttural snarl echoed from the walls of the courtyard as its engine came to life. She shifted into gear and turned around, backing into position among the circle of war cars. When she climbed back out, leaving the engine running, she carried *Firebird* in its scabbard.

The other knights, including the king, had laid their swords in a circle on the stone table, points aimed to the center, but all except King Logan had retreated to their cars. As Valerie approached the Round Table, one engine after another roared to life. By the time she stood beside the thirteenth segment of the table, every war car was rumbling. She unsheathed *Firebird* and held it over the table, lowering it gently into place.

The circle of cars erupted into a gyre of noise, car horns blasting and engines revving, accompanied by the festive shouts of the drivers. Valerie was vaguely concerned about going deaf, but her cheeks hurt from how much she was smiling. King Logan approached and put his arm around her.

Valerie had to yell to be heard over the noise. "What happens now?"

King Logan gave her shoulder a squeeze and shouted back. "Now comes the best part." With his other hand, he made a fast circle in the air, then aimed for the southernmost gate. The circle of war cars pulled away from the table in unison, headlights flashing and horns still blaring. They drove all the way to the perimeter lane, but idled there, a gap left in their ranks.

"It's time to let this city meet their newest knight," King Logan said. "Let's go for a drive."

THE END

Thanks for reading! Word of mouth and Amazon reviews are the two things keeping books like this being written. If you enjoyed this adventure, please tell a friend and leave a review. Thank you for being a part of its success.

If you keep reading, I'll keep writing!

Looking for your next thrilling read? Be sure to check out *Faster Than Falling.*

Born in the sky. Doomed to fall. Destined to soar.

The skylands are in danger. Born in the floating colony of the Skylighters, Samra has yet to master flight, and that's a big problem.

When cutthroat pirates raid her home, she discovers that the aerial ocean is more deadly than she ever imagined. Now she must survive in their world or lose it all.

High in the mountains, a human boy with a homemade skyship takes to the air on a quest to save his family, but he soon discovers that the Heights have already been claimed, and he's far from welcome. The young heroes are caught in a rising conflict between earth and air, with the fate of the entire sky at stake.

Take flight on a bold adventure to an exotic world where dangerous beasts, deadly pirates, and fantastical airships rule the skies. Discover a thrilling new tale of action, villainy, and friendship.

Make the leap into the sky today! Find out if you have what it takes to soar...

"Van Coops beckons the reader through the door, then drags you into a fantastic ride, replete with eccentric tech; alien naturescapes... and good old-fashioned piracy. Storytelling at its finest!"- **Robert Scanlon, Author of Constellation.**

★ ★ ★ ★ ★ *Filled with outstanding characters, bold escapades and breathtaking scenery, it is a fast-paced and brilliant adventure for all ages.* **Bethany Cousins** *(Amazon US review)*

★ ★ ★ ★ ★ *"An epic tale of adventure and coming-of-age."* **Mark Speed, Author of Dr. How and the Illegal Aliens**

Get started HERE: **https://www.books2read.com/u/mgrEq7**

ACKNOWLEDGMENTS

Every book I write has an incredible team behind it. My sincere thanks to the eagle-eyed advance readers that test drive each novel and let me know of any speed bumps along the way.

Special thanks to Kay Dudley Clark, Marilyn Bourdeau, Von Whitlock, Maarja Kruusmets, Sarah Van Coops-Bush, Eric Lizotte, Ken Robbins, Marilyn Gast, Rob Stephen, Lee Inks, Andy Booth, Rick Bradley, Claire Manger, Donnisha Cherelle Jones, Norma Grubb, June Høstan Van Riel, Thomas C. Altman, Andrew Freeman, Ginelle Blanch, Felicia Rodriguez, Mark Hale, Missy Burrows, Amy Estes Spicka, Bruce Green, Diann Marshall, Yvonne Mitchell, Maurice Druck, Karen Stansbury, Elaine Davis, and Bethany Cousins.

H. Claire Taylor helped me align the elements of the story when I was in the darkest depths of writing the second act. Thanks for getting me back on track.

A special thank you to the team at Damonza.com for their gorgeous cover designs.

And to my wife Stephanie, daughter Piper, and my soon-to-be-born son, Morgan, who inspired me to get this story out in the world. I love our family.

OTHER SERIES BY NATHAN VAN COOPS

In Times Like These

The Skylighter Adventures

ABOUT THE AUTHOR

Nathan Van Coops lives in St. Petersburg, Florida on a diet comprised mainly of tacos. When not tinkering on old airplanes, he writes heroic adventure stories that explore imaginative new worlds. He is the author of the time travel adventure series *In Times Like These*, and the YA steampunk series *The Skylighter Adventures*. His third series, *Kingdom of Engines*, explores a swashbuckling alternate history where the modern and medieval collide. Learn more at www.nathanvancoops.com

Cover design by Damonza.com

Map created by Nathan Van Coops

Chapter images designed by Julia Scheiber

Author photo by Jennie Thunnell Photography

ebook ISBN: 978-1-950669-04-2

Print ISBN: 978-1-950669-05-9

❀ Created with Vellum

Made in the USA
Middletown, DE
02 February 2021

32946867R00203